Praise for Nalini Singh and the Psy-Changeling Series

SLAVE TO SENSATION
'I LOVE this book! It's a must read for all of my fans.
Nalini Singh is a major new talent'
New York Times bestselling author Christine Feehan

VISIONS OF HEAT
'Breathtaking blend of passion, adventure, and the paranormal.
I wished I lived in the world Singh has created. This is a keeper!'
New York Times bestselling author Gena Showalter

CARESSED BY ICE
'Craving the passionate and electrifying world created by the
megatalented Singh? Your next fix is here! . . . One of the most
original and thrilling paranormal series on the market . . .
Mind-blowing!'
Romantic Times

MINE TO POSSESS
'Singh has done it again. *Mine to Possess* grabs you and
never lets you go. This may be the best book of an already
outstanding series'
Fresh Fiction

HOSTAGE TO PLEASURE
'Singh is on the fast track to becoming a genre giant!'
Romantic Times

BRANDED BY FIRE
'I don't think there is a single paranormal series as well-planned,
well-written, and downright fantabulous as Ms Singh's
Psy-Changeling series'
All About Romance

Also by Nalini Singh from Gollancz:

Guild Hunter Series

Angels' Blood

Archangel's Kiss

Archangel's Consort

Psy-Changeling Series

Slave to Sensation

Visions of Heat

Caressed by Ice

Mine to Possess

Hostage to Pleasure

Branded by Fire

Blaze of Memory

BONDS OF JUSTICE

A PSY-CHANGELING NOVEL

NALINI SINGH

Copyright © Nalini Singh 2010
Extract from *Play of Passion* © Nalini Singh 2010
All rights reserved

The right of Nalini Singh to be identified as the author of this work
has been asserted by her in accordance with the
Copyright, Designs and Patents Act 1988.

First published in Great Britain in 2011 by
Gollancz
An imprint of the Orion Publishing Group
Orion House, 5 Upper St Martin's Lane, London WC2H 9EA
An Hachette UK Company

1 3 5 7 9 10 8 6 4 2

A CIP catalogue record for this book is available
from the British Library

ISBN 978 0 575 10009 1

Printed in Great Britain by Clays Ltd, St Ives plc

The Orion Publishing Group's policy is to use papers that are
natural, renewable and recyclable products and made from wood
grown in sustainable forests. The logging and manufacturing
processes are expected to conform to the environmental regulations
of the country of origin.

www.nalinisingh.com

www.orionbooks.co.uk

To Kayo, Cynthia, Loma, Emily & Akbar

Because you all rock. Thank you for being my 'tomodachi'!

JUSTICE

When the Psy first chose Silence, first chose to bury their emotions and turn into ice-cold individuals who cared nothing for love or hate, they tried to isolate their race from the humans and changelings. Constant contact with the races who continued to embrace emotion made it much harder to hold on to their own conditioning.

It was a logical thought.

However, it proved impossible in practice. Economics alone made isolation an unfeasible goal—Psy might have all been linked into the PsyNet, the sprawling psychic network that anchored their minds, but they were not all equal. Some were rich, some were poor, and some were just getting by.

They needed jobs, needed money, needed food. And the Psy Council, for all its brutal power, could not provide enough internal positions for millions. The Psy had to remain part of the world, a world filled with chaos on every side, bursting at the seams with the extremes of joy and sadness, fear and despair. Those Psy who fractured under the pressure were quietly "rehabilitated," their minds wiped, their personalities erased. But others thrived.

The M-Psy, gifted with the ability to look inside the body and diagnose illnesses, had never really withdrawn from the world. Their skills were prized by all three races, and they brought in a good income.

The less-powerful members of the Psy populace returned to their ordinary, everyday jobs as accountants and engineers, shop owners and businessmen. Except that what they had once enjoyed, despised, or merely tolerated, they now simply *did*.

The most powerful, in contrast, *were* absorbed into the Council superstructure wherever possible. The Council did not want to chance losing its strongest.

Then there were the Js.

Telepaths born with a quirk that allowed them to slip into minds and retrieve memories, then share those memories with others, the Js had been part of the world's justice system since the world first had one. There weren't enough J-Psy to shed light on the guilt or innocence of every accused—they were brought in on only the most heinous cases: the kinds of cases that made veteran detectives throw up and long-jaded reporters take a horrified step backward.

Realizing how advantageous it would be to have an entrée into a system that processed both humans, and at times, the secretive and pack-natured changelings as well, the Council allowed the Js to not just continue, but expand their work. Now, in the dawn of the year 2081, the Js are so much a part of the Justice system that their presence raises no eyebrows, causes no ripples.

And, as for the unexpected mental consequences of long-term work as a J . . . well, the benefits outweigh the occasional murderous problem.

CHAPTER 1

Circumstance doesn't make a man. If it did, I'd have committed my first burglary at twelve, my first robbery at fifteen, and my first murder at seventeen.

—*From the private case notes of Detective Max Shannon*

It was as she was sitting staring into the face of a sociopath that Sophia Russo realized three irrefutable truths.

One: In all likelihood, she had less than a year left before she was sentenced to comprehensive rehabilitation. Unlike normal rehabilitation, the process wouldn't only wipe out her personality, leave her a drooling vegetable. Comprehensives had ninety-nine percent of their psychic senses fried as well. All for their own good of course.

Two: Not a single individual on this earth would remember her name after she disappeared from active duty.

Three: If she wasn't careful, she would soon end up as empty and as inhuman as the man on the other side of the table . . . because the *otherness* in her wanted to squeeze his mind until he whimpered, until he bled, until he begged for mercy.

Evil is hard to define, but it's sitting in that room.

The echo of Detective Max Shannon's words pulled her back from the whispering temptation of the abyss. For some reason, the idea of being labeled evil by him was . . . not acceptable. He had looked at her in a different way from other human males, his eyes noting her scars, but only as part of the package that was her body. The response had been extraordinary enough to make her pause, meet his gaze, attempt to divine what he was thinking.

That had proved impossible. But she knew what Max Shannon wanted.

Bonner alone knows where he buried the bodies—we need that information.

Shutting the door on the darkness inside of her, she opened her psychic eye and, reaching out with her telepathic senses, began to walk the twisted pathways of Gerard Bonner's mind. She had touched many, many depraved minds over the course of her career, but this one was utterly and absolutely unique. Many who committed crimes of this caliber had a mental illness of some kind. She understood how to work with their sometimes disjointed and fragmented memories.

Bonner's mind, in contrast, was neat, organized, each memory in its proper place. Except those places and the memories they contained made no sense, having been filtered through the cold lens of his sociopathic desires. He saw things as he wished to see them, the reality distorted until it was impossible to pinpoint the truth among the spiderweb of lies.

Ending the telepathic sweep, she took three discreet seconds to center herself before opening her physical eyes to stare into the rich blue irises of the man the media found so compelling. According to them, he was handsome, intelligent, magnetic. What she knew for a fact was that he held an MBA from a highly regarded institution and came from one of the premier human families in Boston—there was a prevailing sense of disbelief that he was also the Butcher of Park Avenue, the moniker coined after the discovery of Carissa White's body along one of the avenue's famous wide "green" medians.

Covered with tulips and daffodils in spring, it had been

a snowy wonderland of trees and fairy lights when Carissa was dumped there, her blood a harsh accent on the snow. She was the only one of Bonner's victims to have ever been found, and the public nature of the dump site had turned her killer into an instant star. It had also almost gotten him caught—only the fact that the witness who'd seen him running from the scene had been too far away to give Enforcement any kind of a useful description had saved the monster.

"I got much more careful after that," Bonner said, wearing the faint smile that made people think they were being invited to share a secret joke. "Everyone's a little clumsy the first time."

Sophia betrayed no reaction to the fact that the human across from her had just "read her mind," having expected the trick. According to his file, Gerard Bonner was a master manipulator, able to read body language cues and minute facial expressions to genius-level accuracy. Even Silence, it seemed, was not protection enough against his abilities— having reviewed the visual transcripts of his trial, she'd seen him do the same thing to other Psy.

"That's why we're here, Mr. Bonner," she said with a calm that was growing ever colder, ever more remote—a survival mechanism that would soon chill the few remaining splinters of her soul. "You agreed to give up the locations of your later victims' bodies in return for more privileges during your incarceration." Bonner's sentence meant he'd be spending the rest of his natural life in D2, a maximum security facility located deep in the mountainous interior of Wyoming. Created under a special mandate, D2 housed the most vicious inmates from around the country, those deemed too high risk to remain in the normal prison system.

"I like your eyes," Bonner said, his smile widening as he traced the network of fine lines on her face with a gaze the media had labeled "murderously sensual." "They remind me of pansies."

Sophia simply waited, letting him speak, knowing his

words would be of interest to the profilers who stood in the room on the other side of the wall at her back—observing her meeting with Bonner on a large comm screen. Unusually for a human criminal, there were Psy observers in that group. Bonner's mental patterns were so aberrant as to incite their interest.

But no matter the credentials of those Psy profilers, Max Shannon's conclusions were the ones that interested Sophia. The Enforcement detective had no Psy abilities, and unlike the butcher sitting across from her, his body was whipcord lean. Sleek, she thought, akin to a lithely muscled puma. Yet, when it came down to it, it was the puma who'd won—both over the bulging strength that strained at Bonner's prison overalls, *and* over the mental abilities of the Psy detectives who'd been enlisted into the task force once Bonner's perversions began to have a serious economic impact.

"They were my pansies, you know." A small sigh. "So pretty, so sweet. So easily bruised. Like you." His eyes lingered on a scar that ran a ragged line over her cheekbone.

Ignoring the blatant attempt at provocation, she said, "What did you do to bruise them?" Bonner had ultimately been convicted on the basis of the evidence he'd left on the battered and broken body of his first victim. He hadn't left a trace at the scenes of the other abductions, had been connected to them only by the most circumstantial of evidence— and Max Shannon's relentless persistence.

"So delicate and so damaged you are, Sophia," he murmured, moving his gaze across her cheek, down to her lips. "I've always been drawn to damaged women."

"A lie, Mr. Bonner." It was extraordinary to her that people found him handsome—when she could all but smell the rot. "Every one of your victims was remarkably beautiful."

"*Alleged* victims," he said, eyes sparkling. "I was only convicted of poor Carissa's murder. Though I'm innocent, of course."

"You agreed to cooperate," she reminded him. And

she needed that cooperation to do her job. Because—"It's obvious you've learned to control your thought patterns to a certain degree." It was something the telepaths in the J-Corps had noted in a number of human sociopaths—they seemed to develop an almost Psy ability to consciously manipulate their own memories. Bonner had learned to do it well enough that she couldn't get what she needed from a surface scan—to go deeper, dig harder might cause permanent damage, erasing the very impressions she needed to access.

But, the otherness in her murmured, he only had to remain alive until they located his victims. After that . . .

"I'm human." Exaggerated surprise. "I'm sure they told you—my memory's not what it used to be. That's why I need a J to go in and dig up my pansies."

It was a game. She was certain he knew the exact position of each discarded body down to the last centimeter of dirt on a shallow grave. But he'd played the game well enough that the authorities had pulled her in, giving Bonner the chance to sate his urges once again. By making her go into his mind, he was attempting to violate her—the sole way he had to hurt a woman now.

"Since it's obvious I'm ineffective," she said, rising to her feet, "I'll get Justice to send in my colleague, Bryan Ames. He's an—"

"No." The first trace of a crack in his polished veneer, covered over almost as soon as it appeared. "I'm sure you'll get what you need."

She tugged at the thin black leather-synth of her left glove, smoothing it over her wrist so it sat neatly below the cuff of her crisp white shirt. "I'm too expensive a resource to waste. My skills will be better utilized in other cases." Then she walked out, ignoring his order—and it *was* an order—that she stay.

Once out in the observation chamber, she turned to Max Shannon. "Make sure any replacements you send him are male."

A professional nod, but his hand clenched on the top

of the chairback beside him, his skin having the warm golden brown tone of someone whose ancestry appeared to be a mix of Asian and Caucasian. While the Asian side of his genetic structure had made itself known in the shape of his eyes, the Caucasian side had won in the height department—he was six foot one according to her visual estimate.

All that was fact.

But the impact was more than the sum of its parts. He had, she realized, that strange something the humans called charisma. Psy professed not to accept that such a thing existed, but they all knew it did. Even among their Silent race, there were those who could walk into a room and hold it with nothing but their presence.

As she watched, Max's tendons turned white against his skin from the force of his grip. "He got his rocks off making you trawl through his memories." He didn't say anything about her scars, but Sophia knew as well as he did that they played a large part in what made her so very attractive to Bonner.

Those scars had long ago become a part of her, a thin tracery of lines that spoke of a history, a past. Without them, she'd have no past at all. Max Shannon, she thought, had a past as well. But he didn't wear it on that beautiful— not handsome, *beautiful*—face. "I have shields." However, those shields were beginning to fail, an inevitable side effect of her occupation. If she'd had the option, she wouldn't have become a J. But at eight years of age, she'd been given a single choice—become a J or die.

"I heard a lot of J-Psy have eidetic memories," Max said, his eyes intent.

"Yes—but only when it comes to the images we take during the course of our work." She'd forgotten parts of her "real life," but she'd never forget even an instant of the things she'd seen over the years she'd spent in the Justice Corps.

Max had opened his mouth to reply when Bartholomew Reuben, the prosecutor who'd worked side by side with

him to capture and convict Gerard Bonner, finished his
conversation with two of the profilers and walked over.
"That's a good idea about male Js. It'll give Bonner time
to stew—we can bring you in again when he's in a more
cooperative frame of mind."

Max's jaw set at a brutal angle as he responded. "He'll
draw this out as long as possible—those girls are nothing
but pawns to him."

Reuben was pulled away by another profiler before he
could reply, leaving Sophia alone with Max again. She
found herself staying in place though she should've joined
those of her race, her task complete. But being perfect
hadn't kept her safe—she'd be dead within the year, one
way or another—so why not indulge her desire for further conversation with this human detective whose mind
worked in a fashion that fascinated her? "His ego won't let
him hide his secrets forever," she said, having dealt with
that kind of a narcissistic personality before. "He wants to
share his cleverness."

"And will you continue to listen if the first body he gives
up is that of Daria Xiu?" His tone was abrasive, gritty with
lack of sleep.

Daria Xiu, Sophia knew, was the reason a J had been
pulled into this situation. The daughter of a powerful
human businessman, she was theorized to have been Bonner's final victim. "Yes," she said, telling him one truth.
"Bonner is deviant enough that our psychologists find him
a worthwhile study subject." Perhaps because the kind of
deviancy exhibited by the Butcher of Park Avenue had once
been exhibited by Psy in statistically high numbers . . . and
was no longer being fully contained by Silence.

The Council thought the populace didn't know, and perhaps they didn't. But to Sophia, a J who'd spent her life
steeped in the miasma of evil, the new shadows in the Psy-
Net had a texture she could almost feel—thick, oily, and
beginning to riddle the fabric of the sprawling neural network with insidious efficiency.

"And you?" Max asked, watching her with a piercing

focus that made her feel as if that quicksilver mind might
uncover secrets she'd kept concealed for over two decades.
"What about you?"

The otherness in her stirred, wanting to give him the
unvarnished, deadly truth, but that was something she
couldn't ever share with a man who'd made Justice his life.
"I'll do my job." Then she said something a perfect Psy
never would have said. "We'll bring them home. No one
should have to spend eternity in the cold dark."

Max watched Sophia Russo walk away with the civilian
observers, unable to take his attention off her. It had been
the eyes that had first slammed into him. *River's* eyes, he'd
thought as she walked in, she had River's eyes. But he'd
been wrong. Sophia's eyes were darker, more dramatically
blue-violet, so vivid he'd almost missed the lush softness of
her mouth. Except he hadn't.

And that was one hell of a kick to the teeth.

Because for all her curves and the tracery of scars that
spoke of a violent past, she was Psy. Ice-cold and tied to a
Council that had far more blood on its hands than Gerard
Bonner ever would. Except . . . Her final words circled in
his mind.

We'll bring them home.

It had held the weight of a vow. Or maybe that's what
he'd wanted to hear.

Wrenching back his attention when she disappeared
from view, he turned to Bart Reuben, the only other person who remained. "She wear the gloves all the time?"
Thin black leather-synth, they'd covered everything below
the cuffs of her shirt and suit jacket. It might have been
because she had more serious scars on the backs of her
hands—but Sophia Russo didn't strike him as the kind of
woman who'd hide behind such a shield.

"Yes. Every time I've seen her." Frown lines marred the
prosecutor's forehead for a second, before he seemed to

shake off whatever was bothering him. "She's got an excellent record—never fumbled a retraction yet."

"We saw at the trial that Bonner's smart enough to fuck with his own memories," Max said, watching as the prisoner was led from the interrogation room. The blue-eyed Butcher, the media's murderous darling, stared out at the cameras until the door closed, his smile a silent taunt. "Even if his mind isn't twisted at the core, he knows his pharmaceuticals—could've got his hands on something, deliberately dosed himself."

"Wouldn't put it past the bastard," Bart said, the grooves around his mouth carved deep. "I'll line up a couple of male Js for Bonner's next little show."

"Xiu have that much clout?" The trial of Gerard Bonner, scion of a blue-blooded Boston family and the most sadistic killer the state had seen in decades, would've qualified for a J at the trial stage but for the fact that his memories were close to impenetrable.

"Sociopaths," one J had said to Max after testifying that he couldn't retrieve anything usable from the accused's mind, "don't see the truth as others see it."

"Give me an example," Max had asked, frustrated that the killer who'd snuffed out so many young lives had managed to slither through another net.

"According to the memories in Bonner's surface mind, Carissa White orgasmed as he stabbed her."

Shaking off that sickening evidence of Bonner's warped reality, he glanced at Bart, who'd paused to check an e-mail on his cell phone. "Xiu?" he prompted.

"Yeah, looks like he has some 'friends' in high-level Psy ranks. His company does a lot of business with them." Putting away the phone, Bart began to gather up his papers. "But in this, he's just a shattered father. Daria was his only child."

"I know." The face of each and every victim was imprinted on Max's mind. Twenty-one-year-old Daria's was a gap-toothed smile, masses of curly black hair, and skin the color of polished mahogany. She didn't look anything like the other victims—unlike most killers of his pathology, Bonner hadn't differentiated between white, black, Hispanic, Asian. It had only been age and a certain kind of beauty that drew him.

Which turned his thoughts back to the woman who'd stared unblinking into the face of a killer while Max forced himself to stand back, to watch. "She fits his victim profile—Ms. Russo." Sophia Russo's eyes, her scars, made her strikingly unique—a critical aspect of Bonner's pathology. He'd targeted women who would never blend into a crowd—the violence spoken of by Sophia's scars would, for him, be the icing on the cake. "Did you arrange that?" His hand tightened on a pen as he helped Bart clear the table.

"Stroke of luck." The prosecutor put the files in his briefcase. "When Bonner said he'd cooperate with a scan, we requested the closest J. Russo had just completed a job here. She's on her way to the airport now—heading to our neck of the woods as a matter of fact."

"Liberty?" Max asked, mentioning the maximum-security penitentiary located on an artificial island off the New York coast.

Bart nodded as they walked out and toward the first security door. "She's scheduled to meet a prisoner who claims another prisoner confessed to the currently unsolved mutilation murder of a high-profile victim."

Max thought of what Bonner had done to the only one of his victims they'd ever found, the bloody ruin that had been the once-gamine beauty of Carissa White. And he wondered what Sophia Russo saw when she closed her eyes at night.

CHAPTER 2

Nikita Duncan, Psy Councilor and one of the most powerful women in the world, scanned the biographical data in the confidential file in front of her, pausing for a second on the attached digital image.

The human male had a distinctive face. Sharp cheekbones, skin that spoke of a complex genetic heritage, and eyes that hinted of a parent from central Asia. But it wasn't Detective Max Shannon's appearance that interested Nikita.

No, she was interested in something far more important—his mind.

CHAPTER 3

The patient is no longer connected to the PsyNct by a single biofeedback link—her mind survived by anchoring its entire consciousness into the fabric of the neural network. Any attempt at separation will lead not only to death, but to the total and complete destruction of her personality.

—PsyMed report on Sophia Russo, minor, age 8

Sophia hadn't slept for twenty-four hours when she walked into the ironically named Liberty Penitentiary the next morning, but no one could've guessed that from the crisp clarity of her tone, the smartness of her dress. She was taken directly to an interview room upon arrival. The assistant district attorney in charge of the case arrived a minute later.

Five minutes after that, she began the memory retrieval. Unlike Bonner's, this inmate's mind was full of nothing but forty years of living and violence. Some young Js got lost in the mess, but Sophia had learned to filter very well. She went directly to the memories of the day in question and took no more than the relevant minutes.

Humans tended to be suspicious of telepaths, and Js in particular, afraid the Psy would steal their secrets. The truth was, Sophia already had too many pieces of other people's lives in her head. She didn't want any more—especially the kinds of memories she was invariably asked to retrieve. In all her years of service, she'd found only four innocents. "I have it," she said to the A.D.A.

Asking the prisoner and his attorney to wait, he walked her to the waiting area outside the warden's office. "Could you project the memories to me?"

Nodding, she did as asked. This little telepathic quirk was what turned a Tp into a J. Most telepaths could transmit words and/or isolated visuals, but Js could not only retract, but transmit the entire memory in a continuous stream. This A.D.A. was human, his shields no barrier. That could have been a handicap in other circumstances—however, given that this case had no associated cost or benefit to the Council, he was safe from Psy coercion.

"Thank you," he said after she completed the projection. "That does put a different spin on things, doesn't it?"

She didn't answer, aware he wasn't talking to her. And even if he had been, she would've made no response. She tried not to "see" the memories anymore. It was a futile effort, but sometimes, she could distance herself a fraction.

The A.D.A. released a breath. "I'd like to go back and chat with the witness and his attorney. The jet-chopper will be arriving to take you back to the mainland soon."

"Please go ahead." She saw him looking around for the warden. "This location is tightly guarded. I'll be safe on my own."

"You sure?" A concerned look.

"I spend a lot of time in prisons."

"I guess you must at that. Alright, you've got my secretary's number. Give her a buzz if the chopper doesn't arrive in the next ten minutes."

"I will." Nodding good-bye as he left, she took a seat, outwardly calm. But the truth was, she should've never, ever been left alone. As she'd told the A.D.A., it wasn't because her physical position put her at risk. There were at least four double-keyed electronic security doors, full of bars and steel, between her and the first inmate.

It wasn't even because she might get scared sitting alone in such a cold, gray place.

She had witnessed thousands of moments of the most depraved violence and pain, but she herself didn't feel fear. She didn't feel anything. The Silence Protocol, the conditioning that chilled Psy madnesses as it chilled their emotions, ensured that. However, in Sophia's case, Silence didn't work as well as it should. And everybody knew it. Most Psy would have been summarily rehabilitated, but Sophia was a Justice Psy. And Js were rare enough and necessary enough that they were allowed their little . . . peculiarities.

Of course, Js were also never to be left alone in "suggestive" locations.

Evil is hard to define, but it's sitting in that room.

The reminder of Max Shannon's grim words stayed her hand for a second. Would he consider this evil? Perhaps. But as her path was unlikely to ever again cross with that of a man who'd made her, for a fleeting instant, wish to be something better, she couldn't let him guide her actions. Because though what she was about to do wasn't in any official manual, like all Js, she considered it part of her job description.

The first scream came four minutes later. In spite of its shrill, piercing nature, no one heard it. Because the man who was screaming was doing so soundlessly, his mind locked in a telepathic prison far more invidious than the plascrete and mortar one that surrounded him on every side.

Even as he screamed, he was moving, unzipping his pants, pushing them down to his ankles, shuffling over to pick up a tool he'd hidden in the hollow leg of the desk his attorney had won for him. The inmate was a learned man, his attorney had argued; it constituted cruel and unusual punishment to put him in a place where he couldn't write, couldn't keep his research notes. The attorney had never mentioned the tiny, helpless victim his learned client had put in a dog cage devoid of the most basic of human necessities.

However, the amenities he had taken such glee in winning were the furthest things from the inmate's mind at that moment. His hand clenched on the tool as he blubbered without voice, his will shredded like so much paper. Then the tool touched the flaccid white of his belly and he realized what he was about to do.

Blood dripped onto the floor almost a minute after that—it took time to achieve that kind of damage with nothing but a shiv, a weapon made out of a toothbrush ground against contraband rocks until its edges were as sharp as . . . well, almost a knife.

The act of amputation was excruciatingly painful.

And it was long over by the time a short, compact man with black hair faintly touched with silver walked into the waiting room. "I'm sorry for the delay, Ms. Russo. Your jet-chopper arrived five minutes ago, but I wasn't immediately able to spare an escort—several prisoners decided to get into a ruckus in the yard."

Sophia stood, briefcase held loosely in her left hand. "That's quite alright, Warden." The otherness in her settled back, its task complete. "I'm still on schedule."

Warden Odess escorted her through the first set of security doors. "This is what, your third visit here this month?"

"Yes."

"Things going well on this new case?"

"Yes." She paused as he cleared them through the second to last checkpoint. "The prosecution team feels certain of success."

"I guess they've got an ace in the hole with you. Pretty hard to argue innocence when you guys can pick the memories out of the accused's mind."

"Yes," Sophia agreed. "However, insanity or diminished responsibility pleas are quite popular in such cases."

"Yeah, I guess so. You can't see into their heads, right? I mean—know what they were thinking at the time?"

"Only by reference to their actions or words," Sophia said. "If those actions or words contain any hint of ambiguity, the field is thrown wide open."

"And, of course, the defense always argues that things weren't as they appear." Snorting, the warden stepped out into the crisp light of the late winter's day. Sophia blinked as she, too, exited. The light seemed too bright today, too intense, cutting across her retinas like broken glass.

Odess watched as she blinked. "Guess it's time for you to go in."

Most people didn't know that Js only worked one-month rotations before returning to the nearest branch of the Center to have their Silence checked. But Odess had been part of the prison system for over a decade. "How do you always know?" she asked, having worked with him sporadically over those ten years.

"That question is your answer."

She tipped her head a little to the side.

"You begin to act more human," he told her, his dark eyes holding a concern she'd never understood. "At the start, when you've just returned from wherever it is you go, your responses are short, distant. Now . . . we actually had a conversation."

"An astute observation," she said, realizing the tilt of her head for what it was—a sign of disintegration. "Perhaps we can have another conversation in a month's time." That was how long it would take for the conditioning to begin to fragment again.

"I'll see you then."

Sophia walked to the waiting jet-chopper with an easy, unhurried stride. She was in Manhattan proper by the time they discovered the prisoner bleeding in his cell.

Max had spent the night going over the Bonner case files, on the slim chance that the bastard would actually give up a body at some stage. In truth, every single detail of the Butcher's crimes was already engraved on his memory banks, never to be erased, but he'd wanted to be absolutely certain of his recall. All that death, the pain, coupled with the smug arrogance of the man who'd ended so many lives—it hadn't exactly left him in the best frame of mind for what had to be some kind of a Psy joke.

"Commander," he said, staring into the aristocratic face of the Psy who ran New York Enforcement, "if I can speak bluntly—"

"You rarely do otherwise, Detective Shannon."

In most humans and changelings, Max would've heard in that statement a wry humor. But Commander Brecht was Psy. He'd look at a rape victim with the same dispassionate gaze as he would a drive-by-shooter.

"So," Max said, pressing two fingers to the bridge of his nose, "you'll understand where I'm coming from when I ask you why the hell you'd put me on this. The Psy hate me."

"Hate is an emotion," Commander Brecht said from his standing position by an old-fashioned filing cabinet that had somehow survived all attempts at modernization. "You are more of an inconvenience."

Max felt his lips curve up in a humorless smile. At least you could never accuse Brecht of not cutting to the heart of the matter. "Exactly." He folded his arms over the crisp white shirt he'd put on in preparation for a court appearance. "Why would you want an inconvenience running an investigation into a Psy situation?" Psy were insular to the nth degree. They kept their secrets even as they stole those of others without pause or conscience. It pissed Max off, but all he could do was keep on doing his job. Sometimes, he won in spite of their interference—and that made it all worth it.

"You have a natural mental shield." Commander Brecht's tone was straightforward. "The fact that you're immune to Psy mental interference may have been a stumbling block when it comes to your career—"

Max snorted. Fact was, with his solve rate and aptitude tests, he should've made lieutenant by now. But he knew he never would—Psy controlled Enforcement, and his ability to withstand their attempts at coercion, to run his cases as he saw fit, made him an unacceptable risk in any position of power.

"As I was saying," the commander continued, his hair solid gilt under the streak of light coming in through the tiny window to his left. "While it may have been an obstacle in your path to a higher position within Enforcement, it is also an advantage."

"I'm not going to argue with that." Unlike so many humans, Max had never had to worry about whether he'd closed a case or looked the other way as a result of subtle mental pressure—many a good cop had broken because of that simmering kernel of doubt, that niggling concern that he'd been led to a particular conclusion. He said as much to Brecht. "I would've gone into private investigation if I didn't have the shield—staying here to get mind-fucked wouldn't have been at the top of my list."

The commander walked over to his desk. "It's beneficial for New York Enforcement that you decided to stay—you have the best solve-rate in the city. And you're also, as the humans would say, mule stubborn."

Max had been called a rottweiler once in a while. He took it as a compliment. "Still doesn't answer the question of why you'd want me on a Psy case." Command always assigned those to Psy detectives.

Max didn't have a problem with that—so long as it was only Psy who were involved. But it angered the hell out of him when humans and changelings got shortchanged because a member of the cold psychic race was part of the equation. "The Bonner situation—"

"Is currently at an impasse according to the report you turned in last night. You're going to wait him out, correct?"

Unfolding his arms, Max shoved a hand through his hair. "I still need to be able to respond quickly if he does decide to talk—I know this case like no one else." And though he'd run the Butcher to ground, his task wasn't yet over—wouldn't be over until he'd brought each and every girl home, giving their grieving families the peace of being able to bury their babies in proper graves.

To this day, he could feel the slight weight of Carissa White's mother as she collapsed into his arms—it had been a snowy winter's night when he'd gone to their pristine little villa, a villa Carissa had decorated with twinkling Christmas lights two weeks earlier. Mrs. White had opened the door with a laugh. Later, she'd gripped his jacket and begged him to tell her that it wasn't true, that Carissa was still alive.

And then she'd made him promise. *Find him. Find the monster who did this.*

He'd fulfilled that promise. But he'd made other promises to other parents.

No one should have to spend eternity in the cold dark.

"That shouldn't be a problem." Brecht's words crashed through the echo of another Psy voice—through the memory of a haunting statement so at odds with her glacial presence that Max hadn't been able to stop thinking about her.

"The case I want you to work is high priority, but with room for flexibility should you need to fly back to consult on the Bonner case." Brecht slid into the chair behind his desk. "If you'd take a seat, Detective." A pause when Max didn't immediately obey. "Your obsession with Bonner ended with the capture of a sociopath who would undoubtedly have continued to take lives if you hadn't stopped his killing spree. However, if you let that obsession control you now, you'll wind up dead of stress while he grows fat behind bars."

Max raised an eyebrow. "Been talking to the Enforcement shrink?"

"I may be Psy, but I was also a detective."

And because Max had seen Brecht's case files, because he knew the man *had* been one hell of a smart cop, he took a seat.

"What I'm about to tell you can't leave this room, whether or not you decide to accept the task." Brecht's eyes were a pale color between gray and blue, shards of ice encased in steel. "Do I have your word on that?"

"If it's an Enforcement matter, it's an Enforcement matter." Irrespective of anything else, he still believed in the badge, in the good that they did.

Brecht gave a nod of acknowledgment. "Over the past three months, Councilor Nikita Duncan—"

A Councilor?

Yeah, that got Max's attention.

CHAPTER 4

"—has lost three of her advisors by three very different methods. One was a heart attack, the second an automobile accident, the third an apparent suicide."

Max's gut went tight as cop instinct took over. "Could be coincidence."

"Do you believe in coincidence, Detective?"

"About as much as I believe in the tooth fairy."

The commander nodded. "Councilor Duncan does not believe in coincidences, either. She wants you to find out who is going after her people and why."

"She's in San Francisco," Max said, the same instinct telling him that far more was going on beneath the surface than a simple—and inexplicable—request for a human cop on a Psy case. But Max didn't go straight for the jugular—there were better ways of getting information. "Cops down there aren't going to like me stepping on their toes."

"For the purposes of this case, you'll be made a special investigator, with the authority to work across state lines.

It's regular practice with detectives who have the specialized skills to work a particular situation."

That much was true. However, something else was equally true. "I've heard the Psy have their own version of a police force. I'd have thought a Councilor"—especially a Councilor with all her secrets—"would want them to take care of it."

"Normally, yes." The commander picked up a small data crystal and placed it on the desk between them, a silent prick to the curiosity that made Max a cop who always, *always* found the answers. "However, the Arrow Squad is loyal to another Councilor, and if that Councilor is behind these attacks, then Councilor Duncan will not get the truth. Her own people have proved deficient in the skills necessary to take care of the task."

Max thought over what he knew of Nikita Duncan. She was an astute businesswoman, one who made money hand over fist—but unlike Councilors Ming LeBon and Kaleb Krychek, he'd never heard her name linked with a military operation, so it might be a legitimate fact that she'd found a gap in her resources once she eliminated this Arrow Squad from the mix.

"Alright," he said, eyes narrowed. "But mental shield aside, there's got to be some other reason the Councilor asked for me. What skills make me so special?" He was damn good at what he did, but there were excellent cops in San Francisco.

"Don't disregard your shield so easily," the commander responded. "It's one of the strongest we've ever encountered in a human." An implied confirmation that Psy had tried to break through it any number of times. "However, you're correct. There is something else—you have friends in the DarkRiver leopard pack. Councilor Duncan seems to believe that that friendship will make it easier for you to run the investigation in her city."

Ice crawled in a slow spread through Max's veins. Clay Bennett, the changeling male Max knew best, was one cool customer. Max wouldn't put it past the leopard pack to whittle down their enemy piece by piece—they were predators after all. But—"Isn't Councilor Duncan's daughter mated to Lucas Hunter, the alpha of DarkRiver?" Sascha Duncan's defection from the Psy world had made news across the country.

"Yes, but they no longer have any kind of a personal relationship."

Max nodded to show he'd heard, but the fact of Sascha's existence, her relationship with Lucas, put his mind at ease. Because while they might be predators, the cats were also big on family. He couldn't see them culling Nikita's people on the sly. "If I do this," he said, knowing he couldn't let it go now, his curiosity a steel blue flame inside him, "I'm going to need full access. If Duncan has her people blocking me at every turn, it's going to be impossible for me to do my job."

"Councilor Duncan understands that." Brecht picked up the data crystal and moved it in front of Max. "This has the basic background information. However, as you can imagine, there are areas of considerable sensitivity. That's why you'll be working with a Psy partner who'll help you in relation to the peculiarly Psy aspects of the investigation, and who will be tasked with filtering certain data."

Max had known he'd need a Psy advisor, but the second part of Brecht's statement made his hand clench on the crystal. "How the fuck is he going to realize what's relevant and what's not?"

"*She*," the commander said, "is to work intimately with you."

"Makes no difference to the question—what qualifications does this 'partner' of mine have to make those decisions?" Max wasn't just used to working alone, he liked it that way.

"She's a J," the commander said. "Has been operative since she was sixteen. She's now twenty-eight."

Anticipation licked along his spine. "What's her name?"

"Sophia Russo."

His mind reacted immediately—an image of haunting

eyes in a face marked by violence, a voice that said things it shouldn't, a body that made his own itch to thaw out all that ice. It was then, as he considered if the latter was even pos- sible, that he was hit by the import of Brecht's words. "Twelve years of active service? Most Js don't last that long."

He'd worked with at least twenty over his eleven years in Enforcement. Each had retired before the age of thirty, and, he realized, he'd never seen any of them again. It hadn't struck him as odd before, because Psy weren't exactly the type to send Christmas cards, but the fact that not one, *not one*, had ended up working in another area of Justice— either they had one hell of a retirement plan or . . . Given the cold-blooded way the Council treated its own people, the possibilities were chilling. And Sophia Russo had been a J for twelve years. She had to be reaching "retirement" age.

When the commander spoke, he didn't address Max's implied question, didn't tell him what happened to Js who reached the end of their working lives. "Ms. Russo has considerable experience in interacting with humans—you should find her a satisfactory partner." A pause. "Detec- tive, I need an answer today."

Max played the data crystal over his fingers. He still wasn't sure what the hell he was doing considering work- ing for the Psy, or the real reason why Nikita had asked for him, but if you stripped away all the bullshit, one thing remained unchanged—he was a cop. And Nikita Duncan was a citizen. "I'll do it."

Sophia sat across from the M-Psy in charge of her eval- uation at the Pittsburgh branch of the Center, her hands placed on the table, her eyes calm.

"There's been," the M-Psy said, "a report of an incident at Liberty Penitentiary."

She didn't fall for that trick, didn't respond. Because he hadn't asked a question.

"Did you have anything to do with that incident?"

"What was the incident?"

The M-Psy looked down at his notes. "A pedophile mutilated himself."

It was easy to keep her face expressionless—she'd been practicing since she was eight years old and about to be euthanized. "Was he human?"

"Yes."

"Perhaps he felt remorse," she suggested, knowing the creature in that cell had felt pity only for himself, for the fact that he'd been caught and locked up. "Humans have emotions after all."

"There's no indication he felt remorse."

At least the man hadn't managed to fool the prison psychiatrists. "Is he speaking?"

The M-Psy shook his head. "Not coherently."

"Then it's impossible to know if he felt remorse," she responded with total equanimity. Perhaps she should've felt guilt, but of course, she was Silent. She felt nothing. But she knew what that prisoner had done, knew every tiny detail of the horror he'd imprinted on a young, unformed psyche. Sophia had buried the memories even as she extracted them from the child's mind, leaving him with a week-long blank in his past that would only unlock when he was old enough and strong enough to bear it.

It was unfortunate that the trick didn't work on children who were born with the J facility. If it had, perhaps she would have had a different life . . . Perhaps.

The M-Psy tapped something on his datapad. "This is the third such incident in the past year where you've been in close proximity."

"I need to be in prisons often," Sophia replied, though her mind was in another room in a well-appointed cabin two decades in the past. "My chances of being near an incident are higher than that of an ordinary individual."

"The J-Psy Management Board has determined that you need to go in for reconditioning"—the M-Psy turned his datapad so she could see the authorization—"especially given your recent contact with Gerard Bonner."

"I have no disagreement with that." They'd poke and

prod at her during the reconditioning process, but Sophia knew what they'd find. Nothing. Complete or partial memory erasure might not work on Js, but a woman who made her living retrieving the memories of others got very good at clouding her own when necessary. "Would it be possible to schedule it today? I need to appear as an expert witness in a case first thing tomorrow morning."

Total reconditioning—known as rehabilitation—effectively turned the individual into a vegetable. But the basic reconditioning that Sophia had gone through any number of times took a bare few hours to complete. Add a full night's sleep and she'd be functioning at peak efficiency again when the sun rose.

The M-Psy checked his schedule. "We can slot you in at six tonight."

And, Sophia thought, she'd lose several hours to a semiconscious state—when time was running out for her at an inexorable pace. But all she said was, "Excellent."

"There is another matter."

Sophia looked up at the comment. "Yes?"

"The Management Board has reassigned you." The M-Psy sent an electronic file through to Sophia's organizer. "You've been selected to work directly for Councilor Nikita Duncan as a special advisor."

The first step, Sophia thought, having expected the transfer on some level. Js who began to show too many cracks were phased out step-by-step. By the time they disappeared, nobody remembered they'd once known a Justice Psy by that name. Nobody realized the J had simply vanished, never to be seen again. "My duties?"

"Councilor Duncan will brief you—you have an appointment with her at one tomorrow. Given the time of your court appearance, you should have no difficulty making your flight." The M-Psy stood. Paused. "I haven't been authorized to inform you of this, but you should have time to put your affairs in order."

Sophia waited. The words were unusual, could well be another trap.

But when he spoke, he gave her the answer to a question that had been circling in her mind for months now. "This reconditioning will be your last—your telepathic shields are too severely degraded to allow for a further reset." Cool green eyes met hers. "Do you understand?"

"Yes." *The next time she walked into a Center, only a shambling, empty-eyed shell would walk back out.*

CHAPTER 5

The child has been damaged on a fundamental level. Any attempt to save her will require the allocation of considerable time and resources with no guarantee of a productive return.

—*PsyMed report on Sophia Russo, minor, age 8*

Just over twenty-four hours after his conversation with Commander Brecht, Max exited his gate at San Francisco's domestic terminal with a single suitcase and one very pissed-off cat in an industrial-strength carrier. A cat whose yowling was starting to make people look at Max with the narrow-eyed stare reserved for those who beat their dogs and ran their horses to exhaustion.

"Max!"

Looking up, he saw a familiar tawny-haired figure. Putting the suitcase and carrier down, he picked Talin up in his arms and gave her a kiss on the lips. "Damn, you look good, Tally." Her face glowed with health, her freckles golden against skin that had managed to retain the burnished hue of summer even in the crisp chill of January.

A growl emerged from the green-eyed man on Tally's right, his gaze vivid against rich, dark skin. "Once, I'll allow. Kiss her again and all you'll be kissing is the asphalt."

Grinning, Max put a laughing Talin on her feet and held out his hand. "Nice to see you, too."

Clay shook it. "Hello, Cop." His eyes went to Max's feet.

And Max realized Morpheus had gone utterly silent the instant they neared the couple. Glancing down, Max saw the black-haired ball of indignant fur staring at Clay. "I think he's trying to figure out what the hell kind of cat you are."

Talin bent, went to reach through the bars as if to pet the cat.

"Don't," Max warned, one hand on her shoulder. "He bites."

"He bites Tally," Clay said, looking at the cat with eyes that were no longer human, "I'll show him *my* teeth."

"Shh, now," Talin said, stroking Morpheus gently on the forehead. "He's just mad about being cooped up, aren't you, gorgeous?" Looking up at Max, she mock-whispered, "Clay gets snarly on flights, too."

"Watch it," Clay said, but the curve of his lips made Max grin. Man was well and truly a goner.

"I'm glad you brought him," Talin said, rising to her feet. "He'd have missed you."

"Nah—he'd have found another sucker to feed him," Max said, knowing the former alley cat had the survival instincts of a rat on a sinking ship. "But since I'm not sure how long this'll take, I figured Morpheus might as well come and see the world with me." Nodding thanks at Clay as the changeling male grabbed his suitcase, Max took the carrier. "I appreciate the pickup."

"I voted to leave you stranded," Clay muttered.

Talin linked her arm with Max's. "Don't mind him. Secretly, he loves you."

"Very secretly." Max's heart went tight in a good way at seeing Talin so happy. They'd become close during the investigation into several missing kids a while back, but he'd known her on and off for years, their beats colliding in New

York. She'd worked with troubled kids—and Enforcement was always picking up those kids.

But it wasn't just that. He and Talin had a connection, one they'd never really articulated but which was simply understood. They'd both been children caught in the foster-care system, understood the scars that could leave. It wasn't the kind of thing you could really explain to anyone who hadn't lived through it.

But Clay got it. Max didn't know the big man's history, but the connection Max shared with Talin was slowly being formed with her mate as well. Max had taken them to dinner the last time they'd come up to Manhattan, had ended up getting well and truly drunk with the leopard. Talin had herded them home from the bar, promising to tear the hides off them the entire time, but she'd tucked them both in that night—pushing Max down onto their hotel couch and telling him to stay put.

Grinning at the memory of the pulsating rock music she'd played the next morning as punishment, he looked down at the wild mane of her hair. "Did you check out the apartment?" He'd e-mailed them the details of the place where he'd been put up for the duration.

"It's near Fisherman's Wharf," Talin said, "not that far from the Duncan building. Nice area—close to the shops."

Clay glanced up as he stowed Max's bag in the trunk of the car. "You sure you don't want to tell us what you're doing for Sascha's mother?" His eyes were human again—and full of a keen intelligence, as befitted one of Dark-River's top men.

"Sorry, can't say anything. Not yet." Max put Morpheus in the backseat. "I might be able to share more once I know what's going on." Getting into the seat beside the still silent cat, he strapped up and waited for Clay and Talin to get in. Except . . . "What the—" Reaching beneath his thigh, he found himself holding some sort of a weird pink-haired doll with joints in impossible places.

"That's a Metamorph," Talin told him, turning to look over her shoulder. "They change into animals."

"Huh." He played with the little toy, managed to figure out the mechanism, and voila, he had an improbably pink wolf on his hands. "Like a changeling."

"Yep. Clay keeps buying them for Noor even though she already has at least a dozen." Talin was twining her fingers with her mate's free hand even as she teased him. "One look from those big brown eyes and he folds."

Clay lifted up her hand and pressed a kiss to her knuckles. "You don't complain when I melt for your big gray eyes."

."*Clay.*" Blushing, Talin nonetheless blew her mate a kiss.

Relaxed by the byplay, Max leaned back in his seat—after checking to ensure a still silent Morpheus was okay—and thought about the e-mail he'd received while waiting to board the airjet. It had come via the commander's office.

Sophia Russo will meet you in San Francisco.

Anticipation thrummed through him—his body didn't seem to want to accept the fact that the woman was more likely to freeze his balls off in the night than consent to tangle with him in the male/female sense.

But Max had stopped being ruled by his hormones around the age of sixteen, no matter that this J with her night-violet eyes full of secrets tugged at him in the most visceral of ways. Using the time he had before his flight boarded, he'd made a few phone calls, including one to Bart Reuben to get an update on Bonner. The prosecutor had had nothing new to report on that front, but when Max mentioned he was going to be working with Sophia, he'd said, "I got curious about her, did some digging."

Max had been startled by a sudden—and forceful—surge of possessiveness. "Why?"

"Those gloves," Bart had replied. "I realized I'd seen them before, on a J I worked with a long time ago. I know they mean something, but I haven't figured out what yet. However, I did find out something else very interesting."

Fighting off his unexpectedly strong response to the idea of Bart investigating Sophia, Max had forced his tone to lighten. "You going to make me beat it out of you?"

"No, a bottle of single malt whiskey will do." He'd been able to hear the laugh in his friend's voice. "Seems like over the past year, our Ms. Russo has developed a curious little habit of being in close proximity to some very nasty people who decided to mutilate themselves in creative ways."

"That's not surprising, given how long she's been a J." A cop would have to be willfully blind to miss that occasionally homicidal "quirk" of J psychology. It was always impossible to prove anything, of course, even if a cop felt so inclined given the nature of the individuals the Js invariably targeted, but the Corps policed itself very effectively—it wasn't good for their image to have their people start going nuts in public.

Even as the thought passed through his head, Max had found himself disturbed by the idea that Sophia Russo might be going slowly insane. "Why hasn't she been yanked from active duty?" It had come out harsher than it should have.

Bart, thankfully, hadn't noticed. "She's very, very good at her job," he'd replied. "But she's reaching her use-by-date. One of these days, she's going to disappear just like every other J I've worked with over the years."

Now, as the car entered the hilly streets of San Francisco proper, Max thought of the last words Sophia had spoken to him, and he felt a low burn of anger in his gut at the idea of her having a "use-by-date."

Sophia took a seat across from the exotic-looking woman who might well sign the order for her rehabilitation once she was deemed obsolete. It should have concerned her, if only on an intellectual level, but Sophia wasn't affected by much at present.

So soon after a reconditioning, with her mind piercing in its clarity, the facts were undeniable: her shields against the PsyNet were rock solid—for the simple reason that all Js were drilled remorselessly until they mastered that skill— but the shields that protected her on a day-to-day basis, her telepathic protections, were paper-thin. Any number of occurrences could incite a devastating mental wave.

Results could range from shock and psychic disintegration to death.

Councilor Nikita Duncan raised her head from the file on her desk as Sophia was thinking she'd prefer a sudden and total death over a psychic collapse. Far better that it all end in a sudden, bright burst of agony, than to find herself weakened and at the mercy of those who had none. She'd been helpless once in her life—never again would she allow herself to be in that position.

"Ms. Russo"—Councilor Duncan's voice was precise—"I believe you had a court appearance this morning?"

"It was at nine," Sophia said without pause. "I was finished and on my way here by ten thirty."

"So you've had a chance to read the file I e-mailed to you?"

"Yes, I went through it on the airjet." What she didn't add was that she'd spent the majority of the time looking at the small digital image of the man she'd be working with, a man she'd never expected to see again in the course of what remained of her lifetime.

The photo had been taken earlier this year, and there'd been something in it that said he'd been laughing just before the photographer pressed the shutter, those uptilted eyes lit from within. She'd found herself fascinated by the difference between that image and the grim-faced man she'd met outside the interrogation room in Wyoming.

"Do you have any questions?" Nikita asked.

"Not at this stage—the assignment appears straightforward." Other than the fact that she'd been paired with a human who made her think thoughts that weren't only impossible, but so outrageously impossible that she wondered if she was already walking the cracked and twisted road to irrevocable insanity.

Nikita's eyes turned into pieces of jet, hard, cutting. "Before we continue, I want to make one thing explicit—I don't want any 'incidents' while you're in my employ."

"I don't know what you're referring to, Councilor." Sophia kept her face expressionless—it was a fiction, but it was a fiction that would keep her alive a little longer. Long enough to speak to Max Shannon again, to find out what it was about him that made the last forgotten slivers of her soul, her personality, shimmer with unexpected fragments of light. At the same time, the otherness whispered that he was smart, that he'd discover everything about her and turn away once he knew. It would hurt. And the broken girl inside of her, the secret hidden beyond Silence, was tired, so tired of hurting.

"I've said what I have to say," Nikita said after a small pause. "Break the rules and you'll pay the price."

Sophia knew enough of Nikita to understand that that was no idle threat. The Councilor was rumored to be a viral transmitter, able to infect minds with the most fatal— and if she chose, viciously painful—of psychic weapons. "Understood." Rising to her feet, she picked up her organizer. "I do have one question that doesn't relate directly to the case."

Nikita waited.

"According to my immediate supervisor, you specifically requested me." Sophia hadn't been aware that Nikita even knew her name. "Was there a reason for that?"

"It made more sense to use you than to take a fully functioning J out of the system." Cool, pragmatic words.

Except for one thing.

Sophia knew Nikita was lying.

Max's mind had circled back to Bonner by the time they arrived at the apartment—having stopped to pick up a few supplies on the way. Forcing himself off the topic, if only to deny the bastard the satisfaction of knowing he'd once again got everyone dancing to his tune, he looked around the apartment while Talin played with a Morpheus who was still miffed at his recent imprisonment. But judicious use of cat treats and Talin's stroking hands seemed to be bringing the sulking beast out of it.

"Nicer place than I expected," he said to Clay. Big bedroom, living area, kitchen, and bath. And he had windows. "Guess being a special investigator pays more than being a detective."

Clay walked to join Max at the window near the dining alcove. "Good view from here. We've had a lot of heavy fog in the mornings, but it makes for some spectacular sunrises."

"Yeah." Lowering his voice, Max asked, "How's Jon?" The teenager had been kidnapped, held in a Psy lab, and tortured before being rescued. Last Max had heard, he was giving Talin and Clay fits with his tricks.

Clay grinned. "Still a smartass teenager."

"So, normal?"

"Yeah. He's got a crush on one of the young dominant females—poor cub. He doesn't realize how nice she's being to him by not kicking his ass."

Max grinned, relief a crushing wave inside him. "I bet she thinks he's adorable."

Clay snorted. "I think it's more a case of 'aw damn, he's a baby, I can't hurt him.'"

"Ouch." Max winced, feeling for the kid. "That's got to bite."

"Uh-huh." A very feline look appeared on Clay's face. "But, you know, he's determined as hell. A few years down the track and who knows."

"Max?"

Glancing around at Talin's voice, he saw Morpheus purring in her lap. Ungrateful alley cat never purred for Max. All he got was sniffs and snarls. "Yeah?"

"Do you want me to take him home with us?" Worry marked her expressive features. "He doesn't look like an inside cat."

Max scowled on Morpheus's behalf. "Damn right he's not. He'll find a way out of here within the day." And probably come home with a few new scars to add to his already prodigious collection.

Talin scratched the traitorous cat behind his ears. Morpheus's eyes all but rolled into the back of his head. "Well," she said, sounding dubious of Max's claim, "if he starts to pine for some greenery, you know where I live."

"Morpheus's favorite hobby involves garbage cans—I think he'd have an aneurysm in a forest," Max muttered. "Is he really purring?"

"Of course he is. I know how to treat cats." A sultry glance aimed solely at her mate.

Max rocked back on his heels, feeling like a voyeur and—if he was honest—a little bit envious as well. He'd give his right arm to be loved like that . . . to love like that. But fact was, he wasn't capable of that depth of vulnerability, and he was honest enough to know it, to never make promises he couldn't keep.

One woman had kissed him on the cheek as they parted and said, "You threw away the key to your heart a long time ago, didn't you, Max?"

He'd smiled that night, because she was a woman he respected, a woman who remained a good friend, but afterward, he'd wondered—had he thrown it away or had the lock become permanently warped, incapable of opening?

The discreet chime of the doorbell silvered into the air, into his thoughts. "I'll get it." Walking across, he opened the door.

And knew he'd been waiting for her since the second he set foot in this city of fog beside a sparkling bay.

CHAPTER 6

Any skin-to-skin contact with a human or changeling, even a Psy with inadequate shields, may destroy what remains of your telepathic protections. Avoid all physical contact.

—*Advisory letter to Sophia Russo from the*
J Corps Medical Division

Sophia was unprepared for the visual impact of Max Shannon, no matter that she'd met him previously. He was the kind of man some women would want to own, she thought, having run across such females in the course of her career several times. They would see him as a trophy, a prize to show off—never realizing that they were attempting to leash a vicious storm.

Though Max was beautiful, what saved him from crossing the line into a more delicate prettiness was the obdurate hardness of his jawline, the unflinchingly adult expression in his gaze. Those eyes said that Max Shannon had looked into the void—and come away with a piece of it in his soul.

Then he spoke, drawing her attention to those well-shaped lips. "Sophia." He'd braced one hand on the doorjamb, didn't pull it down to offer to her.

She appreciated the gesture—many humans took it as an insult when she refused to shake their hands, never realizing that the common courtesy could cost her everything. "I thought I should let you know I'd arrived. I've been placed in the apartment next door."

Max glanced to his right. "That'll make things easier." Easy words, but his tone said something else.

"I won't be spying on you, Mr. Shannon." Something long dormant in her stirred at the challenge she read in him. "To be quite frank, your personal activities hold no interest for either me or Councilor Duncan." Not quite the truth. Nikita might not care about Max Shannon's personal life, but Sophia found herself compelled to know the man behind the enigmatic mask of an Enforcement detective.

The edge of a smile touched Max's lips, but it was his eyes that mattered. They never lost that blade-sharp gleam that told her he was calculating her every move, her every act. "You just want me for my detecting skills, is that it?"

She didn't know how to respond to the patently nonserious question—she'd been dealing with humans her entire adult life, but she'd never dealt with someone who evoked this odd . . . *fascination* in her. It had begun with the way he looked at her but was now a wholly independent thing. And the fact that it was already so strong so soon after a reconditioning, meant she had far less time than she'd previously believed before her telepathic shields sheared forever.

Someone spoke behind Max at that moment, and he turned, dropping his arm from the doorjamb. That was when Sophia saw the two other individuals in the room. A human female and a male who was clearly *not* human. She took a step back and to her left as the couple exited to stand to her right.

"Clay, Talin, this is my . . . partner"—a pause she knew had been intentional—"Sophia Russo."

The man gave a nod, while the woman smiled. "Nice to meet you."

Sophia nodded in response, wondering how this Talin could stand with such calm beside the male who was unquestionably a predator. And since this was San Francisco there were only two possible conclusions—only one once you factored in the way the green-eyed man had moved, with a fluidity at odds with the muscular size of him. "You're members of DarkRiver?"

"You must be new to the city," Talin said, tucking back her hair to reveal an ear adorned with a dangling earring made of irregular glass beads in the colors of autumn. "Most people recognize Clay."

"I've been to San Francisco before," Sophia replied, intrigued by the odd shapes of the beads, the way they'd been put together. There was no conformity, no perfection. "However, I deal almost exclusively with humans and Psy." Changelings had authority over all crimes that involved just those of their race.

"Sophia's a J," Max said, leaning one shoulder against the doorjamb.

She noted the corded forearms revealed by the rolled-up sleeves of his vivid blue shirt, noted, too, the easy grace with which he made even the smallest of movements—this man, she thought, was built along the sleek lines of the low-slung cars preferred by so many of the emotional races.

Her gaze clashed with his at that moment, and the question in them made her aware they were all waiting for something from her. Breaking the contact—which felt oddly, inexplicably intimate—she took a step to her left. "I'll leave you to your visit. Detective Shannon, if you'd just let me know when you're ready to start—"

"We can start now," he interrupted, still in that lazy position against the doorjamb. If she hadn't seen him in Wyoming, she might have been fooled into believing him "safe." But she had seen him in that prison. Not only that, she'd read the file that chronicled his stubborn, relentless pursuit of the Butcher of Park Avenue. She knew the danger that lay beneath the languid charm.

"We'll leave you to it, then." The woman named Talin stepped forward to kiss Max on the cheek, breaking Sophia's line of sight. "But I was hoping you'd have dinner with us," she said, turning to include Sophia in the invitation.

Max glanced at his watch even as Sophia curled the fingers of her left hand into her palm. What Talin had just done, that easy contact . . . it had been ordinary. Human. And it had made Sophia brutally aware of the gulf between her and this cop whose presence, whose watchful eyes, fanned the fires of rebellion in her.

"It's almost three now," Max said, his voice low and smooth—and disturbingly abrasive against Sophia's skin, "so how about dinner around seven? We should be ready for a break by then anyway." A glance up at Sophia from those eyes that saw far too much. "That work for you?"

She didn't know why she said, "Yes, that'll be fine," when she should have demurred from the social invitation. As her response to Max demonstrated with manifest clarity, she'd failed in her attempts to be the most perfect of Psy. But she was in no way similar to a human. She was, in all probability, even less "human" than most of her brethren, her psyche having been worn away by the corrosive acid of the images stored in her brain.

Clay said good-bye then, his voice deep against Talin's softer tone. As the couple left, the leopard male's hand on his mate's lower back, Sophia found herself the sole focus of Max's perceptive near-black eyes, the eyes of a man who was used to stripping shields, unearthing the most deeply buried of truths. "Come on in," he said, "unless you need to grab anything from your place? We should go over the details, make sure we're on the same page."

"Yes, I'll retrieve my organizer." The words came out calm, though her heartbeat had turned erratic. "It'll take me only a minute or two." Stepping to her door, she pushed through and picked up the small case she'd left on the coffee table. She should've walked straight back out, but she took a minute to breathe, to check her PsyNet shields for any minor fractures that might betray the swiftness with which her recent reconditioning had begun to degrade.

Satisfied that everything was holding for now and certain, too, that her secrets were safe from a cop who saw too much, she went to Max's. His living area was empty.

Assuming he'd gone to retrieve his own notes, she closed the door and took a seat at the small table in the dining alcove near the window.

She'd just opened her case when a huge black cat jumped onto the chair opposite, placed its front paws on the table, and looked at her with one gray and one brown eye. Physically startled, she nonetheless contained her reaction—that aspect of her conditioning was so much a part of her, it no longer took much effort to maintain.

The cat continued to stare at her.

Curious as to what the creature would do if touched, she extended a hand and brought her fingers to its nose. It sniffed at the leather-synth of her glove before proceeding to stare at her again.

"Ignore Morpheus." Max walked back into the room and picked up the cat to drop him easily to the floor. The feline padded off, tail in the air. "He likes to stare people out."

"I see." She found herself following Max's movements as he put some cat food and water into a split feeding dish. He'd changed into jeans and a black T-shirt that bared his arms, the color an austere contrast to the golden warmth of his skin tone. "Have you had any further contact from Bonner?"

Sleek black hair fell across his forehead as he shook his head and rose. "No." A single harsh word. "Bastard's probably waiting for us to crawl back to him."

"He'll wait a long time."

To her surprise he said, "If I thought he'd tell us the locations of the bodies if I crawled, I'd do it without hesitation."

The answer added another layer of complexity to his personality, made the fascination inside her grow. "Most males, especially those drawn to a career in Enforcement, would consider that an insult to their pride."

"Pride is meaningless if you can't keep your promises." Washing his hands after making that cryptic statement, he wiped them on a towel and came to take a seat opposite her. "First things first"—all cop, not even a trace of the deceptive charm she'd seen in the doorway—"here's what I know." He recapped the situation. "Do you have any more information?"

"I don't believe so." She made herself concentrate on the screen of her organizer. "As far as I can tell from your summation, we were given identical files." Except that hers had included an image of Max Shannon, an image she'd saved to an encrypted file.

Max leaned back in his seat, waiting to speak until she'd lifted her eyes to him. "Have you been to any of the scenes?"

"No. Kenneth Vale's—the apparent suicide's—apartment has been compromised to the point where it's useless as far as any forensic examination is concerned," she told him, having checked that with Councilor Duncan. "However, it was left intact to give Council psychologists a chance to examine it in case it threw any light on Vale's personality. His suicide is considered an unusual case."

Max narrowed his eyes. "You talking about the method he used to hang himself?"

"Yes." Sophia couldn't imagine the demons that would drive a man to choose such a long, tortuous form of death—if indeed, he had chosen his death. "I've been given the codes to access his apartment."

"Good, we'll go have a look. I'm guessing we've got nothing on the heart attack victim—file says he was cremated," Max said, tipping back his chair.

"They would have taken samples of his blood, checked for—"

"I e-mailed Nikita from New York," Max interrupted, "asked her about that. Seems like the samples have mysteriously disappeared."

"Interesting."

"Isn't it?" He tapped his finger against the table, and it wasn't a restless movement. "What about the car the third possible victim was driving when she had her accident?"

"It's being held at a private facility here in the city."

"Well, that's something at least." Scowling, he tipped his chair even farther back. "Would've been better if Nikita had called us in right away instead of waiting several weeks after the crash—but I guess she figured she could get to the bottom of it herself."

Sophia couldn't concentrate on his words, her attention held by something else altogether. "You'll fall over if you keep doing that."

He shot her an amused look, continuing to hold the precarious balance. "Used to drive my foster families nuts."

His openness about being in the foster-care system was unexpected. And it made Sophia give in to the seeds of rebellion, to ask a question that a perfect Psy would have never asked. "You weren't with one family long term?"

"No. Longest was six months," he said easily, and tipped his chair back down on all four feet. "I assume Nikita had her techs check the vehicle out?"

She nodded, a strange realization taking form inside of her. Max hadn't had parents either, not in reality. He was like her, at least in that way. She wanted to share that with him, with this man who'd seemed to *see* her from their very first meeting, but she didn't know how, having no capacity or experience at building bonds with another individual. "Yes," she said instead, harshly aware of how remote she sounded, how inhuman . . . as if she was already dead. "However, Councilor Duncan has authorized the expenditure required to get an independent report if you think it necessary."

"I'll decide that after I have a chat with the mechanic." Pushing back his chair, he rose to his feet, the scent of his body—soap, warmth, something darker—sweeping across her senses. "But first—Vale's apartment."

"Alright." She stood, aware her movements were not as graceful as his—her body felt jerky, disconnected. "If you'll give me a moment to change out of my suit."

"You had court this morning?" He reached out to open the door for her, the action making her pause for a second. Men never did things like that for her. It wasn't because she was Psy—she'd watched any number of males do the same act automatically for all females. But they always seemed to want to distance themselves from the violence she wore on her face—as if they were afraid it was catching.

"Sophia?"

She realized she'd been quiet too long. "Yes?"

"How did the case go?"

"How it always does," she said, unlocking her door with gloved hands that were a constant reminder of who she was, and who she'd be till the day she died—no matter the need to rebel, to break the chains of a past that refused to set her free, there could be no other tomorrow for her. "I told the judge and jury what I saw. That is all I do."

CHAPTER 7

Men who know their fathers are different creatures from men who don't. It's time I ripped off that particular blindfold.

—E-mail from Max Shannon to Bartholomew Reuben

Max watched Sophia disappear into her apartment and let out a breath he hadn't been aware of holding. The woman got to him, no doubt about it. And she got to him in a way that made a mockery of any thoughts he might've had about keeping his emotional distance.

Heading back to his bedroom with that truth circling in his head, he grabbed a black Windbreaker from his suitcase. It took only a couple of seconds to shove his cell phone inside and shrug into it—walking back out, he leaned against the wall opposite Sophia's door as he waited for her to finish changing. It gave him a couple of very needed minutes to calm down.

And face the facts.

His body not only liked the idea of Sophia Russo, it liked the reality of her even more. She had lush, sensual lips, curves that made a man thank God—and she smelled so good he wanted to bury his face in her neck like the leopards did with their mates. But those eyes that had once reminded him of River's laughing gaze . . . they were utterly flat, so lifeless he may as well have been talking to an automaton.

With most Psy, he would've accepted that lack as an inevitable side effect of their emotionless personalities, but with Sophia, he knew it had to be a carefully constructed lie. Because no one who'd seen the things Sophia Russo had seen, who'd walked in the blood-soaked footsteps of evil, could have remained unscathed by it.

Not unless her emotions weren't simply buried, but excised from existence.

The door opened at that moment, revealing the woman at the center of his thoughts. She'd changed into jeans and a gray sweatshirt that covered those curves he was starting to obsess over. He could see the edge of a white T-shirt beneath the sweatshirt, while plain black sneakers peeked out from under the hem of her jeans.

"Is this appropriate?" she asked. "I assumed we might have time to go to the garage as well."

He ran his gaze not over her clothing, but over the soft curls of her shoulder-length hair. A rich, charcoal black, those curls tempted a man to fist his hands in the softness, tug her close, and sink his teeth—deliciously carefully—into that full lower lip. "Yes." It came out husky.

She hesitated, as if she'd caught the edge in his tone, but her words when they came were pragmatic. "I'll e-mail the Councilor from the car, ensure the chief mechanic knows we'll be coming." Locking her door after picking up that little computronic gadget that seemed to be surgically attached to her hand, she fell into step beside him, her head not even reaching his shoulder.

"You're short." He could tuck her under his arm, and against his body, without any problem whatsoever.

Sophia almost halted. "That kind of observation is rude in all cultures."

He shrugged, but he'd noted the jerky movement before she smoothed out her stride, considered the implications—Psy made it a point to react as little as possible, regardless of the provocation. And Max was very, very good at provocation when he was in the mood. "I didn't say you didn't look good short."

"I am what is termed a 'throwback' to my great-great-grandmother," Sophia said, her tone pure feminine frost. "She had the identical body type. I will never be slender."

"From where I'm standing"—Max couldn't help himself, the devil in him taking over—"slender is overrated."

Ignoring him with a focus that made his lips curve into a slow, satisfied smile, Sophia pressed her finger to the touch pad for the elevator. "Will your pet be alright in the apartment?"

Surprised she'd bothered to ask after Morpheus, he nodded. "I left a window open for him."

"There is only a very narrow ledge, and it's several floors off the ground." A glance back down the corridor, as if she was considering returning for Morpheus. "He is also in an unfamiliar city."

That look, the words, the hint of a personality behind the ice, had every one of his instincts humming—Sophia Russo was no robotic Psy. She was something, some*one* far more intriguing. "Morpheus is an alley cat," he said, remembering the way he'd seen her extend her fingers toward the cat, the inquisitive look on her face when she'd thought he wasn't watching. "He already considers that ledge his own personal egress and the city his very own playground, trust me."

"He is your pet and your responsibility."

Letting her step into the elevator as it arrived, he bit back a grin at that prim reminder and reached for the keypad. "I was told we'd have a vehicle—do you know if it's already here?"

"Yes. I picked it up and parked it in the basement garage." She waited until he'd pressed his finger to the appropriate number before surprising the hell out of him. "You can drive."

When he raised an eyebrow, she said, "I've had enough contact with human males to realize you seem to have a congenital inability to function while a female is at the wheel, and I'd rather your full attention be on the case."

He rocked back on his heels, way past intrigued and well into seriously screwed—because there was only one way this could end. That hint of personality and the inexorable tug of a deeper *something* between them notwithstanding, Sophia wasn't only a J, wasn't only a Psy, she was Councilor Duncan's personal eyes and ears. A smart man would keep his distance, make sure she never forgot that while they might be working together, they sure as hell weren't on the same team.

There was just one problem with that—he, a man known for leaving his lovers with smiles on their faces, and without a backward look, wanted to know every tiny detail about this woman who spoke to parts of him that had been in cold storage so long, his body physically hurt as they woke. It was, to be honest, uncomfortable as hell. More, the shocking intensity of his response went against the pragmatic nature of his mind—he was used to thinking, to planning.

But he was also a man who knew how to adapt. And he hadn't backed down from anything or anyone since the day he'd grown old enough, and strong enough, to defend himself . . . to protect himself.

"You know," he said as the elevator doors opened, determined to uncover the truth of the enigma that was Sophia Russo, "changelings would consider your letting me drive a surrender."

She stepped out into the garage, so prim and proper that he wanted to mess her up three ways to Sunday, the long-forgotten boy in him sitting up in mischievous anticipation. What would she do, he wondered? Did Sophia Russo even understand the meaning of the word "play"?

"I'm sure you realize," Sophia said in response to his comment, "that nothing is that easy with Psy, Detective."

"Max." He wanted to hear her say his name, acknowledge him as a man.

A slight nod. "This is our car." She stopped in front of a black sedan with tinted windows.

He whistled through his teeth. "This is a very well-designed tank." Sleek, meant to mix into ordinary traffic, but—to his experienced eyes—surely bulletproof and with a body built to survive impacts from vehicles twice its size.

"Councilor Duncan thought it prudent since I'll be working with you." A curl of raven black hair swung against her cheek as she began to slide off her right glove. "It's become common knowledge that once a J takes an 'impression' of a memory, that memory becomes inaccessible to another J."

Realization coalesced into a tight line of tension across his shoulders. "How many times has someone tried to kill you?"

"I'm not certain." She used her thumbprint—her hand unmarked, unscarred—to unlock the car and access the computronic control panel. "I can program you in now if you'll come over and press your thumb to the scanner."

He did so, waiting patiently while she ensured he had full rights to operate the vehicle. "Guess," he said afterward, as she got out and walked around to the passenger side door.

"What?"

"Give me an estimate of how many times you may have been the target of an assassination attempt."

She opened her door. "I've only been shot at three times."

Only. A lot of cops didn't get shot at that many times their whole career. Sliding into the driver's seat—after shifting it back more than a foot—he brought up the manual controls, viscerally aware of the delicate vulnerability of her skin bare inches away. "Why is that?" he asked, speaking past a sudden possessive edge that honed his protectiveness to a steely gleam.

And that, too, was a surprise. Though he was a protector at heart, a facet of his personality he'd learned to handle, he'd never been possessive . . . or maybe, a long silent part of him whispered, he'd simply learned not to be. If you didn't claim people, they couldn't reject you, couldn't leave you, couldn't break your fucking heart. Except even that reality didn't stop his primal response to Sophia—it came from some place deeper, beyond the civilized skin of his humanity.

Sophia turned to buckle her safety belt. "I assume," she said in response to his question, "people wanted to stop me from giving evidence—if I die, the impression dies with me."

His fingers almost brushed her hair as he braced his arm on the passenger side seatback in preparation for reversing the car.

The way she shifted to avoid any contact was subtle . . . and a chilling reminder that for all her lush femininity, Sophia Russo would never melt for any man. It should've thrown cold water on his simmering hunger, nipped that dawning possessiveness in the bud, but all it did was make him want to tug at her curls, just to see what she'd do.

There was a reason he'd spent most of junior high in detention.

Fighting the urge, he dropped his arm once he had the car out and angled toward the exit. Slow, he thought, he had to do this slow. She was so skittish, he'd have to stroke her into trusting him. If he pushed too hard, too soon, he'd lose any hope of getting through her shields—and that was unacceptable.

Because Max had made his decision. Whatever it was that burned between him and this J with her haunted eyes and secrets, he wasn't about walk away. "No," he said, making his voice deliberately relaxed, nonthreatening, "I meant why can't another J re-scan a memory?"

"We're not certain." Sophia's voice was steady, but with a husky undertone that brushed a kiss across his skin. "However, the strongest theory is that whatever mental 'door' we enter to take the memory has the flow-on effect of permanently closing that door the instant we leave."

"So with Bonner . . . ?"

"Scans were attempted at his trial but never completed. His mind is still 'open' in that sense."

Pulling out into the traffic, he put the car into hover-drive, but retained manual control. "There's no enforced automatic navigation here, right?"

"No. Manhattan is unusual in its rules—likely because of its geography."

"Hmm." Feeling the powerful vehicle purr under his hands, he relaxed into the seat and turned his mind to the case . . . and to a truth he wasn't blind to, no matter the power of what she incited in him. "Are you planning to fuck with me?"

To Sophia, the question was a rapier sharp thrust between her ribs. "Please explain your words, Detective." He'd been so easy a companion over the past few minutes she'd almost forgotten the lethal man she'd met outside that interrogation room in Wyoming. A mistake.

"You're meant to act as a filter"—a stroke of the steel that lay below the beautiful surface—"but fact is, I can't be effective if you're hiding things I need to know."

Sophia wondered how many suspects he'd fooled into dropping their guard before striking with that precise blade of a voice. "You've just called me stupid."

"Did I, Miss Sophia?"

Again, he unbalanced her, made her uncertain how to respond. Humans asked her for information, for insight into their cases, sometimes making small talk in the process, but this, what Max was doing . . . she didn't understand it. "Be blunt, Detective," she ordered. "I don't handle subtlety well."

Max shot her a look she couldn't read, but he followed her order. "I need to know whether to treat you as a partner or as a stooge for Councilor Duncan."

She thought of the cold-eyed woman who would one day sign her death warrant, ensuring her last days on this earth would be spent as a fugitive; thought, too, of this piercingly intelligent, complex man who made her wish—for one broken second—that she was normal. But she'd lost her chance at any kind of normality in a fracture of razor-sharp glass and screams twenty years ago. "Councilor Duncan wants you to find the mole in her system," she said in a voice that came out coated in ice. "I'm to do everything I can to assist you. That is the extent of my brief."

"So," Max said at last, "this suicide. Kenneth Vale."

Sophia brought up the information on her organizer even as she closed the door gently on the past, so as not to awaken the slumbering otherness inside of her. "He was the Councilor's specialist in stocks and bonds," she said, finding an anchor in what she understood, words and data and fact.

"What were the consequences of his death?" A practical question, but his voice had shifted again, the timbre warm, disturbingly intimate in the confines of the car.

Her hand slipped a little as her palm turned damp. "She lost a certain amount of money when news of Vale's suicide got out. You have to understand, such an act is highly unusual among Psy"—among *most* Psy—"and is considered a sign of severe mental illness."

Max's next words hit her without warning. "You're not telling me everything."

How had he known? She stared at the clean lines of his profile, her eyes lingering at his temple. He was human. All his records proved that without a doubt—and yet the way he read suspects, the way he'd just read her, it reminded her again that she'd have to be very, very careful around him.

If he realized the extent of the fractures inside of her, if he understood the things the otherness had done . . . She took a slow, careful breath. "It has no bearing on the case."

The look he shot her was brutal in its demand. "I'll decide what's relevant."

"Suicide," she finally said, "is considered an acceptable choice in some circumstances. However, in those cases, the suicide is usually undertaken in a quiet, unobtrusive way."

"Suicide's never quiet or unobtrusive." His voice was a whip, cutting across her skin. "I've seen enough shattered families to know that. But . . . Psy don't do love, do they?"

"No." Emptiness in her soul, an echoing nothingness where there should've been family, should've been connection, even if only of the coldest kind. "Often, in cases of severe mental deterioration, the choice is between suicide and rehabilitation."

Suicide is the better option, Sophia. Another J, speaking to her two months before he was discovered dead in a hotel room, having overdosed on a carefully calculated cocktail of drugs. *At least, you'll die whole. If they take you, they'll leave an atrocity behind—a creature that should not exist.*

CHAPTER 8

The minor's parents have willingly surrendered full custody to the state as she does not appear to have the capacity to manage life in the regular population.

—PsyMed report on Sophia Russo, minor, age 8

Max had been a cop for over a decade. It didn't take him long to connect the dots. Staring out at the city streets, he tried to wipe out the image of Sophia slipping softly into the last good night, unable to believe that this smart, steely woman would ever give in to death without a fight. "And do you think suicide is preferable to rehabilitation?"

"I believe the choice is the individual's." A pause. "But if you're asking if I would ever make that choice—no." She tapped the screen of her organizer with a little laser pen. "Would you like to talk about the second suspicious death?"

Convinced by her absolute answer on the issue of suicide, he turned his mind back to the case. "Carmichael Jones," he said. "Massive coronary in his suite while at a meeting in the Cayman Islands. Maid found him— pathologist ruled he'd been dead for at least two, three hours at that stage."

Sophia didn't say anything for almost a minute. Then, "Do you have all this data in your head?"

"Yes." Startled at the question, he glanced over, caught those night-violet eyes watching him with a focus that felt like a touch. "Don't you?"

"No, I have other things in my head." She dropped her gaze to the screen of the organizer, cutting off that topic, but he felt its shadowy echo all around him.

His hands clenched on the steering wheel. "Do you have nightmares?"

"Psy don't dream." It was the nonanswer he'd expected, but then she added, "It's easy for them to say that," and he knew Sophia had looked into the abyss and screamed.

Even as he opened his mouth to reply, she spoke again, and this time, her words were icily pragmatic. "Carmichael Jones was Councilor Duncan's main advisor in relation to the property arm of her business."

Max let her retreat for now. "Construction's a big part of her empire from what I've heard."

"Yes. She's had a lot of success building changeling-aimed complexes."

"Hmm." He considered what he knew of changelings. His friendship with Clay—and another DarkRiver sentinel, Dorian—was solid, but it had been earned through blood. In general, when it came to strangers, the predatory species tended to maintain a reserved distance. "How did she manage that?"

"She has an agreement with your friends' pack. I believe it's proven a beneficial arrangement for both parties." A little movement as she settled against her seat, the scent of her a tantalizing stroke across his senses. "There are rumors the SnowDancer wolves are a silent party in many of these deals, but no confirmation."

Max whistled. If the cats were chilly when it came to outsiders, the wolves were downright glacial. "Did Carmichael Jones deal with the leopards?"

"No. Nikita is the main contact—which is unusual."

Caressing the car through a turn, he shook his head. "Not really—I have a feeling her daughter was meant to be the original lead." He'd never met Sascha, but he had met her mate, Lucas, briefly during his previous trip to San Francisco—on the trail of another butcher, one who'd eviscerated children like they were so much meat.

"Detective . . . Max. Are you well?"

He realized he was squeezing the steering wheel hard enough to turn his skin bloodless. "Yeah."

"You have nightmares, too." Soft words. "They always pass."

The statement hit him with the force of a ten-ton truck—she was trying, he realized, to comfort him, this J who had more nightmares inside her skull than he'd ever see, even if he lived ten lifetimes. "Nikita," he said, his voice dropping as he fought the urge to bring the car to a halt, to take her into his arms, to comfort *her*, "probably took over when Sascha defected."

She didn't pursue the subject of nightmares. "Yes, that makes sense."

"And Sascha *is* her blood"—he knew better than anyone that that didn't always mean what it should, but in this case—"maybe she needs the contact."

Sophia shook her head. "Nikita cut off Sascha the instant her daughter proved flawed."

Her words, coupled with the direction of his thoughts, threatened to pitch him back into the past, into the life of another unwanted child. "Do you think," he said, slamming the door on those memories, "that Sascha is flawed?"

"It doesn't matter what I think, only what Councilor Duncan believes."

"You didn't strike me as a coward, Sophia."

Utter stillness. "What is it you want from me?" It was an outwardly calm question, but he was certain he heard a bewildered vulnerability beneath the surface.

It made him feel like a bastard. "I'm just trying to know who you are." And why she spoke to a part of him that had gone quiet a long, long time ago.

"Nobody," she said, her tone so flat, he could've imagined the soft-voiced woman who'd told him his nightmares would pass. "I'm nobody."

"Sophi—"

Sophia spoke over him, the dark, broken girl inside her panicked. He was pushing too hard, seeing too much. She wasn't ready to be exposed to the light, wasn't ready to bare the scars that scored her from the inside out. "Getting back to the financial situation," she said, the words coming out in a fast, staccato beat, "the cumulative effect of her advisors' deaths, while not huge, has been enough to cause Nikita significant problems in terms of her overall business reputation."

Max didn't speak for almost a minute, but when he did, it was about the case.

She didn't make the mistake of thinking he'd given up. Max Shannon had scented her weakness. And like the puma she saw in his masculine grace, he wouldn't let up until he'd drawn first blood.

CHAPTER 9

Hundreds of miles away, in the dark outskirts of Moscow, Councilor Kaleb Krychek got out of bed, having slept roughly two hours. Knowing there would be no more rest, not tonight, he pulled on a pair of pants in a thin, breathable material and went for a run across the night-draped countryside that surrounded his home.

The earth was hard, almost cutting underneath his uncovered feet, the wind a whip across the skin of his back. He felt none of it, his mind racing through the endless black skies of the PsyNet, the darkness broken only by the stars that represented the minds of the millions of Psy hooked into the network—a network that provided the biofeedback necessary for life.

Kaleb ignored those minds, his focus on finding the one piece of data the NetMind itself seemed to be hiding from him. Tonight, too, the neosentience that was both the guardian and librarian of the Net—a neosentience that in all other things obeyed Kaleb without question—held him at bay, its shields impenetrable.

Dropping back fully into the world, he ran at a pace that would've surprised those who'd seen him only in the suits he wore as a Councilor, pristine and flawless. That would've been their mistake. Because he was a cardinal telekinetic, his psychic strength beyond measure, his eyes—white stars on a spread of black—living pieces of the PsyNet. More, he was the most powerful Tk in the Net—movement was as simple to him as breathing. And tonight, he moved through infinite quiet. Even the nocturnal creatures seemed to have gone to ground.

Perhaps it was because they'd sensed a more dangerous predator in their midst.

Returning home after an hour, his body covered in sweat, he took a shower, then sat down at his desk. The first thing he pulled up was a file on Sophia Russo, not out of any particular interest, but because he made a habit of keeping an eye on what his fellow Councilors were doing. Nikita might've been an ally, but theirs was an alliance of expediency, nothing more.

The J-Psy's file was detailed, as was the case with most of her designation. And notwithstanding her irregular childhood, and recent appearance on the rehabilitation watchlist, her abilities fell within fairly normal parameters for a J. So why was Nikita so interested in this one particular J? There was no doubt that she was—the request to the J Corps had been very specific.

Making a mental note to monitor the situation, he was about to pull up another file when he felt something trigger his outermost shields on the PsyNet. Given that those shields were so complex they were all but invisible, he only spared the incident a cursory glance. Many people contacted his shields without realizing it. But then, the intruder made it *through* those shields.

Kaleb opened his psychic eye between one blink and the next.

The intruder was gone.

Which in itself was an answer—because anyone good enough to have left without getting caught in one of his traps shouldn't have triggered the alarm in the first place. "So," he murmured on the physical plane, "the game has begun."

CHAPTER 10

Sensation builds. You may consider a handshake harmless, but each time you touch a human, it threatens your conditioning.
—Excerpted from lessons given to Psy children during their transition into adult training

Sophia was more than ready to exit the car by the time Max brought it to a stop in front of a mid-rise building not far from Golden Gate Park—the site of Kenneth Vale's apartment, the location of his suicide. Sophia had never suffered from a psychological issue that made her vulnerable to claustrophobia, but being in that car with a quietly brooding Max had been . . . unsettling.

He took up more space than he should, the heat of his body inescapable in the confines of the vehicle. She'd felt as if he was touching her with each wave of that starkly masculine heat—and for a woman who hadn't been touched in years, it had been an experience that left her scrambling for escape.

"Entry codes?" Max asked as they walked up the steps, his voice rubbing against her skin like sandpaper.

Again, it was touch without a touch, something she had no ability to avoid, to process. "I have them here." She let them into the building and headed toward the elevator security console, her gloved fingers slipping off the pad once before she collected herself.

Trembling, Max thought, Sophia was trembling.

"This is a very exclusive building." A calm voice, that betraying hand dropping to her side as the elevator headed down to them. "Vale's position with Councilor Duncan enabled him to secure his privacy to this extent."

"Why bother?" Max folded his arms to keep from sliding his hand under her hair, to the soft warmth of her neck so he could tug her to him, so he could apologize for pushing her too hard, too soon, with a slow, sweet kiss—no matter that they'd been strangers only a day ago.

"Before these deaths," he said, forcing himself to maintain a white-knuckled hold on a need that refused to obey the rules of civilized behavior, "I'm guessing being Nikita's business advisor wasn't exactly a high-risk position, so why the security?"

"Humans," she said, "and the occasional nonpredatory changeling, have a way of expecting things from Psy they shouldn't." A meaningful glance out of those vivid, impossible eyes. "Vale was, in all probability, protecting himself from those who wanted to pitch to him in person."

The elevator opened at that moment. A woman entered the lobby at almost the same instant, swiping a card where Sophia had entered Vale's access code. "Please hold the elevator."

Max did so, conscious of Sophia all but disappearing into a corner.

"Thanks." The woman's ruby red smile betrayed her humanity. "Are you moving in? I haven't seen you before."

Max saw the stranger give him the once-over, recognized it for what it was. Women had been making him offers since before he was legal. And he'd learned to turn them down without hurting their feelings—because in spite of the actions of the woman who'd shaped him, he'd never hated her or those of her sex. Part of him had always wanted to protect her—even as a child, he'd known that no matter what she did to him, her pain was deeper, older, a vicious animal that tore her to pieces from the inside out.

So today, he gave this woman a small smile. "Just checking the place out."

"Well," she said as the elevator opened on her floor, "if you want to ask any questions about the area, call me." Passing over a card, she exited, her musky perfume a lingering reminder of her presence.

Sophia stirred. "She was playing a mating game with you."

Max had been about to drop the card into the small wrought iron recycling bin in the corner, but now slid it into his pocket. If it took jealousy to rouse the real Sophia to the surface, he'd use it without any guilt whatsoever—when a man got kicked this hard in the guts by a woman, anything was fair.

And the unique individual behind the mask of the perfect J, the one who'd told him Bonner's victims shouldn't have to spend eternity in the cold dark—that's who he wanted to know. "It's called flirting." He shot her a slow, deliberately provocative smile. "I'm sure you must've seen humans do it before."

"Is that the physical type that attracts you?" Aware she should back off, but unable to stop pushing for an answer, Sophia stepped out of the elevator on Vale's floor. "Tall, slender, with a fashionable-dress preference?"

Max gestured to the left of the quiet, carpeted corridor. "That's his place." Letting her pass him so she could input the code that would disengage the locks, he pushed open the door. "And," he said in a voice that made the tiny hairs on the back of her nape rise in warning as she walked in ahead of him, "the answer to your question is no. That woman didn't do it for me." He pushed the door shut behind them. "Now a small woman with dangerous curves . . . I could bite into her."

She froze, certain she was misreading the comment, but suddenly very conscious of the way her lower body filled out her jeans. "Detective Shannon," she said, turning to face him, "you're being highly inappropriate."

His lips kicked up at the corners. "You started it."

She wanted to trace the shape of those lips, wanted it so badly her fingers cramped as she fisted them. Her Silence had been fragmenting for years—an inevitable side effect of her work as a J, and one for which the J Corps had a "don't ask, don't tell" policy. So long as the medics didn't find any evidence, the J Corps Management Board wouldn't turn in a fractured J. It was partly an economic decision in order to retain the number of active Js . . . and partly because everyone in the Corps had looked into the chasm of madness at some point in their lives.

Though Sophia hadn't allowed herself to think about the truth even within her own mind, conscious of how deep M-Psy could dig, her conditioning had broken close to completely earlier this year, her mind twined with strange, dark tendrils that rebuffed Silence; and the reconditioning she'd undergone only the previous day had already been sloughed off like so much dead skin. But in spite of it all, she'd been able to hold up the facade, the pretense of being the perfect Psy. Until now.

"Breathe, Sophia." A husky order, and to her surprise, he took a step back, began to walk around Vale's living area. "This room is set up for entertaining—or maybe meetings, since I'm guessing Psy don't do parties?"

She forced her brain to function, to provide him with the answers. "Actually," she said, the words coming sluggishly as she fought the confusion created by his mere presence, "cocktail parties are held when there are human or changeling clients. It's all about putting the other side at ease."

Some Psy could even manage a glacial kind of charm— Councilor Kaleb Krychek had an unusual number of admirers in the non-Psy population. She couldn't understand why. Yes, aesthetically speaking, he was the epitome of a cold male beauty. But he was also, she was certain, quite capable of snapping his admirers' necks without the least pause should the occasion call for it.

"Do you know if Vale received business clients in here outside of any social events?" Max's expression was all cop when she dared meet his gaze again. Yet, embers continued to burn in the depths of those near-black eyes. He made no effort to hide them, no effort to pretend that things were as they should've been between an Enforcement detective and a Silent J.

"It's possible." Could Max share that warmth, she wondered, thaw the frost in her soul, frost that had begun to form when she'd been a traumatized eight-year-old strapped helpless to a hospital bed? *Could he fix her?* "Some humans don't like to be seen consorting with Psy." It was a question—vital, necessary, powerful—couched as a statement.

Max peeled off his Windbreaker, bunching the black material in his hand. "I don't like the Psy," he said with blunt honesty. "I don't like how they mess with human minds and pervert justice so the Council can get what it wants."

She'd known that, of course she'd known that. But she hadn't wanted to know.

"But Sophie"—what had he called her?—"I'm no bigot. And you're a J. Cops and Js have always gone together." He held her gaze until she looked away, scrambling to find her footing by reciting the minutiae of the case in her mind. Because what he'd just offered, it was something she wanted so badly that if she dared reach for it and he drew back his hand, it would push her the final step into an irrevocable insanity.

"Sophie." A quiet demand.

She shook her head. "There's not much left inside me, Max." Sometimes, all she heard were echoes. "I don't know how to play the games that woman was playing with you."

Max sucked in a breath, blindsided by Sophia's stark honesty. It stripped away the sophisticated rituals of the dance between male and female, allowing no room for illusions and half-truths. He could've pulled back, but he'd made his choice—to follow this strange, powerful attraction through to the end. "No games," he said, holding her gaze. "Not between us."

She took a long breath. "I'm Psy, Max." Not a rejection . . . a reminder.

"You're a J." Turning away, he dropped his Windbreaker on the back of a nearby sofa before crouching to examine the small glass cabinet below the comm console. Several data crystals lay neatly within. "Might be something here."

He saw Sophia tug at her gloves to ensure every inch of her skin was covered before she extended her hand to accept the crystals. Reading the tense line of her body, the desolate simplicity of her earlier words still circling in his head, he dropped them into her palm with care, avoiding physical contact. "Not likely to be entertainment," he said, rising to his feet. "News footage?"

She bent to place the crystals on the small beveled coffee table in the center of the room. "He may have kept business documents within easy reach"—the words were cool, Psy, but he'd seen the mask fall, wasn't fooled—"things that weren't sensitive. They were probably left behind to help the psychologists create a full mental profile." She gestured down the corridor. "He took his life in the bedroom."

Nodding, Max walked to the room where Kenneth Vale had spent his last minutes on this earth, slowly, painfully choking to death. "You should look at this," he said to Sophia, "the image in the file doesn't really convey the impact."

Moving to stand beside Max in the doorway, confident that for all his relentless will, he wouldn't touch her without invitation, Sophia looked up and to the gleaming meat hook that hung from the bedroom ceiling. "The fact that he went to the trouble of screwing it into the ceiling was tabled as evidence of his disturbed state." Her thoughts flashed to another crime scene photo—Vale's face contorted, his tongue grotesquely swollen. He'd evacuated his bowels, his expensive wool trousers stained with death.

"I didn't have a chance to read the full report on the

plane," Max said, his gaze still on the brutal shine of the meat hook. "How did the investigators explain the fact that there were scratches around his neck?"

"That he realized the irreversible nature of his actions when it was too late." Death was forever. She'd learned that truth young and had never been given a chance to forget.

"He was a fairly decent telepath, right?" At her nod, tiny lines fanned out from the corners of his eyes. "Then someone must've heard him cry out for help."

"They identified Jax in his bloodstream," Sophia said. "The general consensus is that he was disoriented by a drug haze, couldn't find the door out of his own mind."

"You're my Psy expert—tell me if that's possible."

"Yes, it is." Mental pathways could twist, could turn, could shatter . . . especially if you were a hunted child, terrified and screaming. "However, Vale had no indicators of any prior drug use—and it seems to me that if he was going to take drugs to dull the edge, he would've simply suicided by that method, using far more effective agents."

Making a *hmming* sound low in his throat, Max went to the naked white of the floor below where Vale had taken his life, the carpet having been cut away. "Plus, it just doesn't fit the profile PsyMed had of him before he died." Looking around, he grabbed a chair sitting in one corner of the room and brought it to that barren patch of floor. "The fact that everyone was so ready to believe the suicide verdict in spite of all that tells me the Psy are in more trouble than anyone knows."

She watched him stand on the chair, her fingers gripping the doorjamb at the sudden transposition of his body with Vale's. "Max?" His name spilled out, the broken girl inside of her scared, so scared. He was too close to the evil. What if it touched him, this man with his unexpected smiles and his eyes that *saw* her?

Max tugged on the hook, his biceps defined as he placed his weight on the ugly object. "Strong, but it had to be—he was hanging here for at least an hour or two before he was found, wasn't he?"

She forced herself to think. "Time of death suggests that." Years of experience sparked her neurons to life, notwithstanding the chill of terror. "However, he wasn't seen for two days beforehand."

Max's eyes met hers. "Good girl."

Disconcerted by the moment of perfect understanding outside of any psychic connection, she vocalized her conclusions. "You believe someone was holding him drugged and hostage during the time it took to install the hook."

"Maybe not the whole time, but part of it, yeah." Jumping off the chair, he returned it to its previous position. "The whole thing smells like a setup— theater for the public."

"Councilor Duncan was able to keep a lid on the details."

Max raised an eyebrow. "You telling me no one whispered about it on your PsyNet? According to what I've heard, it's a clearinghouse for pretty much every scrap of data known to Psy around the world."

She rarely entered the Net these days. There was too much there, too many voices, too many thoughts—it was akin to being battered in a storm-tossed sea, each stray whisper, each murmur, a body blow. "Yes, you're probably correct," she said, suddenly realizing that Max had a tiny scar high up on his left cheekbone. The tips of her fingers tingled, wanting to touch, to trace, to learn.

Max's expression changed. "Do it." A quiet, intense command from a human who saw far too much.

"I can't."

Not won't, Max thought, can't. "Why?"

She looked away . . . but then returned to hold his gaze. Strong, he thought, she was stronger than she knew, this J who'd told him she didn't have much left in her. "I'm now a Sensitive." She spread her fingers between them. "I pick up thoughts through touch."

He sucked in a breath as his mind filled with images of her sitting in that room with Bonner's malicious presence only inches away, the skin of her face, her neck so naked, so very vulnerable. "What would happen if someone disturbed touched your skin?"

"If I was lucky, I'd go into shock. More likely, the avalanche of images would shear my telepathic shields and kill me."

He didn't move, staring at those slender gloved fingers he'd fantasized about having all over him. "How long since you've touched another person?" It came out harsh, raw with a need that felt as if it had had years to grow, to mature.

Eyes the color of heat lightning met his, overflowing with a loneliness so absolute, it had no end. "Four years."

CHAPTER 11

Sascha Duncan, cardinal E-Psy, mate to the alpha of the strongest leopard pack in the country, and a woman known for her calm in the midst of a crisis, threw a half-a-million dollar book against the wall.

Regret struck almost immediately, and she caught the book using her minor telekinetic ability before it hit, but frustration continued to churn within her. According to Alice Eldridge's seminal work on E-Psy, a cardinal empath should have the capacity to stop a riot of thousands in its tracks, but Sascha couldn't even control five people. Those five had been volunteers, packmates who trusted her enough to allow her to attempt to feed peaceful emotions into them—after they purposefully got themselves excited.

"But it doesn't work!" Rubbing her hand over the hard mound of her pregnant belly, she stomped outside to find her shirtless mate replacing a window on the left-hand side of their cabin. The aerie above that cabin was now off-limits.

Lucas tended to snarl at her if she even teased him about trying to climb up.

"Sascha darling," he now said, wiping finger marks off the newly installed pane of glass using his discarded T-shirt, "next time your hellion fan club wants to play catch, I suggest Dorian's place."

Her "hellion fan club" was composed of twin cubs, Roman and Julian—and Dorian's house was made of glass. Normally that kind of a distinctly feline comment would've made her laugh. Today, she kicked bad-temperedly at the forest floor. "That book just *assumes* so much knowledge. As if I'm supposed to magically pluck the information out of the ether!" Another kick. "What kind of a thesis is that? Shouldn't a doctoral student know better than to—"

"Sascha?"

She snapped up her head, all but growling, "What?"

Her mate leaned forward in a deceptively slow move, snagged her shoulders, and kissed her. And kept on kissing her until she melted, closing her hands over the warm silk of the skin that covered his muscular shoulders. "You need a haircut," she murmured into the kiss. The black strands were long enough to brush the backs of her hands.

He kissed her again, his lips smiling against hers. "I'm scared of scissors."

"Excuses." She stroked her fingers through the strands. "You just like girls going crazy over your hair."

"Busted." A warm, loving stroke over her belly. "How's our rock star doing?"

"Loud as always." She'd been able to sense the life force of their baby from a couple of weeks after conception. At five months, that tiny life was now a constant presence in the back of her mind, normally content, often happy, and sometimes delighted. Like now. Their baby knew its father's voice, his presence. "Thank you for the kiss." The unspoken support.

"It's a hardship keeping up with your demands"—a mock sigh—"but someone's got to do it." Another nibbling, laughing kiss when she snarled at him—and she was getting quite good at it after the number of times he'd done it to her.

"So," he said after he had her breathless, "the funneling emotion trick didn't work?"

"No—it did. But only for a short period. I can't hold it for longer than maybe thirty seconds." Turning, she leaned her back against his chest. "There's something I'm missing."

Lucas's arm came around her upper chest, holding her to him. "Have you considered talking to Dev?" he asked, referring to the leader of the Forgotten—Psy who'd left the Net over a hundred years ago and formed their own society.

"I was thinking of doing that." She gripped his arm. "I wish . . . I wish Nikita had known the joy I feel now. I wonder sometimes if she heard me like I do our baby, or if Silence blocks that connection."

"It must," Lucas said, brushing his lips over her temple, the scent of him a stroke of wildness touched with clean male sweat. "How else could a woman carry a child for nine months and not love it with every beat of her heart?"

Sascha felt a deep sorrow for the indescribable beauty of what her mother had missed. "Do you think she'll care that she'll soon have a grandchild?" They'd managed to keep the pregnancy under wraps from the general public so far—helped in part by the way the baby sat on her frame, and by clever use of clothing—but it'd soon become impossible to hide the wonderful truth.

Lucas's free hand slipped between them to massage her lower back with strong, circular strokes. "Better?"

"How did you know?" She pressed a kiss to his biceps. "I'll melt if you keep doing that."

But her panther had turned serious. "Do you want to see your mother, kitten?"

"I don't know."

CHAPTER 12

The records of your birth were destroyed during a fire twenty-five years ago, unfortunately before they had been archived. We are very sorry to be unable to help you in your search.

—*Sisters of Hope Hospital, City of New York,*
to Max Shannon, January 2079

Max and Sophia didn't speak again until they were well on their way to the private garage where Nikita had stashed the vehicle the third presumed victim had been driving when she died.

"Is it just the disturbed that you have to be careful of?" Max's mind was still reeling at the realization that this woman whose skin he'd wanted to stroke from the very first, whose body sang a siren song to his, might be forever out of his reach.

"Most cops," Sophia said in a quiet, even tone that cut as deep as a scalpel, "carry as many nightmares as a J. Touching one would be akin to slamming a lightning bolt into my head."

His hands clenched on the steering wheel as she continued to speak. "All Psy run the risk of becoming Sensitive, but Js tend to have the highest rates of actual onset. To counteract that, the Council once considered banning touch from the instant of birth, but there proved to be certain . . . undesirable consequences to such a course of action. Tactile aversion is taught to us as part of the final stages of our conditioning."

Max thought of the hours, the days he'd spent locked in a dark box, without any hope of a kind touch when he was finally let out, and knew that no matter the horror, he'd been lucky. Because he'd seen pictures of twentieth-century orphanages where babies had been left to rot in their cribs. Those children had been damaged beyond repair. "I can't see a Psy rocking her baby to sleep," he said, feeling a tug deep in his soul.

He'd rock his child to sleep, no damn question about it. No son—or daughter—of his was ever going to wonder what was so wrong with him that his own parent couldn't bear the sight of him. "What kind of touch," he said, swallowing the knife blade of pain that was his past, "is permitted during childhood?"

"Nurses hold children during feedings, walk around with them at times. Contact is prescribed at the optimal level to ensure psychological health."

It sounded so cold, so clinical. But the hell of it was, it was better care than he'd ever had. When he'd been very small and helpless, perhaps his mother had felt a surge of maternal love? But Max didn't think so. Hate that deep, that violent, took time to grow, to mature.

A small light flashed once on Sophia's organizer, snapping his attention back to the present. "Anything important?"

"No, just an update on one of my cases from the prosecuting attorney. We won." She put a hand on the dash to brace herself as the car came to a sudden halt upon sensing the dog that had darted into the road.

Max scowled at the owner of the little terrier but let it go at that. Getting the car running again, he glanced to his left. "This is it." Time to focus on the case—rather than his impossible fascination with a J who might go mad . . . might die, if he touched her.

* * *

"**Do you know** much about cars?" Sophia asked as they walked to the garage entrance, tugging at her gloves in a gesture she recognized as anxious. She couldn't help it, her nerves abraded—the more she was around Max, the more she found herself thinking about the faint hope that had taken shape in the back of her mind when she'd read his file.

Max shoved his own hands into his pockets, his stride unconsciously graceful. It made another forbidden thought surface in the darkest, most secret corner of her mind—a thought tied to the whispered intimacy of sex. She'd never before considered the act, one that would tear apart the final fragile threads of her psyche, but today she found she didn't want to die without seeing Max Shannon's naked body move with that powerful liquid grace.

She was so consumed by the fantasy it took her a moment to realize he was speaking.

". . . hoping to talk to the mechanic who actually went over it. If she's not on shift, we'll just take a look at the vehicle, come back later to talk to her face-to-face. I'm no expert on cars, but I want to read her."

"Yes," Sophia managed to say as they reached the entrance—to be met by a well-groomed young female in blue overalls. Her name tag identified her as the chief mechanic.

"Detective Shannon, Ms. Russo, please follow me." With that, she led them toward an isolated and sealed workroom at the very back of the garage. "This was Allison Marceau's car."

Eyes on the crumpled wreck of what had once been a dark green sedan, Max blew out a surprised breath. The majority of cars these days survived most impacts with the passenger cage intact. This was so much spaghetti. "Car versus tree?"

"Out near Modesto," the mechanic answered, heading to the computer station built into the large workbench at the back of the room. "She was discovered by the leopards after they heard the sound of the initial impact."

Max made a mental note to talk to Clay, find out

anything that may not have made it into the official files—Psy, and even many humans, had a tendency to disregard the acute nature of changeling senses. Could be the cats had scented something that could've caused the crash—maybe even caught a hint of another person in the vicinity. "You did the work on this yourself?"

"Yes." She pulled up something on the screen in front of her. "According to the data stored in the onboard computer," the mechanic continued, "Ms. Marceau didn't brake but accelerated on the turn."

Sophia stepped up beside the other woman. "That's not in the file."

"Councilor Duncan asked me to keep it out of the official record."

Sophia glanced at him, her unspoken thought clear. *Suicide?*

"Funny coincidence," he murmured under his breath. "Is it possible," he said, "that the car could've been rigged so that the brake was read as the accelerator by the computer?"

The mechanic replied with a positive answer, but said she needed more time to investigate. "The computer's memory chip was severely damaged in the crash—it took me close to two weeks to retrieve what information we have at present."

"Anything you find out," Max said, writing down his cell code for her, "I want to know."

Ten minutes and a few more questions later, Max and Sophia exited the garage into the crisp air of San Francisco. "Let's walk. I need to think."

"Alright."

They were almost a hundred yards down the slight slope before he vocalized his thoughts. "Humans aren't the only ones vulnerable to psychic attack. If the car's systems prove clean, then Allison Marceau could've been coerced to do what she did."

Sophia realized she was walking too close to him, close enough to feel the rough caress of his body heat. "The psychic control of the aggressor would have to be considerable." His arm brushed hers, a hard, warm stroke. "Marceau was a Gradient 7 telepath." A warning shrieked in her head, but she didn't move away. "Her shields would have been airtight."

"All you need," Max said, his gaze distant, "is a crack, a fissure."

Her arm burned where he'd touched up against it, and though she knew it for a psychosomatic reaction, the contact having been muted by the layers of clothing between them, she clung to the sensation. "I'm certain Councilor Duncan would've weeded out anyone whose conditioning was suspect."

"Maybe, maybe not."

"You're thinking of Sascha," she said, shifting a single dangerous inch closer to the living heat of him. "I wouldn't consider that a parallel."

"No?" His hair lifted in the breeze blowing off the bay, baring the clean, perfect lines of his face.

"Psy are almost obsessive about bloodlines," she said, her thoughts buried in memories of a past that proved the truth of that assertion beyond any doubt. "It's a loyalty unlike human loyalty; nevertheless, it is loyalty." Compared to human love, Psy familial loyalty was a wintry, practical thing. And it was very much conditional.

Sophia had failed to meet those conditions as a child, and it had cost her her parents' allegiance. Yet it seemed to have held for the Duncans, notwithstanding the very public nature of Sascha Duncan's defection. "It may be that the Councilor protected her daughter because Sascha is her genetic offspring."

Max gave a humorless smile. "Funny—Nikita's about the coldest woman I've ever met, but she was probably a better mother than mine."

It was an open door. And the lost, painfully lonely part of her wanted to walk through that door so desperately that she found the words. "Your mother was inadequate?"

"She hated me," he said, his tone austere, as distant as

his expression. "Truly *hated* me. I don't know why she carried me to term, because I'm certain she wanted to kill me the instant I was born."

Sophia tried to glimpse in this hard-edged cop the vulnerable child he must've been. She couldn't. But she did understand a truth that "real" Psy weren't supposed to understand. "It hurt you," she said, attempting to say the right thing, to hold on to his trust. *No one* had ever shared such a private thing with her out of choice. It made her heart turn oddly heavy, a thick ache in her chest.

"She died when I was fifteen." Words that sounded calm, but his voice was sandpaper against her skin, harsh, rough. "And the hell of it was, I missed her. Even though she'd given me up to foster care more than once, treated me worse than you would a dog when I *was* home, I missed her." A rush of wind rippled through his hair at that moment, and it seemed to act like a spray of cold water. He blinked, shook his head. "I don't know why I'm telling you this."

She didn't know either, but she hoarded the memory in the secret part of her that no reconditioning had ever been able to reach or erase. Everything in her wanted to return his gift in kind, to tell him that she comprehended the agony he must've gone through, but trust was such an unfamiliar territory that she floundered, the words stuck in her throat.

And Max blew out a breath. "Must be the sea air, bringing up old memories." He glanced at his watch. "Looks like it's time for dinner."

The dinner proved interesting. Sophia, this J who kept short-circuiting Max's defenses with her gift of listening with a total and absolute focus, was less Psy in her mannerisms than others he'd met, and though she was reserved, she did join in the conversation—dominated by Clay and Tally's two adopted children, Jon and Noor.

It made Max's protective instincts relax to see them all so robustly happy. But what intrigued him most was that

Sophia ate the sweet crab flesh he put on her plate—though she'd ordered a simple fillet of fish in white sauce for her own meal. There was nothing on her face to betray whether or not she enjoyed the taste of the crab, but she didn't reject any of his offerings. And several times, he caught her looking at him as if she wanted to speak, those amazing eyes almost indigo.

He'd glimpsed that same look on her face when he told her about his mother. That was a truth he'd never shared with anyone—that he'd told her, a woman, a *Psy*, he'd barely met, scared the hell out of him. It was tempting to pull back, to raise a wall of formality between them—he knew she'd get the message, she was too smart, too perceptive not to—but he'd made a promise.

No games.

And, the fact of the matter was, her ability to unsettle him notwithstanding, he didn't want to keep his distance from Sophia Russo. No, he wanted her from the lush beauty of her mouth to the ripe curves of her hips, to the unadorned honesty that had slapped him sideways more than once already.

If this was obsession, he thought as they exited the elevator and headed down to their apartments after returning home, then so be it. "Sophia," he said, staring at her gloved hands and—driven by the determination he had to possess her, hold her, break through the veil of her Silence—seeing a sudden, gaping hole in the web of her logic.

"Yes?" She spoke again before he could respond. "Did your friend confirm whether Allison Marceau said anything when she was found?"

He hadn't realized she'd picked up on that short conversation he'd had with Clay when they'd gone for a walk along the pier following dinner. "He said the boys who found her were adamant she didn't speak. No suspicious scents at the scene either."

Taking out her keycard, Sophia unlocked her door, the movement a fraction too fast. Max's instincts uncurled in anticipation—she was trying to get away from him, which meant she already knew what he'd just realized . . . and she was sensitive enough to his moods that she'd picked up the tension that had turned his muscles rigid.

He tried to catch her eye, failed. "I have a question."

She pushed open the door. "We can talk tomorrow. I should get some rest."

Max wasn't about to let her escape. "Have you ever," he said in a low murmur, "tried to touch someone with a natural mental shield?"

Sophia froze. "No, such people are rare." And none of them had ever been *right*.

"How long have you known I had one?" A dark, intense question.

"From the start." She walked inside the apartment, conscious of both the corridor surveillance and the fact that the pristine surface of her Silence was beginning to crack like so much glass.

Max followed, closing the door with a muted snick that did nothing to lessen the tension that made her chest tight, the air suddenly too thin. "Then why did you let me think my shields would make no difference?"

Because she'd break if this failed, Sophia thought, scrabbling to find a mental foothold. Max, with his intelligence, his smiles, his will to find those lost girls . . . he wasn't only *right*, he was the embodiment of every forbidden dream born in the forever shattered part of her psyche. This man would've come for her—when she'd been hurt and bleeding in that cabin where the others had died, he would have come for her.

"Answer the question, Sophia."

She hadn't realized she'd already become used to hearing him call her Sophie. The loss sliced a line of blood across her soul. "It wasn't relevant." She had to fight this pull, had to keep him at a distance. To take the chance and destroy that final flickering hope . . . no, she couldn't bear it. "We're colleagues—touch has nothing to do with it."

"Now who's playing games?" A single calm sentence that tore her defenses apart.

She looked up, saw the embers in that near-black gaze. And watched as he walked forward until they were separated by a bare foot of distance . . . to hold out a hand, his jaw a taut line, challenge in every part of him.

She stared at that hand. If she took it and his natural shield wasn't protection enough, Max's memories would punch into her with the force of a raging tornado—and if she somehow survived the vicious power of that telepathic blow, she'd know him without ever *knowing* him, all his secrets, all his yesterdays an endless roar inside her skull.

"Come on, Sophie." A command that vibrated with masculine anger . . . and a darker, richer emotion that caressed a burn across her skin. "We need to know the answer—and don't you dare tell me you don't understand why."

CHAPTER 13

At that moment, faced with a Max who was making no effort whatsoever to hide the steel of his nature, a Max who was forcing her to confront the truth of this strange, unexpected something between them, Sophia discovered she had another flaw—a hitherto unknown susceptibility to that tone in his voice. "I need to check if I sense you through the glove." Reaching out before the fear could take over, make her turn back, she grazed the tips of her fingers across his palm.

His fingers curled inward even as she retreated—as if he'd hold her. "So?" A rough demand that rubbed the sandpaper deeper across her skin.

"I sense only your body heat." Wild and hot and an invitation that made a sumptuous warmth ignite in her abdomen, the broken part of her craving more . . . and yet utterly terrified at taking this chance. "I'll recite the alphabet," she said, knowing he wouldn't allow her to turn back, wouldn't allow her to hide. "If I go quiet"—she tugged off a glove—"break contact."

Max dropped his hand without warning. "Those eyes . . . the things I see in them." A low, harsh word. "I promised myself I wouldn't push you, and what the fuck am I doing but exactly that? Jesus." He shoved his hands through his hair, his shoulders twisting as if he'd turn, walk away.

And she knew the decision was hers. To hide, to pull back before promise ever broke under the pressure of reality . . . or to defy fear and reach for a man who made her wish for something so impossible, it was surely a little piece of madness.

"I would know you, Max." Soft words in a voice that had already become exquisitely, intimately familiar, gentle bonds that held Max in place. "Before . . . I would know you." Closing the distance between them, Sophia waited until he lifted his hand . . . and then she stroked her fingers across the very center of his palm.

It was an electric shock that went straight to Max's gut. Hissing out a breath, he curled his fingers into a fist even as she dropped her own hand and took a jerking step backward.

"Sophia?" Deep-seated instinct shoved at him to go to her, cup her face in his hands. Keeping himself in position was the hardest thing he'd ever done. "Are you in trouble?" It savaged him that he might have hurt her.

"No. I apologize—I'm fine." But she was staring at his hand, a quaver in her voice. "I felt none of your memories. You're as blank as a piece of wood."

Relief was a fucking fist inside his chest. "I've been called hardheaded before, but never wooden."

"I didn't mean to offend."

It was oh-so-tempting to touch his lips to hers, to tease her by telling her that she could make it up to him, but given the way she was standing so stiff and shocked, he knew he'd have to wait for his first taste of the lushly enticing Sophia Russo. "I was playing with you, Sophie."

"Oh."

He flexed his hand, saw her eyes go to it. "You felt it, too, didn't you?"

Shifting away in a sudden movement, she walked around him to open the door to her apartment. "I'll see you tomorrow, Max."

Sophia stood with her back to the door she'd closed behind Max until she heard his own door open and close. Only then did she slide down the wall to sit with her legs stretched out in front of her, her entire body buzzing in a way that was simply not in the realm of her experience.

She looked at her right hand, running the pad of her thumb over her fingertips in a bewildered attempt to understand that electrifying burst of sensation. It had been . . . she had no words for it, no way to explain something so wild, so extreme it defied her efforts at categorization.

The true paradox was that she hadn't lied—no matter the almost painful sensation of the contact, Max was as silent to her psychic senses as a piece of wood or a block of plascrete.

Silence.

For the first time in her life, that word meant something other than the conditioning that had acted as a cage even as it kept her alive. Max had been a wall of pure silence, an unexpected oasis in a world filled with noise. But her response to his touch had wiped out that startling peace.

She stared at her hand again. "I don't understand."

Max knew the answer, she thought, she'd seen it on his face. But the question was—did *she* want to know the answer?

A telepathic knock sounded in her mind the instant after that thought passed through it. Recognizing the signature of her boss in Justice, Jay Khanna, she pulled together the threads of her perfect facade and said, *Sir.* He wouldn't guess at the reality of her condition. No one else ever had. Even the M-Psy saw only the fragmentation of her telepathic shields—to them, it was a simple psychic issue, nothing to do with the scars she wore deep inside, where no one could see them.

Ms. Russo, I need to go over part of the Valentine case with you.

Sophia waited. She'd long ago learned how to bury her true thoughts, her true self, in order to survive.

According to your notes, when you recovered Ms. Valentine's memories, you saw her stab her husband seventeen times?

That's correct, sir. A human-to-human spousal murder wouldn't normally have merited J involvement, but Ms. Valentine was the daughter of an influential individual with a controlling interest in a major power plant. Valentine Senior had used the same thing Max had—a natural shield—to ruthless advantage in business, until even Psy "played nice" with him.

Sophia had often wondered why the Council hadn't had him discreetly assassinated, and come to the conclusion that the male provided undisclosed goods or services that were valuable enough to afford him some protection. Humans, driven and shaped by their unpredictable emotional natures, often came up with ideas and concepts that were staggeringly unique. It was why Max had caught Gerard Bonner while the Psy profilers were still arguing about the "psychological parameters" that defined the sociopath.

How many times, Jay Khanna now said, *did you see her husband abuse her in the days leading up to the murder?*

Sophia betrayed no surprise—part of her had been expecting the question since the moment she met the arrogantly beautiful Emilie Valentine. *None, sir.*

Think about that carefully, Ms. Russo. We'll speak again before the case goes to trial.

Letting the veiled order fade from her mind, Sophia considered what her response would be on Jay's next telepathic visit. The ability to "bend" memories was the most tightly guarded secret of the Justice Corps. Everyone thought Js could only project what was already in a defendant's mind. In most cases, yes.

But there was a select group of Js who had the ability to manipulate memories without leaving a trace, changing images and words, sounds and actions until a simple tumble down a set of stairs could be made to look like an abusive push.

Sophia was one of the best, had been brilliant at it even as a child. Because she'd spent every spare moment honing the skill, aware that that nascent ability was one of only two reasons why the decision makers had let her live after she'd been ruined from the inside out, her mind a place where nothing quite made sense anymore.

Nobody ever asked, and she never told . . . but the splinters in her soul were permanent. She'd never recovered from the terror-filled days she'd spent trapped in that cabin in the mountains, never again understood the world as she had before the glass cut her face to shreds.

Max finally fell asleep late into the night, his body still humming with his violent response to Sophia's fleeting touch. So in a sense, he'd expected the intensity of his dreams . . . but not their subject.

"You little shit!" Hands shaking him hard, so hard, as a screaming mouth spewed obscenities at him.

He stood frozen, trying not to cry. He couldn't cry. That would only make her more mad.

"Just like your father." It was screamed into his face. "Piece of filth."

"I'm sorry," he said, and he couldn't help it, his voice broke.

For an instant, her face went unnaturally calm. There were no more screams, no more painful shakes. She just stared at him.

And he knew that his mother wanted to suffocate the life out of him.

Max's eyes snapped open, his hand going for the stunner under his pillow. It took him close to two minutes to realize the danger was only in his head. She'd almost killed him in the memory, come so close that sweat broke out along his spine even now, his skin taut with remembered terror.

Getting up, he walked into the bathroom to throw cold water on his face.

It snapped the remaining threads of the dream, his mind beginning to function again. The connection was indisputable—Sophia, a *J*, had touched him . . . and he'd had a dream from when he'd been small, so small that he couldn't have been more than three at the time. He'd never before remembered anything from that period of his life.

The consequences of further contact didn't escape him—but when it came to Sophia Russo, Max had no intention of retreating.

Max invited Sophia into the privacy of his apartment the next morning when she came to meet him for the drive to Nikita's office. Shadows bruised the skin beneath her eyes, her bones cutting blades against that normally lush skin. "Tough night?" he murmured.

"I should know better than anyone that memories are never gone," she said in an echo of his own thoughts, "but even I, it seems, have some delusions left."

Raising his hand with a slowness that gave her plenty of warning, he began to play with a lock of her hair. She went preternaturally still, but she didn't stop him. "Memories aren't always vicious," he said, speaking to both of them. "I'll remember the softness of your hair each time I smell your shampoo. Let's see, vanilla and"—he paused, took a long, indulgent breath—"below it, some kind of a flower?"

To his surprise, she answered. "Lavender soap. I use it on my body." Then she lifted her own hand, hesitated.

He bent his head in invitation, his heart kicking against his ribs. *Slow, Max,* he ordered himself, *take it fucking slow.* He waited for her fingertips to stroke through his hair, however she touched not his hair . . . but his lips.

He couldn't control the shudder that rippled through him. The leather-synth of her glove was warm with her body heat, the pressure so slight as to be nonexistent—but it held him captive, slave to her desires.

"This," she whispered, tracing the shape of his mouth, "will be a good memory."

It was tempting to surrender to the pleasure, but she'd come to him with nightmares in her eyes. "Tell me about your dreams."

"You said your mother hated you," she said, the harshness of the words nullified by the delicate way she stroked over his lower lip, as if fascinated by the feel of him. "Mine rejected me as absolutely."

The hunger to hold her strained at every one of his muscles, the butterfly flirtation of her touch fuel to his instincts. "Why?" The cop in him said this was important, that it held the key to understanding her.

"I was imperfect." Dropping her hand, she took a step back. "We should begin the drive to Nikita's."

Imperfect. Anger burned a steel flame inside him, but he angled his head in acquiescence, not trusting himself to stop with a simple comforting touch—not when he wanted to crush her to him, teach her that he saw her as anything but imperfect.

Neither of them spoke again until they were in the car and on the road. "My knowledge of Nikita is based on what I've seen in the media," he said as they merged into the morning traffic. "She comes across as intelligent, a cut-throat businesswoman."

"I agree." Sophia felt her muscles relax at the realization that Max didn't intend to press her to take the next step in this unforeseen, unpredictable dance. The part of her that had been waiting for him for a broken, tormented eternity wanted to rush, to race, but the simple fact was, she didn't have the capacity to process anything more than what they'd already done. Not yet. "Nikita also seems to be one of the few high-level Psy who thinks in truly global terms—she is, as far as I know, the solitary Councilor who has such close ties with a changeling group."

"I heard that Anthony Kyriakus is still subcontracting foreseeing work out to his daughter, Faith."

Sophia nodded, having followed the news of Faith NightStar's defection. Foreseers were rumored to be even more mentally unstable than Js—and yet Faith had survived. Though Sophia had always known that any such defection was out of the question for her, her mind woven inextricably into the fabric of the Net, Faith NightStar's survival had seemed a victory for all of them who were labeled mad and had their lives erased from existence.

"Yes," she said in response to Max's question. "Anthony is also involved with the changelings, but according to my research, Nikita was the one who took the first step into such an arrangement when she formed a business alliance with DarkRiver's construction arm."

Max switched lanes, his brow furrowed in thought. "Could be something there," he murmured, and she could almost hear his brain working, making connections with a speed that many Psy, certain of the superiority of their mental abilities, would find extraordinary. "Any more details on the construction deals?"

Forcing herself to look away from the clean lines of his profile, the sleek strands of black hair that glimmered with hidden red highlights in direct sunlight, Sophia checked her data. "It looks like her firm is gaining changeling housing contracts not only in the U.S., but also internationally. The murders may be motivated by professional rivalry."

"It would fit." Max tapped a finger on the steering wheel. "Each of the victims died on the verge of a major deal."

Surprised, Sophia quickly skimmed through the relevant parts of the file and realized he was right. "All three were linchpins, bringing something unique to the table," she said out loud. "Their deaths derailed the entire process in each case."

"Nothing obvious connects the three deals," Max said.

"We need to find out if there's a link beneath the surface, if one particular competitor benefits with Nikita effectively out of the run—" A beeping interrupted his words. "That's my cell." He nodded at where it sat in the holder on the dash. "Can you check the caller's name?"

"Of course." Picking it up, she glanced at the ID . . . and felt her mind go quiet, cold, the otherness stirring to life. "It is the prosecutor, Mr. Reuben."

CHAPTER 14

I can only show you what the defendant did in that room ten months ago. To ask me whether or not he is a monster is to presume I have an intimate knowledge of monsters.

—*Response by Sophia Russo (J) to a question posed by the prosecution in case 23180: State of Nebraska v Donnelly*

Mouth a grim line, Max brought the vehicle to a stop in the half-empty car park of a restaurant that hadn't yet opened.

Listening to his end of the conversation, she'd divined the reason for the call by the time he hung up. "Bonner wants to talk to me again." The thought of trawling through that mind full of malice made her entire body stiffen in revulsion.

Better to kill him.

Because he might just be the final weight, the one that would cause her shields to shred beyond any hope of repair. And Sophia wasn't ready to have her brain crushed, her psyche, her personality, wiped from existence. Not when she'd just found Max, found this man who made the cold, dark places fill with light. Clenching her fingers on her organizer, she fought past the whispers of vengeance that seemed to originate in the dark tendrils snaking through her mind and soothed the otherness back to sleep.

"Bastard says he's got something to share, some memory he's apparently been able to dig up." Max braced his arm on the back of her seat, playing with a strand of her hair as he'd done in the apartment.

She didn't pull away. They had trust between them now, a fragile thing born in the electrical storm of their first real touch. "I suggest that this one time, we let him play his games." No matter her hunger to *live*, to steal and claw every extra day she could out of this life, she couldn't walk away from Bonner's evil. Not when the cost of protecting herself would be to abandon those lost girls, leave them buried and forgotten in the dark. No one should be forgotten. *No one.*

"If we play it right," she said, remembering three other young lives that had been willfully erased from every mind but her own, "it'll only increase his frustration, make him more malleable."

Max's eyes filled with raw, edgy emotions she'd never get the chance to study, to truly know. Not in this lifetime. So she asked, "What are you thinking?"

"That it's a pity torture is illegal." A visceral anger in every world. "We'll set up a comm-conference. We're not traipsing up to him so he can have a convenient memory lapse."

"The comm systems at our apartment won't have the necessary encryption." Sophia's own anger was a colder thing, a thing that saw nothing wrong in taking an eye for an eye, a life for a life. "We could ask Enforcement if they have a secure link."

"Their system was pretty good last time I was here." Releasing her hair with a little tug that made her scalp prickle with sensation, the ice thawing in a flare of white-hot heat, he rubbed at his jaw. "But they have leaks."

"There are leaks in every Enforcement building." Facilitated, in most cases, by the Psy.

"I think I know someone else who'll have a secure link."

So it was that half an hour later, Sophia was ushered

into a small conference room in the medium-sized office building that was the DarkRiver leopard pack's city HQ. "They're not worried?" she asked after their escort—an auburn-haired young male—withdrew from the conference room. "The changeling distrust of Psy is well-known."

"This is where the cats do business," Max replied, setting up the comm-conference using the touch pads. "Some of that business is with Psy. And don't forget—DarkRiver has several Psy defectors in its ranks."

"This building is full of changelings." The statement of the obvious slipped out.

Max turned to pin her to the spot with his eyes. "Are you having trouble?"

"No." She tugged her gloves more securely over her wrists and snugly below the cuffs of her white shirt, the action more of . . . comfort, than necessity. "Changelings are actually restful."

A raised eyebrow, those solid shoulders relaxing as he returned his attention to the comm controls. "Not many people would describe them that way. They tend to have this wild energy below the human surface."

She wanted to point out that he burned with that same wild energy—though in his case, it was contained so well, most people would never guess at it. All those women who wanted to own him, she thought, they didn't understand what it was they dared attempt to harness. But she knew. And she wondered what it would be like to stroke that sleekly muscular body with her bare hands.

He looked up, caught her watching him. "When we're alone." A tease . . . and a warning.

Closing her hand over the arm of her chair, she jerked away her head. "Changelings all have natural mental shields."

"So why are you tense enough to snap?"

It was impossible not to glance back at him, to watch him as he rechecked the encryption, lines of concentration across his brow. At that moment, the leash slipped free, the reins broke, and everything disappeared but the promise and the danger that was Detective Max Shannon—she wanted to touch the skin exposed at his nape, wanted to know if it was soft or rough, wanted to strip off his shirt and rub her lips over the muscles that shifted beneath that honey-colored skin, wanted to stroke and know and possess. She simply *wanted*. "Changelings like to touch." It came out soft, husky.

Max's shoulders grew tight, but he didn't turn. "I asked Clay about that while you were in the bathroom just before. They don't presume skin privileges, so you're safe."

"Skin privileges." She tested the unfamiliar term, gleaning its meaning from the context. "And you, Max?" Thought translated into words so fast, she had no chance—or will—to hold them back. "Are you easy with skin privileges?"

Max moved to brace his hands on the back of her chair, leaning down until his lips threatened to brush the tip of her ear. "It depends on who's asking." The scent of him surrounded her as he placed his hands on the table on either side of her. A sensual trap. "But if you're talking about a certain J, well, for her, I might be very, very easy."

A tight kind of heat bloomed in Sophia's stomach, a strange fire that burned even the darkest, most secret part of her. "Max." She didn't know what she was asking for, her heartbeat an erratic tattoo against her ribs.

Max pushed off the table with a groan. "We can't do this here. It's almost time for the conference." A light touch on her shoulder, holding a protectiveness that shook her, disarmed her. "You ready, Sophie?"

His voice, his presence, his willingness to be her shield . . . it shook her, but she nodded. "Yes." This had to be done—those girls had to be brought home.

Even a Psy without any family of her own understood the importance of children, the ties of blood. To lose a child in the Net was to lose not only your immortality, but also your chance to gain the unqualified loyalty of at least one individual. Unless, of course, you were young enough to sire or carry other progeny.

Sophia's parents had been in their early thirties the summer she turned eight and everything fractured. They'd gone on to have two more children—both with each other. Their genes, after all, had already proved a complimentary set. Her siblings, too, were high-Gradient telepaths. Not as strong as her. But they weren't broken.

Bartholomew Reuben's face appeared onscreen at that moment, slicing away the heart pain of the past with the sadistic evil of the present. "Max, Ms. Russo, good to see you. You'll be transferred to Bonner in a few seconds."

"You flew there, Bart?" Max asked. "Waste of time."

"No, I'm in another prison." The prosecutor's lips curved in a humorless smile. "Bonner's not going to be pleased we didn't all start running when he said fetch."

A warning countdown appeared in the corner of the screen.

Ten.

Max snorted. "I'm not exactly worried about pleasing the bastard."

Nine.

"I'll be hooked into the comm-conference—"

Eight.

"—but Bonner will see only Ms. Russo."

Seven.

The scrape of a chair.

Six.

"I'll move a little," Max said, "make sure I'm out of the shot."

Five.

"You good, Sophie?"

Sophie. Tenderness in the way he said that name, making it something special between them, a gift.

Four.

"Yes." She held his gift tight to her heart.

Three.

"Instant you want out—"

Two.

"—say the word."

One.

Reuben's face disappeared, to be replaced by the gilded blond looks of a killer so vicious, the tabloids had fought to tell his story. He was a megastar in the shadowy under-world of serial-killer groupies, his "authorized biography" read with religious fervor. She wondered how many of his fans realized the book was mostly fiction.

Bonner was incapable of truth.

"Ms. Russo." That charming smile, but there was an edge to it. "I was so looking forward to seeing you in person."

"That would have been an inefficient use of my time," she replied, keeping her hands loosely in her lap.

"But how will you take my memories if you aren't nearby?" A slow raising of his shoulders. "I'm afraid my mind isn't cooperating with my need to share." Deep blue eyes filled with rueful laughter, the charming apology of a man who'd done something a little naughty.

It would, Sophia thought, be so easy to kill him. She'd just have to be in the general vicinity. Her telepathic reach was long enough—she could make him suffocate himself with a pillow, maybe beat his skull against a wall until pieces of bone pierced his brain. The terror would make him mindless.

A tap on the table to her left.

Max. The reminder of the gift she'd been handed, the gift she was determined not to lose, made her snap back to attention, the otherness retreating in the face of her resolve. "The prison officials stated that you'd remembered a place we'd be very interested to learn about."

Bonner displayed his teeth in a smile that could've graced a toothpaste commercial. But his eyes. Reptilian eyes. She'd seen eyes like that before—on the powerful in the Net, men and women for whom the sanctity of life meant less than nothing.

The man who'd done her last childhood evaluation—making the final call on whether she was useful enough to be saved or should be put down—had had eyes like the Butcher of Park Avenue. "Mr. Bonner?" she prompted when the killer didn't reply.

"The memory seems to have faded away." A disappointed sigh. "I know it had something to do with trees, but . . ." Another shrug. "Maybe if you came here, used your abilities to jog my recall . . ."

"It seems even this was a waste of time." Glancing to her left, she gave a curt nod. "Cut the connection."

Bonner's face twisted to reveal the monster within for one violent second. "Ms. Russo, I don't think you realiz—" The empty slate of a blank screen.

"I want to kill him with my bare hands," Max said in a voice so calm it made every single hair on the back of her neck rise in warning. "It's not a need for justice or anything pure. I want vengeance. I want him to suffer as those women—those *girls*—suffered."

"We all have the capacity to kill," Sophia said, telling herself to stop, but unable to keep quiet—she needed to know what he thought of the broken part of her that knew only the most lethal kind of justice. If he was going to reject her, better that it be now, when she'd only touched the wild heat of him once, when she'd just begun to learn him . . . when she might survive the denunciation. "The lines are simply different for everyone."

Max's eyes met hers, piercing in their intensity. "And yours involve children. Sometimes women, but most often, children."

Sophia swallowed, uncertain how to answer, uncertain how to read *his* answer.

Bartholomew Reuben's face reappeared on the comm screen at that moment. "He's pissed. Never saw that ugly face of his until today."

"Not even at trial?" Sophia asked, her confused terror translating into a rigid composure.

"Cool as a cucumber, that one," Reuben said. "Smiled at the jurors, flirted with the gallery. If we hadn't had airtight evidence, he might well have charmed himself out of a conviction." A small pause. "Please be careful, Ms. Russo. Bonner is under constant supervision, but he does have rabid fans. If he manages to get out a message to one of them, you could be in danger."

"Don't worry, Mr. Reuben." Sophia took the small, folded note Max passed her under the table. "Right now, he needs me alive. He wants to awe me with his brilliance." After that . . .

Max felt his gut grow painfully tight as he thought back to the expression on Sophia's face before Bart signed off. He'd known exactly what she was considering, his complex, dangerous J, knew, too, that he couldn't let her do it. But they were geographically far enough from Bonner right now that Sophia's tendency to hurt nasty people in creative ways was something he had time to deal with.

He knew it wouldn't be easy. Not when her actions— and the crimes of those she'd punished in that peculiarly J way—all added up to a past that spoke of a brutal kind of hurt. Those scars, he thought, were invisible. But they were far more important than the thin lines that marked her face.

"Max," she muttered under her breath as they headed up to Nikita's office.

He knew why she was giving him that perplexed look— and it soothed him to know the ploy had worked, drawing her back from the edge of the void. "Hmm?"

"You can't write me notes like that." It was a hissed order as the elevator doors opened on the correct level. "What if someone had seen?"

Max shot her an innocent look. "I just asked a simple question."

"*What do you think of boardroom sex?*" A raised eyebrow. "That is not—"

"Well, since you asked," he interrupted, walking into the outer section of Nikita's office, "I vote in favor."

At that moment, his entire being filled with the sensual delight that came from teasing Sophia, Max had no idea of the bloody consequences that would result from this meeting.

CHAPTER 15

Some women are not meant to be mothers.
    —From the private case notes of Detective Max Shannon

Councilor Nikita Duncan, he thought as they entered her private office, was a beautiful woman. If you liked beauty cut in ice. Perfect. Distant. Cold. According to public records, she was part Japanese, part Russian. That explained the combination of high cheekbones, almond-shaped eyes, above-average height. She'd passed on the height to her daughter, but from the images Max had seen, Sascha's black hair curled rather than ran a slick dark rain, her skin a warm golden brown to Nikita's flawless ivory.

"Detective Shannon, Ms. Russo." She gestured for them to take the chairs in front of her desk.

"Actually, Councilor," Max said, "I think better on my feet." Walking to the huge plate-glass window that was the back wall of her office, he looked down into the active buzz of San Francisco and played a hunch. "I need you to share the information you've withheld."

He felt Sophia's eyes on his back, and had it been any other woman, he'd have been prepared to get a royal reaming later on for springing this on her. But Sophia was unlike anyone he'd ever before met. He had no idea how she'd react—and that both delighted him and frustrated him.

"It would," Nikita answered, "be illogical of me to conceal information when I'm the one who requested this investigation."

Max turned enough that he could meet those cool brown eyes. "Three deaths—one car accident that you weren't sure was suspicious, one suicide that could've been caused by mental illness, one heart attack—that's not enough for you to pull in an outsider." A human.

Nikita stared at him, a lethal adversary for all that she wore a crisp skirt and shirt, her makeup professional, her hair perfect. "It's gratifying," she said into the silence, "to know that you have the intelligence to get this task done." With that, she tapped something on her desk—Max guessed she'd activated some kind of an aural shield as a defense against high-tech spies. "There was an attempt on my life approximately four months ago."

"I heard rumors. Something to do with the Human Alliance?" he said, referring to the most powerful human organization on the planet. On the surface, it was all about business, but word was, the Alliance had a strong paramilitary arm.

Nikita gave a regal nod in response to his question. "They placed an explosive device in the elevator I use to access this office and my penthouse, their apparent plan being to detonate the charge while I was inside."

"They hooked into your surveillance system?" Max asked, supremely conscious of Sophia's silent presence, though his eyes remained on Nikita.

"Yes." Nikita rose from her chair and, using a thin silver remote, activated a comm panel on what had appeared to be a blank wall.

The boy in Max was intrigued enough to have him walking over. "This isn't on the market yet."

"I purchased a small company last year—their engineers

are brilliant, but it's the designers who have proven truly exceptional."

Another click in the back of his mind, another piece of the puzzle coming into view. "A human company?" He caught a hint of vanilla and lavender as Sophia moved to stand on Nikita's other side, and the scent was a slow stroke across his senses, a sensual reminder that his body had chosen this woman and had no intention of changing its mind.

"Yes," Nikita said. Then, using the command pad on the side of the screen, she brought up a three-dimensional model of the Duncan high-rise, drilling down until they were staring at a cross section of the relevant elevator shaft. "Access to this elevator is difficult but not impossible. However, access to the shaft itself is strictly controlled—computronic security, twenty-four-hour surveillance."

"Emergency hatch in the elevator?" Max asked.

"Sounds an immediate alarm if it's so much as touched."

Max understood the import of her statement when she used a red *X* to mark the place where the charge had been laid.

Above the elevator.

Mind beginning to hum with the exhilaration that came from knowing a case was starting to take shape, he tapped the screen, rotating the image until he could've drawn it from memory. "Someone inside had to have either greased the wheels for the saboteurs or done the job himself." And the two, he thought, weren't necessarily connected. A smart man might've become aware of the Alliance's plans, used them to further his own agenda. "Surveillance footage?"

"By the time I realized the significance of where the charge had been placed, that footage was gone, erased."

Sophia stirred, bringing up something on her organizer. "The list of those with the security clearance to success-fully execute such an erasure is very short and includes every individual in your inner circle."

"Precisely, Ms. Russo."

"I don't seem to have the name of your security chief."

"He's dead." Brisk words coated in frost. "He was killed in an accidental fall three weeks before the assassination attempt."

Max folded his arms, his gut tight. "He was the first victim."

"Yes, I've come to believe so."

Sophia looked up from her organizer. "You haven't hired a replacement."

"No—I haven't found the right candidate. The assistant chief is doing an unobjectionable job at present."

Max stared at the image of the Duncan building, but he wasn't really seeing it. There was dedication here, he thought, a long-term commitment that had to rise from a very specific motive—and whatever that motive was, it was about more than the thrill of murder. "You're telling me," he said to Nikita, "that you no longer trust anyone in your inner circle."

"No. I—" She cut herself off as her phone began to beep. "It must be something critical. I ordered no interruptions." Picking up the handset, she said, "Yes?"

Max glanced at Sophia, caught by the way a sudden sliver of sunlight glimmered off the rich ebony silk of her hair. He could play with the soft strands for hours, intended to do exactly that once he'd coaxed his J into bed.

"Don't disturb anything. Don't enter."

Nikita's words had his attention whiplashing back to her. "What is it?"

She hung up. "It seems you will no longer have to satisfy yourself with cold case data. My international financial advisor, Edward Chan, has just been found dead."

This time, Max thought, there was no question of it being murder. Either the people behind the acts were getting impatient, or this was a message. "Sophia, you recording?"

"Yes." She'd clipped a small wireless camera over her ear, curving the lens in front of her left eye. "Go."

Having barred anyone else from entering, Max took his time looking over the scene, which happened to be on the second-highest floor of the Duncan building, right below Nikita's penthouse. The murdered man lay on the otherwise undisturbed bed, his legs hanging over the side. His pants were slate gray, his belt sedate black leather, his white shirt stained like a Rorschach painting in red.

"No bruises, no defensive marks on his hands." The only evidence of violence was the bowie knife thrust hilt deep in his sternum—solid, thick, and Max guessed, with a wicked curved edge. The kind of knife you might use to bring down game or skin the pelt off a downed animal. "Looks like a single blow, directly to the heart."

Sophia continued to film as they spoke. "Either the victim allowed his attacker close, or the killer used Tk to punch the blade home."

"Tk—telekinesis?" That would explain how the knife had ended up buried so deep—though a burst of cold rage might well have sufficed to give the killer enough strength.

"Yes. I'll go through the personnel files"—Sophia moved to his left, capturing images of the body from every angle—"find out how many telekinetics the Councilor has in her organization."

"Nikita said Chan got in from Cairo last night," Max murmured, "but that he had a number of informal meetings scheduled here in his home office this morning." Which meant someone had known his schedule well enough to time the murder when Chan would've been alone and vulnerable.

As she shifted position again, the clean purity of Sophia's scent swept over him, providing a much-needed antidote to the ugliness of death. Psy, human, or changeling, Max thought, murder always had the same putrid stench. And the dead always screamed for the same justice. Edward Chan was one of Max's now, just like every single one of Bonner's lost victims.

"It was an individual he trusted," Sophia said. "That's the

only way a telepath of his strength—8 on the Gradient—could've been taken by surprise."

Raising his gaze from Edward Chan's cold flesh, Max put his hands on his hips, pushing back his jacket. "One problem though—even the most perfectly aimed stab wound wouldn't have caused death instantaneously and a telepath could get out an emergency message within seconds, if not less." Unlike with the Vale scene, everything here suggested a quick, brutal operation. No time to drug the victim into compliance. "Why didn't he call for help?"

"Turn his head a fraction."

"What're you looking for?" He saw nothing remarkable except for a couple of droplets of blood below the—*Damn.* "Telepathic blow."

"If someone hit him with a hard enough one at the same instant that he was stabbed, while his attention was splintered by shock, it would've torn through his shields, destroyed his mind."

"Cold, calculated." A one-two hit to ensure success.

"Max." Sophia's voice was almost soundless.

Spine prickling with awareness, he followed her gaze to the bathroom mirror—just barely visible through the half-open door on the other side of the bedroom.

The single word was written in blood that had dripped onto the white porcelain of the sink. But the accusation was still very legible.

Traitor.

CHAPTER 16

The space for your father's name is blank in our records. Such an action is permitted in some limited circumstances, but the cause must always be noted. There is no such note on your file. We apologize for the error.

—*Office of Births and Deaths: City of New York,*
to Max Shannon, June 2079

Nikita handed Max a data crystal as soon as they returned to her office. "I've downloaded the security footage for you—it covers the period since Edward's return from Cairo."

Max slipped it into his pocket. "Are private comm conversations backed up on your main servers? The killer dropped a corrosive acid in the computronic 'brain' of the system in the victim's room." And they'd found neither a cell phone, nor an organizer.

"Edward's entire file was wiped using his own security override," Nikita said, the words succinct. "The murderer must've torn it from his mind."

The callous nature of it all might've shocked other men, but Max knew that no matter the race, some were always born with a capacity for evil. "We thought we might have a pattern of deaths—each of your other advisors was hit before a major deal. Does Chan fit?"

Nikita was shaking her head before he finished speaking.

"Edward had a lot of things in play but nothing close to completion."

Frustrated at the sudden end to that line of inquiry, Max focused on another. "Sophia says the victim was high profile enough that he was known outside business circles?"

A quick nod that sent her glossy hair swinging. "It was part of his job description to wine and dine human and changeling businessmen and women. As a result, he occasionally found himself in the society pages."

Max felt Sophia glance at him with those amazing, perceptive eyes, knew she'd made the same cognitive leap he had. "Would it be fair to say he'd made some personal connections within those groups?"

Nikita took a moment to think about it. "Not in the human or changeling sense. However, certain individuals had come to have a measure of trust in him because of a shared history of successful deals."

"An unquantifiable loss," Sophia said. "One that you will feel the effect of for some time."

"Yes." Nikita looked at Sophia for a long, quiet moment before returning her attention to Max. "I'm beginning to see the pattern it appears you already have, Detective."

"So my next question won't come as a surprise—who doesn't like you getting into bed with the other races?" Edward Chan, Max was certain, had only been considered a traitor by association. It was Councilor Nikita Duncan who was the key.

"That," Nikita said, "is something I'll have to think about."

Sophia spoke into the small pause. "I've heard rumors of a group called Pure Psy—the members seem to believe that contact with the other races is tainting the purity of our Silence."

"Yes. They've begun to gain a measure of support in the Net." Nikita returned to her desk. "I have some additional data on them that I'm sending you now—please brief the detective, Ms. Russo."

It was a dismissal from a woman who was used to

obedience, but Max wasn't finished. "Whoever's behind this, he or she is getting bolder—they're going to come directly after you sooner rather than later."

"I'm protected. That's why Edward and the others are dead—the assassin went for the next best thing." A razor of a glance. "You'd do well to protect yourself. You are, after all, only human."

Sophia didn't say anything to Max until they were in the car heading out from the Duncan building. "Does it bother you?"

"What?"

"Being thought of as less because of your humanity?" It bothered her a great deal. Max was worth far more than any other man she'd ever met.

But he shook his head, his lips curved in a distinctly satisfied smile. "Nikita felt the need to point out my humanity because she's been forced into a position where she has to rely on a measly human. That has to bite."

"It's an irony, is it not?" Sophia murmured, thinking of connections, of mothers and fathers. "She's one of the most powerful people in the world, her net worth in the billions—and yet she doesn't have a single person in her life whom she can trust not to thrust a knife into her back."

"She made her choices." Max had no sympathy for a woman who'd disowned her child. He knew exactly how bad that had to have hurt Sascha.

When Sophia didn't say anything, he glanced at her. "What about you, Sophie? Who do you trust?"

Her answer rocked through him. "You're the only person I've ever told of my parents' rejection of me."

"Strange, isn't it?" His voice came out harsh, raw with emotion.

"What?"

"That the two people Nikita chose to work this case are both people whose mothers threw them away." It couldn't be a coincidence, not with the resources Nikita had at her disposal.

Sophia's organizer flashed at that moment. "Nikita's lab techs have done a first-look analysis of the forensic data—the blood on the mirror was the victim's, the DNA and prints in the public areas belong to either Chan or Nikita's other employees, all of which can be explained by the meetings he held in his home office. No unexplained or suspicious DNA in the bedroom."

"That was fast."

Sophia's answer was practical—and said a thousand things. "She's a Councilor."

"Hmm." Pulling to a stop in front of a small, bustling restaurant, he turned off the engine. "It's almost half past two. You can tell me about Pure Psy over lunch." From what he'd heard so far, the group sat in diametric opposition to Nikita's growing business alliances with the other races—but he needed to know more about their tactics to judge whether murder might be part of their arsenal.

Sophia didn't move to step out of the car. "We can't risk being overheard."

"Takeout it is, then." He wanted nothing more than to be alone with her, to take the next step in this strange courtship of theirs. "What do you want?"

"It matters little to me."

Max had already slid back his door, but now he paused and looked at her, realizing how far she'd retreated within herself, her expression so remote he knew it was a front, meant to hide the vulnerable truth. "Damn. I'm sorry." Every protective instinct he had, awakened to quiet, intense life. "I didn't think about it."

"It's alright." Those night-violet eyes held a surprise that rubbed those same instincts very much the wrong way. "It's not something you need to think about."

That she'd say that after the unspoken depth of this connection between them made him want to reach forward and tug her into a hard, hot kiss—remind her of the truth in a way she couldn't ignore. But he couldn't touch her, not yet. "Yeah," he said, "I do." Because slowly, inexorably, she was becoming his . . . to watch over, to know.

A wash of shadows in that stunning gaze, a silent indication that she'd heard the message behind the words. "Thank you."

Such a polite statement hiding so much emotion. "Don't worry," he said with a slow smile that made the polite mask slip, her expression flickering with suspicion, "I intend to take my payment in kisses."

Exiting the car to her sharply indrawn breath, he headed into the restaurant. The buzz of human and changeling energy surrounded him from every side—voices rose and fell in animated conversation, the odd burst of laughter punctuating the hum. A woman brushed by him as she left, throwing him an apologetic glance over her shoulder. Another patron almost ran into him as he got off a stool around the island that surrounded the chefs in their open-air kitchen.

Ignoring what for him were distractions, but would for Sophia be a small slice of hell, Max placed his order using the built-in pad on the counter.

The waitress put the order in front of him less than five minutes later. "You look like a cop."

He raised an eyebrow as he scanned his debit card over the reader.

Laughing, she leaned forward, her cleavage displayed to cheerful advantage. "We get a lot in here—there's an Enforcement station two blocks over."

"You've developed excellent radar."

"You're not from around here—I can hear the accent." Taking something from her pocket, she slid it across the counter with a smile. "For you."

Picking it up when she turned to deliver another order, he saw that it was a small personal card made out of Japanese *washi*, bearing the name Keiko Nakamura and a cell phone code.

"Lucky man," a morose male said from his left. "I've

been trying to get her to go out for a coffee for months."
Envy was a thorny vine around every word.

"I'm off the market." It had been true since the instant
he first laid eyes on Sophia Russo, whether he'd known it
at the time or not.

A gleam of interest. "Can I have the card then?"

"Sorry." Max dropped it into the takeout bag. "Keep
trying."

Keiko's rejected suitor scowled into his udon soup as
Max walked away, his mind already on a woman with eyes
full of secrets dark and painful. *My Sophia*, he thought,
and it was a vow.

Sophia lifted the takeout containers from the bag as
Max went to grab the plates from his kitchen area. When
she saw the small white card, she assumed it held the number of the restaurant. Then her eye fell on the text. "Who's
Keiko Nakamura?"

"What?" Max walked out with the plates. "Oh, don't
worry about that. It's going in the recycling." Putting down
the plates on the table, he plucked the card out of her hand
and placed it in the bin marked for the recycling chute.

But Sophia couldn't let the point go. "You met her at the
restaurant?"

"Yes." Placing two glasses of water on the table, he
pulled out a chair with a spare efficiency that struck her as
quintessentially male. "Waitress."

"When a female gives her contact details to an otherwise unfamiliar man," she said, trying not to be distracted
by the heated strength of him so close . . . so touchable, "it
is for private reasons." As with that woman in the elevator
at Vale's apartment. "Women seem to always be giving you
their cards."

Max opened one of the containers and served some
sushi onto her plate using the disposable chopsticks. "That
bother you, Sophie?" A low, deep tone, a masculine smile
that made her skin go tight with warning.

Remembering too late that Max Shannon was a cop used to digging deep, reading truths and lies, she opened the other container. "What is this?"

"Tempura." Max put what appeared to be a battered prawn onto her plate, his voice holding a distinct male amusement. "Try it. And you haven't answered my question."

Having removed her gloves and washed her hands earlier, she used her fingers to pick up a piece of sushi. "I suppose I should become accustomed to women . . ." She paused, unable to think of the correct term.

"Hitting on me."

"Yes, I should get accustomed to women hitting on you," she said. "After all, you are a beautiful man."

Color flagged Max's cheeks. "I'll let you—and *only* you—get away with that. But never in public. Got it?"

She was so fascinated by the disarming glimpse of embarrassment that she blurted out a need so deep, it would ravage her if he refused. "I would rather you not respond to any such invitations while we are . . ."

His gaze met hers, his attention so total that she felt as if she was in the sights of some great bird of prey. "While we are?" he prompted when she didn't continue.

She'd come this far, couldn't go back now. He knew about the otherness, about the cold justice she'd delivered to those who'd hurt society's most vulnerable, and he hadn't turned away—she was still too terrified to ask him why, but it gave her the courage to say, "While we are learning each other."

"Learning each other," Max repeated, as if measuring the words. "And will you let me in, Sophie?"

"Yes." Something stirred deep within her, something that was at once dark . . . and lonely. Unutterably, absolutely lonely. "Be with me, Max." Saying that was the hardest thing she'd ever done—it felt akin to tearing out her heart and placing it at his feet . . . and hoping, just hoping, that he wouldn't crush it.

Max didn't say anything for several long moments.

When he did speak, his voice seemed to have dropped an octave. "Do you know what you're asking, what I'll demand of you?"

The tiny hairs on her arms stood up at the leashed intensity of the question. "Yes."

Max picked up a piece of tempura, but instead of putting it on her plate, lifted it to her lips. His eyes held a silent challenge. And Sophia found her bone-deep vulnerability retreating under a wave of determination—Detective Max Shannon was not going to disconcert her so easily. She parted her lips and took a bite. Eating the other half—a shocking intimacy—he returned his attention to her face. To her mouth. "Won't whatever you experience spill out into the PsyNet?"

"It's a risk, yes," Sophia admitted, feeling her lips turn dry, her throat seeming to swell. "However, like all Js, my PsyNet shields are airtight, so the risk is acceptable. Even if there is a leak, any irregularities will be attributed to my disintegration as a functioning J, rather than to such a blatant breach of Silence."

His lips thinned. "And once those irregularities become too strong, you'll be taken away to be retuned."

"Reconditioned," she corrected automatically. Part of her wanted to tell him the final truth—that her chances had run out, that their relationship would accelerate her disintegration . . . and that she'd choose a fugitive's death before allowing her personality to be erased, her memories of Max scrubbed away to leave her a hollow shell.

But if she shared that, he'd never agree to her request, this man who looked at her as if she mattered, as if she was worth protecting. And she needed him to agree—the hunger inside of her, it was so vast, so endless, so dark and cold, she didn't know how she'd borne it this long. "I've survived reconditioning a number of times." When he didn't say anything, she rubbed her damp palms on her thighs. "Max?"

Max heard the well-hidden tremor, the touch of vulnerability, and had to force himself to keep from soothing away her worry. Because that would be a lie. He was well and truly hooked on Sophia—but no matter how easy he was with others, how laid-back, he'd never be that way with this woman he was coming to consider his. No, with her, he might play—*would* play—but he'd also push and demand and take. And she needed to understand that.

Making a decision, he stood and walked around to brace his hands on the table on either side of her, his breath stirring the tiny curls just above her ear. He saw her hands clench on her thighs, the scent of her a mix of vanilla, lavender, and something a little wilder, uniquely her own, a flower that had never known the hand of man. "Be sure, Sophie." Today, this minute, he might possibly be capable of walking away. But if he touched her, if he claimed her . . . there'd be no going back.

CHAPTER 17

Sophia's answer was immediate. "I am sure."

But he saw the strained angle of her jaw, the taut line of her body. "Are you?" When she remained stiff within the bracket of his arms, he drew in a deep breath . . . and let go of the reins. "If we do this today, if you accept me, then you take me as I am." He forced himself to give her one final chance, though the need to take her at her word, to finally taste the temptation that was Sophia Russo, was a pounding beat in every cell of his body. "I won't be controllable, and I sure as hell won't do only what you ask of me." He brushed the shell of her ear with his lips.

Sophia sucked in breath.

"Okay?" he murmured—he'd challenge, coax, seduce, but he wouldn't hurt her. Never would he hurt her.

A jerky nod. "But I need space." She went as if to stand up.

He kept her in place by the simple expedient of remaining in position. "Like I said, baby—we do this, you'll have to let go, trust me." He let his lips stroke over the tip of her ear again, felt her tremble.

So sensitive, so exquisitely sensitive.

But no pushover.

"I may be fractured," she said in blunt response, "but I am not a submissive personality."

He felt his lips curve, delighted. "Did I say I wanted a submissive? I just want to make sure you don't expect one either."

"Do you know how I see you?" A husky question. "As a tiger who has decided to behave for the time being—I'm not stupid enough to attempt to leash you."

The maleness in him settled at the verbal stroking. "I'll teach you how to make me come willingly to your hand," he murmured, pressing a single, gentle kiss to the sweet slope of her neck. "Anytime you want."

A long, shuddering exhale, her skin shimmering with heat. *"Max."*

"Ride it," he said. "Don't fight, just ride the wave."

Sophia shook her head. The impact of his touch—hard, jagged, almost painful—shoved through her. "I can't. It's too much."

For an instant, she thought he wouldn't shift and she'd drown in the avalanche of sensation, but then he rose to his full height, releasing her from the sensual prison of his arms. Pushing back her chair, she got up and stumbled to the bathroom. The cold water she splashed onto her face snapped some semblance of control back into her, but it still took several long minutes before she got herself under enough control to dare check her PsyNet shields.

Holding—a hard carapace that left her battered inside. Battered but protected. A strong PsyNet shield was a J's sole protection against early rehabilitation, and as such, was an unspoken secret in the Corps, the shield techniques passed on from J to J outside of any scheduled lesson. Even her boss, who played politics with cold-blooded ease, would never divulge that one truth. Because no one in the Corps was ever safe.

"Sophie." Max's voice, shaping her name like a caress. "Either you come out or I'm coming in."

Tucking her hair behind her ears, she opened the door and walked toward the table. "I'm fine." A lie. She was terrified he'd decided against her, a woman who couldn't handle a simple kiss. "It was just a shock to my senses."

Max pulled out her chair. "Tell me."

She didn't sit, didn't dare go so close to the temptation and danger of him. "I miscalculated how big the impact would be." How visceral. Her hands trembled as she went to pick up her discarded gloves. "We should work on the case." It was a jerky, unsophisticated attempt to change the subject.

Max smiled, and it felt as if he'd stroked a fingertip across the most sensitive parts of her. "We'll watch the data files from the security cameras in the corridor outside Chan's apartment—you can finish your lunch at the same time."

Her stomach felt tight, twisted into knots. "I don't really need any more—"

"You'll eat." Cool words. "You'll need your energy."

Her negative response whispered away as she read the intent in those dark, dark eyes. "You still want to be with me? Even though I couldn't even handle . . ."

"I figure it just means you need more practice."

The provocative words turned the knots in her stomach into butterflies. "You mustn't say things like that."

"Why?" A slow, deep smile that revealed a lean dimple in his cheek. "Practice will be fun—I intend to be a very demanding coach."

She stared, wishing she could kiss her way down that dimple.

"Come on." Smile widening and filling with a wickedly sensual heat, he turned to head to the comm screen in the living area. "Bring your plate." A coaxing glance over his shoulder as he inserted the crystal into the built-in player on the side of the screen. "I promise to behave."

She wasn't sure she believed him, but she couldn't resist. He stretched out an arm on the sofa behind her head as soon as she sat down. "Max, you need to sit a little farther away."

"No." The dimple disappeared, but his expression remained warm . . . intimate. "No backward steps." He turned on the comm screen using the remote, even as his fingers began to play with strands of her hair.

For the first time, she found herself wondering what she'd taken on.

A tug on her hair. "Focus, J."

J. It had always been, if not a curse, then a symbol of the inevitable. But when Max said it . . . Her eyes lifted to the screen as it filled with a shot of the corridor leading to Edward Chan's room. As she watched, Max programmed the screen to skip to anything that disrupted the image of the empty corridor. The first time, it was a cleaning bot, buzzing its way industriously along the carpet.

"I don't think he did it," Max murmured, his focus very much on the screen.

Sophia took the chance to watch him. His profile was all clean lines, his skin that strokable dark honey, his bone structure flawless. But Sophia had seen beautiful men before. Objectively speaking, Councilor Kaleb Krychek was one of the most devastatingly attractive men on the planet—but the one time she'd been in his vicinity, he'd made her blood run cold. Max, on the other hand . . .

Her eyes went to the triangle of flesh bared at the open collar of his shirt. Other men sometimes had hair there, but she could see only smooth, unblemished skin. It made her want to ask him to unbutton the shirt farther so she could kiss her way across his chest, learn him with her mouth.

"Now who's this?"

Sophia jerked her head to the woman onscreen. Dressed in a deep green pantsuit, she stepped out of the elevator and headed toward Chan's room, but entered the suite opposite his. Putting down her plate, Sophia reached for her organizer. "That has to be Marsha Langholm, Nikita's most senior advisor. She uses that apartment while in the country."

"We'll need to talk to her." Reaching over, Max took her organizer so he could read the notes she had on Langholm. "If you didn't like sushi, you should've spoken up."

She ate another piece. "I've never tasted it before. It's fine."

"What about the tempura?" He kept his eyes on the screen as it skipped to show a young male who slid an envelope beneath Chan's door before returning to the elevator.

"I recognize him—Ryan Asquith," she said. "He's the same intern who later found the body. And tempura is quite . . . enjoyable." Never before had she considered food anything more than nourishment that kept her alive—like most Psy, she'd been conditioned against falling victim to the inherent sensuality of taste and pleasure.

"We'll try something else next time."

"There's Marsha again." The woman walked over to Chan's with a briefcase in hand, exiting two minutes later to re-enter her own room.

"Quick visit." He froze as the screen skipped forward and stopped on another individual. "Hell."

Sophia looked up. The female onscreen was tall, with black hair that spilled past her shoulders in soft curls, and skin that was dusted a golden brown. Unlike the others, she wasn't wearing a suit, but a shapeless coat in royal blue that swamped her frame.

But no matter the ill-fitting clothing, even Sophia knew who that was. "I thought," she said, "that Sascha was estranged from Nikita?"

"There are the business ties DarkRiver has with Nikita. But what was she doing on a private floor?" He went silent as Sascha knocked on Marsha Langholm's door, was admitted.

The screen skipped forward.

Two more men appeared a short time apart, neither of whom they could immediately identify. The first—a slender black male who looked to be in his thirties—spent approximately ten minutes with the victim before leaving.

The second—an aristocratic man with prematurely silver hair—stayed five minutes longer than that before being shown out, and the victim was alive at that stage. They saw him step out into the corridor, walk his colleague to the elevator while they apparently finished up their conversation.

The next piece of movement showed Sascha exiting Marsha's apartment with the other woman by her side.

"Wait." Max paused the screen, rewound it to the image of Edward Chan disappearing into his apartment. "Look at the time stamp."

"Ten fifteen a.m."

"I'm resetting it to playback continuously from this point." But when he pushed Play, they saw Sascha leaving Marsha's apartment.

Sophia blinked, staring at the time stamp. "It's over an hour and a half later."

"From the looks of the file data," Max said, bringing it up on the side of the comm screen, "someone input a 'do not record' order for that period." He restarted playback.

The next movement came barely five minutes after Sascha's departure, when the same intern who'd left the envelope returned—eventually entering the apartment to discover Chan's body. "Why was Asquith given not only permission, but the code to override Chan's security?" Max asked Sophia, stopping the playback.

"He must've gone into the Net to contact Edward, found him gone." Sophia had seen J minds blink out like that, known that death had claimed one more of her own. "Psy who drop out of the Net without explanation are always tracked down to verify the reason for their disappearance." For Sophia, that reason would only ever be death, her mind too deeply integrated into the Net to survive any separation. "How long it takes depends on the circumstances, but here it was obviously very close to the time of the murder."

When Max didn't say anything in response to her statement, she glanced over to find him pinching the bridge of his nose in an uncharacteristic gesture of frustration. "Max?"

A low, hard word as he dropped his hand. "I'm about to piss off the few friends I have in this city."

Sophia went to reach out, touch him. But Max thrust both hands through his hair and got up from the sofa before she could transform thought into action. Her fingers curled into the sofa cushions—just as something walked across her feet. She jerked back in response, making Morpheus yowl. "Oh, my apologies, Morpheus."

The cat gave her a baleful glare before hopping up to sit on the sofa beside her.

"He wants you to pet him," Max said distractedly, pulling out his cell phone. "I'll give Clay a call, set up a meet."

"What about Marsha Langholm?"

"We'll talk to her after Sascha."

Morpheus put a clawed paw on Sophia's thigh, insistent. Taking the hint, she ran her fingers through his fur. It was far softer than she'd imagined, the living warmth of him making the experience nothing akin to touching a faux-fur coat, as she'd once done in a department store.

When Morpheus spread out over her thigh, eyes closed in feline bliss, she knew she'd passed muster. However, her attention was no longer on the temperamental cat, but on his master. Max stood by the window, cell phone to his ear. He moved, she thought, with the same grace as the feline under her hand—with a muscled ease that told her he was in full and total control of his body, his strength.

What would it be like to stroke *him*?

He turned, met her eyes. She wondered what he saw, because his expression changed to a look she knew instinctively she'd only ever see in a sexual context. Closing the phone, he walked over and brushed back her hair, stroking his finger along the very tip of her ear. "Sascha's at the city office."

It was the lightest of touches, but she shivered. "That is not an erotic zone."

"Oh?" Leaning down, he closed his teeth gently over the same spot.

And Sophia saw stars.

They were met at DarkRiver's city HQ by the leopard alpha himself. Lucas Hunter was obviously not pleased to find his mate in the crosshairs of an investigation, but he said nothing except, "Max, Ms. Russo," before showing them up to the meeting room.

Entering, Sophia tried not to stare at the woman seated on the other side of the round table. But that proved impossible. The image on the screen hadn't done Sascha Duncan justice. Not only did she bear the startling night-sky eyes of a cardinal—white stars on a sweep of black velvet—she was beyond beautiful, her face holding a glow that didn't seem real.

"This is Sophia," Max said to Sascha, his fingers pressing lightly on Sophia's lower back.

Her clothing did nothing to mute the impact of his touch, the tiny hairs on her arms rising up in vivid response. "Ms. Duncan," she somehow managed to say.

"Please call me Sascha." Glancing up, the cardinal Psy touched her fingers to Lucas's as her mate walked around to stand by her side, his hand on her shoulder. Something unseen passed between them, because the leopard alpha angled his head in a move that was very feline, before saying, "Take a seat," and folding his own body into a chair beside his mate.

"Sophie." Max pulled out a chair, taking his own after she'd seated herself. "I'll be upfront with you both," he said to the DarkRiver couple, one arm braced on the table. "Sascha, you were in the Duncan building this morning in the apartment across from an Edward Chan."

Lucas leaned back in his chair in a seemingly casual pose . . . except that his eyes weren't quite human—Sophia could see an areola of gold around the green, as if the leopard was simply waiting for an excuse to get out.

"What're you getting at Max?" A question that held a warning.

"Just doing my job," Max said easily. So easily you could've almost overlooked the fact that he was holding Lucas's gaze with unflinching confidence.

Dominance, she thought, it was all about dominance with males.

"Lucas," Sascha murmured, and Sophia saw the other woman's shoulder muscles shift in a way that meant she had, in all probability, placed her hand on her mate's thigh. An intimate gesture between male and female, one she knew Max would allow her . . . and not another woman, no matter who she was. Not now. A strange new thing unfurled inside of her, tight and hot and determined.

"Yes, I was there," Sascha said to Max, even as Sophia fought the urge to push herself, to stroke Max, feel his muscles bunch under her touch. "I went to speak to Marsha Langholm."

"The thing is"—Max's tone was gentler than Sophia had ever heard it—"Edward Chan was murdered in the room across from Langholm's while you were in there with her."

Sascha's eyes went wide, her distress open. "Oh, God. That explains it."

CHAPTER 18

Lucas ran a soothing hand along Sascha's spine. "Shh, kitten. Don't let it stress you out."

"I'm okay—it was just the shock of it." Taking several deep breaths, she looked straight at them. "How much do you know about my abilities?"

Max glanced at Sophia, and she took that as a cue to answer. "They say you can sense emotion, heal wounds of the heart. There are rumors you're an E, a designation that doesn't exist."

"Oh, it exists," Sascha said with a firmness at odds with the incredible warmth of her presence. "I'm an empath, not a particularly useful thing in the Net under Silence. But that doesn't matter—only two things matter. One—I couldn't murder anyone, not without it rebounding back on me. I'd feel the impact of the victim's death, and I'm fairly certain it would kill me. Nikita can verify that for you."

Sophia found herself believing Sascha. There was just something about the other woman that made her *want* to believe. If all Es motivated the same response, then it might go toward explaining why their designation had been buried—they were a threat, because they inspired loyalty without the fear that was the Council's favorite weapon. "You said two reasons," she prompted in a tone that held genuine respect. "What's the second?"

"I think I felt him die." It was a whisper. "It was just before I left Marsha's room. I felt a wave of nausea, then everything went black—I thought I was going to faint. But it passed within seconds, so I put it down to getting up too quickly from the sofa." She leaned into her mate's embrace—Lucas's face was set in lines of savage protectiveness, but he held her with open tenderness. "Poor Edward. He always worked so hard."

"Sascha." Max's tone was oddly careful as he said, "Did you see or hear anything that might help? I've got a gap of ninety critical minutes in the security footage."

"No." Frown lines marred her brow. "The rooms are all soundproofed, and I was intent on my conversation with Marsha. We were together the whole time except when I got up to go to the bathroom." Those extraordinary eyes met Max's. "I'm the last person who'd hurt anyone."

Max thrust a hand through his hair. "Look," he said in the tone of a man who'd made a decision. "I think it's about time you know what's going on." A searing glance out of those near-black eyes. "Sophie, it might be better for you to leave the room."

She remained in her seat. Max tapped her foot with his in playful approval—making her heart slam against her ribs, her fingers curl—before turning his attention back to the other couple. "Someone's attempting to derail Nikita's organization by taking out her people because he or she can't get to Nikita herself. It's looking like the bombers four months ago only got to the elevator shaft because someone on the inside made sure they did."

Sascha's hand clenched into a fist on the table. "You don't think they'll facilitate another attempt on her life?"

"Your mother," Max said, "is forearmed and very

security conscious. That's why the killer has become frustrated, started to target those around her." He blew out a breath. "Sascha, if you're still in contact with her, you're a prime target."

Lucas Hunter tangled his fingers with his mate's, his lethal anger turning into an intense, protective focus. "Sascha isn't Nikita's heir."

"She's Nikita's daughter." Max shook his head, his jaw a stubborn line. "I don't care what anyone says about the Psy ability to cut off people without a thought—if a Councilor's daughter is taken out, it *will* have an impact."

"You may not be Councilor Duncan's financial heir," Sophia said into the silence, "but you remain her genetic heir, the only one she has." And genetics were very, very important in the Net. Those of her race had no love, no hate, to tie them together, but they had blood. "As far as I know, she hasn't arranged for a second child or a surrogate."

"No," Sascha whispered. "I've never understood why."

"My pack will protect my mate," Lucas said to Max. "Thanks for the heads-up."

Max gave a wry smile. "Thanks for not ripping my face off before I could get a word out."

"It's such a pretty face," the leopard alpha responded, a feline smile warming those feral green eyes, "the women in the office would probably string me up if I messed it up."

Sophia felt the tension level in the room drop even before Max's expression shifted to pure male amusement. "I thought Dorian was considered the fairest of them all."

It was Sascha who replied. "I don't know, Max"—a tight smile, as the empath fought her worry for her mother—"you're giving him serious competition. I'm certain I heard Zara say something about wanting to lick you up like strawberry ice cream."

Sophia decided this Zara person couldn't be allowed anywhere near Max. Who tilted back his chair in that way he had and laughed. "Since I've already broken the rules, if either of you have any idea of who might want to go after Nikita, I'd be happy to hear it."

"Let us discuss it and get back to you." Squeezing his mate's shoulder, Lucas rose to his feet.

"Fair enough." Max stood as well. "Clay knows where I'm staying, and he's got my cell code." As the men shook hands, Sophia got up, taking one last look at the extraordinary daughter Councilor Nikita Duncan had borne. Sascha's head was bent, her smile having faded away to reveal a haunting worry.

"Sophie."

She turned to see Max holding the door. Walking out beside him, she considered whether she'd mourn her own parents when they died. *No*, she thought. They'd erased her from their lives so cleanly that she'd had to erase them from hers in order to survive. It had been hard, so hard to do that. She'd written letters at first. She'd begged.

Finally, a response had come . . . one that had made her parents' position clear with brutal precision—she was no longer, it had stated, an "acceptable genetic heir."

A wolf whistle pierced the air, slicing neatly through the pained numbness of her memories of the day she'd realized her parents were never returning for her. The whistle originated from the mouth of a small woman with coffee-colored skin. "I hear you're single, Cop." A blinding smile.

Max's responding smile revealed the lean dimple in his left cheek that Sophia wanted to kiss each time she saw it. "Your intel is out of date."

"I knew it—I'm going to die an old maid." Her face drooped. "I shall now go drown myself in fantasies where three—no *four*—hot men await my every whim."

Sophia didn't say a word until they were back in the car. "I'm . . . glad that you no longer consider yourself single." It took considerable willpower to say that, to admit how much his commitment meant to her. No one had ever before chosen her. No one.

Reaching out with a deliberate slowness, Max brushed

his knuckles over her cheek. The sensation was a hot whip over her skin. "The things I plan to do to you, Sophie," he whispered in a deep voice that made her toes curl. "Zara's fantasies have nothing on mine."

Lucas waited until after Max and Sophia Russo had left to turn to his mate. Fighting the urge to just cuddle the worry out of her, he leaned back against the wall by the door and folded his arms. "Now, kitten, how about telling me exactly what you were doing in the Duncan building?" His heart had almost stopped beating when she'd confessed her little field trip.

"Lucas," Sascha said in a voice that would've normally made him calm down.

"That isn't going to work." He dropped his hands, moved to brace them on the tabletop. "I thought we agreed you'd stay out of the limelight while you're so vulnerable. And God, you went—" He grit his teeth, unable to get the words out.

"No one realized I was pregnant," Sascha said, rising to move around the table, "not even Marsha. She thought I'd put on weight because of my unregimented existence." Her hand curved over his cheek. "I needed to talk to her."

"Why?" He thought he knew, but he wanted to be certain after she'd sucker punched him with this stunt. "And sit." Pulling out a chair for her, he took one to her right.

Placing one hand on his thigh in that way she had, his mate took another deep breath. "I wanted . . ." Her voice shook, and he could no more stop from reaching out to kiss her, pet her, than he could stop breathing.

"Kitten, you know you can tell me anything, *anything*." Why had she felt the need to hide this? That was what had him so lost.

"I planned to tell you as soon as I got back," she said at once, her fingers tightening on his thigh, "but you were so busy I thought I'd wait till tonight."

"You're supposed to tell me things like this *before*." The panther snarled in agreement.

"I knew you wouldn't let me see Marsha on my own," she said, a stubborn angle to her jaw. "And I didn't want you to worry—you do so much of it already."

"Of course I do. You're pregnant with our child—I have the right to go nuts looking after you."

"And I love you for it." An affectionate wave of emotion down the mating bond tied them together on the level of the soul. "But this, I needed to do alone."

His panther caught the vulnerability beneath the steely will. Reaching out, he curved one hand behind her nape in a hold as protective as it was proprietary. "I still haven't heard what you went to do."

"Marsha's been my mother's advisor since before Nikita became a Councilor, since before she had me."

The tenderness he felt for her made his soul hurt. "You went to ask her what Nikita was like during her pregnancy and when you were born." His mate was so scared she wouldn't be a good mother—when everyone around her knew she'd be an amazing one.

"Yes." Her eyes were almost starless when she looked up. "But I couldn't make myself ask any of those questions. I guess part of me was afraid of what she would say—that Nikita never loved me, not even when I was in her womb."

It tore him apart to see her hurting. "Kitten."

A reassuring squeeze of his thigh. "It hurts, but it won't ever break me again like it almost did once. Not when I can feel you loving me every moment of every day." Eyes shiny with emotion, she reached up to stroke her fingers through his hair. "Mostly, I think I need to hear the answers from Nikita herself."

Lucas shifted closer, so she could more easily pet him with those hands he adored. "I'll call her, organize a meeting." He'd dance with the devil himself if that was what it took to ensure his mate's happiness.

"Marsha missed my pregnancy because she's so focused

on work she's oblivious to anything else," she said, playing her fingers over his jaw and along his neck. "Nikita won't."

Lucas laid his hand over the curved mound of her stomach, knowing that if he pressed his ear to that same spot, he'd be able to sense the heartbeat of their unborn child. "We've managed to keep it quiet this far, but I think unless you plan to stay in seclusion, the jig is up. Max knew you were pregnant the instant he looked at you." At five months along, she was gorgeously, radiantly beautiful—any man with a working heart would realize she carried a life in her womb.

"Are you calling me fat?"

He caught the gleam of laughter in those stunning cardinal eyes and knew his Sascha was more than tough enough to handle the woman who'd given birth to her. "According to Dev *should mind his own business* Santos, I should be feeding you more." She'd gained little extra weight through the pregnancy. "Are you sure you're eating enough?"

"Lucas, did you or did you not go out at three a.m. to get me a pizza with all the fixings?"

"Did you say thank you for that yet?" He leaned forward to speak with his lips against her ear.

Making a small, pleased sound, she nuzzled into his neck. "I seem to remember you purring."

"Even though all I got was a single measly slice."

"I rest my case." A kiss pressed to the beat of his pulse. "I eat like the proverbial horse." Sascha patted her hand over the one Lucas had placed on her abdomen. "We're both doing more than fine according to the doctor and Tamsyn." The DarkRiver healer had examined her only yesterday.

A shift inside her, a strange, beautiful thing, then a tiny foot slamming into her with a strength that surely came from the baby's father. "Oof."

Lucas beamed with pride. "That's my girl."

Sascha made a face. "Why are you so convinced it's a girl?" They'd made the decision not to ask the doctor or healer to confirm gender, though Sascha couldn't help but know—her baby's mind was developing day by day, becoming a stronger and stronger psychic warmth inside of her. Still, she liked to play with Lucas. He'd ordered her not to tell him.

"I just know." Bending his head, he pressed a kiss to the top of her abdomen, much as he had a habit of doing late at night, saying good night to their babe.

She ran her fingers through his hair. "I love you so much, Lucas." Her eyes teared, her voice got thick.

"Hey now." Raising his head, he touched his forehead to hers. "Pregnancy hormones strike again?"

A jerky nod as she melted into his embrace. "I should've told you about visiting Marsha, but I swear I wasn't in any danger."

Lucas went predator-still. "Who went with you?"

"I'm not telling you if you're going to go snarl at them."

"I'm their alpha—they should've told me."

She thumped a fist against his chest. "I'm their alpha's mate."

And, Lucas thought, she'd earned her packmates' loyalty in her own right. "Dorian," he said, knowing the sentinel had a mile-wide soft spot for Sascha. "Why wasn't he on Max's surveillance?"

"He was less than thirty seconds away, in the emergency stairwell, monitoring the corridor with his super-duper high-tech gee-whizz surveillance equipment, while I had the meeting. He even had me wired in case Martha suddenly went insane and tried to kill me by throwing her organizer at my head." A theatrical gasp.

Lucas nipped her lower lip in punishment for the smart-aleck response—and because he was proud of his mate's strength, no matter that he hadn't gotten his own way. "Come on then, let's go see what Blondie has to say."

"Lucas, did you notice?"

"What?"

"Max and his J."

Lucas leaned one arm against the table, scowling. "No, I didn't notice."

"Sophia Russo's almost impossibly good at hiding her disintegration," Sascha said. "I only picked it up because of my empathy. So much pain, so *much*." She closed her hand into a fist, rubbed it over her heart. "I wanted to reach across and tell her it was alright, that she was safe, that we'd help her."

Lucas was used to his mate's empathic nature. But he was also an alpha, pledged to protect his people. "She's in the Net, Sascha. No way to know if she can be trusted."

"*I* know." A stubborn look. "And if she decides to call me one day, I won't say no to any request she makes."

"Were you this hardheaded when I mated with you?" A growl formed low in his throat.

"No. I think I'm maturing with age."

"Well, stop it." In spite of his teasing words, her responses, he caught the edge of fear in her eyes. "Don't worry, kitten. The cop knows what he's doing." Max Shannon, Lucas thought, might appear nonthreatening with that easy smile of his, but it was deceptive—the cat had sensed the truth, sensed the hunter that lurked beneath the human skin. "He won't stop until he brings down his prey."

CHAPTER 19

No one ever expects betrayal. No one.
—*From the private case notes of Detective Max Shannon*

Making it back to the Duncan building by five, Max and Sophia managed to round up the other four people who'd appeared on the surveillance footage.

The intern, Ryan Asquith, was unable to provide any useful information, but Marsha Langholm was far more forthcoming. "Detective," she said. "I'll get straight to the point. While I did see Edward for a brief period this morning so he could sign a contract, I was in a private meeting at the time of his murder, and I'd rather not—"

Max held up a hand. "Sascha told us she was with you."

A slight nod. "In that case, you'll understand the need for discretion."

"The Councilor wasn't aware Sascha was in the building?"

"I have no way of knowing that."

An artful dodge, but Langholm's loyalty to the Duncans—even to the extent of protecting one who had defected—was clear. "You're one of Nikita's highest-ranking people," Max said. "Is there anything you can tell us that might help with tracking down the person or people behind these murders?"

The woman didn't pretend not to understand. "I knew Vale didn't commit suicide—it was simply not in his psychological profile." A pause. "I can't give you names or any concrete details, but there have been ongoing . . . ripples from Sascha's defection."

Tapping Max's foot beneath the table in a silent signal, Sophia put down her organizer. "Surely no one holds the Councilor responsible for her daughter's so-called flaw? In any case, I thought it was common knowledge that Nikita severed all familial ties with Sascha."

Marsha responded directly to Sophia. "There were questions after Sascha left the Net, but they calmed once it became clear the Councilor was going about her business as normal. Eventually, Nikita's business association with the changelings began to be considered an asset because they are an unusually difficult market to capture."

Max sat back—it was clear Sophia knew precisely the right questions to ask. But he couldn't resist tapping at her foot in playful response. She put the high heel of her pump over the front of his leather shoe in silent reproof.

"What's changed?" In sharp contrast to her foot, Sophia's fingers lay unmoving on the glass-topped table.

He remembered those same fingers weaving through Morpheus's fur, remembered, too, the expression of discovery on her face, as if she'd never before petted a living creature. He wanted to share a thousand other pieces of his world with her—but to do so, he'd have to plumb her secrets, discover everything the Justice Corps kept hidden. Because he wasn't letting this J disappear into the dark.

"The Councilor hasn't changed her business practices." Marsha Langholm's voice broke into his thoughts. "However, there have been certain subtle changes in the Psy-Net."

"The political winds are shifting," Sophia murmured.

"No," Marsha Langholm said to Max's surprise. "I'd say it's more of a split. The lines are very, very fine, but the division is starting to take form. Nikita stands on one side, those who support Pure Psy on the other."

Max decided to reenter the conversation. "Explain Pure Psy to me." Sophia had told him what she knew about the group—including the extra intelligence Nikita had sent her, but this was an opportunity to get the perspective of another powerful Psy.

"Of course you wouldn't have heard of it," Marsha said, and it was—no doubt about it—condescending. "Pure Psy's guiding aim is to strengthen and preserve the integrity of Silence, a concept they term Purity. They've come to believe that contact with the other races is contaminating us—and that that contamination is a direct cause of the rise in defections and whispers of rebellion."

"So Nikita is considered a problem—because of her increasingly strong ties with the changelings." Sophia's tone was as pragmatic as Marsha's. "How about other businesses? Are they pulling back from their non-Psy connections?"

"Some are considering it—while Nikita has recently entered into another construction deal in partnership with DarkRiver and SnowDancer."

"If it is Pure Psy," Max said, telling himself to behave when he got the urge to ruffle Sophia, sneak under that prim composure of hers by tap-dancing his fingers along her thigh, "why single out Nikita? She's one of seven Councilors."

Marsha Langholm touched the screen of her organizer where it lay on the table in front of her, not a restless motion—fully conditioned Psy never made those—but an indication. "I looked you up, Detective Shannon. For a man with such a high solve rate, you're a rare presence in the news media."

Max shrugged, let it rest at that.

"It makes me willing to share this information. I've heard murmurs that Henry Scott has aligned himself fully with Pure Psy, and that Shoshanna, as his wife, is aligned with him."

Max made a mental note to ask Sophie how that worked—the Scotts couldn't truly be husband and wife, not in the emotional sense. "That still leaves Anthony Kyriakus, Tatiana Rika-Smythe, Ming LeBon, and Kaleb Krychek."

"All four have undeclared political loyalties," Marsha Langholm said. "Pure Psy might be suspicious that Anthony doesn't stand on their side of the line, but then again, his action in subcontracting foreseeing work to his daughter is an understandable business decision, given Faith NightStar's sheer value. And, the NightStar clan has little contact with changelings beyond that subcontracting arrangement."

Sophia spoke again, her voice a stroke against Max's senses. "Do you have any idea where the other Councilors might stand?"

"Tatiana Rika-Smythe recently bought significant amounts of shares in human companies. If she continues on that track, it will by default put her on the other side of the line from Pure Psy. Ming LeBon and Kaleb Krychek are unknowns. They've done nothing that could be considered either for or against the group."

"I don't get one thing," Max said, tipping back his chair. "Psy are all about logic, right?"

"Correct, Detective."

"Then Pure Psy makes no rational sense." A pointed tap on his foot. Hiding his grin, he put his chair back down on all four legs. "If they succeed, they'll isolate the Psy, cut off huge sources of revenue."

Marsha Langholm didn't answer. Sophia did. "It is logical, in a way," she said. "Pure Psy believes that if the Net is 'closed' again, then Psy power will grow to the extent that our race will eventually be able to exterminate the changelings and humans both."

"Even if such an act means a loss of power—of personnel," Marsha Langholm added, "in the short term."

It was the most cold-blooded description of murder Max had ever heard.

Dorian looked up from the computer where he was doing something that disappeared the instant Sascha and Lucas walked into the second subbasement of the Dark-River building.

"He knows," Sascha whispered to her co-conspirator.

Dorian grinned at Lucas. "So how mad are you?"

"If you didn't have a mate, I'd consider making you a eunuch," Lucas said, watching Sascha walk over to stand on Dorian's other side, her hand on the back of the sentinel's chair.

Turning, Dorian angled his head, asking for permission. When Sascha smiled, he pressed his ear against her belly, touching his hand protectively to the swell. If any man outside the pack had dared to do that, Lucas would've torn him to shreds with his bare claws. But this was Dorian, Sascha's favorite sentinel, and one of the best friends Lucas had ever had.

His panther sat up in inquisitive interest when Sascha laughed at something Dorian whispered to the baby. "Hey," the sentinel said in a louder tone, "you never know. Kid could come out wanting to know all about advanced martial arts."

Sascha messed up the sentinel's distinctive white-blond hair. "According to Vaughn, *she's* going to be a painter, he's sure of it. According to Clay, *he's* going to be a sentinel-born. According to Hawke—"

Lucas growled at the wolf alpha's name.

Laughing, Sascha continued. "According to Hawke, *her* purpose in life is going to be to make Lucas insane. He's already bought Lucas a woolen hat—for when he tears his hair out," she explained at Dorian's confused look.

Lucas felt his lips tug upward at her gentle teasing. "You know what I can't wait for? That wolf to get his comeuppance. I'm going to throw a party when he gets mated—then take a front-row seat while his mate makes mincemeat out of him."

Sascha's expression softened, and Lucas could guess the direction of her thoughts. Accepted knowledge said the wolf alpha would never mate, but things had shifted in the past year. It was beginning to look as if there *might* be a chance for the SnowDancer. And no matter how much they antagonized each other, Lucas would never wish anything but good luck to the other male on this one point. Because when it came to mating . . .

His eyes met those of the cardinal Psy who was his mate, his heartbeat. "Stop flirting with Dorian and come over here."

Taking his hand, she moved to fit herself against his side. "I wouldn't dare flirt with Dorian. Ashaya would turn me into chopped liver."

Dorian gave a smug grin. "My mate thinks I'm the most gorgeous leopard she ever saw."

"Show us the footage before your head explodes," Lucas muttered, but his own cat was grinning to see Dorian so happy. The sentinel had been latent most of his life, unable to shift into leopard form. Now that he could, he did so at every opportunity. "Have you managed to catch a rabbit yet?"

A single eloquent finger. "Fuck you."

Lucas snickered. "What about trying for a turtle?"

Dorian lunged out of the chair and went for Lucas's throat.

Laughing, Sascha watched the two men fall to the floor. Neither had released claws, and it was obvious they weren't doing anything much more than wrestling. Men, she thought with a fond shake of her head, turning to take Dorian's chair.

Oooh, that felt so much better.

Though her energy levels had increased over the past week or two, her ankles were persisting in their attempts to turn into miniature logs. A little bump in her stomach, a reminder that it was all worth it. *Yes,* she thought to her child, *you're worth everything.*

A sense of happiness, warmth, belonging.

She stroked her hand over her belly, keeping one eye on the two boys still rolling around on the floor. *You're incredibly loved, my sweet baby.* The entire pack was waiting for the birth, as they did for every birth in DarkRiver. Each child was treasured, celebrated.

None would ever be rejected as flawed.

Smiling, she tapped the screen to bring up the correct files. Dorian hadn't actually listened in on her conversation with Marsha—instead, he'd monitored the tone of her voice with one of his gadgets, ready to break down the door the instant it indicated distress. However, he'd also kept an ear on what went on in the corridor, recording it as a matter of course.

Something thumped behind her as she opened the file. "Dorian?" she said. "Is this audio only?"

"What—*umfh!*" Another thump. "Yeah. Haven't had a chance to—"

A loud crash.

Trying to keep a stern face, she turned. "If you mess up this lab, I'll rat you out to Ria." Lucas's administrative assistant had ordered all the hard-to-find equipment Dorian had specified, helped put the place in order to the last rivet and bolt.

Lucas lifted up his face, his hair messy and so gorgeous, she wanted to tumble him to the floor herself. "Aw, come on."

"Yeah," Dorian muttered, pushing himself up into a sitting position, his T-shirt rucked up to bare part of his muscled abdomen. "That's just mean, siccing Ria on us."

"She's five feet and zero inches," Sascha said, noting that between them, Lucas and Dorian probably outweighed and out-muscled Ria four times over. "Why are you all so scared of her?"

"You don't know 'cause she likes you." Getting up,

Lucas held his hand down to Dorian, who took it and bounced up to his feet.

Neither looked anything but a little rumpled. Cute, she thought, they looked cute. And they'd snarl if she even dared utter the word. "I'd like to listen to this audio now." Her joy dimmed. "Someone's trying to hurt my mother."

Lucas squeezed the back of her neck in silent reassurance, his love a protective shield around her. When Dorian queried her words, Lucas gave him a short précis of events—the sentinel touched his fingers to her cheek before turning to fix something in the audio file. "I was monitoring the live feed the whole time and heard nothing suspicious, but I was only listening out for threats to Sascha. Here we go."

There was a whole lot of nothing, and more nothing on the tape.

"New plan," Dorian said after several minutes, "I'm going to skip to any incidents where the noise level went over the baseline."

There were several noises that made the computer stop, people coming and going. Then, a bare few minutes before Sascha left Marsha's apartment, the sound of footsteps, a knock, a door being opened.

"I see you received my message," said a male voice, with a slight French accent. "Come in. The papers are sitting on the coffee table where you left them earlier today."

"Ah, fuck," Lucas muttered, thrusting a hand through already tousled hair. "If that's what I think it is, Max is going to be pissed."

CHAPTER 20

Like the majority of telepaths born with the J facility, this female has a minor ability in the F spectrum, limited to the potential for backsight. Her ability measures at 1.5 on the Gradient and may never activate.

—PsyMed report on Sophia Russo, minor, age 8

Max wasn't pissed when Lucas called him. He was beyond pissed. "Damn it, Luc. You should've told me this when we met."

"It's evidence you wouldn't otherwise have," the Dark-River alpha said as Sophia got up and closed the door to the interview room, ensuring privacy. "And for the record, I didn't know. I've already snarled at the two culprits for you."

Recognizing the peace offering for what it was, Max blew out his breath. "Can you send the segment through to my phone? I'll pick up the original later."

"I'll get Dorian to do it. And, Cop"—his voice dropped— "you need us, we're there. Don't hesitate."

"I'll hold you to that." Closing the phone, Max told Sophia what the DarkRiver alpha had shared.

Sophia tucked her hair behind her ear, baring the marks on her face, marks that were becoming intimately familiar to Max. "They take the protection of their mates seriously."

"Do you think it's only changelings who do that?" Max raised a hand, waited until she leaned a wary fraction toward him. Then, his eyes on the sweet curve of her lips, he danced his fingers over her temple, the edge of her cheek, and along her jaw.

Sophia's heart was a stampede in her chest, her skin prickling with a near-painful heat, but she didn't move away. And when Max stepped even closer, until her breasts brushed his chest with every breath, she found her free hand rising to press against the warm resilience of his pectorals.

"I want skin," she dared confess, though she wasn't certain she'd survive the sensual impact.

"Yeah?" Max bent his head, his breath hot against her cheek as he stroked his lips over her skin in a slow, sweet glide, his hand closing over her hip in a grip so proprietary, it felt akin to a brand.

"*Max.*" Her legs trembled with the effort to stay in place, to soak in the feel of him—hard and strong, an erotic temptation.

"Enough." Max stepped back. "Next time, I get your mouth."

Gripping the back of a chair, she swallowed, tried to find her voice. It was gone, lost in the rush of thunder that was her bloodstream. Her eyes met Max's again, and she saw the glitter in his gaze, saw, too, the skin pulled tight over his jaw. "It can't affect you like it does me," she finally managed to say, her throat raw. "You must be used to it."

"So another man would work just as well for you?"

The answer spilled out of her. "Only you." A dangerous confession, but Sophia didn't have time to play games. Bitterness threatened to rise in a sharp, acidic burst, but she crushed it, determined not to give in to useless anger. "Only ever you."

Max sucked in a breath, swearing low in his throat. "Good—because I sure as hell am not the sharing kind."

With that harsh statement of claim—and she understood that that was exactly what it was—he turned to the door. "I'll be back in a second."

Max leaned against the wall outside the meeting room, his breath coming in jagged gulps. The cool air did little to clear the scent of Sophia from his lungs. She was nothing he'd ever expected, everything he wanted.

And she was Psy.

Just now, when he'd touched her, when she'd touched *him*, her eyes had drowned in black. No iris, no pupil, no whites, nothing but an endless spread of black. It had shaken him, not because he was afraid—but because it was a reminder of the gulf between them. He'd seen the PsyNet in her eyes, a vast emptiness that he could never enter, and she could never leave.

Sascha Duncan did, his mind whispered.

The elevator doors opened on the heels of that thought, disgorging Quentin Gareth, one of the two men Max and Sophia hadn't been able to initially identify on the security footage.

"Detective Shannon." The male's prematurely silver hair glinted under the overhead lights. "I was told you had questions for me."

"Thanks for coming." Pushing off the wall, he opened the door to find Sophia sitting in a chair on the other side of the table.

The distance did nothing to eliminate the thrumming tension between them, so thick and hotly sexual that Max wondered how Gareth could miss it.

"Detective," the man said as soon as they were seated, "if this could be as fast as possible, I'd appreciate it. I'm scheduled to catch an airjet to Dubai."

Max was aware of Gareth's travel plans, but unlike with human criminals, Psy—especially Psy this high up in the power structure—were far less of a flight risk. Nikita could track Quentin Gareth across the PsyNet if it came down to it. "How about you just run us through your meeting with the victim," he said in a tone he kept casual. Maybe Psy didn't feel, but from what he'd seen, they were very, very good at reading and manipulating those who did.

"Our meeting was prearranged, but Edward reconfirmed once he returned from Cairo. The meeting covered a number of general ideas for expansion—we wanted to talk before I got caught up with the Dubai negotiations and he with his own projects."

Responding to Max's questions, Gareth told them he knew of no reason why anyone would've targeted Edward Chan. Max ended the interview on that point. "We need deep background checks on all four possibles," he said to Sophia after Gareth left. "My gut says Marsha is clean, but she could have a skeleton in her closet that leaves her open to blackmail."

"I'm already working on it." Her voice was husky, a rough caress, a reminder of the sensual fever that had almost consumed them earlier. "I have contacts in Justice who can do it under the radar."

Max clenched his hand on the arm of his chair. "You know," he murmured, needing to release the tension in some way, "I think this table is strong enough to take your weight. You never did tell me what you thought of boardroom sex."

She jerked up her head, a slight flush on her cheeks. But she didn't back down. "I think we'd need a stronger lock on the door—and I'm not sure I'd enjoy being pounded against a hard surface."

The word "pounded" acted like an aphrodisiac, sending his good intentions all to hell. "Then you can ride me," he said, his cock a steel rod in his pants. "The view"—he ran his gaze over her breasts—"would make me more than happy to be pounded."

"Max," Sophia said in a very tight voice, "if you don't behave, I'll—"

It was probably for the best that Andre Tulane, the final

individual on the surveillance footage, arrived then. He gave them the same basic story as Quentin Gareth.

"Any one of them could've done it," Max said after the man left, "even Marsha. All she'd have needed was a couple of minutes while Sascha went to the bathroom."

Sophia's responding words were practical . . . even if her voice continued to rub across his skin in sweet, hot strokes. "Maybe. But according to my recollection of the interview with Sascha, they were together when she felt Edward die."

Max frowned, thought back. "You're right. I'll confirm with Sascha in any case."

Nodding, Sophia said, "We should listen to the audio made by DarkRiver."

Taking out his cell phone, Max played the file. "Edward Chan's bio said he grew up in France"—a sharpening of interest, the first scent of their prey—"so that's got to be him. Which means Chan welcomed someone *back* into his apartment just prior to his death. The time stamp on this file fits the time line perfectly." Getting up, he walked to lean back against the table beside Sophia, unable to resist running his finger down her arm. "The wording tends to clear Ryan Asquith, even if he is a telekinetic."

She shivered but didn't pull away, her hand dangerously close to his thigh. He wanted her to raise it, place it on him, go higher. Smothering a goan at the erotic image, he focused on her mouth instead. "Yes," she said, her lips soft and lush, "Asquith only went inside the apartment at the end. But by the same token, he is the newest, least known member of Nikita's staff."

"Yes"—his own voice was sandpaper rough—"but he wasn't working for her when the elevator charge was laid." Remembering the note he'd written while she'd been out of the room earlier, he took it out of his pocket and dropped it into her bag, making certain to just barely brush the back of her hand. It was a silent continuance of their play, a dare.

Sophia parted her lips, but whatever she was going to say was lost as she sucked in a breath, a spread of black staining her eyes. *"Max."*

Sophia felt herself kicked into a memory retrieval with ruthless force. Except this was different. Not only the violence with which she'd been plunged into the memory, but her orientation within in. Usually, with other people's memories, she saw what the individual in question had seen, looked through his or her eyes.

Here, it was as if she was an impartial observer, a third party wholly unconnected to the events playing out below—in what appeared to be a filthy alley crushed between two dirty tenement buildings.

They were children. Two boys. The dark haired one was painfully thin, his legs too long for his body, his eyes liquid dark in a face that was so beautiful, she knew he must've gotten teased for it—but he'd grown into that face, turned it savagely masculine with sheer strength of will. "You gotta stop this," he said to the boy opposite him.

He smiled, that boy with his incredible lilac eyes and hair the color of ripe wheat turned to gold. If the first boy was beautiful, this one was a young god. His lips were flawlessly shaped, his skin porcelain, and his voice, when he spoke, as clear as the purest of bells. "Why?"

"Why?" The first boy, the boy Sophia knew, grabbed his friend's arm, turning it over to reveal the ugliness of needle tracks. "If this is what it's doing to you on the outside, what do you think it's doing to you on the inside?"

The other boy smiled again and this time, Sophia caught it, that odd disconnection in his gaze, the stare of someone who wasn't quite present. "It takes me flying, Maxie."

"It's fake." Max's hands on the other boy's face, forcing the golden child to meet his gaze, his voice flint hard. "It's just make-believe. You know that. When you crash, it hurts."

A moment of strange clarity. "So what? What's so good

about our life? Huh?" The golden child cupped Max's face in turn. "One of her men tried to touch me last night."

Cold rage turned Max's expression to ice. "I'll kill him."

Truth, Sophia thought, that was the unvarnished truth.

"It's okay. Mum screamed and kicked him out." He pressed his forehead to Max's in a painful kind of affection. "She protects me. Why doesn't she protect you?"

Thin shoulders sagging for an instant. "I don't know, River."

A vivid blackness, a connection being cut, and Sophia felt air whistling into her lungs in a violent, biting rush.

"Sophie! Look at me." Max's hand on her cheek, a tactile shock that made her eyes snap open.

He dropped his hand at once, white lines bracketing his mouth. "Talk to me."

"Not here." Her throat was shredded, lined with a million splinters. "Get me home. Please, Max."

And somehow, he did.

Her knees buckled the instant they were inside his apartment.

"I've got you." Catching her up in his arms—and being careful to avoid any skin-to-skin contact—Max carried her to the sofa. But instead of setting her down, he took a seat with her in his lap. "Shh," he said when she grew stiff. "Let me hold you."

"Max—"

"I need to do this." A fierce whisper.

When he did nothing except hold her, she relaxed, laying her head on his shoulder. It was so tempting to place her hand on his other shoulder, but he was only wearing a fine cotton shirt and she wasn't sure if the barrier would be strong enough. Not after the impact of what she'd seen, and with him so warm and solid around her, the scent of him an unambiguously masculine blend of heat, soap, and a fresh pine that she knew was his aftershave.

Drawing it in, she sighed, melting into his embrace. She could have cuddled into him forever, but she had to know, had to ask. "Who is River?"

Max froze at the quiet question, his heart punching against his ribs so hard, he half expected to see blood dot his chest. "My younger brother."

Sophia stilled within his arms, but her question, when it came, was practical. Psy. "You have clear markers of Asian descent, while he was unquestionably Caucasian."

The logical query calmed him, gave him an anchor. "He looked—looks exactly like our mother." River had been her shadow and her mirror. And in the end that knowledge had broken his brother. "We had different fathers. His was as blond as our mother." While Max's was an unknown, a man who'd given him only the genetic heritage of another culture. "No one ever believed we were brothers." But they were. They'd come from the same womb, grown up in the same hell.

"Is he—" A pause, a long breath. "You wanted to use the past tense."

Another stab of pain, but he didn't tell her to drop the subject. It had been so long since he'd spoken of River to someone who'd known him—and somehow, he knew his J did. "River disappeared when I was almost fourteen and he was eleven. He was so lost in the drugs by then that I know he can't have survived long . . . but part of me wakes up every morning hoping that when I open the door, I'll see him on the other side."

Sophia shifted position, her gloved hand rising to curve hesitantly over the back of his neck. "I'm sorry, Max. I didn't mean to invade your memories."

"I thought my shield—"

She shook her head. "Most telepaths who are born with the ability to be Js often also have some latent or weak F abilities."

Max frowned. "Foreseers see the future."

"Usually, yes. But there is a small subgroup that sees the past. It's termed backsight."

He knew she was talking so factually because she'd read his pain, was trying to distance him from it the only way she knew how, his vulnerable J with a heart that understood how much memories could hurt. "You saw River in a flash of backsight."

"Yes. It's the first incident I've ever had." Eyes haunted, she placed her hand on his shoulder. "If statistics hold true, that's probably the single one I'll ever experience."

"You sound glad."

"I've never felt so helpless," she whispered.

"What did you see?" His heart twisted—there'd been no horror in her eyes, so perhaps she'd seen a slice of happiness.

"You and your brother in an alley. You were trying to talk him out of doing drugs."

"I tried so many times." Max dropped his head against her. "He was the one person I loved, the one person who mattered. But I couldn't save him."

"He was so young," Sophia said.

"And damaged—so much that he couldn't see any other way out." Max wished he could go back in time, convince River that none of it was his fault. "He blamed himself for things over which he had no control."

Her hand stroked his nape, soft, hesitant, but gaining in confidence. "He said . . . he said . . ."

And he knew she hadn't missed out on the horror. "Tell me."

"He said she didn't protect you."

The pain of the child he'd been speared through him. "It was as if my mother had two personalities." One for each son. "As an adult, I know I could've done nothing to bring on the kind of hatred she felt toward me—but part of me still believes that I did something to make her treat me the way she did." His voice broke.

Sophia's breath whispered over his hair as she held him, as she, a woman born of a race with no emotion, gave him more affection than the woman who'd given birth to him.

CHAPTER 21

Sascha lay curled up in bed around six that evening, tired though she'd done very little. But she didn't feel the need to move—it was nice to lie surrounded by the warm, masculine scent of the panther who was her mate. Snuggling into his pillow, she opened up the text that was her own personal guidebook—and an endless source of frustration.

However, she felt more hopeful of deciphering the oblique nature of some of the chapters today, after having spoken to a Forgotten empath, an elderly lady named Maya.

"Only cardinals could stop riots," Maya had said in response to Sascha's question, her trim figure active as she paced in front of her comm screen. "So I wasn't taught how, but I have a vague memory of my grandmother talking about a 'terminal field.'"

Maya hadn't been able to dig up any memories of what

the term might actually mean, but it was a start. With that in mind, Sascha was about to reread the section on riot control when she heard Lucas moving about in the living area. "Lucas." She kept her tone soft, knowing he'd hear.

He filled the doorway, all green eyes and dark hair. Such a beautiful man, was her mate. Such a dangerous one, too, especially when the protective streak that had been honed in blood was riding him. "Do you have time to discuss something?"

His expression gentled. "Two minutes? I want to send this note off to Zara."

"I'll be here." Watching as he left, she played with the spine of the Eldridge book.

"You need a better bedtime story." Lucas prowled in to sprawl on his back beside her.

She raised her head instinctively, and he slid one arm beneath before turning to curve his big body around hers. It had become their favorite sleeping position.

"I'm not sleepy," she said. "Just wanted to rest my feet."

"I'll give you a foot rub."

Joy shimmered through her, an incandescent light. "Lucas, you do realize you're spoiling me beyond redemption?"

"Don't worry—I plan to ignore you once you give me my baby princess."

She laughed, secure in the knowledge of his love. "Did you manage to talk to Sienna?" The teenager, part of a family of Psy defectors that had found sanctuary with the SnowDancer wolves, had been staying with DarkRiver on and off for the past few months.

"She got up to the SnowDancer den safe and sound." A kiss pressed to the sensitive skin below her ear. "She's a very good driver."

"And Kit?" The DarkRiver male was a young soldier, a future alpha—and appeared to be forming an attachment to Sienna.

"He's still down here." Lucas sounded as if he was frowning in thought. "I don't know if we have any right to say anything. They're both adults."

"I'm not sure if Sienna is thinking straight." The Psy teenager had been close to the breaking point when she first came to stay with DarkRiver. She'd stabilized since then, but . . . "How's Hawke?"

Lucas didn't curse at the mention of the SnowDancer alpha, an indication of just how seriously he was taking this. "Seems fine, but it's hard to read another alpha—we get pretty good at keeping our thoughts to ourselves when necessary."

"Hawke and Sienna—there's something there." A raw, almost angry fury. "With Kit, it's harder to pinpoint. I can sense something between them, but what, I can't yet tell."

"Kit would be the better choice for her," Lucas said in a quiet tone that did nothing to hide the depth of his concern for everyone involved. "Hawke isn't going to be easy on any woman he takes as his own. And the fact is, he lost the girl who would've been his mate as a child. I don't know if his wolf will allow him to accept another female on that level."

Sascha had no answer to that. Like changeling leopards, wolves mated for life. She'd sensed Hawke's anger, his wolf's tormented rage, but she'd also sensed Sienna's anguish at her response to the SnowDancer alpha. And then there was Kit—gorgeous, loyal, strong Kit.

"Is that what you wanted to discuss?" Lucas took the book from her hand and put it on the bedside table before returning to hold her close again.

The imp of mischief that had awakened after she mated with Lucas made a sudden appearance. "No—did you hear the wolves are calling Mercy 'their' sentinel?"

A growl that made every hair on her body rise in primal response. "She might've had the bad taste to mate with a wolf, but she's ours. They try to co-opt her, I'll be giving you a nice, new Hawke-fur coat for your birthday."

Unable to withhold her laughter, she patted his arm. "You're so easy."

"Brat." But the panther was laughing with her. "You okay?"

She knew he was talking about Nikita, about the confused emotions in Sascha's heart. "I'm getting there."

CHAPTER 22

Sophie, my sweet, sexy, Sophie, I do think I'd like to unbutton that perfect little suit jacket. After that, I'd like to slip each and every tiny pearl button out of its slot to open your shirt to the waist.

—*Handwritten note from Max to Sophia*

Max walked out of the shower an hour later to find Morpheus glaring at him from the bed. "What?" he asked, pulling on a pair of jeans and a dark green T-shirt.

The cat continued to glare.

"I fed you," Max muttered, glad for the prosaic reality of life for giving him a way out of the memories that had haunted him for over a decade. "Don't scowl at me because you snarfed it in one minute and now have a stomachache."

Morpheus licked his paw. He was *not amused*.

Deciding not to pet the damn cat right then in case it decided to bite off his hand, he ran a comb through his hair and walked out to the kitchen. Thanks to the grocery shopping he'd done the day he arrived, he had all the ingredients for the dinner he planned to cook for Sophia.

"Shouldn't we focus on the case?" she'd asked before she left his apartment, her eyes huge. "My incident has already taken time we could've spent going over the evidence."

He'd realized, with a strange warmth in his chest, that she was once again trying to help him in her own way—that smart mind had figured out he'd feel better if he buried himself in work. "We can discuss as we eat," he'd said. "And, I think we've got time."

"Why do you sound so certain?"

"You know the pattern we talked about?"

"With the victims all being murdered on the verge of a major deal?" An intent look. "Edward Chan's murder doesn't fit."

"I did some digging on that." He'd set his cell phone to run a number of Internet searches, glanced at the results as they finished up the final interview today. "Chan was scheduled to speak before a group of changeling alphas in South America later this week. No Psy has ever before been acceded that right."

Sophia had gone very quiet. "Did they kill him because he was about to get Nikita access to a major untapped market—"

"—or because the contact would've violated a belief in Purity?" From what he'd learned of Pure Psy, he was convinced they wouldn't shy away from murder. "No way to tell. But I'm going to call Nikita, alert her to the possibility."

When he did contact Nikita, she'd not only agreed with his theory, she'd confirmed that no other project was at a stage which might trigger a kill. "I've also got twenty-four-hour surveillance on all my high-level people. They won't be easy targets—and if one of them is behind this, it should give him pause."

Now, as Max began to prepare dinner, he considered the possible impact of his and Sophia's investigation on the conspiracy. Not significant, he decided. Whoever was behind this—the kingpin—was running things with a cool, clear head. He or she wouldn't be put off their game by a mere human and a J at the end of her useful life.

His jaw went tight just as the doorbell chimed. Putting down the knife he'd been using to chop up some herbs, he went to the door and pulled it open. The woman at the center of his thoughts stood on the other side dressed in jeans and a cardigan in a delicate cream shade that made him want to peel it open—to expose skin of an even richer cream.

"Max?" Her voice was tentative when he continued to block the doorway.

He stepped back, waiting until she was inside and away from the cameras before he gave in to the urge to touch her. Lifting away her hair, he pressed a single kiss to the soft skin of her nape.

Her shiver was violent, but she didn't pull away. "I wasn't sure if I was meant to contribute anything to the meal." A breathy voice, her head angled slightly to the side, as if she was welcoming another kiss.

Unable to resist the exquisite temptation, he moved behind her, put his hands on her hips, and said, "You'll be dessert."

Sophia felt her throat lock, her skin stretch painfully taut over her body. "Are you playing?" she finally managed to say. "Like with the notes?"

Max's breath against her neck. "No."

She balled her fingers into fists. An emotional reaction. One that would've concerned her before she'd decided to *live* . . . to love. She wasn't sure she knew how, wasn't sure the capacity hadn't been cut out of her with brutal efficiency. But Max was *important*. She'd kill for him, she thought, this man who saw in her a woman worth trusting . . . a woman worth teasing. "This cardigan has pearl buttons, too," she whispered.

His body seemed to relax a fraction at her reference to the note he'd dropped into her bag earlier, and she hoped she'd brought some light into his heart. "Witch."

Releasing her clenched fingers one by one, she lifted her hands and then, very deliberately, stripped off her gloves. Dropping them to the floor, she reached for his hand.

His palm met hers, his fingers twining with her own to curl into her palm.

For an instant, everything went black. When she could see again, she found herself leaning against Max's chest, his free hand curved over her abdomen as he held her against the masculine heat of his body. "I'm here." A rough murmur.

She clung to the strength of him, the lean muscle of his body a solid wall in a shifting universe. It was difficult to breathe—he was in the air, too, an invisible caress. Dark, potent, male, Max surrounded her.

"Your shields," he said against her ear, his lips touching her skin in small, erotic bites. "Are you safe?"

Knowing he was right to be concerned, she opened her psychic eye and checked her protections against the Psy-Net, ready to patch any fractures, hide any weaknesses. What she saw made her go motionless. "They're holding, but not in a normal way."

"Explain."

"My shields have always been rock solid, but now . . . they're moving. It's as if I'm in the middle of a tornado." The psychic wind blew back her hair as she stood shocked in the center of her mind. "Nothing can get in or out because the layers shift constantly, tearing apart anything that attempts to penetrate."

"Is it harming you?"

"No. It's efficient beyond anything I've ever seen, but it may bring attention to me." She'd survived this long by being faultless when it came to her work, but deliberately unremarkable in any other way—the perfect Psy.

Even as she spoke, there was a mental knock on her mind. "Someone's seen," she said, before answering the telepathic contact. *Sir.*

Jay Khanna's psychic voice was clear, direct, his telepathic reach close to 9.8 on the Gradient. That reach had given rise to speculation that the reason Khanna had been taken off the active roster at an early age was because the Council had other uses for his telepathy. *Ms. Russo,* he said now, *there's been a significant change in your shields. Do you need assistance?*

It was a thinly veiled query about whether her conditioning was close to total collapse. If she said yes, she'd be picked up for emergency reconditioning—and find herself undergoing total and comprehensive rehabilitation, her memories of Max scrubbed away, her mind broken until it was nothing but an empty shell.

Silently thanking the M-Psy who'd told her the truth about her status, she said, *My shields appear to have evolved to provide better protection.*

Shields do not evolve.

No, she thought, they didn't. *I misspoke, sir. I've been working with the idea of this type of a shield for a while— they simply went into effect before I planned.* It was a reasonable response—all Js tinkered constantly with their shields in an effort to eke out another day, another hour of life.

Khanna accepted her explanation, his tone retaining its professionalism as he switched topics. *Have you reviewed the Valentine file?*

Yes, sir.

And your conclusions?

Remain unchanged.

Very well. Continue with your current assignment.

Ending the telepathic conversation, Sophia sagged against Max, telling him what had occurred. Max moved the hand he had on her abdomen, inciting a strange twisting sensation in her body. It wasn't painful. No, it was . . . interesting. "What else is up?" he asked.

"What?"

"Your expression changed toward the end."

She thought about what her boss had asked her to do, thought, too, what it would mean to share that with Max. He'd *know*. What she'd done. The lines she'd crossed. Pain rippled down her spine. "I don't want to tell you," she said, incapable of any sophisticated evasion when it came to this man.

To her surprise, Max squeezed her hips and said, "Keep

your secrets"—his voice an intimate darkness in her ear—
"for now."

Max felt Sophia's hand tighten on his, wanted only
to bend his head even farther and put his mouth on the
unsteady beat of her pulse, suck hard. The possessive urge,
the violent need to claim her to the core was a gnawing
ache in his gut. He wanted the world to know she was
his—make certain no one would dare lay a finger on her.

It took every ounce of will he had to fight the craving
and lead her to the bar stools on this side of the kitchen
counter. Dropping her hand, he put both of his around her
waist and lifted her onto a stool.

Her hands flew to his shoulders. Gripped.

A sweep of black erased her irises between one blink
and the next.

"Sophie." He squeezed her waist. "Stay with me."

"I'm right here."

"Your eyes."

"Oh." She blinked, but the black remained. "It happens
when we utilize a strong burst of psychic power, or . . . I
suppose"—a wash of color across her cheekbones—"feel
an intense emotional response."

The maleness in him smiled in sensual satisfaction. "I
like the sound of that." Leaning forward, he slicked his
lips over her own, a tease that made his cock throb—but
conscious of how far he'd already pushed her, he was on
the other side of the counter before she exhaled and swiv-
eled to face him.

"That," she said, "was . . . interesting." Her chest rose
and fell in long, deep breaths, her skin colored with a heat
that invited a man's mouth.

The excruciating pulse of his body, the unremitting
hunger, might've consumed him if he hadn't had something critically important in mind for this evening. "Let me
finish making this sauce," he said, voice rough with sexual
desire. "You want to shred the lettuce for the salad?"

He waited until she'd washed her hands and retaken

her seat before asking the question to which he needed an answer before he could begin to work out how to engineer her defection, how to keep her forever. "Sophia—I've been patient." His hand fisted, because he knew this truth would be nothing good, but at least he'd have a starting point. "Tell me where Js go when they stop working."

A quiet, quiet moment. "Some who are removed from the active roster early enough take up desk jobs in Justice," she said in a voice so soft he had to strain to hear her, "others go insane, and the rest of us . . . we die."

CHAPTER 23

Max staggered, bracing his hands on the counter. *"Tell me."*

"My Sensitivity"—she glanced back at her discarded gloves—"is a result of failing telepathic shields. They're so thin now that when they shear, the thoughts of every man, woman, and child in this city will smash into my brain, crush my mind."

The brutal forecast had Max clenching his jaw. "How long?"

"Not long."

Anger—hot, protective, violent—was a rush of white noise in his ears. "When were you planning to tell me?"

Sophia swallowed at the tautly held fury in that question. "I'm sorry." It hurt her to see him so angry with her. "I thought if you knew how . . . broken I truly was, you wouldn't want me."

"Sophie." A low, dark word, a shake of his head that made the sleek black strands of his hair catch the light.

"They'll rehabilitate you if they find out how close you are to the edge, that's the bottom line?"

"Yes."

His shoulders firmed, the intelligence in his eyes a razor. "They can't do that if you're out of the Net. We'll figure out a way to fucking rebuild your shields once you're safe."

He was fighting for her, she thought with a wrench deep inside of her. *Never* had anyone fought for her. She'd never been important enough. It broke what fragile defenses she might've still had—she couldn't, wouldn't, hold back the final truth. "Without the biofeedback my mind needs from the Net," she began, "I'll die within seconds." Realizing she'd somehow shredded the entire lettuce, she began to peel the cucumber on the counter.

"Sascha isn't dead." Max pushed back from the counter, folding his arms across his chest. "Neither are the other Psy in DarkRiver."

"Yes, they've found an exit route." Finished with the peeling, she began to slice the cucumber into precise, thin slices. "However, even should such an exit be open to other Js, I couldn't take it."

A silent pause, his thrumming anger a whip against her skin.

"I function as a minor anchor." Sophia knew she shouldn't be speaking of this. The agony spearing through her nerves, a conditioned response, told her it was deeply forbidden. But she wanted, *needed*, Max to understand.

"Keep talking." It was an order.

Part of her wanted to rebel, but she knew she'd pushed him too far—anything more might destroy this bond between them, this beautiful thing that had never been meant for someone so broken—but that she refused to give up. Max was *her* gift. "Anchors are literally that," she said, fighting the pain with the stubborn possessiveness inside of her. "They're born with the ability to merge into the Psy-Net itself. They help keep it stable and are almost always cardinals."

Max tapped the counter in front of her. Jerking up her head, she saw him holding out a hand. "Knife."

She gave it to him, realizing the cucumber was now in hundreds of tiny, tiny squares. "Oh."

No shrug, no smile that revealed the lean dimple in his cheek. The loss speared through her. She'd seen human and changeling women coax their men into smiles, but had never imagined she might one day need to do the same. Or that she'd so desperately want to. Getting off the stool, she wiped her hands on a towel. "Max—"

"No." He pinned her with his gaze. "So help me, Sophie, I'm so fucking mad at you right now—" He blew out a breath. "Help me set the table."

She gave in, aware for the first time that Max's relentless will would, of course, translate into an inexorable kind of anger. Neither of them spoke again until they were seated across from each other, their meals in front of them. Morpheus appeared out of nowhere to sit on her feet.

"Don't feed him," Max said. "He's getting fat."

She gave him an innocent look even as she discreetly dropped a piece of bread for the cat—who seemed to have a strange predilection for it. "Of course not."

A glint of amusement lit the cold fire in his eyes. "If"—he sat back, a tiger momentarily at rest—"anchors are usually cardinals, why are you doing their job?" His biceps drew her eye as he clasped his hands at the back of his head.

It was difficult to think past the compulsion she had to get up and peel Max's T-shirt off his body, long-dormant instincts awakening to tell her that touch would reach him far faster and deeper than words ever could.

"You don't get to play"—a low, dark voice—"until you're straight with me. Then we'll talk about punishment."

Her toes curled. "Cardinals," she managed to say through the crashing wave of need, "are rare, and cardinals who can be anchors are even rarer." Agony spiked out of nowhere, wiping out the other sensations. There was, it seemed, one thread of conditioning still active in her—the Council did not like Psy speaking about the critical network of anchors.

"However, non-cardinal individuals can sometimes develop the ability to merge with the Net." She gripped her knees tight in order to ride out the increasing waves of pain. "We're not true anchors—more like . . . small weights on the net, helping to keep it in shape, in place. There aren't enough true anchors to do everything."

Morpheus patted her foot with a paw. Glad for the touch of reality, she snuck him another piece of bread as Max spoke. "Now *that* doesn't make sense. No self-supporting ecosystem would effectively cripple itself."

She blinked, having never thought of it that way. While she was still trying to figure out how the shortage could have occurred, Max forked up a bite of rice, lifted it to her lips.

She opened her mouth without thought, let him feed her. The feel of the tines sliding out from between her lips was a cool, slow pleasure. "Why did you do that?" she asked after swallowing the unexpected bite. "I thought you were angry with me?"

A faint smile. "I find myself fascinated by your mouth. The things I'd like to do to it . . . Even when I'm furious, you make me crazy, J."

A brush of heat across her body, a physiological reaction she didn't quite understand . . . but one that wiped out the pain. *Oh*. She looked at him, at her cop. "How did you know?" About the pain, about the hurt.

"Because I know you." The sensual teasing disappeared from his face. "Now tell me why anchors can't leave the Net."

"Most Psy have a single link to the Net deep within their mind, and the defectors must have cut that link to leave, but anchors are woven into the PsyNet's very fabric by millions upon millions of fine connections." The Net was both safety and a steel cage. "If I tried to leave, death would be

instantaneous—but that's not the worst part. Because of
the particular way I'm integrated into its framework, part
of *me*, my memories, my personality, is anchored in the
Net."

Max put down his fork, appetite gone. "You're saying
you'll effectively rehabilitate yourself if you try to leave."

"Yes."

Max wasn't sure he believed that. From what he could
tell, Silence was a form of brainwashing. And what better way to ensure compliance than by convincing someone
they couldn't leave the Net?

"You think I've been blinded to the truth."

It didn't surprise him anymore, that she was able to read
him with such ease. "You've been in that world your whole
life. It's hard to see what's right in front of you sometimes."
He'd spent his childhood pretending his mother loved him.
It had been necessary for his survival, but it had been a
willful blindness. In Sophia's case, it was more likely a
conditioned response.

But she shook her head, her eyes bleak. "Js are, by the
nature of our work, far more aware of the harsh realities of
life than other Psy. I've looked at the issue from every angle,
and the unavoidable fact is that once integrated in such a
complex way, a mind cannot physically disengage—even
if I somehow survived the physical brain damage, the person who remained wouldn't be Sophia Russo."

Cold spread through his veins, but he wasn't about to
give up. "Are you going to tell me how you developed the
ability to merge with the Net, why you're so inexorably tied
to it?" He'd heard something in her words when she'd spoken of it, a slight hesitation that pricked at his instincts.

She put down her own fork. "Can we sit nearer to each
other?"

His gut clenched at the polite way she'd asked for
comfort—ready for rejection. Always so ready to be rejected.
He wondered if she was even aware of it, but he was, and it
savaged him to realize how badly she'd been hurt. "Yeah.
Let me clear the table first."

"I'll help you. We may as well wash them so that we can concentrate on the case later on." It was as she was drying a dish—having replaced her gloves—that Max couldn't stand the painful quietness of her any longer. Moving behind her, he pressed a kiss to the curve of her neck.

She dropped the dish.

"Got it." Placing the unbroken item on the counter in front of her, he pushed back and forced himself to head to the coffeemaker, though he wanted only to wrap his arms around her and hold her tight, so tight. "Something to drink?"

Sophia answered without thought. "Yes." Hands still trembling, she watched as he poured a single cup of coffee, then heated up a mug of milk. She wanted to touch her fingers to her neck, to feel the echo of his kiss, the slight rasp of his unshaven jaw against her skin.

"Come here." A quiet command, eyes that drew her forward.

Closing the small distance between them, she parted her lips to ask for another kiss—driven by her need to be with him—when he took the spoon he'd been using to stir a dark mix into the milk and put it to her lips. "Taste."

It was impossible to do anything else. The burst of sensation was sharp, almost bitter, exquisite in its richness. She put her hand on his wrist when he would've withdrawn the spoon, the feel of him solid and tempting under her glove.

Shaking his head in a gentle tease, Max drew away the spoon, slow, so slow. "The whole cup's for you." Then he leaned forward and kissed her, licking his tongue over the seam of her lips as if to steal the flavor.

She gripped his T-shirt as the floor disappeared from beneath her. Groaning, Max pulled back—but only after grazing her lower lip with his teeth. Liquid warmth pooled between her thighs, making her body clench.

"Take your chocolate"—an order in a voice gone sandpaper rough—"and go sit before I give in to temptation and unbutton your cardigan, put my hands on your beautiful breasts."

He turned away even as she tried to process the searing sensuality of that image. The idea of those strong, clever hands on her flesh, that sleek hair brushing over her as he bent closer . . . How did women survive such vicious cravings? Holding the chocolate he'd made for her, she watched her cop's T-shirt stretch across his shoulders as he raised his arm to put the mix back into an upper cabinet.

He was beautiful.

And he'd given her the right to touch him. Even mad, he wouldn't push her away, wouldn't reject her as imperfect.

Not giving herself a chance to change her mind, she put down the mug, closed the distance between them, and wrapped her arms around him from behind, resting her cheek against his back.

"Sophie."

The masculine fire of him soaked through her skin, a near-painful bite. "When I began to show J tendencies as a child," she said, holding on, holding tight, "I was placed in a residential facility with other telepaths who needed specialized training."

Max's hands closed over her gloved ones, but he didn't turn, letting her use his body as a shield against the dark that had never set her free. "Someone hurt you there." His voice was jagged, his muscles rigid.

"We were in a remote location," she said, finding courage in his strength. "Because young telepaths, especially those with unusual abilities, tend to have trouble with shields, it's easier to train us out of the cities." Practical words, but the other half of her, the half that had been born that summer two decades ago, clung to the solid wall of Max, afraid, so very afraid. "So there was no one to notice that our instructor was beginning to act beyond Silence. Like Bonner."

"He was a true sociopath." Icy rage in every word.

She held it close, used it as a weapon against the past.

"The summer I turned eight, he took four of us—four trainee Js—to another, even more remote location for intensive drills. Before we left, he requested and received permission to enclose us in his shields so that we could drop ours without consequences should we have trouble during the drills." Her fingers dug into Max's chest, and she wanted to tear through the fabric, press her skin to his, bury the past under an agony of sensation.

"Sophie." A voice scraped raw. "I can wait, baby. I'm sorry for—"

She shook her head. "No." She wanted him to know, needed him to know. "Once our instructor"—she couldn't say his name, her terror too deep—"had us alone and in the cage of his shield . . . he hurt us." Sophia could still remember their shock, their inability to understand. "Carrie died the first day. She was the smallest, the weakest." And the monster had broken her in his eagerness.

"He was more careful after that. Bilar died on the third day." He'd convulsed in front of her and Lin, and they could do nothing to help, their hands and feet tied behind their backs, their mouths taped shut. Sophia had dared the monster's anger and reached out with her telepathy, refusing to let Bilar die alone. His screams had echoed inside her mind for hours.

Max's hands tightened on hers. "Why didn't your parents, the watchers in your PsyNet, sense his deviancy?"

"Don't you see, Max?" Her voice shook. "He was the perfect Psy." Silence didn't differentiate between those who had been conditioned and those who simply *did not feel*.

"Is he dead?" A quiet question asked in a voice that made the other half of her, the scared broken child, go motionless, wondering . . .

"Yes." When he didn't say anything else, she continued. "Lin and I, we were the last two left. He was nine, I was eight." She felt her heart begin to speed up, her spine to knot. "The monster didn't want to break us too fast, so he was careful. But one day he did something to me, and I didn't respond like he wanted. I didn't scream. So he threw me headfirst through the large glass window at the front of the cabin." Pain, blood, the glitter of glass in the sun, she'd never forget any part of it.

"Enough, Sophie." Max's entire body was so hard, so unmoving, she'd have thought him stone but for the furious beat of his heart.

"I want you to know. *Please.*"

"You never have to beg me for anything." A harsh order.

"Lin saved me," she said, clasping his words to her soul. "While the monster was outside, checking to see if I'd survived, he somehow managed to get to the comm panel, input the emergency code." And then Lin, the sweet, talented telepath who might've been her friend in another life, had died, his internal injuries too massive. "Everyone's forgotten them. Carrie, Bilar, and Lin, but I remember. Someone should *remember.*"

This time, Max did move. Pulling away, he turned. She went into his arms, ready for the heat, the almost violent pleasure-pain. "People talk about how the Psy are starting to break," he said in a fierce whisper, "but nobody ever speaks about the victims."

He understood, she thought, he *understood.* "We're as dirty a secret as the monsters. Those of us who survive are damaged goods, never quite the same. My parents wrote me off, turned me over to the state. I heard them in the hospital. . . . talking about whether it would be better to just put me down."

CHAPTER 24

Your request to have Sophia Russo, minor, age 8, removed from your official family history has been granted. The state will pay the costs of her care and education until she reaches her majority. You are no longer considered bound to her or responsible for her in any way.

—*Final decision of the Council Subcommittee on Genetic Inheritance, November 2060*

Max's embrace tightened until it almost hurt. But she needed it, craved it. The lost, indelibly fractured half of her clung to him, realizing it was being accepted, no matter the extent of its flaws. "The anchor thing," he said. "That's what saved you. Because it's a rare ability."

She nodded. "When the monster threw me through the window, he didn't just scar my face. He also broke my mind." She'd been a terrified child who'd finally realized that no help would come, that she'd soon be buried in an unmarked grave beside Carrie and Bilar. "But my brain didn't give up. It 'rerouted' itself directly into the fabric of the Net, the only thing big enough to hold together what remained of my psyche."

"I am so damn proud of you," he said, his voice low and husky.

She wanted to grab onto the commitment, the promise, implicit in his words. "I'm really broken, Max." It was the final secret, the final truth. "I can pretend to be normal, but I'm not. I never will be."

"You survived—how you've done it doesn't matter. The fact that you have? It's better revenge on that bastard and the ones that allowed him to do what he did than anything else."

Shuddering at the unflinching acceptance in his tone, she moved one hand lightly over his back. His muscles shifted beneath her touch, as if in response. Growing bolder, she pressed harder, felt his abdomen grow taut against her. It was instinct to spread out her hand, run her fingernails over the fabric in sensual exploration.

Swearing low under his breath, Max moved back a step, gripping her arms at the elbows. "Aren't you going too fast?"

"No." She could feel her nerves, ragged and frayed, close to overload, but still she wanted more, wanted to fill herself to the brim with him, until she had enough for a lifetime. "Don't stop, Max. The touch keeps me here." Not in the past.

Max groaned. "Drink. And behave." He put the hot chocolate in her hands and picking up his coffee, headed to the couch.

Left with no choice, she followed a second later. Putting her drink beside his on the coffee table, she turned her body sideways on the couch, terrified she'd scared him with the voracious depth of her need . . . but not ready to accept his decree. He'd told her she'd never have to beg. He'd accepted her. He was hers. "I'm not misbehav—"

Max had his mouth on Sophia's before he could think about the consequences, his hand tangled in her hair. God, he was so angry over what had been done to her, so fucking pissed at the parents who'd rejected her when they should've stood by her. And because he'd die before he hurt her, his anger had nowhere to go—except into a raging protectiveness. Running his tongue along the seam of her lips, he urged her to part for him. And when she did, he swept in without hesitation, taking, tasting, claiming.

Her hands fell to rest on his thigh, excruciatingly close to his cock. Releasing his grip on her, he picked up those delicate gloved hands and put them on his shoulders. She clenched her fingers on him, her nails biting just enough through the thin gloves and the material of his T-shirt to make him want to strip it all off and tell her to use those nails on his flesh. *Hell.* Breaking the kiss, he put his hands on her waist. "Straddle me."

She was all huge eyes and kiss-bruised mouth, but she did as he asked, her curvy body coming down on his thighs even as she leaned in and took his mouth. He hadn't expected that, hadn't expected her to seize the reins. But he was more than willing to let her have her way.

Her kiss was inexperienced, hesitant, and so arousing, he had to lock his muscles to keep from pushing up that primly buttoned cardigan and cupping a sweet, plump breast in his palm even as he took her mouth in a much more sexual fashion. Instead, he let her sip at him, let her stroke and taste and lick. The last made his fingers clench on her hips. She did it again.

Sophia Russo was a quick study.

Feeling his lips curve in a smile that was more than a little feral, he sucked at her upper lip, bit down on the lower. She jerked, then pressed into him, her arms weaving around his neck. Taking that as a yes, he repeated the caress, moving his hands down her hips and over the taut length of her thighs at the same time. A shuddering moan before she finally tore away her mouth.

Her eyes were awash in black, a sea of purest midnight. He'd been ready for that. But he wasn't ready for the fever in her cheeks, the thumping beat of the pulse in her neck, the way her body turned all loose and limber, as if she was drunk. Alarm spiked. "Sophie, talk to me."

"Mmm?" Dropping her head to his shoulder, she rubbed her cheek against his T-shirt, a lazy kitten. "I think you blew my circuits."

The dazed comment made him want to laugh in spite of the savagery of his emotions—but worry cut the impulse midthought. Maybe this was as close as they'd ever come, him and his Sophie. "Are you in pain?"

Another lazy rub against him, her hand clenching and unclenching on his other shoulder. "I never realized men and women were so different . . . not really." Her breath blew hot on the skin of his neck as she spoke, her body a warm, luscious weight against his aroused form. "It's quite extraordinary."

"Baby, you can't avoid the question." Brushing her hair very carefully off her face, he looked down to find her eyes closed. "Are you in pain?"

"Have you ever had your foot fall asleep after a period of inactivity?"

"Yes."

"And the sharp stabs afterward when you try to use it?" A smile flirted with her lips. "That's what it feels like." Her eyes opened. "I'm waking up, Max. A little pain won't make me take a step backward."

Protectiveness and pride smashed up against each other. "No more tonight."

"No, Max." She moved slightly across his body, an erotic stroke and a stubborn will. "No, please."

He let her kiss him again, let her convince him. But when her skin flushed fever hot, when her muscles began to quiver, he broke the contact, lifting her off his body and onto the couch. No matter how much he wanted to claim her in every way a man could claim a woman, he wouldn't do it if it would destroy her. "No more, Sophie. You can't process everything at once."

"But—"

He placed a finger against her lips. "That foot that falls asleep? It doesn't wake up all at once."

She stared at him for long moments, but he got a nod at last. Leaving her to repair her shields as much as she could—and it was a fucking fist in his heart that their touching hurt her on any level—he got up, splashed ice water on his face, then returned with the case files. "Ready?"

"Yes." Taking a sip of the hot chocolate he'd made her,

she met his gaze, those eerie eyes of endless black impenetrable, unreadable. "Max?"

"Yes?"

"Will you remember me?"

His heart broke into a thousand pieces. "Always."

Early the next morning found Sascha sitting across from Nikita in a conference room at DarkRiver's business HQ. "I didn't think you'd come."

Nikita's response was pragmatic. "DarkRiver is an important business partner."

"This isn't a business meeting," Sascha said, refusing to let her mother ignore the truth. "I thought I made that clear in my request. I'm sorry if you were misled."

Nikita remained an ice sculpture on the other side of the table. "Every contact with you is business. If you weren't part of DarkRiver, there'd be no need for contact at all."

It hurt, yeah, it hurt. But Sascha was stronger now. And she had the strength of the pack behind her. She could feel their wild protectiveness on the other side of the door that enclosed her in this room with Nikita. But most of all, she could feel the love of her panther. "I wanted to tell you—"

"You're pregnant," Nikita said without ceremony. "It's difficult to miss."

But so many people had, Sascha thought, trying not to read in Nikita's keen eyes any kind of an emotional meaning. "I'm about five months along."

"You must be able to feel the fetus move."

Sascha curled her hand into a fist under the table, trying to keep her emotions in check. "Yes. The baby is rather feisty, especially at three a.m."

A pause. "You were the same."

And there, in that instant, Sascha knew she didn't understand her mother as well as she thought she did, that Councilor Nikita Duncan had secrets even an empath couldn't plumb.

Nikita spoke again before Sascha could. "I've heard rumors that the leopards isolate their pregnant mates during the final months of their pregnancies."

Sascha rolled her eyes. "The tabloids made that up after one of the women in the pack was prescribed bed rest because of complications—you must know how they sensationalize everything." Her panther, overprotective as he was, would never try to keep her apart from those she considered hers—both in the pack and outside of it. But that wasn't what she'd asked her mother here to discuss. "Why did you send me the book by Alice Eldridge?"

"You're a cardinal with the strength to control tens of thousands," Nikita answered, picking up her organizer. "Having an individual of your strength in my corner would be an asset—the benefit would outweigh any cost associated with your flaw."

Once, that would've cut Sascha to the quick. Now . . . now she wondered just how many lies Nikita had told her over her lifetime.

Sophia woke from the most sleepless of nights, her body aching from the inside out, her skin too tight, her nerves shredded. Everything was "off." Irritation burned inside her, and it had no target, no focus.

Showering helped calm her body a fraction, and so did an intense ten-minute meditation. Feeling slightly more in control, she dressed in a black pantsuit paired with a white shirt, dried then plaited her hair—baring a violence-touched face Max didn't seem to find the least objectionable—and forced herself to eat a nutrition bar for breakfast. Her cop, she thought, would not approve.

Strange twisting sensations in her abdomen, the renewed prickling of her skin. Heat was just starting to spot her cheeks when the doorbell rang. Throwing the wrapper of the nutrition bar in the recycler, she walked over and opened the door.

It was his scent that hit her first. Exotic and familiar,

male in a way she couldn't explain. But she knew she'd be able to distinguish it from a million others. "Max."

His eyes narrowed as he entered, closing the door behind himself. "You're flushed. What's wrong?"

She rubbed gloved hands over her arms. "I don't know. I feel . . . edgy. My skin, my body—"

The worry disappeared from his face, to be replaced by something darker and full of a quiet masculine amusement. "It's called frustration, sweetheart."

Frustration: synonymous with aggravation, irritation, dissatisfaction.

Yes, she thought. *That's the word.*

"I'd have more sympathy for you except that I spent the night with a permanent hard-on."

Her eyes dropped to his groin. He groaned even as his body reacted rather spectacularly.

Sophia wanted to touch. "Fix it," she ordered. "You know how to end my frustration and yours, and I'm no longer as overwrought as I was last night."

He blew out a breath. "Yeah? Maybe I do. And maybe so do you." There was something exquisitely sensual in his words. "I—"

She never got to hear what he would've said, because his cell phone beeped at that moment. And everything changed.

"It's Bart." All hint of sensuality leaving his expression, Max put the phone to his ear, his responses not telling Sophia much. "I'll talk to her." He snapped the phone shut. "Bonner's broken sooner than we thought."

"He's angry," Sophia said, feeling a layer of ice form around her, an impenetrable barrier threaded with dark tendrils that "tasted" of the Net. "His ego can't take that I ended yesterday's comm-conference before *he* was ready." Turning, she headed to her bedroom.

Max caught her arm, felt her tremble though he'd been careful not to touch skin. "What're you doing?"

"Packing an overnight case," she said, her voice firm, though her body swayed toward his before she caught herself. "He'll talk this time, I'm sure of it." She nodded at his cell phone. "Call Nikita."

"We can't leave midcase," Max said, because though those lost girls owned a piece of his heart, they were already gone, their lights doused. But Sophia, she was alive, her flame flickering against the violent storm of Bonner's evil. He couldn't believe that Carissa White and her sisters in death would want him to sacrifice Sophia to bring them home.

"Nikita will allow us to take a short break," Sophia replied. "As you said yourself, this killer is unlikely to strike in the near future." She kept talking, though he could see the jagged rise and fall of her chest, the glittering pain in her eyes. "The forensic data from Edward Chan's murder scene will have been more thoroughly processed by the time we return, and we've already spoken to the witnesses. We can continue to run deep background checks and verify their alibis for the earlier murders from a distance."

Max waited until she paused for breath. "You have to turn this over to another J."

"No. This is mine." Tiny lines fanned out from the corners of her lush mouth, an indication of stubbornness—one he'd just learned to read. "I'll do this. I'll finish this."

Max didn't budge—he had a whole streak of stubborn in him, too. "You've told me how close you are to losing your telepathic shields. Working with a mind like Bonner's will only put more stress—" He froze as she pressed a finger to his lips.

"They're lost, Max." A bleakness in her eyes it hurt him to witness. "I have to find them, bring them home from those unmarked graves."

He heard in those words an echo of the nightmare summer that had almost destroyed her, a silent, painful ache, and knew he had to let her do this. "Even a hint of a problem and you get out. Agreed?"

It was more an order than a question but she nodded. "Agreed."

"I'm letting Bart know he needs to have an M-Psy on standby."

"That's a good precaution." No M-Psy could heal the telepathic deterioration of a J, much less of an already damaged one like Sophia, but they could perhaps help her handle any physical symptoms. "However, make sure the M remains outside the interrogation room—Bonner will pounce on even a hint of weakness."

"Don't let the bastard get to you." Tugging down her glove to expose a patch of naked skin between glove and cuff, he bent his head as she watched in thrall. His kiss branded her from the inside out. "We have the little matter of frustration to discuss."

CHAPTER 25

Sometimes evil wins. But not here. Not today.
—*From the private case notes of Detective Max Shannon:*
State of New York v Bonner

Nikita wasn't pleased at the interruption in her investigation, but she didn't attempt to stand in their way after Max made it clear that not only would they continue to work her case while in Wyoming, but that Bonner's victims had a prior claim on his loyalty.

"How long will this trip take?" she asked.

"If Bonner gives up the bodies"—a grim hope—"I'll have to inform the parents." They knew him, trusted him . . . would know why he'd come after so long. "After that, forensics will take over. Since Bonner is already in prison for the length of his natural life, it's not imperative I be there at every moment." Though before, he would've been, would have wanted to see it through to the bitter, destructive end.

Now, he had other priorities. "I can delegate the supervision to one of the other detectives"—good cops, cops who'd sacrificed weekends, given up vacations, to help Max in the hunt for the Butcher of Park Avenue—"and keep an eye on things from a distance." Of course, he'd never be free of the Bonner case, not truly. And perhaps he didn't want to be. A man carried scars on his heart. They made him who he was.

Sophie would leave the biggest scar of all.

No. He refused to lose her, this J with her hunger for touch and her gifted mind.

"Very well, Detective." Picking up a cell phone call, she turned to the plate-glass window. "I expect you to keep me informed."

Max found himself momentarily caught by the image of Nikita standing silhouetted against the glass, her gaze somewhere far in the distance. Powerful. Lethal. Alone.

Sascha stretched out her legs on the ottoman in Tammy's living room and leaned back against the softness of the couch. Like everyone else in DarkRiver, she'd headed to their healer the instant she'd needed comfort of a feminine kind. Lucas had dropped her off after lunch with a kiss—though she knew it was only because Tammy's mate, Nathan, was home. Likely, there was another sentinel prowling around outside anyway—DarkRiver took the protection of its healer dead seriously.

Suspicious scrabbles sounded from behind her. Feeling her lips tug upward, she remained in place, her eyes closed. Little *click-clacks* on the wooden floor, silenced as they hit the rugs. Then a few whispering scratches and she felt a warm, playful presence walk along the top of the sofa back to lie down a few inches from her ear. Another presence, just as playful, a little more mischievous, settled beside her thigh.

She'd half expected a baby roar to make her jump up in surprise, but when she opened her eyes, Julian and Roman, Tammy's twins—both in leopard form—were looking at her with expressions so innocent, her heart melted. "How am I supposed to resist?" she murmured, stroking Jules while she glanced up at Rome.

Getting up, he padded over to nuzzle at her ear. She tried to catch him in one arm to bring him down, but he jumped onto the couch beside her so she could pet him, too.

"Are my little demons bothering you?" Tammy asked, walking into the living room with a tray piled high with Sascha's favorite chocolate-chip cookies hot from the oven.

"They're being sweethearts," Sascha said, as Rome settled down with his paws on her thigh, his eyes closing in bliss as she petted his gorgeous little head with firm, sure strokes. "They're not as rambunctious with me anymore."

"What do you expect?" Tammy rolled her eyes. "They're growing up around Nate and the others. They've figured out you're to be 'looked after.'"

Sascha laughed as Tammy took a seat opposite her. Ferocious, the twins' pet kitten, immediately made himself at home in the healer's lap. "Shouldn't they both be in kindergarten?"

"They're doing half days at the moment—just got home a few minutes back," Tamsyn said with a fond smile. "They both got a good-behavior report from the teacher."

Kissing the pad of her index finger, Sascha touched it to the tip of Julian's nose. Lifting a paw, he nipped playfully at her finger. "Why do you sound so surprised?"

"Tell me you're not."

Sascha couldn't help it, she laughed again, even as Jules and Rome both gave little growls. "They'll grow up into wonderful young men, you know."

Tammy's eyes softened. "I know." Petting a purring Ferocious, she leaned back in her seat. "So, you saw your mother today."

"Yes." Roman butted against her hand when she stopped stroking him, and she continued at once, scratching him behind the ears in that way he liked before moving up and down through the beautiful gold and black fur of his back. "I don't know if I'm fooling myself, but I think . . . there's something different about her."

Tamsyn didn't say anything, just let Sascha talk. And

she did. She talked about her hopes, her worries, her fears. "Do you think," she said at last, "it's just the emotions of pregnancy? I mean, I love our baby *so much*. I can't imagine any mother not feeling this way." Under her now unmoving hands, Jules and Rome lay curled up, fast asleep, two exquisitely precious lives.

"Psy are different," Tammy said at last, "you know that far better than I ever could. But you're also an empath, and if your heart tells you there's some hope of a healthy relationship with Nikita . . ."

"I don't know," Sascha said. "I just know I'm not ready to give up on her yet."

Tammy's smile was slow, strong as her healer's heart. "Then I guess Councilor Nikita Duncan had better watch out."

Having dropped a dubious-looking Morpheus off at DarkRiver HQ—to be taken home by Clay—Max and Sophia arrived at the closest airport to the D2 penitentiary less than three hours after Max's meeting with Nikita. A twenty-minute drive later and they were at the facility.

"Bonner still refusing to talk?" Max asked Bart after Sophia returned to the room, having undergone a quick preliminary checkup at the M-Psy's hands. Max met her gaze, caught the very slight shake of her head. Relief twisted around his heart—she was hanging on, refusing to surrender to the death that had been stalking her her whole life.

"Bastard hasn't said a word since he asked for Ms. Russo," Bart said, glancing at Sophia. "Be careful, Ms. Russo. I have a feeling he's enraged after we sent in a male J to do a follow-up on his comm-conference with you."

Sophia's expression didn't change. "I expected that, Mr. Reuben. Bonner isn't used to being denied."

Max folded his arms across his chest. "That's an understatement." Bonner had been born into wealth, gone to the most exclusive private schools, summered on a vineyard in

Champagne, wintered at a ski resort in Switzerland. He'd had simply to ask and his parents had given it to him, their only son—a hundred-thousand-dollar car at sixteen, a trip around the world at seventeen, a private residence on their extensive property at eighteen.

"He'll try to play you," Bart said, tapping a pen on the old-fashioned legal pad he insisted on using. "He's had a few days to do some underground research, maybe find out things about you—"

Sophia shook her head. "I've survived worse monsters." Her eyes met Max's. "It's time for me to go in."

Every single muscle in his body went rock hard in rejection of the idea, but he nodded. "I'll be right here—one small signal and I come get you."

Sophia walked into the same room she'd entered only a few days prior, but this time, she was viscerally aware of Max's gaze on her no matter that he stood hidden behind the wall that separated the room from the observation chamber. And though a prison guard stood with his back to the wall behind Bonner, it was the knowledge of Max watching over her that kept her calm, focused.

Her cop would never let the monster touch her.

With that knowledge in her heart, she said, "Mr. Bonner," as she reached the table.

Gerard Bonner's smile presumed an intimacy that made her skin crawl. "Sophia. I'd rise to welcome you, but alas . . ." He gestured to the clamps that kept him immobilized, his hands jerking to a halt.

"It's for my protection that you can't move," she said, taking a seat across from him. "You have very strong hands." After torturing Carissa White in a multitude of horrific ways, he'd finally killed her with the intimacy of his hands.

"Are you attempting to shock me?" A warm chuckle from the outwardly handsome man in front of her. "I enjoyed it, you know. Poor Carissa. She begged me to do it in the end."

So clever, she thought, always couching his words in a way that it was never quite a confession. Not that they needed it, not for Carissa White. "I was told you were ready to cooperate."

"Did I put you to too much inconvenience with my request?" he asked, his expression filling with what many would've mistaken for the sincerest of apologies. "I find that I like you the best. You're so much . . . gentler than the other Js."

"Did you know, Mr. Bonner," she said conversationally, "that in the early part of this century, they still incarcerated males together in the same cell? Tell me"—she held his gaze, let him see that she'd looked into the abyss, that nothing he said could touch her—"do you think you would have . . . enjoyed"—a deliberate echo of his word, his tone—"being in a cell with another inmate who might not have shared your more sophisticated tastes?"

Bonner didn't like that, his eyes showing the sadistic bite of malignant rage before he got it under control. "I'm sure I would have survived, Sophia. Hmm, does anyone call you Sophie?"

She hated that he'd used Max's pet name for her, hated it so much that for an instant, she wondered if she'd betrayed herself, because Bonner's blue eyes glinted with pleasure.

"You may call me anything you wish." A facsimile of calm, good enough that it had fooled the medics all these years. "All I care about are your memories."

Another crack in the facade, the ugliness inside him rising to the surface for a fleeting instant. "Then take them, *Sophie*." Vicious words laced with charm. "Take what you came to find . . . then maybe you can tell me how you got such a pretty, pretty face."

She did nothing, felt nothing. His words didn't matter— not when Max *saw* her, knew her, accepted her. "I'm not going on some kind of a scavenger hunt in your brain, Mr. Bonner. If you want to cooperate, then cooperate. If not, I'll make a final recommendation that your offers to share information have been nothing but a waste of time and that all further approaches from you be ignored."

"Bitch." It was said in that same charming voice, his smile never slipping. "Is the rest of your skin marked? Or are you a blank canvas just waiting for the right artist?"

"One last time, Mr. Bonner—are you ready to cooperate?"

"Of course."

She held the eye contact, sweeping out with her unique telepathic gift. Some Js needed physical contact with those they scanned, but she never had. And now, with her Sensitivity, touch would take her too deep, lock her into another's mind. And if there was one consciousness she did not want to be trapped within, it was that of the sociopath on the other side of the table.

Moving effortlessly through the easily permeable barrier that was the weakness of a human shield, she stepped into his mind. It was as calm, as orderly . . . but the pieces had shifted. Bonner was rearranging his memories of the past, perhaps to better fit his own personal view of the world.

A woman's screaming face, her back contorted in agony, her eyes bleeding at the corners. Sophia recoiled inside, but years of training kept her from betraying her abhorrence on her face. "We already know what you did to Carissa White," she said. "If that's all you've got—"

A small wooden glade, peaceful almost.

She felt the handle of the shovel vibrate under her hands as he/they drove it into the earth, heard the eerie quiet, felt the cool crackle of the plastic under his/their hands as he/they rolled the body into the shallowest of graves. Bonner didn't waste any time covering his victim up again, his/their actions as impersonal as if he/they were raising a garden. The body had ceased to have any meaning once it stopped screaming. Not long afterward, the earth covered the plastic, and then they were walking through the forest, exiting less than five minutes later onto a rugged track swathed in fog.

Firs—deep green, thick with foliage—their tips disappearing into the fine white mist, surrounded them on all sides, but there was a lot of undergrowth, a few spindly trees of other species. So not a tree farm, but something more natural. She got into the vehicle, started the engine after stripping off heavy gardening gloves. The four-wheel drive took the rickety road with ease, until half an hour later, she appeared out of the fog and found herself at a T-junction, a sealed road in front of her. Her heart was calm, her body relaxed. It was—

Sophia realized she was losing herself in Bonner, fought to bring herself back. "I need a location." She could see nothing but the infrequent car zipping by fast—a lonely highway.

"Patience, my sweet Sophia." Bonner was breathing hard, excited by the memory . . . by making her relive it with him.

That was when she saw it, the board on the left that marked the entrance to "Fog Valley Track."

She took note of the kinds of flowers she'd seen, the angle of the sun, the weather, everything she could.

Then Bonner's memories shifted sideways, a twisting kaleidoscope.

She'd expected something of the kind, pulled back before it could affect her. "That doesn't give us much."

"You'll find her." He drew a long, deep breath. "You'll find my lovely Gwyn."

Gwyneth Hayley had disappeared six months after Carissa White and was widely considered to be Bonner's second victim. Sophia tried to pry further details out of the Butcher, but he just smiled that intimate, satisfied little smile and told her she'd have to do some of the work herself.

Exiting, she let the medic scan her. "You need nutrients," was the response.

She drank the energy drinks he gave her, then let Bartholomew Reuben lead them up out of the bowels of the building and to a conference room on the upper floor. "If everyone could drop their shields," Sophia said, "I can project the scan into your minds." This was part of what made her a J, rather than a simple telepath—the ability to literally project entire memories. She could only do five people at a time, but other than Max, there was only Reuben, the warden, and Reuben's assistant. "I'm sorry, Detective Shannon, I can't project through your natural shield."

Max shrugged. "Projecting is tough on a J, right?" He continued without waiting for an answer, "Why don't you give us a recap instead?" His eyes were piercing. "If Bonner really is in a cooperative mood, we don't know how soon you might have to scan him again."

He was protecting her. The knowledge made her heart expand until it threatened to consume her. Taking a deep breath, holding that powerful emotion like the treasure it was, Sophia described what she'd seen.

"Fog Valley Track," Max said, already on the phone to the computer techs at Enforcement. "Yeah, how many hits?" A pause. "Narrow it down to a location with a lot of firs, relatively isolated—or it would've been five years ago; maybe off a highway."

Sophia raised her hand to catch his attention. "The temperature was cool, though the position of the sun suggested it was close to midday." Her mind filtered out the distractions of the other cars, Bonner's thoughts, and saw through to the other side of the road. "There was a billboard advertising a harvest festival as he turned out of the track."

Max repeated her words to the computer tech, waited a few moments. "I owe you a drink. Send everything through to D2, comm station three. And encrypt it, just in case someone's scanning the prison line." Hanging up, he said, "We've got three mentions of a Fog Valley Track that might match," he said.

"The track was very rough," Sophia pointed out. "Could be it's not on the maps at all."

"Yeah." A grim look. "But we'll worry about that after we check out these images."

Those images were transmitted moments later. Sophia

said, "That one," almost before she was aware of opening her mouth.

Gwyneth Hayley's last resting place lay deep within a snow-capped mountain range.

CHAPTER 26

Faith NightStar, daughter of Councilor Anthony Kyriakus and the most powerful foreseer in the world, walked out into the forest that surrounded the home she shared with her changeling mate, hoping the fresh air would melt away the fog that clouded her mind. Deep and viscous, damp and clammy, it felt almost real—the chill of it making her rub her hands up and down her arms.

"Something bad is coming," she said out loud, trying to think past the thick gray soup that hid everything from view. "Fire and fog and screams and metal." They were all connected. The fog touched those in the center, but so did the flames and the stabbing, cutting violence of metal.

She began to pace restlessly across the pine needles that littered the forest floor, her gut twisted up with the knowledge that someone was going to die. Tears pricked her eyes, burned in her throat. "Fire and fog and screams and metal."

But no matter how many times she repeated that, no matter how many times she tried to part the fog, all she got was a crushing sense of impending horror.

CHAPTER 27

Evil does exist. It may not be listed in any official manual, may be considered an emotional construct, but as Js, you must accept that there will come a time when you will be faced by such malevolence that it will challenge all that you know, all that you believe you are.

—*Sophia Russo (J) to trainee Js (unofficial seminar held at an undisclosed site)*

Four hours after Sophia pinpointed the location, the entire team, complete with a forensic unit, got out of their vehicles at the forested end of Fog Valley Track. Though the ground was currently clear, the air up here carried a touch of ice, the threat of snow lingering in the air.

"You, me, and Bart," Max said to Sophia. "We go in, see if we can eyeball anything. If that fails, we send in the dogs." It was just nudging five, but the winter sunlight was fading fast. It would've been more sensible to wait until the next day, but an unspoken thought united them all—they couldn't bear to leave Gwyn alone and cold in the dark any longer.

Nodding, Sophia took the lead. "The undergrowth has gotten considerably thicker in the years since Bonner was here."

"At least the path's still negotiable," Bart said, pushing a branch out of his way as he and Max followed Sophia's shorter form. "It'll be a bitch to process though once we find the grave."

Max shot out a hand to grip Sophia's upper arm when she stumbled over a rock. "Thank you, Detective." A calm, even voice, but Max had felt the slight tremor in her muscles, knew his Sophie was hanging on through sheer, stubborn grit.

"Anything look familiar?" Dropping her arm, Max backed off, aware of Bart staring at him.

"Not so far."

Bart nudged Max, his voice low. "You know Psy don't like to be touched."

"They also probably don't like to fall flat on their faces."

"True." Blowing out a breath, Bart shook his head. "I haven't called Gwyn's parents yet." The name fell easily from the prosecutor's tongue—like Max, he'd come to intimately know the short life and lost dreams of each and every girl.

"Neither have I," Max said, remembering Gwyn's mile-wide smile, her long runner's legs, with an anger that hadn't dulled in the intervening years. "No use ripping the scab off that wound unless we can give them some peace."

Sophia went motionless up ahead, her head angled toward a twisted old tree on the edge of the path. "I saw that." It was almost soundless.

Max kept an eye on her as she stepped off the path and began to jog forward. Not more than five minutes into it, she jerked left and clambered onto a fallen log. But she didn't step off on the other side. Reaching her, Max jumped up on her right, as Bart did the same on her left.

There was no need to ask her what she'd seen.

"It's like the land died here," Sophia said, her eyes on the lifeless patch of earth in front of them, which though bordered by the living beat of the forest, tiny shoots and greenery, was itself as browned and dry as dust.

As if Gwyneth Hayley's lifeblood had soaked into the soil and turned it barren.

* * *

The forensic team worked deep into the night, under brilliant lamps. By midnight, they'd found only seven discrete bones, the others in all probability having been carried away by forest creatures, but amazingly, one of those seven was the skull. And there were teeth still attached to that skull.

A positive dental match was made on the spot using mobile equipment.

Sophia saw Max's shoulders shudder and drop the instant after the forensic technician made his pronouncement. "I'll do it," he said to Bart Reuben.

Bart's face was drawn, his eyes full of old pain as he acquiesced. "They trust you more."

Letting the prosecutor walk past her and back to the site, Sophia went to stand beside Max as he moved away from the group and into the night-shadow of a giant tree with sweeping arms. "You're calling her family?"

A nod, his face lined with angry sorrow. "I'd prefer to do it in person, but I have to make sure they get the information before it leaks to the media." His fingers clenched on the phone. "It'll tear them apart all over again."

Hidden in the darkness, she dared lay her hand on his arm. "But it will give them peace—and Gwyneth a safe place to rest."

Max didn't reply, but he leaned into her touch. It threatened to shatter her.

Because Max Shannon was not a man who leaned on anyone.

As she stood there beside him, he coded in a number from memory and raised the phone to his ear. And then he did what had to be done.

The next two days passed in a blur. Sophia had another comm-conference with Bonner. However, he wasn't in the mood to cooperate. "I'm enjoying my extra hour in the sun far too much," he told her. "So obliging of the prison authorities to stick to their bargain with me."

Knowing he'd string them along now that he had their attention, she didn't squander her time and, instead, asked Max if there was anything she could do to assist him.

"Keep an eye on the Nikita situation," he told her. "Go over the forensic reports as they come in, compare the results sent in by Nikita's people against those of the independent lab we contracted." As the lead detective on the Bonner case, he wasn't only dealing with the families of the victims, but also the brass and the media; his eyes bloodshot with lack of sleep. "Did we receive the report from the mechanic on the crashed car?"

"Yes. She confirmed the computer was tampered with." Sophia wanted to touch him, give comfort in the human way, but they were in the hastily thrown together "war room"—located in the closest Enforcement station to where Gwyneth Hayley's body had been found. Activity buzzed on every side, crashing against her senses. "The second autopsy you ordered on the driver has also been completed. There were no drugs in Allison Marceau's system."

"Makes sense if the car was the weapon." He glanced quickly at the report. "Even if she sent out a telepathic scream, it wouldn't have been noted as anything suspicious."

"It might be better if I went back. I can deal with things—"

"Stay." It was a single quiet word, but it carried a thousand unsaid things.

Bound to him now by threads she didn't quite understand, but that had become the defining truths in her life, she stayed—setting herself up in her hotel room, away from the constant storm of the war room.

To everyone's surprise, the Council dispatched several Ps-Psy to help with the search around what had been dubbed Bonner Site #1. "Psychometrics sense the imprints of the past," Sophia explained to Max when he asked for a quick précis. "They usually work verifying the age and provenance of works of art, other expensive objects—but I've heard it said that some can also pick up 'echoes' of events that took place in a particular location."

"I had a look at the title of the land," Max told her a few hours after the psychometrics arrived. "It's owned by a Psy conglomerate and earmarked for development."

That, Sophia thought, made much more sense. "They don't want any unanswered questions lowering the value of the land and subsequent development."

"Not that it matters why they're here. Tanique"—he named one of the Ps-Psy—"already located two of Gwyneth's bones almost half a mile from the gravesite."

That was one of the few conversations they managed to have in the bleak, exhausting hours that followed. It was on their last night at the search base—right after it was announced that no evidence of further bodies had been found within a mile-wide radius of the site—that she discovered something interesting.

She'd been digging deep into the backgrounds of all the individuals of interest, tapping her connections in Justice when necessary. The aristocratic Quentin Gareth came across as a ruthless businessman, but seemed otherwise clean. Andre Tulane, in contrast, had repeating weekly meetings that she could tie into nothing official, while the intern, Ryan Asquith, had a note on his file that meant he'd been reconditioned within the past year as a result of a court order.

All merited further investigation, but the most interesting data resulted from a logarithm she'd been running on news uploads at around the time of the killings: Councilor Kaleb Krychek had been in the relevant area at the time of every single murder. He'd even been snapped by the *San Francisco Gazette*—leaving an early morning meeting with Nikita—on the day Edward Chan had a knife thrust into his heart.

"It ties up so neatly—but at the same time, it doesn't make sense," she said to Max the next day as she finished locking up her bag for the return trip to San Francisco. With the families of all the victims having been notified of what was happening behind the scenes with Bonner, and with no hope of finding any further remains, Max had decided they needed to turn their attention back to Nikita's situation.

"Isn't Krychek a telekinetic?" Max asked, shadows under his eyes from the lack of sleep.

"Exactly—and he's teleport capable." It hurt her to see him hurting—she couldn't wait until they were home, where she could wrap her arms around him, give him the surcease he'd given her so many times. "He would've been smart enough to teleport in to do the kills while he wasn't officially known to be in the region."

Taking her bag and slinging his own duffel over his shoulder, Max headed to the elevators as she pulled the door to her hotel room closed. "From what I know of Councilor Krychek," he said as she came to stand beside him, "he's a stone-cold operator. I can't see him wasting time with the theater of a fake suicide."

"I've never heard a confirmation, but there are constant whispers that he was raised by a sociopath, that he's a murderer at heart." She'd seen Krychek once—on the other side of a hotel lobby—but his presence had made her alter her route, take the long way to her destination in order to avoid him. It had been self-preservation, the otherness in her recognizing an intelligence as lethal—and far, far colder.

Max rubbed his hand over the jaw she'd watched him shave a few minutes ago when she'd gone into his room ostensibly to talk about the case. The experience had been starkly, beautifully intimate. "The pattern's too political for a serial killer," he said, waiting until she stepped into the elevator before following. "That kind of a sociopathic drive wouldn't have allowed him to keep his urges leashed to the extent of only committing murders on the verge of a big deal."

"There's another rumor that might be more apropos," Sophia said, curling her fingers into her palms to keep from touching the smooth skin of his jaw, breathing in the fresh pine of his aftershave. "That Nikita and Krychek have some kind of an alliance."

"Now *that* fits the pattern," Max murmured as the doors

opened at the garage level. Heading to the vehicle they'd rented at the airport, a vehicle that had spent the entirety of the past forty-eight hours sitting in the garage—Max having had access to an Enforcement car, while Sophia remained in the hotel to work—he dumped their bags in the trunk. "Someone's trying to cause suspicion between the two."

"Do—" She was cut off by the beeping of her cell phone. Pulling it out, she said, "Sophia Russo."

"Thank God I caught you—Max's phone won't go through." It was an unfamiliar voice, trembling as if the speaker had run a hundred miles. "This is Faith Night-Star."

Getting into the car when Max opened the door for her, Sophia immediately realized the reason for the call. "You had a vision." And the visions of a cardinal F-Psy were accurate to within a hundredth of a decimal point.

"Yes," Faith said as Max snapped on his safety belt and went to put his thumbprint on the starter. "The car is rigged. Do you understand?" Frantic words. "Don't start the engine."

Max's thumb brushed the ignition switch.

"No!" Sophia jerked Max's hand away from the ignition with a wrench that had his head snapping toward her.

"Sophia!" Faith's voice merged with Max's demand to know what was going on.

"I'm fine," she said to Faith, tremors shaking her frame. "We're both fine. Here, you better speak directly to Max."

Leaning back in her seat, she tried to get her heart to beat in a normal rhythm as Max had a short, sharp discussion with Faith. Closing the phone, he ordered her to step out of the car. Neither of them said a word until they were standing in front of the innocuous-looking vehicle.

"I'm getting the bomb squad," Max said, using her cell phone to make the call when his own proved to have a flat battery. "They'll be here in five minutes, tops."

"So soon?" She had to focus on the mundane, on the

practical . . . rather than on the fact that Max had come terrifyingly close to death.

Max touched her lightly on the back, and she realized just how much she'd missed the contact in the frenetic pace of the past two days. No one had ever told her that touch was something you became addicted to, the loss of it a hunger, an ache deep within.

"They work out of the same Enforcement building we used as a base." His hand dropped away as an Enforcement vehicle drove into the garage. "Still, that was damn fast."

Two men and one woman stepped out, all three in the protective gear of the bomb squad. "Tell me what you know," the woman said.

"We got the heads-up from an F-Psy—" Max began.

"Foreseer?" The woman whistled. "I didn't realize they made civilian predictions—heard it was all business."

"Faith NightStar," Max said. "She's part of DarkRiver. She saw the car explode after I started the engine."

"Hmm. Given current technology, it's got to be some kind of a detonation message being sent to the actual device." She was already moving toward the car, equipment in hand. "You two might want to clear the garage. You're not wearing protective gear."

Max nodded to the entrance ramp. "We'll be waiting outside."

"I'll give you a yell soon as we locate anything."

Faith paced across the beautifully lighted cave that was her home office, rubbing her hands up and down her arms.

"You cold, sweetheart?"

Looking up, she found Vaughn in the doorway. Her jaguar had a streak of white dust on his face, a rip near the bottom of his T-shirt, and was so wonderful she still couldn't believe he was hers. "No." But she walked into his embrace. "Hold me."

"Hey." His arms came around her, strong and warm, one hand gripping a chisel he'd clearly been using on his current sculpture. "I thought you said the cop and his J were all right?"

"They are." She ran her fingers over the gritty dust that covered the skin of his arm. "But I still have this *knowing* that something bad is coming." She hated the amorphous knowings even more than the dark visions. At least the visions showed her something concrete, something she could fight or avert. "It's an emotional knowing—connected to someone who's important to me."

"Did you try the exercises you've been working on to fine-tune your control over your abilities?"

She nodded, sliding her hands under his T-shirt and to the muscled warmth of his back. "I can't break through the veil. And Vaughn, it's something really, really bad." Ice filled her heart, coated her veins. "What if I can't stop it?" What if she lost one of the people she loved?

Vaughn pressed his lips to her brow. "We discussed this. You'll go mad if you take responsibility for every evil you can't stop." His tone was gentle but absolute. "You saved two lives today. Celebrate that."

Raising her head, she met those golden eyes—eyes of a jungle cat made human—that had become the fulcrum of her universe. "It's hard." And part of the reason why so many F-Psy had gone irrevocably mad in the past—that need to save every life, avert every sorrow, could devour the unwary.

"That's why you have me." Lips against her own, intense protectiveness in the way his body curved over hers. "Let's see if we can't get you into a better frame of mind." And then her jaguar was purring low in his throat as he peeled off her clothes. "It'll come to you if you're relaxed."

She felt her heart lighten with sensual humor. Oh, how she needed him. His ability to play, to laugh, to love, made every darkness bearable. "So you're stripping me naked for my benefit?"

A look so innocent, it would've done one of Tammy's rambunctious twins proud. "Of course."

Faith let him love her, let him comfort her . . . and hoped it would break open the deadlock on her mind. Because whatever was coming, it was a crushing, terrifying blackness that only ever meant one thing.

Death.

CHAPTER 28

We don't choose our parents. And their mistakes aren't our own. You are what you make yourself—don't ever forget that.

—Max Shannon in reply to an e-mail from the sole survivor of the Castleton murder-suicide

Sophia allowed herself to lean against the garage wall once they'd exited onto the quiet street outside. She wasn't concerned about setting off alarm bells if caught on surveillance—even Psy sometimes lost the perfect posture that had been drilled into them as a symptom and indication of control.

Max braced himself with one arm on the wall beside her, his eyes ablaze though he kept his distance. His earlier touch everyone would discount as a human action inspired by the emotions of the moment. But if he touched her now, Sophia knew she wouldn't be able to resist crumbling into his embrace.

"You okay?" Rough tone, violence contained.

She wanted so much to crawl into his arms, to hold the solid reality of him to her until she believed he was alive, was safe. "Yes."

Lines bracketed Max's mouth. "This has to be connected to the work we're doing for Nikita."

"Not necessarily." Realizing that he was focusing his anger into work, she kicked her sluggish brain into gear. "Bonner is very wealthy, and Bartholomew said that he has many groupies."

"I'll have his visitor logs and mail records checked out. But fact is, he likes playing with you—I don't think he'd have you killed."

"He has no way of knowing I'm working with you on another case," she said, her hands clammy inside her gloves, her heartbeat erratic, "especially if this particular plan was put in motion before we met. He considers you his adversary, doesn't he?" She'd seen the notes, notes Bonner had sent to Max while he'd still been an unknown serial killer. Each had been a taunt, a declaration of his superiority.

But then Max had caught him.

"Fuck." Blowing out a breath, Max clenched his fist against the wall, the rough texture of the plascrete rubbing against his skin. He wanted nothing more than to grab Sophia and drag her to his chest, to crush her close until the thudding fear of his heartbeat decreased to something less agonizing.

"Max," a soft word, a warning from a J with eyes full of remembered terror.

Shoving his other hand into a pocket to stop himself from reaching for her, he said, "Bonner likes to get up close and personal."

Sophia nodded, her hair lifting in the breeze that sent a discarded soft-drink bottle rolling down the otherwise empty street. "Yes, a bomb is something more apt to be used by those of my race—especially if the aim was expediency."

"Let's see what the bomb squad has to say."

They had to wait fifteen more minutes before the squad called an all-clear, having removed the device and placed it into a blast-proof container. "High tech," the female member of the team said. "Nothing your average malcontent could make on his own."

Max hunkered down beside her, aware of the two males

giving Sophia the once-over. If they so much as smiled wrong in her direction, those faces would be hitting the old-fashioned concrete of the garage floor—he was not in a rational mood right now. "Someone wealthy?"

"Sure. The rich can source anything, but they'd have to have some fairly strong contacts—this stuff is Defense grade."

"Is it from a Psy company?" Sophia came to stand so close beside him, he could've reached out and curved his hand around the smooth temptation of her calf. Though he forced himself not to touch, her proximity soothed the clawing edge of his protectiveness.

"Can't tell from a surface look, but they're the leaders in explosive technology, so I'm guessing yeah." She locked the box. "You want me to call forensics?"

"Thanks." Rising, he said good-bye to the bomb experts just as two uniformed officers arrived to hold the scene secure. "Detective Chen is on her way," one of them said.

Grabbing Chen's number from them, Max made a call to her, then one to Bart, telling him of the incident and asking him to have his people go over Bonner's mail and visitor records.

"I'll organize it," Bart said. "Glad you're safe."

"Thanks." Ending the call, Max made another one asking for a ride to the airport.

"Shouldn't we stay for the investigation?" Sophia asked.

"No point." Max wanted Sophia out of here, wanted her safe. "I know Chen, and she's a hell of a detective. She'll keep us in the loop if they discover something—and she's okay with taking our statements over a comm link."

"And if this *is* connected to Nikita rather than Bonner," Sophia said, "then we need to be in San Francisco."

"Yeah, because even Psy sure as hell wouldn't attempt to blow up a cop five minutes from an Enforcement station unless they were planning something damn spectacular. Either we've gotten too close to something—"

"—or we were meant to be a distraction," Sophia completed.

The question was—Who or what target was important enough to chance taking out a cop? The fact that he was human didn't negate the danger—all politics aside, Enforcement command would take the murder of one of its officers as a personal attack.

Sascha grinned as Lucas stopped at a small corner shop to buy her an ice cream. "Thank you, Mr. Hunter."

"You're welcome, Sascha darling." He shook his head as they pulled away from the store. "I don't know where it all goes."

She took a contented bite of her chocolate-coated chocolate ice cream. "Don't make me mad."

He shuddered. "I think you've fulfilled your quota of crazy today."

She made a face at him, able to hear the cat's humor in his voice. "There is no quota, not once you start carrying around a bowling ball in your belly." A little pat to reassure the baby, who appeared to be fast asleep. "Not that I don't adore our little bowling ball."

A fond glance from the cat beside her. "Why are we going into work?"

"Because they need you to sign documents." Savoring the delicious treat, she sighed. "It's such a beautiful day."

"Let's take a drive through the Presidio before we head in," he said, referring to the forested region just outside the city. "You can find a nice sunny spot to eat your ice cream while I take a nap."

She shot him a laughing glance, warmth filling her body at the remembrance of exactly why he was so sleep-deprived. "Are you complaining?"

"No"—a wicked smile—"I'm planning my revenge."

Max and Sophia had gone over every piece of evidence related to Nikita's case twice by the time they were twenty minutes into their flight. "What are we missing?" Max muttered, frustrated at the feeling that they were being blind to something critically important. Bonner and his twisted games just didn't fit.

The vanilla of Sophia's shampoo whispered across his senses as she bent her head over her organizer, an invisible caress. "Whatever it is, it must be taking place soon if they came after us in such a high-risk location." They'd both realized the bomb could've been planted anytime in the past forty-eight hours. Which meant—"We have to work on the assumption that the timeline has to be very, very short by now."

"A strike anytime soon will break the pattern of murders before a big deal." Max had spoken to Nikita prior to boarding the airjet, reconfirmed that nothing was even close to final. "Why?"

"Something's made them push their schedule forward." Her thigh brushed his.

The fleeting touch was a balm, centering him. "Nikita's people—anyone who'll be out of easy reach for a long period?"

Sophia tapped the screen of her organizer with quick motions. "Prague, Berlin, Tokyo, hardly out-of-the-way locations. And any who are going are coming back within a week or two at most."

"It has to be an issue of access," Max muttered. "And for some reason, they were worried we'd figure it out—"

"*You*, Max." Sophia's eyes turned an intense, incredible night violet. "They were worried you would figure it out—you're the wild card in this situation, a human whose thought processes they can't predict."

"Okay, so a target a Psy wouldn't immediately think of, coupled with a deadly—" Ice crawled through his veins, right to his heart. *"No."*

"Max?"

"Where the hell did I see it?" Reaching into the seat pocket in front of them, he pulled out the entertainment module. "They were flashing the selections on the big screen when we boarded, remember?"

"Yes, but what did you—"

"There!" He stopped on the front page of a national tabloid. The headline was: *Scoop! Sascha Duncan Pregnant!* Below that was another headline in a slightly smaller font: *DarkRiver Alpha Keeps Pregnant Mate Captive!*

Max put down the module. "Bastards are afraid the cats really are about to put Sascha into hiding."

A sick feeling bloomed in the pit of Sophia's stomach as she remembered the glowing warmth of Sascha's presence. The E-Psy was something incredibly good, something their race needed to protect, not harm. "Our cell phones won't work." As a result of accidents in the twentieth century, all devices were now automatically blocked while an airjet was in the sky.

Max was already rising. "I'll talk to the steward, get an emergency call out."

"Wait," Sophia said. "That'll take too long. I'll do it on the PsyNet." Though she was a very strong telepath, her shields were viciously degraded. If she attempted to send that far without the aid of the Net, they could collapse, killing her before the message reached the intended recipient.

"You do it on the Net, I'll make the call, cover our bases."

Nodding, she closed her eyes to ensure total focus and opened her psychic eye. She hadn't tried to cross her new shields before today, but if they were hers, they should obey her—and they did, wrapping her in distinctive mobile firewalls as she exited out into the PsyNet.

Forcing herself to ignore the battering influx of information that was the endless river of the Net, she arrowed straight to Nikita's mind. As expected, the Councilor's shields were beyond impenetrable, but Sophia began to try to break them. It was the easiest way to ensure she'd get Nikita's attention as fast as possible.

It only took a split second. "Ms. Russo." Nikita's icy presence. "People who attempt to hack my shields don't usually survive."

Sophia knew full well she'd risked infection from a

mental virus if the Councilor had laced her defenses with her own personal brand of poison. "You need to get a message to Sascha. We think she's the next target."

"Details?"

"Nothing concrete—but it'll happen very soon."

Nikita broke contact.

Dropping out of the Net, Sophia found that she was gripping the armrests so tight, her tendons showed white against her skin.

"Sophie, sweetheart, talk to me." It was a soft-voiced command, meant to carry to her ears alone as Max returned to slide into his seat.

"I told Nikita." She swallowed, realizing something too late. "I just hope she was the right person to tell."

CHAPTER 29

One thing I've learned after so many years on the job—no one is simple, no one is one-dimensional. And still, people surprise me.

—*From the private case notes of Detective Max Shannon*

Sascha's and Lucas's phones both started beeping with the pack's emergency code when they were two streets over from the HQ. Then the car phone started beeping.

"What the hell?" Lucas double-parked beside a bright magenta monstrosity that Sascha had been teasing him about buying.

"I'll get mine," Sascha was saying when she felt a telepathic knock on her mind. Firm, familiar. *Mother.* Her own telepathic reach was small, but Nikita's was so wide, she'd hear Sascha's weaker voice.

You may have been chosen as a target by my enemies.

I understand.

The methods they've used thus far suggest they do not have a teleport-capable telekinetic at their disposal.

I'll make sure I'm careful about my physical surroundings.

Don't forget about explosives.

No.

I'll organize protection—

Thank you, Mother, Sascha said, emotion a rock in her throat, *but the pack will take care of me. I promise.*

Very well.

Nikita's mind dropped away, but Sascha didn't take it for disapproval. Glancing at Lucas, she saw his green eyes had gone cat. "My mother just warned me I might be a target," she said.

"I thought you were 'pathing to someone." Starting up the car, he turned back the way they'd come, heading out of the city and toward their cabin. "Faith had a vision—that was your phone. Dorian cornered a sniper on his security rounds—that was my phone. And Clay got a call from Max before his own informants told him about another suspicious man in the apartment building facing the HQ—that was the car phone."

Sascha blew out a breath. "Darling, you do realize that means the baby and I were never in any danger?"

Lucas squeezed the steering wheel as if he'd like to rip it off. "I'm not going to calm down for a while, so deal with it."

Reaching out, she rubbed the back of her hand over his cheek. "Since we're going home, I'll have lots of privacy to pet you." A nudge in her stomach, a thump in her heart. "And you can pet me back."

The leopard shot her a quick glance.

"They would've hurt you, too." How *dare* they!

Lucas took her hand, brought it to her lips. "The pack would've never let that happen."

The cunning way her leopard had turned her words back on her when it suited him thrust past the anger to leave only a deep need to touch, to love, to cherish. "Take me home, Lucas."

Max called Lucas the instant they landed. "She's safe?"

"We're both fine—you the reason Nikita knew?"

"Sophie managed to pass on a message through the PsyNet."

"Clay and Dorian have some intel out at our HQ that you should see—probably shouldn't come over the comm lines." A long, indrawn breath. "And, Cop—thanks."

Hanging up, Max nodded to Sophie. "She's fine. And we might have a lead." He waited only until they were inside the car before reaching over to close his hand over her thigh, his palm separated from her skin by nothing but the material of her skirt. He understood exactly how feral the DarkRiver alpha was feeling at that moment. If Faith hadn't warned them about the bomb . . . "I want to strip you to the skin and drive into you until we both scream."

"Max."

It took him three minutes of teeth-gritting control before he could begin driving. Neither of them said another word until they walked into the DarkRiver building. Clay met them in the lobby and led them upstairs to a meeting room, where Dorian was waiting.

The sentinel with his blue-eyed, blond good looks raised a hand. "Here's the lowdown—the assassin I found ate some kind of a fucking suicide tablet. I haven't seen anything like it outside of historical dramas."

"I worked a case where a small cult committed suicide en masse," Max said, his mind cascading with bleak images of small bodies curled up beside larger ones that should've protected, not harmed. "They used a wine laced with poison."

"It speaks of fanatical devotion," his J said, "rather than professionalism."

"But he was a professional, too." Dorian showed them some images on the comm screen. "His gear, the way he'd been waiting there long enough to have left DNA behind, if you know what I mean—the man knew what he was doing."

"Where's the body?"

Clay was the one who responded. "Enforcement morgue."

"And the other one?" Max asked.

The sentinel looked disgusted. "He figured out we were

on to him and rabbited. I had to bring him down in a public area—Enforcement was there within a minute. He's sitting in a cell not talking right now. No doubt he's Psy."

"There's something else." Dorian picked up what looked like a business card off the table. "This was left behind in the room where the second sniper was hiding."

"That's evidence." Max scowled. "You've fucking contaminated the hell out of it."

"Trust me," Dorian said, "you don't want that in the system. And we processed it."

Max glanced down to see that the card carried a single line of text—what looked like a comm code. Turning it over, he read the handwritten note: *Sascha, DR HQ*

"I recognize that code," Sophia said in a quiet voice. "It's Councilor Duncan's private line."

"Very well guarded," Dorian said. "And available only to a select few."

Max shook his head. "Nikita isn't behind this. And the handwriting—the time's missing."

Sophia took it from his hand. "They were going to insert that once they'd hit Sascha, make it seem as if Nikita had given them the location and time." She placed the card back on the table. "But the fact that they have this number further implicates someone in Nikita's inner circle."

"Another Councilor would also have it—or be able to get it," Max said, eyes narrowed. "No question that Nikita has a mole inside her organization, but there's a much larger power behind this."

"I've already got our informants on alert for anything that might be related." Clay said with a tightly held fury. "You need us, we're there."

Max tapped the card. "What did you find?"

Dorian's scowl did nothing to lessen the sheer beauty of his face. "Only usable print was—surprise, surprise—Nikita's."

"They really thought you were going to fall for that?" Max had seen the way the cats operated—they were highly intelligent predators.

Dorian's mouth went grim. "If they'd succeeded in hurting Sascha, we wouldn't have been thinking too straight. The leopard would've gone for blood."

And, Sophia realized with a chill in her heart, the ensuing carnage would have begun a war.

CHAPTER 30

Nikita thought long and hard about her next move, considered, too, what it might betray. Nothing. If she was careful.

Picking up her cell phone, she input a code.

Anthony Kyriakus answered after a few seconds. "Nikita, this is unexpected."

Yes, Nikita thought, it was. Though they occupied the same basic area of the state, their paths rarely collided. The NightStar empire was built around the foreseeing abilities so prevalent in their genetic line, while Nikita's own company had a much more prosaic base in housing and design. But—"We do have certain commonalities."

A pause. "Is this a Council matter?"

"No." That left them with only one common thread, a thread they'd never before discussed. "Sascha was targeted by my enemies today. You may wish to ensure Faith's safety."

"I don't think you're doing this out of the goodness of your heart."

Nikita had no heart. What she had were brains and a survival instinct that saw nothing wrong with killing, manipulation, and betrayal. But she wasn't fickle. That was bad for business. "It strikes me," she said, "that our aims have coincided more often than not in Council matters of late."

"You're allied to Krychek."

"So are you." It was, she knew, less of an alliance than she had with Kaleb, but it existed. "They are attempting to take our territory, Anthony."

"That's their mistake." And, for the first time, she heard the pure steel that had made Anthony Kyriakus a threat long before he became Council.

CHAPTER 31

*To my Cop—I never imagined you could exist, that you would
exist, for someone like me. I never imagined that you'd look
at me the way you do. I never imagined how hard it would be
to say good-bye.*

*—Sophia Russo in an encrypted and time-coded letter to
be sent to Max Shannon after her death*

The main Enforcement station in San Francisco was a
sprawling complex full to the brim with humanity—and at
present, a Psy assassin.

Sophia took a deep breath as they were led down through
the bull pen and to the short-term holding facilities at the
back of the station. So many voices, so many people, so
many memories and dreams—it was a ceaseless buzz in
her head, her shields already strained after the time spent
in the enclosed space of the airjet.

Though she kept her arms tight to her body, her face
turned away, people still bumped into her. She'd managed
to avoid skin-to-skin contact so far—mostly because Max
had been using his own body to shield hers in the most
subtle of ways, but it was impossible to do anything but grit
her teeth against the onslaught of psychic noise.

Hopes and wishes. Hates and loves. Joys and sorrows.

Even though she couldn't read any specific thoughts, she
could feel the colossal weight of those thoughts battering

at her. The pressure against her shields was immense—she was terrified it would create a break, crushing her under an avalanche of other people's nightmares.

"Here you go." The cop who'd escorted them stopped in front of a cell. "He hasn't said a word."

"Thanks." Max held out his hand. "I appreciate the cooperation."

The cop shook it, but his eyes were flat. "You have Psy backing. Call me when you're done."

White lines bracketed Max's mouth as the other man walked away. She wanted to comfort him, but what could she say? She was Psy, part of the very race whose history of arrogance meant Max was being seen as a traitor to his own people.

His gaze met hers at that moment and something in him seemed to ease. Walking up to the old-fashioned steel bars of the temporary holding cell, he said, "Keeping your mouth shut isn't going to achieve anything, not while you're in Nikita's territory."

The man sitting on a bunk on one side of the room didn't so much as turn his head. Max tried again. With the same result. Shifting to glance at her, Max raised an eyebrow. She took a step closer to the bars. "Fanaticism," she said, keeping her tone clear, Silent, *pure*, "is a breach of Silence."

No response, but she knew he was listening.

"The fact that your colleague committed suicide when he was of sound mind and body speaks to that fanaticism."

The man lifted his head. "It could as well have been a tactical decision to deprive the enemy of an individual to interrogate."

"But you didn't follow that path," she pointed out. "You didn't agree with his actions."

"I have nothing to hide." Cool words. "It's no crime to be in an apartment in San Francisco. Even one with a view of the DarkRiver building."

Sophia wondered if the male had truly thought through

the consequences of his actions. Legalese wouldn't save him, not when he'd proven himself part of the conspiracy against Nikita. Stepping back, she lowered her voice so that it would carry only to Max.

"Nikita doesn't know yet." That much was apparent because if she had, this man's mind would've been torn apart like so much paper before they'd ever had a chance to talk to him.

Max set his jaw. "I don't care who the fuck she is—she does that, I'm done with this case. They can blow her up for all I care."

Nikita would bide her time, Sophia thought. Because right now, she needed Max. "Do you want to attempt further questioning while I—"

The scream was sharp, high pitched. Even as the medical alarms began blaring, the Psy male fell forward and to the floor, his body flopping about in the throes of a seizure that had his head thumping over and over against the plascrete floor.

Max had run to grab the guard with the key the instant after the first scream, but Sophia knelt by the bars, her heart twisting in pity. The would-be assassin's face was contorted, blood leaking out of his ears, and there, in those final moments, Sophia saw fear fill his soul. Reaching through the bars, she gripped the hand that flailed toward her. "Hold on, help is coming."

His hand spasmed on hers, pulling down her glove.

And he touched one finger to the skin bared at her wrist.

A scream of sound, images and thought, yesterdays tangled up in dying agonies.

Someone—Max—wrenched back her hand. "Sophia!"

She blinked, desperately trying to control the ugly roiling in her stomach. "Help him." It came out husky, rough.

Max shook his head, his eyes solemn. "It's too late."

Following his gaze, she saw another Enforcement officer

inside with the prisoner, his head bowed in defeat. The Psy male's eyes stared unseeing at the ceiling.

Nikita was adamant she hadn't killed the man. "He was eliminated to prevent me from discovering what he knew," she said when they confronted her. "If I had taken his mind, ripped away his secrets, I'd have no more use for you and Ms. Russo, Detective—and I'd make sure you knew it."

Sophia watched Max hold that chilling gaze. "Now that, I believe."

"This wouldn't have happened if I'd been notified at the start."

It was true. Because she'd have done the job herself.

But she hadn't.

And right then, Sophia was too numb to consider anything further. She felt battered and bruised by the time they arrived back home. She didn't make the slightest protest when Max ushered her into his apartment rather than her own. "Go take a hot shower," he ordered, nudging her toward the bedroom and the bathroom that flowed off it. "I'll make you something to eat."

She felt her lower lip tremble and it was such a strange sensation that she stared at him, uncomprehending.

"Come on, sweetheart." Soft words, a gentle tone as he walked her into the bedroom and turned her in the direction of the bathroom door with his hands on her shoulders, careful to keep his fingers away from her skin.

He was taking care of her, she thought, her shocked state leaving her without defenses of any kind. "You're the first person who's ever taken care of me." Even before her parents had rejected her, she'd been nothing but a practical responsibility.

Max went very, very still behind her. Then, releasing a long breath, he leaned in close enough that their breaths mingled. "Yeah?" A slow smile. "I guess that makes me a lucky man." Moving to face her, he tugged at her arms until she lowered them from around her waist. Then he pulled off her jacket. "Baby, if I strip you, I'm not sure I'm going to be able to keep on being noble."

Something snapped awake inside of her, electrified at the idea of Max seeing her naked. "I'll be all right."

Shifting back, Max took out something from the closet. "You can put this on after."

It was, she saw, one of his shirts. She could've as easily asked him to go into her apartment and retrieve some of her own clothing, but she took the shirt . . . took the scent of Max into her hands. "Thank you."

"There's a spare towel on the rail. Leave the door open," he said. "I'll be in the living room—I want to be sure I hear you if you call out."

She couldn't find the words she wanted to say, so she forced her feet forward and into the bathroom. Leaving the door ajar, she listened to the sounds of Max moving about in the bedroom as he changed. By the time she peeled off her clothing and stepped into the shower, she no longer felt so close to breaking. Still, there was a new fragility inside of her, a new fracture in her innermost psychic shields.

I can't break, she thought to herself, obdurate in her anger, her need, *not yet. I haven't lived yet.*

Turning off the shower only after her skin was pink from the heat, she got out and used the spare towel to dry herself, then picked up Max's shirt and brought it up to her nose. It had been laundered, but she could sense echoes of Max's innate scent beneath the freshness of the detergent.

It slipped easily over her body, hanging to midthigh. The color was white, but the fabric was thick enough that she didn't have to worry about her lack of underwear being embarrassingly obvious. Not that Max wouldn't already be aware that she was naked beneath his shirt. Feeling her cheeks color, she put her dirty clothes—and gloves—in a neat pile to the side, then stepped out into the bedroom.

It was empty.

Glad for the reprieve, she found herself walking to the

dresser. A plain black comb lay on the surface, along with a wallet and a keycard. The austere nature of it suited him, she thought, because for all his masculine beauty, Max was a cop through and through. Taking the comb, she lifted it up to her hair. It felt wonderfully intimate to run it through the damp strands, and she imagined what it would be like to have him stroke her scalp with those strong fingers of his instead.

"Sophie."

Startled, she dropped the comb on the dresser, turning to find him leaning against the doorjamb. He'd changed into faded blue jeans and a plain black T-shirt that caressed his lithe frame with soft ease. "You look so young," she said. With his hair sliding over his forehead and his expression outwardly relaxed, he could've been a college kid . . . but there was too much knowledge in those uptilted eyes.

"Look who's talking." With that, he pushed away from the doorjamb and closed the distance between them with that inherently masculine grace. "You look good in my shirt."

She tugged at the cuffs she'd rolled up to her wrists, nervous in a way she couldn't explain. "Max, I—" The words stuck in her throat, hard, jagged.

Eyes of near black met hers as he bent his knees to bring himself down to her height. "What do you need?"

The dam burst. "Will you hold me, Max?"

Max stepped closer. "Always. But are you sure? Your shie—"

"Please."

His arms came around her, gently, so gently, as if he was afraid she'd shatter. But when she locked her own around his waist in an iron-tight embrace, his hold turned unbreakable. The electricity of their contact arced through her, but beneath it all was a tranquil, pure silence.

A sigh rippled out of her, as she found sweet relief from the unremitting pressure of the millions of minds in the vicinity, the billions of thoughts pressing down on her. When Max shifted his embrace to cup the back of her head, she shuddered.

He froze. "Sophie?"

"All I feel is you," she whispered against his body, the warmth of him making her want to rub her face against him, rub her skin against him until he was a part of her. "Just you."

"More?" A husky question.

"More."

Bending his head, he touched his lips to her temple, one of his arms moving up to curve around her shoulders, his fingers tangling in her hair. She expected him to speak, but what he did instead was drop a line of kisses along her cheekbone and down over her jaw. Shivering from the sensation, from the near-painful pleasure of the contact, she stood on tiptoe, trying to get closer. A raw male chuckle.

And then Max kissed her.

This was no brush, no teasing taste. He took her mouth with the contained intensity she could feel thrumming beneath her fingers, his muscles taut, his entire body held barely in check. And she realized he was savagely angry, a tiger no longer on the leash.

His tongue swept against hers, buckling her knees. She gripped his shoulders, tried to hang on, drowning in the dark, masculine taste of him. Her heart was a rapid beat within her rib cage, her mind a place of splintering chaos. The only anchor, the only reality, was Max. His shoulder muscles shifting beneath her grasp, he moved one arm down to clamp over her lower back, his hand scrunching up the material of the shirt.

Air brushed the backs of her thighs, and she remembered she was standing in front of a mirror. But the thought was gone in the next instant as he tugged at her hair to angle her head for a deeper, hotly sexual kiss. Wet and open and demanding, it was the most intimate contact of her life. Her chest grew tight, so tight.

"Breathe." A harsh order as Max broke the kiss.

Sucking in a gasping breath, she pressed her mouth back to his. Kissing was . . . wild and exhilarating and so shockingly intimate, she wasn't sure she could handle what came afterward. But she would. "No." The protest was rasped out as he broke the kiss a second time and gripped her arms, holding her hands from him.

A red flush rode his high cheekbones, and his voice, when he spoke, trembled with the force of emotion, "You're not thinking straight."

"I can't be alone, Max." She tried to close the gap between them, but he was too strong. "I want you."

"You had one hell of a psychic shock today," he said, refusing to budge. "I'm not about to let you cause further damage by overloading your—"

"Stop it," she snapped out in spite of the fact that her skin was all but crawling with need, and had the satisfaction of seeing his eyes narrow. "I'm not a child you have to protect. I know what I want."

Max hissed out a breath. "Your shields—"

"I don't know what's happening with my shields," she said, blunt in her need, "but I know that right now, I'm an enigma to those in the PsyNet. This is my chance. If that shield fails tomorrow, if my mind is torn open, so be it— but don't you dare deny us this because you think you're protecting me. Don't you *dare*."

Max's fingers flexed on her wrists, but he didn't pull her forward. "What about me?" he asked, anger a vibrating thread in his voice.

She was taken aback by the question, by the glittering emotion in his eyes. "Max—"

"What the fuck do you think it'll do to me to love you, then watch as your mind breaks?" Veins stood out along his arms, as if he was having to hold himself in vicious check to keep from shaking her.

CHAPTER 32

Sophia's expression shifted from one emotion to the next with lightning speed, but Max had anticipated her, held her tight when she tried to tug herself out of his grasp.

"No," he said, "you don't get to be a coward and back away now."

Her eyes blazed with fire. "I'm not being a coward. You're right—it was selfish of me to ask this of you."

"So you'll walk away? Just put it to one corner of your Psy mind and forget we ever touched?"

A tremble of her lower lip that she tried to hide from him. "Yes. I'm Psy." Rote words, her face turned to the side. "I've learned to compartmentalize."

"Liar." And then he kissed again, unable to stop, whatever remaining barriers he had shredded by her nearness, her scent, her presence, the fucking way she was trying so hard to fight the painful depth of her need because she didn't want to hurt him.

Her mouth opened under his even as she tried to pull

away her wrists. He held her in place for a second before releasing her. Instead of pushing at him as he'd half expected, she wrapped her arms around his neck and met him stroke for stroke, lick for lick. Groaning, he bunched up the shirt she was wearing with one hand, reaching down to cup her buttocks with the other.

Sophia moaned into his mouth, and he somehow found the presence of mind to lift his head, to ask, "Is this hurting you?"

"No." Pulling him back down, she used the skills she'd just learned to drive him insane.

He felt his fingers digging into her soft flesh, made himself soften his hold. Her response was to scrape her teeth over his jaw, along his neck. His hands clenched again, his eyes flicking to the mirror at her back. The raw eroticism of the image was beyond anything he'd dared imagine. Her skin was delicately flushed, a creamy softness against his rougher, darker hands.

Realizing she'd gone still, he looked down into her face. Her lips were parted, swollen from their kisses. "Is the visual impact very intense?"

It was such a Sophia way to put it that the almost violent edge of his hunger shifted into something different, exquisitely tender. "I don't think you're quite ready for it yet," he murmured, indulging himself by stroking his hand across her lush flesh.

"Later?"

"Later." Sucking on her lower lip, he nudged her away from the mirror and toward the bed, not sure he could leash himself in the face of such delicious temptation. She didn't resist, letting him touch her as he would, lead her as he would.

It was a heady sensation, and one that paradoxically gave him more control. Nipping at her lower lip, he pulled back a little. She looked lost for an instant, until he raised his hands to the front of the shirt she wore to undo the top button. Her head dipped, watching him release button after button until the shirt hung completely undone. Lifting a hand, he touched a single finger on the dip of her breastbone, catching her attention.

Her chest rose up and down in a jagged rhythm as he ran that finger slowly down the valley of her breasts and over the softness of her abdomen to circle at her navel. Making an inarticulate sound, she gripped his biceps. "That is not an intimate region."

It took him a second. "Oh yeah?" Spreading his fingers on her, he just barely brushed the curls at the apex of her thighs.

Her fingers tightened on him, her breaths turning shallow. Leaving his hand where it was, he tugged back her head and took another kiss, but this one was slow, lazy, as he attempted to seduce her into relaxing. She responded like wildfire, but her body remained on edge, almost quivering with tension. Kissing his way along her jaw, he said, "Take off the shirt."

She went motionless, her breath hot against his neck. For a moment, he thought he'd pushed her too far, and went to back off. But she lifted her hands to the lapels of the shirt at that moment, her fingers bloodless from the force of her grip.

"No?" he asked, nuzzling at her, taking the scent of her into his lungs. "Want to stop?"

The answer was soft but immediate. "No."

"Want me to help you?"

An almost imperceptible nod.

Forcing himself to keep a stranglehold on his own hunger, he lifted his hands to close over hers. Together, they peeled apart the edges of the shirt to her shoulders. "Let go," he said against her lips.

It took several seconds, but her fingers opened. He held the shirt at her shoulders for a long moment before releasing the fabric. She could've stopped its descent using her arms, but she relaxed them and the material slid off her with the hushed grace of a lover's caress. Instead of gorging himself on the lush beauty of her, he held her close, placing his hand very carefully on her lower back, his eyes locked with hers, his mouth a whisper's breath from her own.

There was, he was glad to see, no fear in her. A little trepidation, but that, he could understand. Smiling, he kissed her again, lazy, easy, undemanding. Her mouth opened under him, but her body continued to thrum with tension. "What're you afraid of?" he finally asked, cupping her cheek with his free hand. "And don't say nothing."

A long, shuddering breath. "I just want to get it over with once—then I'll know what to expect."

Tenderness swept over him, along with a touch of chagrin. "That's not exactly the kind of thing a man wants to hear when he's trying to seduce his woman."

"*Max.*" A worried look. "I feel as if I'm stumbling in the dark. If I knew, then I could . . ."

"Control it?" A gentle tease.

Her hands fisted at his waist. "You think I should just let go."

"No," he said, sipping at her mouth between words. "Everyone's a little edgy their first time."

"So you'll—"

"How about instead of rushing it," he murmured, "we do what feels good? No expectations, no end goal."

"But I want to finish." A stubborn look.

Affectionate hunger rocked through him, at once savage and playful. "Yeah?" He couldn't help his smile. "Alright."

Her eyes widened, as if she'd read something on his face that worried her. "Max?"

But he was already swinging her up in his arms and placing her on the bed. Coming down over her, he settled himself in the vee of her thighs. "Wrap your legs around me."

"That feels . . ." Breathy, almost shocked. "Your jeans . . ."

He shifted against her delicate flesh, knowing the rough material would intensify the sensations. Giving an inarticulate cry, she arched her body. It was all the invitation he needed. Dipping his head, he took one dark little nipple into his mouth and sucked hard, even as he insinuated a hand between their bodies, reaching for the tiny bud in the liquid-soft center of her that could give so much pleasure.

Her fingers dug into his shoulders as she tried to pull him closer and push him away at the same time. Shifting his attention to her neglected breast, he began to play with her clitoris, hard then soft. *There.* He felt it the instant she reacted, modified his stroke to what brought her the most pleasure, lifting himself off her enough that he could stroke downward to rub at the sensitive entrance to her body as well.

She was wet, slick. He couldn't resist the temptation to dip his finger within. That was all it took.

A choked scream. Her body arching bowstring tight.

He could feel the edge of the pleasure that pulsed through her, wanted only to bury himself inside her, feel those muscles clench around his cock. Sweat beaded along his spine as he stroked her down from the orgasm instead.

The single thing that made it bearable was that *he'd* done this to her, to his smart, sexy, stubborn . . . and vulnerable J.

Rising to brace his palms on either side of her when she slumped onto the bed, her chest heaving, he took a kiss. Another. She gave of herself without hesitation, her body limp beneath his, her skin sheened with perspiration. "Feeling more relaxed?" he murmured.

Sophia lifted her lashes to see pure wickedness in the gorgeous bitter-chocolate eyes looking down at her. "Yes, thank you." Her own lips curved—something that felt sparkling, new, and sublime in its perfection. "Did I rush you?"

"A little, but I plan to get my revenge." Another *Max* kiss—as if he had all the time in the world to taste her. "Now, just lie back and enjoy."

Right at that moment, she couldn't have done anything else. Intellectually, she'd known about orgasms, but it was quite a different matter to have one tear through her body. "Is that what it'll be like when we have sex?"

"Yes. Exactly. So don't worry."

She thought she caught a strangled edge in those words, but Max had dipped his head to kiss his way along her collarbone and it became difficult to think. Managing to raise her arms enough to touch his back, she pulled at his T-shirt. "Will you take this off?"

He raised his head. "You okay with that much tactile contact after what we just did?"

It was tempting to say yes at once, but she took a moment to think about it. "Yes." A strange feeling in her chest, a mix of pleasure, anticipation and . . . laughter. "You're wonderfully blockheaded."

His laugh sounded startled out of him. Getting up to straddle her on his knees, he grinned. "Guess being wooden's taken on a whole new meaning around you." He stripped off his T-shirt with an economy of motion that struck her as very male. It was as he twisted to throw the T-shirt off the side of the bed that she caught it.

"Wait." Rising up on her elbows, she tried to see around to his back. "What is that?"

To her surprise, color streaked across his cheekbones. "A memento of my misspent youth."

She was even more curious now. "Show me."

Muttering under his breath, he leaned down to kiss her instead. "You can look at it later."

"But—"

His mouth swept over hers, all demand and a tightly wound hunger. *Oh,* she thought, *oh.* And that was all her mind had the capacity to think because he was pressing her down onto the bed and the skin-to-skin contact was a shocking whip of fire through her body. But rather than drawing back as she would have once, she arched toward him. *No more fear,* she thought. This was *life.* This was *Max.*

"Sophie, my sweet, sexy, Sophie." His jaw brushed over

her neck as he lowered his head to kiss her breasts, his mouth possessive in a way she'd never known she craved until this moment, until this man. Twisting under the grip he had on her rib cage—holding her in place for his maddening caresses, she felt the oh-so-intriguing outline of his erection pressing against her thigh.

"Max, please." She pushed at the sleek heat of his shoulders.

He lifted his head, his hair hanging messy and touchable across his forehead. "Sophie?"

"I want to see."

Shuddering, he let her roll him onto his back. His jaw was a brutal line, the muscles in his arms rock hard as he gripped the bars in the headboard, but he said nothing as she rose beside him, as she ran her hand down the muscled plane of his chest in sensual exploration. "Your chest is smooth." Dark gold and free of hair. "Except here." A thin line of black that began just below his belly button and arrowed inexorably downward.

Max hissed out a breath as she followed that path with her finger. Looking up at him through her lashes, she felt something a little bit sinful come to purring life deep within her soul. "I'm a very quick learner, you know."

He said a word that turned the air blue. "I'm not exactly in the mood to be teased."

"Are you sure?" Feeling an odd exhilaration in her blood, she went to the button of his jeans and found it already undone. She could see why. He was straining against the zipper. Tugging at the metal tab, she went to pull it down when Max said, "I'll do that," and reached for it.

She caught his hand, lacing her fingers through his. "Don't you trust me?"

A heated look. "You touch me and it's over."

"So we'll start again." Pressing her lips to their clasped hands, she untangled their fingers. Though he gave her a scorching look, he didn't try to halt her again when she skimmed her hands over the lean-hipped beauty of him, began to tug at the zipper. She was careful, but not hesitant.

And that was Max's gift to her. With no other man could she imagine being this open, this vulnerable.

Max's abdomen relaxed a fraction as she finished unzipping him. He was—only just—contained within his briefs. Curiosity swept over her in a wave of unashamed lust. She'd seen medical images of men, been taught about sexual organs in her health lessons, but no one had ever told her that everything would change when it was *her* man. Her fingers itched to stroke him, her heart thundering in excitement, mouth dry with anticipation.

Looking up, she saw that he'd closed his eyes, the cords of his neck strained white against the warm tone of his skin. And she knew he wouldn't stop her, no matter what she desired. Trembling with need that made her skin tight, her body slick, she gave in to the luscious molten heat uncurling in her stomach and began to kiss her way down that thin path of hair. The texture of it was surprisingly silky rough against his heated flesh, and it was instinct to stroke her hand over his skin as she tasted.

"Jesus baby." Strangled words as she lay her cheek on his abdomen and reached down to close her fingers over the stiff length of him through the black fabric of his briefs. Max's entire form went rigid . . . and it just felt exquisitely right to lick her tongue across the very edge of his briefs, to squeeze her hand firmly along the masculine heat in her hold.

"Sophie!"

Max walked out of the bathroom to find Sophia curled up under the sheets. There was a look of distinct guilt on her face. Joy warmed him up from the inside out, but he kept his expression stern. "That's twice you've rushed me." He hadn't lost control like that . . . well, ever. "Don't think I'm not going to punish you for it."

Color tinged her cheeks as he slipped in under the sheets beside her. But no matter the temptation, he didn't pull her into his arms, having noticed that she was reacting much more quickly to even the slightest touch. "It'll take a while for you to recover."

A stubborn look that faded into a sigh. "You're right. I think I've pushed it as far as my senses will take today."

"I guess it's like a person who's been starving," Max murmured. "When you start to eat again, you have to do it in small bites at first."

"Can I bite you?" A teasing question that didn't surprise him now that he'd met the wicked side of her.

"If you ask nice."

They lay together for a time, talking about nothing, and then later as they sat side by side in the living room, about the complex jigsaw that was the Nikita investigation. But eventually, she had to go to her own apartment. "I wish I could spend all night with you," she said to him as he walked her over. "But it'll be too much today."

"Next time," he said, keeping his distance as she unlocked the door and entered. "Sophia?"

She glanced back, so beautiful with those amazing eyes and that soft dark hair.

"Tell me if anything happens." His hand tightened on the doorjamb at the thought of losing her to the ferocity of her gift, of never again seeing her lying rumpled and smiling in his bed, never again hearing her talk in that prim tone that held an undertone of wild emotion.

"I will." A steady answer, but when she looked up, her eyes were bruised. "I'm so *angry*, Max," she said in harsh whisper. "How am I supposed to fight my own mind?"

CHAPTER 33

Sophia Russo may require further persuasion re the Valentine case.

—Jay Khanna to unnamed contact via e-mail

Frustrated, choked up with a rage that had nowhere to go, Max made a cup of coffee and tried to lose himself in work. Sophia had updated him on everything she'd discovered during the time he'd been tied up in the wrenching aftermath of the discovery of Gwyn Hayley's body, but now he began to read her notes in depth. She had one hell of a brain, he thought. The information was not only neatly bullet-pointed and outlined, but cross-referenced in a way that told him she had an innate understanding of how his own mind worked.

Near the end of the file, he came across something that made him frown. Knowing he needed Sophia to explain the relevance of the information in a Psy context, he began to get up—when he caught the blinking time code on the comm panel.

One a.m.

His gaze went to the wall that separated his apartment from Sophia's, and he couldn't help but remember the softness of her skin, the way her pulse had rocketed under his touch, the delicate, enticing scent of her. His body, having finally stopped riding the steel edge of need, grew hard, heavy once more. Sucking in a breath through clenched teeth, he threw down his pen and got up, intending to take a cold shower when something stopped him.

A noise.

Angling his head, he listened again. A soft thump. Once. Just once. But he'd heard.

Sophie.

He grabbed his stunner and walked quietly to the door. Activating the outside cameras, he checked that the space immediately outside his door was clear before exiting—with a vigilance all cops learned on their first day on the job. The corridor proved empty, the lighting muted to night levels. Stepping to Sophia's apartment, he scanned himself in using his palm print, his access courtesy of Sophia herself.

Worried that she'd had a blackout as a result of the previous day's events, but forcing himself to move with caution in case of an intruder, he made his way through the unlighted living area and to her bedroom.

The bed held only rumpled sheets and an organizer with a bright, glowing screen. She'd been awake, too, he thought. Whatever had happened, it hadn't taken her unawares.

Fur across his foot. *Morpheus.*

Following the cat's night-glow gaze, he felt his toes nudge something on the floor.

He froze, bent down. The feel of cotton covering warm skin. *No.* Continuing to hold his stunner at the ready, even as he checked Sophia's pulse, he said, "Lights, night mode." The lights came on, on a dim setting, making the transition from dark to light much easier. No one jumped out, the shadows hiding nothing malignant. He looked over the bathroom quickly just in case. Nothing. Whatever had happened, it had happened in Sophia's mind.

Returning, he bent down to check her for injuries, found no cuts, no abrasions. But when he lifted her eyelids, it was to see her eyes swallowed by black. "Sophie," he said again, his tone firm though an anguished rage tore through him—driven by a part of him that didn't understand logic, only a powerful, visceral need for her voice.

No response.

Sliding his arms beneath her body, he lifted her up and took her to the bed, pulling a comforter over her before his hand went to the pocket of his jeans, where he'd left his cell. Pressing in a familiar code, he said, "I need Psy help."

But the Psy who turned up a bare ten minutes later with a tall amber blond male wasn't anyone he'd expected. He recognized her of course—that distinctive red hair, those cardinal eyes. Faith NightStar was said to be the strongest F-Psy in or out of the Net, her ability to see the future a gift and a curse both. But Max knew he'd always see it as a gift after the way she'd saved their lives. "Thanks for coming."

As Faith hurried past and unerringly to the bedroom, Max paused long enough to say, "You got here quick."

"Faith," the changeling male said, "woke me up an hour ago and told me we'd be needed in the city around now."

Max, walking back to the bedroom, stopped for an instant. "I guess I never thought about the reality of being mated to an F-Psy."

Vaughn slapped him on the back. "Ask me sometime about how fucking difficult it is to surprise her with a gift." It was said with affection, his tone that of a man who wasn't only delighted in his mate, but didn't care if the whole world knew about it.

They entered the bedroom at that moment, and everything else faded. Faith was sitting beside Sophia's stiff form, her hand on his J's forehead. "Her telepathic shields are terrifyingly thin, but they *are* continuing to protect her," Faith said, before pausing for almost ten seconds. "Her PsyNet shields appear fine. A little unusual according to my contact, but not damaged."

Max didn't ask about Faith's contact, taking it as a given

that that contact would soon be dead if it became known he or she was sharing information outside the Net. "Do we need to get her to a hospital?"

The foreseer's endless eyes met his. "No. She'll wake up soon."

A simple, absolute answer, and yet . . . "What aren't you telling me?"

"There'll be time after she wakes." Faith looked up at her mate as he came to stand beside her, his fingers playing through her hair. "Coffee?" she asked.

Vaughn's smile was indulgent. "Addict."

"Your fault." The foreseer's expression was somber, belying her light words. "We'll need to talk once she wakes."

Smile fading into an expression of intense tenderness, Vaughn untangled his fingers from his mate's hair and went to exit the room. "Come on, Max. You can't do anything here."

"I'll stay." No way in hell was he leaving his Sophie alone.

Faith seemed to struggle with something as she rose to her feet. But in the end, she followed Vaughn out in silence.

Faith walked straight to where Vaughn was measuring out coffee grounds. "Hey." Putting an arm around her, he hugged her to the solid strength of his side. "The answer's no."

She rubbed her face against his chest as he turned to embrace her fully, loving the scent of him. "How did you know what I was going to ask?"

"We *have* been mated over a year. Give the cat a little credit." A teasing kiss from her jaguar, his hand curving around her throat in gentle possession.

"You said it yourself, Faith." A quiet reminder, the jaguar looking out of his eyes. "The future isn't fixed. It wasn't for Dorian."

"Yes." She'd seen the sentinel's future blacked out, had

thought it meant death, but he'd survived. "It's different this time, Vaughn."

"How?"

"I saw bits and pieces of reality—the fact that Sophia would need us for some reason tonight, other events that may or may not happen, but I *felt* this gathering wave. I can't describe it, but I know something huge is about to happen, and it's centered around Sophia Russo."

"You're talking about more than the life of one person . . . two people," he added, and she knew he'd seen the way Max looked at Sophia. So had she.

Her foreseer's heart hurt for them, for the future they didn't have. "I've never felt anything like this, but from the research I've been doing"—using the records her father had managed to unearth then smuggle out to her—"F-Psy in the past noted the same kinds of sensations before major catastrophic events."

Vaughn cupped her face, an areola of pure gold around his irises, the jaguar rising to the surface. "Are you talking earthquake, plague, political turmoil?"

"Any, all," she whispered. "But whatever it is, Sophia Russo is the domino that will begin an unstoppable cascade." The J was the leading edge of a perfect storm, one that might annihilate them all.

"Max?"

"It's as if he simply doesn't exist in Sophia's future," Faith said, tugging at the tie that held back her mate's hair. It fell over her hands in a stroke of rough silk, a familiar anchor. "But I don't get that same sense of blankness as I did with Dorian. Instead, it's this feeling that he's never been a part of her life. Which is impossible."

Vaughn stilled. "Not if the Sophia you see is Sophia after rehabilitation."

Faith shook her head in stunned horror, but he was right. Full rehabilitation wiped out the psyche, creating a slate so blank that nothing of the mind, the soul, remained.

*   *   *

Max argued with himself about whether or not to touch Sophia, knowing it had to have been their sexual play that had caused this, but driven by gut instinct, he got on the bed and cradled her in his lap. And the instant he did, it felt right. She was a soft, warm weight on him, her breathing easy, her heartbeat steady. Something wild and panicked inside him settled.

She hadn't left him, this J who'd become the fulcrum of his universe.

A quiet sound, so quiet he hardly heard it. Shifting his hold, he pushed midnight strands of hair off her face, keeping his hand on her cheek. "Sophie?"

A hitched breath, eyes fluttering open. They remained drowned in black, endless and mysterious. "Wh—" A gasp, her hand flying up to close over his.

His soul went cold. Driven by primal need, had he made a fatal error? If he had, the shock would plunge her back into unconsciousness . . . or worse. But before he could break contact, she gripped his hand, tight, so tight. And as he watched, the liquid black began to recede from her eyes, until finally, only the violet of her iris, the normal black of her pupil was visible. "Max?"

He tried to catch her gaze, but it kept shifting. "Focus, Sophie. Focus." Her disorientation worried him, could well be a signal of some kind of brain damage.

All at once her eyes locked to his. "Name's not Sophie."

"No? What is it?"

The most minute of pauses. "Sophia Russo." It almost sounded like relief. "Sophia Russo," she repeated, "Gradient 8.85 J-Psy, employed by the Justice Corps, temporarily attached to the office of Councilor Nikita Duncan."

"Good." Relief washed through him as well. "And who am I?"

"Max Shannon, Enforcement detective, highest clearance rate in New York, natural mental shield, and . . . and hands that touch me." Her own hand spasmed around his, as if she'd only just become aware of how hard she'd been holding on.

"Shh." Taking that hand in his, he pressed a kiss to her palm. "You're okay." His heart shuddered though he fought to keep his voice calm.

"Max, you can call me Sophie," she said in a quickness of words, as if afraid he'd take her earlier statement the wrong way.

"I plan to do it for a long time." He'd lost everything else and survived, but he couldn't lose her, not his J. It would break him.

Intertwining her fingers with his, she turned her head a little. "Someone else is here. I can hear sounds."

"Faith NightStar and her mate, Vaughn D'Angelo."

"Faith, foreseer." She dropped her gaze to their hands. "What happened?"

Faith and Vaughn walked back in at that moment, with four mugs of coffee in hand. "We were hoping you could tell us," Faith said, placing two of the mugs on the bedside table.

Sophia looked up but didn't move off Max's lap, which told him more about her condition than anything else. Because his Sophie had a quiet reserve about her in public, or when they were around others, one that he'd come to realize was part of her nature, not a product of Silence. She'd never be comfortable with open displays of emotion—but that was fine with Max, because with him, she lowered her guard, gave him her trust.

Breaking their handclasp, he picked up one of the mugs and urged it into her hands. "Drink."

She took an obedient sip, her eyes not on Faith, but on Vaughn. Max felt a sharp tug of irritation. He recalled hearing that Vaughn wasn't a leopard, but the male was a cat of some kind. He had the same feline grace that Max had seen in Lucas, in Dorian. And Max had been in the world long enough to know that women were drawn to the cat changelings.

Sophia's eyes didn't move off Vaughn even when the cat stretched out his arm on the sofa behind Faith's head, curving his hand around his mate's nape in a blatant display—and statement—of his loyalty. It was Faith who broke the odd silence. "If you don't stop looking at my mate that way, I might have to unsheathe my claws." Her smile took any sting out of what was clearly a tease.

But Sophia didn't laugh. Keeping her eyes on Vaughn, she spoke to Faith. "He's not safe, you know. He could snap your neck with a single move. You should shift away from him."

Delighted at the reason she'd been staring, Max fought not to laugh. But the look of affront on Vaughn's face was priceless. Burying his own face in Sophia's hair to muffle his laugh, he tugged her a little closer, just in case the changeling was annoyed enough to snarl at her. But Faith put a hand on her mate's thigh, and cardinal eyes gleaming with laughter, nodded at Sophia. "I wouldn't throw stones. Look where you're sitting."

Sophia belatedly seemed to realize her position. Color tinged her cheeks, but she didn't move. *That's my girl.* Running a hand over her hair, Max asked her if she knew the reason she'd fallen unconscious.

"Yes." She cuddled impossibly closer to him. "An attempted hack into my brain."

CHAPTER 34

Max sucked in a breath, but it was Faith who next spoke. "That should be impossible. I know some F-designation men and women who see only the past, and they work for Justice—their shields are impenetrable. I assume Js are the same."

"Yes, we are," Sophia said, giving him the coffee so he could place it on the nightstand. "But the attempt was intense enough to cause near-unbearable pressure on my brain." Her body trembled just a little, but Max felt it.

Placing her on the bed with all the tenderness he had in him, he swung his legs over the side and said, "We can discuss this more later. Right now, Sophia needs to get some rest."

"Yes, of course." Faith stood up at once. Vaughn followed a little more slowly.

Walking them to the door, Max was ready for the DarkRiver sentinel's final words. "She's still hooked into the Net, Max. Means she can't be trusted."

He felt his hand clench on the door. "So was Faith when you met her if I'm right."

"Not the same situation, and you know it." The changeling didn't sound angry—if anything, there was a gut-deep understanding in his tone. "Faith was watched, but in an isolated setting. Sophia is in the middle of the Justice Corps. There are all kinds of eyes on her."

And though the sentinel didn't say it, Max knew the implications—Sophia might already have something in her head, something that *had* penetrated her shields without her knowledge.

Having changed into a loose T-shirt to sleep in, Sophia returned from the bathroom to find Max waiting by the bed. He looked strong and beautiful . . . and remote, the stunner he held loosely by his side a stark reminder of who he was, what he did.

"Stay with me." It came out without thought, the heat of his body still imprinted on her skin. "I think I can handle the sensations now." The invitation took all the courage she had. She bit her lip to quiet the plea that wanted to escape. She didn't want him to pity her—but oh, how she needed him.

No words but he placed the stunner on the bedside table and ripped off his T-shirt. She clenched her hands on the bottom of her own. Angling his head, he tugged down the comforter and waited for her to get in. As he went to follow, his jeans still on, she had a thought. "Max, what if I'm compromised in some way? You shouldn't leave a weapon that accessible to me."

"Safety's on, release programmed to my active thumbprint," he said, pulling the comforter over them. "And no offense, Sophie, sweetheart, but you'd make a very bad assassin."

"I could blow out your mind," she reminded him.

"Not easily," he answered. "According to what I've picked up over the years, a natural shield means I'd have enough of a warning to go for my weapon, or considering the fact that you're a little bit of nothing—knock you out cold." The words made him scowl.

"Good." Relieved—in spite of the fact that she could see he hated the idea of hurting her—she let him slide an arm under her head, the other going around her waist. That much sensation, that much contact, still burned a hot, wild flame across her skin, but she was, she thought, becoming used to it. With Max it wasn't an intrusion but a choice on her part. Turning, she placed her hands flat on his chest.

Heat. A sudden fever. Almost pain.

"But no voices in my head," she whispered. "No memories, no thoughts, no yesterdays but my own."

Max squeezed her gently, and she knew he understood. "Don't push it," he said. "Small bites, remember?"

She didn't listen, lost in the storm of sensation, the world a kaleidoscope around her. "We never finished."

Max's hand stopped its soothing strokes over her back. "You're not exactly in any shape—"

Tilting her head, she kissed the line of his neck, taking the taste of him into her lungs. *"Sophie."* Then his hand was on her cheek and she was being turned onto her back and he was kissing the breath out of her. The kaleidoscope spun and spun until it exploded.

As the pieces rained around her, she found herself gripping Max's shoulders in an attempt to hold on. His muscles shifted beneath her palms, liquid and powerful. Instead of trying to control the amount of sensory input, she gave in, drowning in the wild heat of him, the delicious pressure of his lips, the way his thumb pressed down on her jaw to open her mouth to him.

Max felt the instant Sophia let go. Her entire body melted for him, every inch of her open in invitation.

It was the most luscious of temptations.

But he wasn't about to take advantage of her when she'd been disoriented and lost only minutes ago. Breaking the kiss, he looked into eyes that had gone pure black again—but he could distinguish a difference, though he'd have been hard-pressed to describe it. He just knew this time, it wasn't a marker of danger. "Do all Psy eyes do that?" An intimate murmur against her lips, his legs tangled with hers, his hand in her hair.

Her fingers stroked over his shoulders with quick, hungry movements, and he was male enough to adore her for being so very delighted with him. "It's more apparent at the higher end of the spectrum . . . but I think I may be even more susceptible to it, given the nature of my mind." Calm words, but her eyes, her body, told a different story.

He could almost feel the vibrating tension in her, every tendon held taut. "I know who you are," he said, holding her gaze. "I'm not going to be scared away because of your 'imperfections.' "

A sheen of wet in her eyes, turning the midnight iridescent.

"We fit, you and I," he whispered looking into that haunting gaze. "Two broken pieces making a whole." It wasn't the most romantic of statements, but it was torn from his soul. "I am not losing you."

She tugged him down, kissing him until his body hummed for her, until her breath came in choppy gasps. He broke the kiss. "Is this much contact causing you pain?"

A pause. "No."

Swearing, he rolled off to sit on the edge of the bed, looking back at her over his shoulder. "Why the hell did you—"

"I wasn't lying, Max." Curling onto her side, she watched him with an intense interest that told him he was the absolute and utter focus of her world. Some men would've been scared away. Max knew he watched her the same way.

Her chest rose as she took a long, shuddering breath. "I don't know how to describe these sensations. The closest word is pain, but I know that's not right. I don't crave pain. And yet I crave what happens when you touch me."

Max twisted so he could face her, one hand braced

palm down beside her leg. "It sounds like your nerves are raw—overloaded."

"Maybe." Clear words, a steel will. "But I don't want to slow down."

He had a will as strong. "No more touching. I will *not* hurt you."

Her shoulders slumped.

Sensing his advantage, he pushed. "Why did someone try to hack your mind tonight?"

"Probably because they wanted to contaminate the evidence I'm due to give in a high-profile murder case," she said, her eyes not meeting his.

Shame, he thought, that's what he read in her expression. "Sophie?"

"I'll tell you . . . just give me a little more time?" So vulnerable, her emotions stripped bare. "Please, Max?"

He blew out a breath. "I'm starting to think you're using the world 'please' to get around me."

A startled flicker of light in her eyes. "No, I'm not . . . but could I?"

He felt his chest shake with unbidden, unexpected laughter. "Do you think I'm going to answer that?"

"That means I can." She sounded astonished and delighted in equal measures. "I promise to use my powers for good."

Reaching over he slapped her lightly on the bottom through the comforter. "You have the makings of a brat in you."

A slow, so-slow smile, his Sophie beginning to wake from a decades-long sleep. "I need to tell you something about the Nikita investigation that I forgot to mention earlier."

He kept his hand on her hip, enjoying the warm curves of her even if he couldn't touch skin. "I meant to ask you something, too. About Ryan—"

"That's who I wanted to discuss," she interrupted, "specifically, the reason for his reconditioning six months ago."

Max frowned. "The file's sealed." He'd already tried to access it tonight.

"I called in a favor from another J." Pushing up into a sitting position, she shivered when he slid his hand over to her thigh. "Ryan killed someone, but it was an accident. His telekinetic powers went out of control."

Stroking her through the comforter once more, Max got up to walk to the window and back. "How much would the reconditioning have messed with his head?"

"No way to know—the process is intense, but it leaves the mind intact. That's the whole purpose—to eliminate fractures so the individual can function." Her words held the knowledge of experience. "It would make sense that he'd be sympathetic to Pure Psy if his own abilities are spiraling out of control."

"But"—Max folded his arms, leaning back on the wall beside the window—"we come back to the fact that he wasn't working for Nikita at the time of the elevator sabotage. One mole I can accept. Two? No. Not in Nikita's organization."

"He's still the best lead we've got."

Max straightened. "And he won't be going anywhere tonight. I'll call, make sure security has him in their sights. We can talk to him tomorrow."

She knew he was going to leave. Sliding down under the comforter, she turned her back to him. She'd accepted his will, but that didn't mean she had to like it.

"Sophie."

She thumped her pillow into shape.

A low blue word, then the bed dipped. "I can't stay tonight, baby." His hand on her hip, a blaze of heat even through the comforter.

He'd promised to fight for her. Well, she was going to fight for him, too. "We don't have to be skin to skin." She turned to face him, keeping her hands to herself. "You can sleep on top of the comforter." Then she gave a small smile. "Please?"

"You've definitely got the makings of a brat." But Max

stayed, sleeping beside his J for the hours till dawn. The dream came just before he woke, a dream in which River ran laughing behind him as they chased a stray dog they'd made into a pet.

He opened his eyes to find his throat thick with tears, his heart a swelling ache in his chest. And he knew he'd dreamed the joy because of the woman who woke a moment later. "Thank you," he said.

Sleepy eyes, dark curls falling across one cheek. "For what?"

"For making me remember." He'd buried his past because it hurt too fucking much. But in doing so, he'd buried River. "I think," he said, "you would've adored River. He could've taught you every trick in the book on how to be a true brat." Then, as they rose, dressed, and ate, he told her about the brother who'd left a mile-wide scar on his heart.

Sophia halted Max when he would've gotten out of the car at the Duncan building. "I want to tell you about the reason for the hack." She couldn't hide anymore, not after the raw honesty of the memories he'd shared, of the *family* he'd shared. Her heart was so full it was hard to breathe, hard to speak.

"Whatever it is," Max said, his hand along the back of her seat, "you know it doesn't matter. Not between us."

"I can alter memories." She made no effort to dress it up.

"I know."

She jerked up her head. "What?"

"I'm a cop, Sophie." A wry reminder. "I hadn't been in the job two years before I realized what Js could do."

"Then why don't you hate us?"

"I always figured you had no choice in the matter. And, I did my job. I got the evidence. Not every major case is won or lost on the evidence of a J."

She should've ended it then, but now that she'd begun, she couldn't stop. She would not steal his affection, his loyalty, through fraud. It would violate the trust between them, taint everything they had. So though the terror of rejection was a chill hand around her throat, she smoothed her flawlessly straight skirt down her legs and said, "Do you remember Dr. Henley?" The famous geneticist had killed his pregnant wife in cold blood, then sliced her up into neat little pieces and dumped those pieces in the sea when he'd gone out for a Sunday fishing trip. There was even speculation that he'd used some pieces as bait.

"Not a case I could ever forget."

"The Council planned to transfer him to a Psy facility where he could continue his groundbreaking work." The callous murder of an innocent woman and her unborn child had been considered a mere inconvenience. "All the Js knew."

"Pity then," Max said in a hard voice, "that he had a sudden, violent embolism that stopped his heart on his first day in prison, died before the medics could get to him."

Sophia sucked in a breath. She'd guessed he understood what Js were capable of, had wanted to drive home the point so that there would be absolute honesty between them, but from the way he spoke . . . "Have you always known?"

"Cops call it the J-penalty." A grim look. "You weren't in the vicinity. I've seen your record. You weren't anywhere near Henley's prison when he died."

"No." Then, "Not me. Not that time."

He slid back his door. "Come on."

She got out to walk beside him, her heart a tight, hopeful knot. "I know you've accepted me"—and that remained a deep source of wonder—"but I still thought you'd be more . . ."

"Hard-assed?" A snort. "I've seen rich men skate off rape charges, politicians bury abuse claims, young girls commit suicide after being hurt. I don't agree with vigilante justice, but Js aren't exactly vigilantes are they? They know the exact nature of a particular crime, and they tend to give out punishments perfectly calibrated to that crime—and only in cases where justice would otherwise be defiled."

"We aren't judge and jury." She'd never talked openly about this. Even among Js, it wasn't ever actually discussed. But they all knew the parameters, understood what the Corps would overlook as the cost of having Js in the system. "We're the last resort when the tools of justice fail the victims."

"What," Max said, coming to a stop in front of the elevators, his body angled to hide her from the surveillance cameras, "is the impact on a J who acts as that last resort . . . as an executioner if necessary."

"'Every action has an opposite and equal reaction,'" she said, quoting the well-known law of physics. "That maxim holds true on the psychic plane."

White lines bracketed Max's mouth. "So a J would be damaged by the event?"

"Not exactly damaged. I would say . . . changed."

A long, still pause. "You can't do it anymore," he finally said very, very quietly. "Do you understand me, Sophia?"

Her lips quivered for the barest fraction of a moment. "Max, are you trying to fix me?" It was impossible, and she couldn't bear for him to realize that too late, walk away.

"No. I'm trying to save you." An implacable, absolute answer. "It's about choices. I need you to make one to fight those instincts—every time you give in, it eats away a little bit of your psyche."

The otherness in her—twined with those dark threads that tasted of the Net—stirred, considered, bowed its head. "I can do that." For Max, only for Max. He was a cop. He'd accepted her past with open eyes and an open heart, but what she did from now on, even if only a few individuals realized the depth of the connection between them, would reflect on him, stain his career—and she was too proud of him to chance that. "It's a small price to pay to be with you."

"No price, Sophie, no ultimatums." An unqualified reassurance that made her want to pull him forward by the lapels of his suit jacket and kiss him again and again. "You belong to me—and I'm keeping you no matter what."

"That means you belong to me, too." It came from the dark heart of her, the place where no light had ever shone . . . until this man looked at her with eyes that said she wasn't a piece of trash to be discarded because she'd proved imperfect. For the first time in her life, she had started to feel whole, the scars, the fractures, simply a part of her.

Max shrugged, that lean dimple flashing in his cheek. "I'm not arguing."

"So," she said, everything in her—even the once scared, lonely girl who'd only ever spoken through the hand of cold justice before—determined to stake its claim loud and clear, "if I find a business card from a female in your jacket, she had better be a colleague."

Max felt a laugh build in his chest, had to fight the urge to tug Sophia into his arms and bite down on that full lower lip in a gesture of open possession. "No one will dare hit on me after I mention my wife is a J with a jealous streak."

Wife. Her composure splintered. "Max, no matter what, we could never—"

"I told you, Sophie. You're mine. End of story."

CHAPTER 35

In certain types of cases, most cops immediately suspect the
father. Nobody thinks of the mother, not at first. Except me.
And I wish I didn't.

—*From the private case notes of Detective Max Shannon*

Ryan Asquith entered the conference room looking as
unruffled as ever, but that, of course, was de rigueur for the
Psy. Max didn't say anything for several long seconds after
the intern arrived. Taking her cue from him, neither did
Sophia. Finally, Ryan glanced at his watch. "Am I early,
Detective?"

"You didn't tell us you'd undergone reconditioning,"
Max said, instead of answering his question.

The young male didn't so much as blink. "Everything
is in my file."

"And you didn't think to mention the fact that you'd
killed using Tk when we're investigating a murder that
may have had a Tk component?"

Ryan's eyes skated away from Max's. "I assumed you
already knew. The personnel department did a full screen
on me when I applied for this position."

"Interesting thing is," Max murmured, "seems the department just does a basic screen for short-term interns."

Sophia put her organizer on the table. "The detective doesn't understand, Ryan," she said in a quiet, calm tone.

"Oh?" Max raised an eyebrow.

"Those of us who go through a reconditioning," Sophia answered, "aren't considered criminals for any acts committed during the period of fracture, because there is no intent."

Ryan nodded, holding Sophia's gaze. "Exactly. I knew if I told you of the incident, you would focus on me, leaving the true murderer to go free."

"But you can see," Sophia said, "how this places you in the center of the investigation."

Ryan glanced down, then up, saying nothing.

Sophia tapped Max's foot at almost the same instant. Getting the hint, he rose to his feet. "I'm going to grab a bottle of water from outside while Ryan gets his thoughts in order. Sophia?"

"Thank you, some water would be great."

Watching the door close behind her cop, Sophia turned her attention to the boy in front of her. And he was just that, only a boy. A boy, who, somewhere deep inside, was terrified of his own abilities. "Tell me what you were hesitating to say in front of Detective Shannon."

"Will you keep it confidential?"

Right then, Sophia saw something in Ryan's eyes that she'd never expected. "As long as it doesn't affect Councilor Duncan's safety, it won't go beyond these walls."

"At the time of Edward Chan's murder, I'd locked myself in one of the meeting rooms that almost no one uses because I needed to meditate."

"Do you continue to have trouble with your Silence?"

"Yes."

It was a confession that could have this boy sent back to the Center, which made Sophia more inclined to believe him. "Why did you tell me?"

Dark gray eyes locked with her own. "You're a J. I

thought if anyone would understand the pressure, you would."

Sophia wondered if she was being played very skillfully. "Which meeting room?"

Ryan gave her the details without hesitation. "And I'm not strong enough to teleport," he said, confirming what they'd already determined. "That's never been in my skill set."

"Thank you."

Ryan opened his mouth, paused, then said, "Nobody really pays attention to an intern."

"What have you heard?"

"There are rumors in the city that Nikita is as flawed as her daughter." Ryan's tone dropped. "I thought, at first, that it was just uninformed talk, but the whispers are gathering in momentum—and that kind of thing doesn't happen without something, some*one*, feeding the fire."

"Do you have any idea of who it could be?"

"Not Marsha," Ryan responded. "She has no genetic offspring. I believe she has given all her loyalty to the Councilor. I can't narrow it any further."

The door opened then and Max walked in. Sophia said, "Keep your ears and eyes open, Ryan. Let me know if you hear anything."

"I will." Rising, he glanced at Max, his expression opaque, his dress faultless—the perfect Psy . . . on the surface. "Do you have any further questions for me, Detective?"

He left as soon as Max shook his head. "I believe him," Sophia said after filling Max in. "I think he applied to work for Nikita because of Sascha."

Max tipped back his chair. "Explain."

"It's obvious his reconditioning didn't work as well as everyone believes." Reaching out almost automatically, she pushed his chair back on all four feet. "I think he's hoping that since Nikita has a daughter who feels emotion, she'll go easier on him if the truth comes out."

"Nikita's got a heart of fucking stone and I'm being cruel to the stone there."

Sophia had heard whispers of how Nikita had ascended to the Council—her sheer cold-blooded nature couldn't be doubted. "Yes."

"I hear a 'but.'"

"She allowed her daughter to grow to adulthood, when it would've been far easier for Sascha to have had a fatal 'accident' in childhood," Sophia said, knowing he understood what she didn't say, the parallels she'd drawn. "And in the end, the reality matters less than the perception. Ryan wants to find something, someone who'll be on his side."

"I get why he'd latch on to her," Max said, "but if Nikita's the best he can do, the kid's in serious trouble." He tapped the two printouts he'd just put on the table. "We take Ryan and Marsha out—I'm with the kid on her loyalty, plus Sascha confirmed they were together when Chan died—and we're left with Andre Tulane and Quentin Gareth." Tiny lines fanned out from the corners of his eyes. "I've got a couple of things I want to check where those two are concerned."

"Including Tulane's mysterious weekly appointments?"

Max nodded. "He's been very careful not to raise any red flags. Could be a case of hiding in plain sight." It would, Max thought, require balls of steel to pull that off in Nikita's territory.

"If you don't need me," Sophia said, her lips lush and distracting, "I want to go back to the apartment and look through the PsyNet. I have a few ideas."

He frowned. "I don't know much about the PsyNet, but what I do know tells me it'll put a huge amount of pressure on you to be surrounded by so much data, so many minds."

"My PsyNet shields appear to be adapting to my increasing . . . need," she said, and he heard the thread of confusion in her tone, "so that shouldn't be an issue."

"I don't like it." His protective instincts burned a hot white flame. "You'll be alone if something happens."

That gave her pause. "There is a risk, but—"

"Faith," Max interrupted, recalling the almost protective way the F-Psy had looked at Sophia. "Call her. Ask if she'll spot you while you go diving through the Net."

"She's a cardinal F-Psy," Sophia said. "Her time is worth hundreds of thousands, if not millions, of dollars. Why should she agree to waste it on me?"

Max saw that she truly didn't understand. "Because DarkRiver's come to consider me a friend." And the cats understood—even if they didn't exactly approve—that Sophia was his. Plus—"You got the message to Nikita when Sascha was threatened. Changelings don't forget things like that." He saw her absorb that, give a small nod.

"I'll call her—but doesn't the fact that Faith saved our lives cancel out any obligation on their part?"

"It's not obligation. It's about building bonds." Placing his hand on the back of her chair, he met her gaze, the luxuriant softness of her hair brushing his skin. "Promise me you'll be careful. I don't want you bleeding out because you've been taking risks."

Her expression never changed, but he could see steam coming out her ears. "I am not stupid, Detective Shannon. Kindly get that thought into your head."

He wanted to kiss her.

Kaleb walked into Nikita's office to find her just ending a conversation with a tall male of mixed ethnicity who didn't move like a changeling but a human. Kaleb knew who the male was, of course. He'd known all about Max Shannon almost the instant after Nikita requested him. The Enforcement detective wasn't only good at his job, he was as tenacious and stubborn as a bloodhound.

"Councilor Krychek," the detective said with a small nod as he walked out of the room, closing the door behind himself.

"What do you need with an Enforcement agent?" he asked Nikita as he took a seat in the chair across from her. "We have Arrows for a reason."

"The Arrows are Ming's," she said. "I needed an impartial party."

Kaleb thought of the continued attempts to hack his shields, the sense of being very closely observed—and the failed tries to track him through the PsyNet when he didn't want to be tracked. He could have ended the game days ago, turning the tables on his trackers—though, given their skill, it would've taken a concentrated amount of time and effort—but he was intrigued enough to let it continue. Because there was one group and one group alone in the Net with the covert skills to evade the traps he'd laid to date—and if that group had decided to shift its allegiance . . .

"You're hemorrhaging people," he said to Nikita, keeping his other thoughts to himself.

"The fact that you've noticed puts you at the top of the suspect list."

"On the contrary. We both know that I do what needs to be done myself. I don't need to rely on others who might make mistakes."

Nikita settled back in her chair at his plain speaking. "Have you noticed something in Henry's pattern of behavior?"

Kaleb hadn't, and being out of the loop was not something he appreciated. "Tell me."

"I'd rather show you." Turning her chair toward the thin comm screen mounted on one wall, she darkened her windows and brought up a map of the world. "The red dots indicate the places where Henry has been in the past six months. The blue dots indicate incidents that took place at the same time."

There were clusters of blue around every single red dot.

"Incidents have been increasing," Kaleb said. "It's not impossible that he could have coincidentally been at the same locations—but I'm assuming the incidents were major enough to have caught your notice."

"Not the first five or so, no," Nikita said. "As you say, there have been little outbursts of violence here and there, so I paid them no notice. But these incidents don't involve violence—except of the self-inflicted kind."

"Suicides?" That pricked his interest. Suicide wasn't considered taboo in Psy culture. The majority of those who recognized their mental patterns as aberrant chose to end their existence rather than face rehabilitation. But the chances of the suicides—ten or more in each location—lining up so neatly with Henry's travels was exceptionally low.

"I'm certain he's used the tactic before," Nikita said.

Kaleb agreed. There'd been a string of violent incidents several months ago, with Psy breaking conditioning in public. All of those Psy appeared to have been programmed to suicide after completing their task, or if caught. "His recent behavior does, however, suggest that he's seen the error of that line of thinking." Given the way the PsyNet functioned, violence only spawned more violence. A constant feedback loop.

Nikita put down the remote but didn't erase the image. "Several of the individuals who suicided were on the rehabilitation watchlist. The others could've been fragmenting."

"So Henry could see it as removing violence from the Net." Kaleb considered the idea. "Can you send me the full data on the suicides?" The file was telepathed into his mind an instant later.

Nikita checked messages on her organizer as he went through the list.

"He eliminated an erratic but highly intelligent chemist," Kaleb said, "two medical specialists, and at least one trained sharpshooter. And that's at first glance."

"It continues like that," Nikita told him. "He might see it as erasing the weak from the Net, but he's also shoving the balance toward mediocrity."

Kaleb looked at her. "Or perhaps Henry hasn't yet given up on the idea of a fully coherent Net." Before her defection, Council scientist Ashaya Aleine had been close to developing a neural implant that would've instituted Silence at the biological level, creating a true hive mind. She'd destroyed all the pertinent data when she'd defected, but that knowledge could've been recreated. "He may be pruning those he thinks will prove a challenge to that goal."

"In that case, I suggest you be careful."

Kaleb turned away from the screen as she flicked it off. Her windows cleared a moment later. "I appreciate the information—we'll have to consider how to proceed with this. But I wanted to speak to you about another matter."

Nikita waited in pristine silence.

"I've discovered some rather interesting facts about E-Psy." Facts that could turn Nikita's "failure" into an asset.

Nikita put aside her organizer. "Really?"

CHAPTER 36

You make me feel strong, make me feel as if I can fight fate
itself. If you're reading this letter, I failed. But be proud of me
Max—I tried *so* hard.

*—Sophia Russo in an encrypted and time-coded letter to
be sent to Max Shannon after her death*

Sophia wasn't used to having anyone but Max in her
living space. Faith NightStar wasn't anywhere near as
physically imposing as Max, but she had a presence. Then
there was the long-limbed female who'd accompanied her.
"Sophia," Faith said. "This is Desiree."

Recognizing Desiree for what she was—a bodyguard—
Sophia told her guests to make themselves comfortable in
the living area before she walked into the bedroom and
took a cross-legged position in the middle of the bed.
Surfing the Net didn't require much preparation for most
people, but the more centered she was, the less chance of
an accidental breach. Because even in the Net, there were
individuals with weak or useless shields. Their thoughts
leaked out in a constant barrage.

A Sensitive could easily get caught in the psychic
storm.

But Sophia had no intention of being thrown up against
the rocks.

Narrowing her thoughts to a fine, fine point, she took a careful step into the dark skies of the PsyNet and dropped her highly effective automatic firewalls, wrapping herself in much more mundane ones instead—so she could go where she needed to go without being noticed. There was an element of risk to her choice. If any of her fragmentation . . . her feelings, leaked out, she'd be hunted down in minutes. And once they found her, rehabilitation would follow so fast, she'd have no chance of escape. "So I'll be very careful," she muttered, and went to merge into the slipstream of the Net.

Except her shields reset to the distinctive new formation without warning. And no matter how many times she tried, they wouldn't remain ordinary, unremarkable. "I need you to behave," she finally muttered aloud in frustration. "I might as well be wearing a target on my back if I go out like this."

Her shields turned the exact velvet black of the Net, making her effectively invisible.

Sophia swallowed on the physical plane. "Oh . . . that'll work."

No response, but she had the impression that something was watching, listening. It should've disconcerted her, and it did to an extent. But whatever that something was, it was also protecting her. And she wasn't about to reject it . . . not when the otherness in her, the broken girl who'd finally become an integrated part of her after two long decades, recognized the pain in that entity, as if it expected to be kicked aside, to be shoved into a corner, to be forgotten. *I accept*, Sophia thought deep in her mind. *Thank you.*

No response, but her shields seem to strengthen even further as she slipped into the Net—sleek, dark, impenetrable. The psychic network around her was the biggest data archive in the world, its information highways updated every second of every day by uploads from the millions of minds jacked into its psychic fabric, but as a J in possession of often confidential information, Sophia was trained to be far more careful about what she shared. The majority of the time, the only things she uploaded were the official, court-approved results of her cases.

But it wasn't just purposefully uploaded data that filled the Net. There were fragments of thought, images, things that had escaped as a result of inadequate or fragmented shielding, conversations that had taken place in the Net outside of a mental vault. Things did decay after a period of time—but that period could never be predicted. She'd once caught whispers that had mentioned events of a hundred-years past. Other comments decayed almost as soon as they were spoken.

You could spend an eternity surfing the slipstream. However, as a young intern, Sophia had been taught to search using highly refined filters—she'd worked for a prosecutor one summer, a judge another, tracking down specific pieces of data. Now, she used those same skills to search for any mention of Pure Psy.

A significant number of hits.

Rumors mostly, as Pure Psy didn't officially exist. And yet almost everyone in the Net knew about them. It was a very effective technique, Sophia was forced to admit. Those in agreement with Pure Psy's worldview made the effort to find them. On the flip side, those who didn't share that view tended to dismiss the group as nothing but a small fringe element.

As she drilled down layer by layer, sorting through massive amounts of data, she began to glimpse the full extent of the group's insidious growth. Pure Psy was whispered of in French, Malayalam, Russian, Maori, Tongan, Greek, Swahili, Urdu, and a number of other languages she couldn't immediately identify. Saving as much of the data as she could for future translation, she focused on the pieces she could understand.

. . . good of the race.
Pure Psy have the right . . .

Outside Council control . . .
. . . backing. Definitely Council backed.
I don't see the validity in closing the Net.
They've been behind the Jax cleanups . . .

That last whisper caught Sophia's interest. Jax was the scourge of the Psy, a drug that many said broke conditioning on the most basic level, allowing the user to feel emotion. True or not, it was a cancer no one had been able to excise from the population. But, Sophia thought, she *had* noticed a decrease in the number of addicts on the streets of late—and she hadn't seen any at all since coming to San Francisco.

Of course, that could be as a result of the heavy changeling presence in the city. Jax users tended to stick to more Psy-friendly locations.

My family is still discussing the matter.
. . . good of the Psy. It'll bring us back into . . .
The changelings and humans are irrelevant. It's only the
PsyNet that matters.

That last summed up the tenor of the more clandestine discussions, and of Pure Psy. The group was intent on an isolationist policy. It believed the PsyNet had been corrupted by outside influences and was bent on bringing all Psy back into the fold.

Whether they wanted to come or not.

Having managed to get his hands on the nav file from Andre Tulane's personal vehicle—thanks to some discreet help from the Duncan Corporation's head mechanic—Max was on his way to where the slender black male disappeared every second Tuesday, when his stomach growled. Dropping into a nearby deli, he placed his order then made a call to Sophia's.

"She's fine," Faith answered, her voice consciously quiet. "Catching a nap after the exertion, but otherwise okay."

The image of Sophie cradled up in bed made his body fill with a warmth that had nothing to with sex and everything to do with a harsh, protective tenderness. "Call me if that changes."

A slight pause. "Max, she's a J. You understand what that means, don't you?"

It was the care in her tone that stopped him from snapping at her. Faith, he thought, probably comprehended more about the pressures that faced a J than almost anyone else outside the Corps. "I know. Doesn't mean I have to accept it."

"You sound just like Vaughn."

Since the changeling had managed to save his mate, Max figured that was a good thing.

Hanging up after a quick good-bye, he grabbed his chicken and avocado sub and took a seat at one of the tables. He was in the process of demolishing it when Clay slid into the seat on the other side, his own sub in hand. "I got something for you," the sentinel said, taking a long draw of the energy drink he'd ordered along with the sub.

"Yeah?"

"Rumor on the street is that Psy are meeting in little groups all over the place," the sentinel said. "But they're being covert about it."

"Avoiding Nikita's eyes?"

"Possible. Don't forget, Anthony Kyriakus is also in the general area."

"That's right—he's out by Tahoe." And though Faith's father kept a lower profile than Nikita, he controlled a vast network of foreseers—an immeasurable advantage over his enemies. "So what, you were just passing by, saw me?"

"Heard you were around, needed to talk to you and eat lunch." A shrug.

"Funny how you hear things."

"Yeah, funny." The sentinel's expression didn't change,

but Max had the distinct impression the leopard was laughing.

Max gave the changeling male a look that promised retaliation. "You have any specific addresses for these covert meetings?"

"A few—they tend to move around." Pulling out a folded piece of paper from his jeans, Clay passed it over. "We've been keeping an eye on the situation, but since it's accountants and teachers, we put it low down on the priority list."

Glancing at the list, Max noted that none of the locations correlated with Tulane's unexplained trips. "Thanks." Finishing off his lunch, he tucked the slip of paper safely in his jacket. "I'll let you know if anything comes of it."

Clay put his empty drink bottle on the table. "How's your J?" His tone said far more than the words.

"She can't leave the Net." Saying it out loud seemed to make it inescapably more real. "Ever."

"Ah, shit. I'm sorry Max—we would've helped you if she'd wanted to defect."

Max hadn't been part of any kind of a family since River disappeared, but he understood what this was, understood the value of Clay's offer. "Her telepathic shields are close to total collapse," he found himself saying, the words torn out of him. "She's 8.85 on the Gradient, so when they fail . . ." No place in the inhabited world would be safe for her. His Sophia's amazing violet eyes would go black under an avalanche of *noise*—and then there would be only silence in his life.

Endless.

Relentless.

Forever.

Twenty minutes later, Max parked his car a block away from where Andre Tulane disappeared at regular intervals, and strolled down the cheerfully painted suburban street.

The houses wore shades of bubblegum blue, candy pink, and meringue yellow, almost all with white trim. Human. Very human. The sole reason a Psy might wind up living amongst such brightness would be if there was some city ordinance that stipulated the colors in order to retain the area's historical character.

Psy understood the value of architectural tourism.

Seeing an old lady tending her winter-quiet garden a couple of houses over, he wandered across. "A pretty face doesn't do it for me," she said without pausing in her task. "Never has—not since Bobby Jones broke my heart in junior high."

Max didn't much feel like smiling—time was slipping by so fucking fast—but he made his lips curve. "I don't suppose you know who lives in number nine?"

"She's never done anything to hurt anyone"—a suspicious glance—"so you leave her alone."

Max frowned. "Human?"

Her snort was inelegant, her words acerbic. "You think a Psy would live on this street?"

Max made a decision. If it was the wrong one, it could tip off their quarry—but Max had just remembered something else he'd read in Tulane's recent history and realized the answer to this mystery might be both logical . . . and utterly inexplicable. "Thanks for your help." Turning away, he walked to the door of number nine and knocked.

The petite woman who opened the door had arms covered by computronic black carapaces and scars on her face that still bore a hard pink shine—vivid against the naturally mocha color of her skin. "Yes?"

Gut tight with the knowledge that he was right about Tulane's motivation for visiting this house, Max showed her his electronic ID. "Ms. Amberleigh Bouvier?" It wasn't a guess, not given her physical condition.

"Yes. What's this about?"

"Could we talk inside?" He could feel the gardener glaring at him.

A hesitation before she nodded and led him down the corridor and into the kitchen.

"Is this about Andre?"she asked, taking a seat at the table set by the window. When he raised a surprised eyebrow, she continued, "I figured someone would come sooner or later, but I thought it'd be another Psy."

Max leaned one shoulder against the doorjamb. "I need to know the reason for Andre Tulane's visits."

"Penance," Amberleigh said in stark response. "His car blew a fuse and he lost control of it on a rainy night six months ago. Unfortunately, I happened to be on the curb when he drove over it." Amberleigh shook her head, her cropped hair blue-black in the sunlight. "I don't understand it myself, so I can't expect you to. Everyone—even I—agreed it was an accident, but he said he was responsible, so he paid all my medical bills, made sure I got the best treatment."

"Your arms?"

"They'll be back to full strength in another couple of months." She touched her face. "And these scars are going to be all but gone after they heal enough to begin laser treatments."

Those treatments, Max thought, hadn't been around when Sophia had been a child. He might've asked why she hadn't taken advantage of them as an adult, but he knew the answer—it was a quiet, powerful rebellion. Sophia wanted to remember the past, remember the three children who'd been lost. He was fucking proud of her for finding a way to speak even in Silence. "Why does Andre still come to see you?"

"To do any work around the house or yard that needs to be done." Amberleigh sounded bewildered, her eyes huge in that small face. "He doesn't speak more than three words to me, but by the time he's done, the lawn is mowed, anything broken is fixed, and my car's running smooth as Irish whiskey."

Max didn't need to hear any more. Whatever the demons that drove the quiet black man, Andre Tulane was deeply entangled with a human—in direct violation of Pure Psy's aim of absolute racial Purity.

In the Pure Psy world, Max thought as he stepped out into the crisp afternoon air, a human cop would never meet, never love . . . and never lose a violet-eyed J.

CHAPTER 37

There's always a price when you begin to ask questions.
Sometimes, the answers aren't what you hope to find. And
sometimes, there are no answers.

*—From the private case notes of Detective Max Shannon
on the file labeled "River"*

Clay, having driven straight from lunch to take up a
watch position around his alpha pair's home, looked at
Sascha as they walked outside her and Lucas's cabin. He
wasn't as close to her as some of the other sentinels, but he
deeply respected the woman his alpha had chosen. She was
strong, and she made their pack strong.

"I didn't say anything to Max," he said, continuing a conversation they'd had on the phone on his way over, "didn't
want to get his hopes up. But can Noor help Sophia?" His
adopted daughter—the owner of a great big chunk of his
heart—was part human, part Psy. She'd also formed a
soul-deep friendship with another gifted child, Keenan.
And that amalgamation of factors had created something
amazing.

Sascha put a hand on his arm to steady herself as they
stepped over a fallen log, easy with claiming the skin privileges that were a packmate's right—but that she'd never
presumed on until Clay had told her it was okay. "I asked

Faith to see if her father could get us Sophia's medical scans after you called."

Anthony Kyriakus, Clay thought, was an enigma, a Psy Councilor with an apparent heart. "He came through."

A quick nod, a tendril of rich black hair escaping her braid to curl over her cheek. "Tammy, Ashaya, and I all had a look at them." Her expression was bleak when she glanced up. "According to those scans, her organic brain is fine."

Ah, damn. "That's what the kids fix, isn't it?"

"As far as we know—yes. But the fact is, we're learning as we go with Noor and Keenan." She caught a leaf that had floated down through the gold-hued forest light, worrying it between her fingers. "Js have also been a mystery since the dawn of their existence. My best guess is that the damage is psychic and cumulative. When I met her . . . I sensed this incredible will containing a vast pain." Her voice was taut, her bones strained against her skin. "Her shields aren't broken—they've been worn away by a thousand slow drips of acid."

Clay shoved a hand through his hair. "Is there anything that can be done?" He wanted to help the cop who'd been a friend to his mate when she'd been alone, who'd shed blood in the hunt to find a monster experimenting on vulnerable children like Noor.

Sascha looked so distressed, he knew the answer before she spoke, this empath with her huge heart. "I was going to try to see if I could do something on the psychic level, but according to a note in her file, she's a minor anchor." A single tear streaked down her face, her sorrow so heavy he could feel it in his bones. "She's mainlining the Net—and that Net is slowly going insane."

Clay released fisted hands to reach out and close one over Sascha's shoulder. "Did she ever have a chance?"

Sascha's fingers gripped his in painful sympathy. "No."

* * *

Max returned to his apartment to discover that Morpheus had defected for good. The well-fed cat was purring happily on Sophia's coffee table when she let him in. "I missed you today," she said with a smile, but he saw the shadows under her eyes, the new lines of strain on her face.

Heart tight with the force of what he felt for her, he waited only until the door was closed before cupping her cheek, before taking her mouth in a kiss that held as much savagery as tenderness. She responded with a moan low in her throat. "Max, wait."

He bit her lower lip, furious with her for what she would soon do, the betrayal she would soon commit.

Her eyes shimmered. *"Max."*

It wasn't the tears that stopped him. It was the way she said that, the way she looked at him. Not afraid of him, but *for* him. "What is it?" He gripped her hips, unable to let her go.

She dropped her forehead against his chest for a moment. "Will you hate me, Max?"

"Every moment of every day."

"Good."

Anger whiplashed inside him, at this woman who needed him to remember her. Didn't she know he'd never forget? "What," he said, his voice rough with rage withheld, "did you want to tell me?"

A long breath and she raised her head. "While I was in the Net, I did some searches outside the parameters of the case." Those unusual eyes shifted away, then back. "I found some information for you."

He wasn't used to this kind of evasion from her. "If you don't know that I'll stand by you—"

Her fingers on his mouth. "I *know*." Glittering eyes, a tone that left no room for doubt. "I don't want this knowledge to hurt you . . . and I know it holds the capacity for enormous pain."

He took her hand, kissed her knuckles. "I'm tough.

I'll survive." That's what he did—survive. But this scar, Sophie's scar, was never going to heal.

She placed her hand on his cheek in gentle affection, and he knew she understood what he hadn't said, the hurt he hadn't vocalized. "River may have been alive as of two years ago."

His heart stopped. When it kicked out again, he found himself shaking his head, his hands clenching on her—he'd searched for River ever since he became a cop, through every known database and come up blank. "Why would there be anything about him on the PsyNet?"

"His path crossed with that of a human researcher doing a study on adults who'd been drug addicts as children." Gentle words, a worried gaze. "That researcher's paper was footnoted—and linked to—by a Psy scientist's paper on Jax addiction."

"Where—" he began, but Sophia was already pulling away to pick up a sheet of paper from beside Morpheus's purring body. Taking the printout, he went straight to the part she'd highlighted.

There it was. River's name in black and white. The citation noted that the subject had been free of addiction since his fourteenth birthday, when he'd voluntarily entered a program run by a charitable organization.

"Max." Sophia's fingers closing over his wrist.

It was only then that he realized his hand was trembling. "They just used first names—this could be someone else altogether."

"It's an unusual name and coupled with his age at the time the paper was written, and the addiction . . ."

His mind wasn't working too well. He looked up, to see her holding a small piece of notepaper. "What's that?"

"The phone number of the researcher who wrote the original article. He's currently lecturing at the University of the South Pacific and is stationed in Vanuatu." There was a near-painful hope in her eyes. "You should be able to get him in his office a little later on, check if it's your brother."

Reaching forward, he tugged her into his arms, crushing the feminine softness of her to him, burying his face in her hair. "You don't know what this means."

Her fingers dug into his back, her emotions as clear as if she'd spoken.

"You do, don't you?" he whispered against her ear, the scent of her a balm across his ravaged soul. "You know exactly what this means."

"Family, Max. You'll have family." Fierce, hopeful words. "You won't be alone." *After I'm gone.*

Max clenched his hand in her hair, drawing back so he could look down into her face, so he could speak with his lips against hers. "*We*," he said. "We'll have family."

Her eyes filled with light, with untrammeled happiness. "Max." She pressed a kiss to his jaw just as his cell phone began beeping.

It was Bart. "Bonner's escaped."

"**How is that** even possible?" Sophia stared at Max when he shut off the phone and told her what had happened. The prison was underground, all access points securely guarded. Even the emergency exits were set with pressure-sensitive alarms that would activate upon perceiving anything bigger than a field mouse.

Max's anger was a cold, hard thing. "He had an 'accident,' had to be taken to the medical bay. From the sound of it, he'd been working on the doctor for months. He must've convinced her he was innocent."

"Even so"—Sophia couldn't imagine the sly evil that was Bonner back out on the streets—"the doctor couldn't have had the necessary clearance to get him out."

"But she had access to tranquilizers—she took out the warden, then ransacked his office for the override keys." Max clenched his jaw so tight, he could hear his bones grind against each other. "Manhunt's in progress and they're fairly certain he's driving the doctor's car."

Sophia sat down on the arm of the sofa, her fingers digging into the fabric. "And the doctor?"

"If she's lucky," Max said flatly, "she's already dead. If she's not . . ." He knew Sophia understood better than anyone what Bonner was capable of, the pain that would be the doctor's reward for being foolish enough to believe in a sociopath.

A quiet nod. "Do you need to join the manhunt team?"

"I can liaise with them from here." Bonner was not going to fucking steal Max's time with Sophia. And— "They have the numbers on the ground." The team was huge and growing bigger by the hour. "What they need me to do is predict where Bonner might go, update the search grid as we get sightings." The first thing that had come into Max's mind had been Bonner's twisted interest in Sophia. "Sophie, there's a chance he'll head to you."

Sophia swallowed, nodded. "I'll be with you the majority of the time, and when I'm not, I'll be in secure buildings. I'll take one of the security officers with me if I need to go out on my own."

He loved her for not making him fight to protect her. "Right now, he's on the ground, so there's not much danger." But if he managed to get on a flight . . . "I'll alert Enforcement here, let DarkRiver know so their network can keep an eye out."

"Why is Enforcement having such trouble tracking him? Wasn't he embedded?" Sophia asked, referring to the transmitter all violent offenders had placed under their skin for the duration of their sentence.

"He managed to disable it soon after his escape—most likely possibility is that the doctor dug it out for him."

Sophia took a deep, trembling breath. "Will she—the doctor . . . satisfy him for a period?"

Max's stomach turned. "He's been behind bars long enough to have built up his needs." Refined his perversions.

"What can I do to assist?"

He didn't want her anywhere near Bonner's evil—she'd walked into the void enough for ten lifetimes. "Take another look at Quentin Gareth—I have this gut feeling there's something we've missed. Especially with Tulane out of the running." He told her what he'd discovered at Amberleigh Bouvier's house.

"Interesting—the dynamics of Nikita's workforce." A reflective statement. "I'll look at Gareth's file now."

As she did so, he hunkered down to cross-reference the location of the D2 penitentiary with Bonner's known bolt-holes, sending the list to the manhunt team as soon as it was in any kind of shape. "He's smart," Max told the team over the comm line that he'd secured, after discussing the possibility that Bonner might try to get to Sophia, so that they could put alerts on the relevant routes. "I don't think he'll go anywhere near his old hidey-holes." But the team would still have to check each and every one, just in case. "I've also sent you some properties I *know* were his, but that I couldn't ever legally link to him—those were never in the police files, so he didn't have a right to see them during the trial."

"Fuck it, Max—why can't he just die and do us all a favor?" The lead on the team, a man who was legendary for never losing his cool, broke for a second before taking a calming breath. "We're sure the doctor's already dead—dogs led us to a patch of forest not far from D2. Lot of blood.

"Some of it was Bonner's—they cut out the transmitter there. From the high-velocity spray, he thanked the doctor for her help by slitting her throat. He's never been this impatient before—we didn't even have a chance to save her."

Max shook his head. "The doctor was a necessity." A tool. "She was too old to satisfy him in any other way—in his mind, she was probably happy to die once she'd outlived her purpose."

The other cop shook his head in angry disbelief. "What do you need from us?"

"Any confirmed or credible sightings—send the details

to me as soon as you get them. Even a general direction will help me narrow down possible sites. With the amount of money he has at this disposal"—and Max knew there were Bonner family members who still believed in the innocence of their blue-eyed boy—"he could go anywhere."

"We've got the airports covered."

"Good. He might try to fly domestic"—especially if his fixation on Sophia was stronger than his drive to find other prey—"but I don't think he'll leave the country. He enjoys being a star here too much." Ending the call after a few more quick words, he went to sit beside Sophia on the couch. "Now we wait."

Sophia couldn't stand to see the weight on Max's shoulders, the strain around his mouth. "Don't hurt, Max." She cupped his cheek, her emotions stripped bare. "Bonner doesn't deserve to have you beating yourself up for his evil."

"Sweetheart." Max's kiss was so tender, tears burned at the backs of her eyes. It felt different—more than sexual, more than intimate. If felt as if he was handing her a gift she didn't understand. Holding on to him, she gave herself to the kiss, gave herself to Max. When his lips wandered over her cheek and down her jaw, she shivered and wove her fingers through the thick silk of his hair.

Nikita could wait, she thought. The whole world could wait. Tonight, this moment, she was stealing for her and the strong, loyal, beautiful man who'd seen every broken part of her—and yet looked at her as if she was perfect. "Max. Don't stop. Not today."

Lifting his head from hers, he rose to his feet in a smooth move that spoke of a very masculine strength. When he held out a hand, it felt impossibly right to place her own against his palm and allow him to lead her to the bedroom, to watch him put his fingers to the buttons of her shirt, slide them out of the slots one by one.

His knuckles brushed the side of one breast, making her shiver.

"Cold?" An intimate murmur against her neck as he

dropped the shirt to the floor and moved to curve his body around hers from behind, a hard, sleekly muscled male with an arousal he made no effort to hide.

She'd never felt more alive, more sensuous in her femininity. "No."

"Good." His hands shifted up to close over her breasts through the practical cotton of her bra. "If I bought you naughty lingerie"—shaping her, possessing her—"would you wear it?"

Joy rippled through the sensuality, a piquant spice. He was as determined as her, she thought, to make this time *theirs*, something no one would ever be able to steal from them no matter what the future held. "How naughty?"

"Very." He pinched her nipples lightly—a quick, sharp bite—rolled them between his fingers. "The pieces might even make you blush."

Heat was already rising over her body, but it was a languorous, seductive thing. "That sounds like a dare." Reaching back with one arm, she tangled her fingers in his hair, holding him to her. "And I accept."

A smile she could feel against her skin as his hands slid off her aching flesh. Dropping her own arm to the side, she let him undo the clasp of her bra, then reached up to pull it down and off her body. "Why is it"—she shivered as he kissed the top of her spine, went lower—"that I always end up naked while you remain dressed?"

A husky masculine chuckle, his lips moving over her shoulder, his hands on her hips. "Because I'm a smart man." Playing his fingers across her abdomen, he undid the top button of her jeans. "Take these off for me."

That slow, slumberous heat flamed, *burned*, but she took a step forward, lowered the zipper and then—taking a deep breath—pushed down both the jeans and her panties. Leaning forward to pull them off her feet, she could barely hear anything through the thunder of her heartbeat. Max didn't say a word until she straightened back to her full height. But then he spoke . . . and she melted.

CHAPTER 38

"Beautiful." A rough sound, impatient hands that turned her to meet his kiss.

And oh, his kiss.

It held the same wild tenderness, the same protectiveness that had torn through her every shield from the very first. But it also held something else—a raw, dark pleasure, a hotly sexual aggression. Shuddering, she pulled at his shirt. Buttons went flying every which way as he cooperated with her frustrated need to touch him, but his attention was on her mouth, his hunger inexorable.

His hands back on her body as soon as his shirt fell to the floor, he squeezed and petted until she broke the kiss, unable to take any more. But he wouldn't let her go. Kisses on her jaw, on her neck as he walked her backward, the heat of his chest an exquisite caress. She was more than ready to fall onto the bed when it hit the backs of her knees. Not waiting for him to nudge her, she crawled on and turned over to brace herself on her elbows.

He was watching her with a glittering kind of focus, one that made her skin tighten until it almost hurt. She swallowed as his fingers went to his jeans, as he undid the snaps and peeled the denim down his legs, along with his briefs. Her eyes were riveted to the thick length of his erection . . . to the hand he clasped around it. He stroked once, and her body arched. She couldn't explain it, didn't understand it, but the sight of him stroking his own flesh was the most erotic thing she'd ever seen. "Max." A shuddering plea.

Coming over her as she lay back in unspoken invitation, he lowered himself just enough that their thighs brushed, the hardness of his erection pushing at her abdomen in blatant masculine demand. Sucking in a breath, she slid her hands up the beauty of his chest and over those magnificent shoulders. "Yes." It was an answer to a question he hadn't asked.

But he understood. Relaxing his muscles, he allowed his body to touch her all over. The full-body contact was an erotic lightning strike, an electrical storm. Moaning at the pleasure-pain of it, she tangled her fingers in his hair and took his mouth in a kiss of her own. He shuddered against her, his hand clenching on her hip. When he moved that hand to push at her thigh, she spread her legs in silent invitation.

He touched her slickness, and it made her tremble. But he didn't stroke her with lazy patience as he had once before. This time, his touch was deliciously, demandingly rough, as he used his knowledge of her body to make her twist beneath him. "That's it," he murmured, his shoulder muscles bunching against her palms as he played with her. "Scream for me, Sophie."

She managed to tighten her thighs, trapping his hand in between. "I," she gasped out, "am not a screamer."

A wicked, unexpected smile, that lean dimple flashing in his cheek. "Well now, a man's got to take that as a challenge."

She adored him. Tugging down his head, she pressed a line of kisses along the dimple, even as he began to tease her with small movements of his finger against her clitoris. Her breath caught. "Max, you're rushing me."

The sensual complaint made him chuckle. "Fair's fair." But he withdrew his hand, leaning down to kiss her slow and lazy though his body thrummed with tension above her. His hair was a cool stroke across her skin as he moved lower, nuzzling at her breasts before taking a tight little nipple into his mouth.

It was an agony of sensation, and it was magnificent. "Oh!"

Grazing her with his teeth, he released the nipple. "That," he said, circling the wet nub with his tongue, "was close to a scream."

"Gasp," she breathed out. "It was a gasp. Now please do that again."

"What?" Another wicked smile.

"*Max.*"

Chuckling, he dipped his head to tease her neglected nipple, curving his hand possessively over the roundness of her other breast.

Shivering, she found she'd spread her thighs again, that she was cradling him in the most intimate of ways. The depth of pleasure was a knife, sharp and edgy—she shifted restlessly, her hands running up and down his back. *Mine*, she thought with a primal possessiveness, *he's mine.* Her hands touched his buttocks when he raised his head to kiss her on the lips, and she found she really, really liked stroking her hands over the sleekly muscled strength of him.

A groan against her. "Stop that." He nipped at her lower lip when she didn't comply. "Or I'll play the same game with you . . . in front of the mirror."

Her hands went motionless.

Max braced himself on his forearms, intrigued enough to fight the pulsing need of his cock, the drive to sink into Sophie's silken heat. "So, Ms. Sophia Russo has kinky fantasies about mirrors. Interesting."

Heat colored her cheeks, but she tilted up her head. "Tell me one of your fantasies."

He loved that she trusted him enough to not back down. Fighting fire with fire, he made a slow, deliberate move . . . until his erection nudged at her clitoris. *Lord have mercy.* It felt so good, he wanted to slip a few inches lower, take everything. But this was Sophia's first time, and he damn well intended to drown her in pleasure—it was a matter of determined male pride . . . and of how much he felt for this woman.

Whose eyes drowned in black as she said, "Don't think you'll distract me."

Smiling, he kissed her, nuzzling at her throat as he spoke, "You know those suits you wear? The prim ones with skirts to the knee and jackets that button below your breasts?"

"Mmm." She made one of those little movements that drove him insane, rubbing herself against his cock. "My suits are boring."

It took him several seconds to find his voice. "Au contraire." Husky words, his breath caught in his throat. "Those suits give a man ideas. Like, for example, catching you alone in a deserted office"—he gripped her earlobe in a quick, teasing bite—"bending you over a big wooden desk, pushing up that sedate skirt to find you wet for me." The image drove him one step closer to insanity.

Then Sophie said, "Would you touch me?" in a sultry voice that wrapped around his cock and squeezed.

Shuddering, he lowered his head, sucked hard at her neck, leaving a little red mark. "No, this is a Neanderthal fantasy"—one of his favorites—"I just rip off your panties and thrust into you."

"That—" She swallowed, wet her lips. "I have . . . um, nothing against that fantasy."

Now that deserved a hot, open-mouthed, inferno of a kiss. "I have another version," he told her afterward.

Fingers clenching on his biceps, her breasts rising up and down in jagged breaths.

"This time, I get you to stand in front of me, and I push up your skirt inch by inch, while stroking my thumbs along the insides of your thighs." Rising to kneel above her, he mirrored actions to words, parting her thighs to afford him the most delicious of views. "I know you're not wearing anything underneath—though sometimes, I let you wear silk stockings and a suspender belt—"

Her breasts turned a hot blush pink as heat rolled over her body. *"Max."*

He moved his hands over her in a sweeping caress. "Shh, this is getting good." She shivered under his touch. "And so I shove the skirt to your waist, bare you all pink and damp for me"—sliding his hands under her bottom—"tug you close"—positioning himself lower down her body—"and eat you up like candy."

And then he took her. Hot and deep and with an open possessiveness. She bucked under him, lush in her femininity, making small sounds of pleasure that urged him to drive her ever higher. But today, he didn't want her to go over without him. He needed to hold her in his arms, feel her pleasure. So when he felt intimate little muscles clench, her breathing alter, he took one final taste and rose over her body, his hand on her hip. "Together this time, Sophie." The words were so deep, so hoarse, as to be almost unrecognizable.

Sophia realized her cop had reached the end of his control. "Yes, oh, yes." Feeling wild and needy and hotly female, she wrapped her leg over his hip, opening herself even further for him.

He didn't ask again, kissing her with a gut-wrenching blend of tenderness and an almost violent need as he nudged at the entrance to her body. The sensation was . . . indescribable. It might have driven her to madness if she'd tried it when they first met. But now . . .

Burying her face in his neck, breathing in the intoxicating blend of his scent, she gripped his body tight as he slid inside her. His entry burned a little, but that was a small thing subsumed in the agony of sensation. Shaking, she wrapped her other leg around him. The sudden act opened her up, made him slide inside faster than before.

They both cried out, and Max froze above her. "Sophie?"

She ran her teeth up the line of his throat. "Yes." Always, yes for this man.

Tugging off her hands, he twined them with his own as he pressed her to the sheets, his mouth claiming hers. She felt deliciously exposed and shockingly exhilarated as he flexed his hips and buried himself to the hilt inside her. Her cry was torn out of her, her body arching toward his in primal response. When he began to move, she tried to follow. She was a fraction of a second out of sync . . . but only for the first few strokes.

And then, there was no more thought. Just the slick, hot glide of his body against hers, *inside* hers, the rasp of his jaw against her cheek as he lowered his head . . . and finally, the turbulent beauty of a sexual storm that threw them both against the rocks and broke them wide open.

"Hey you." Braced on his side beside her, Max ran his hand down her front. "You look like a well-fed cat."

She scrunched up her face. "That is not a sensual image, not when I know it's Morpheus you're likely using as a comparison."

The tart response got her a kiss, a deep, intense claiming. "How're you feeling?"

"Fine. My inexplicable"—but viciously strong—"shields are still holding on the PsyNet."

"That's good, but I was talking about the physical."

Her body flushed. "Oh." She'd made a visit to the bathroom, had looked at her face in the mirror, amazed at the rumpled, pleasured woman with the kiss-bruised mouth who'd stared back at her. "I'm a little tender, that's all." It felt strange to have such a conversation, and yet she could. Because it was Max.

He smoothed his hand over her abdomen. "Let me know when you're ready for round two—like I told you, practice, lots and lots of practice, makes perfect."

Catching the teasing light in his eyes, she punched him lightly on the shoulder, before turning to face him. "Thank you for making the experience so very . . ."

"Interesting?" A flash of the lean dimple she adored.

"Yes," she said, tracing the laughter with her fingertip, feeling her own lips curve. "It was *supremely* interesting. That's a high compliment."

"I'm so glad." Sliding one arm under her head, he draped the hand of the other over her hip. "For a Psy, you were okay."

"And you weren't bad for a cop."

They looked at each other, both of them utterly delighted in the moment. She wanted to snuggle closer to him, but her body was still humming with sensation. Better to wait a while, she thought, let things quieten a fraction. "Turn around."

To his credit, he didn't pretend not to know the reason for her demand. Scowling, he did as asked. The tattoo ran along the length of his spine, a sword with the tip just below his nape and an intricate hilt at his lower back. It was a gorgeous piece of art.

Fascinated by the spare beauty of it, Sophia pushed down the sheet so she could view the whole thing. "When did you have this done?"

"Sixteen," he said. "I thought I was hot shit."

She considered the boy he must've been—tough but slender, his musculature still developing, and wanted to trace every inch of that tattoo with soft, adoring kisses. "The blade's so empty in comparison to the artwork on the hilt."

His muscles bunched. "I left it blank on purpose. For you."

Her throat locked. She wanted to give him a gift, too . . . a gift as precious, as enduring. "It's near lunchtime in Port Vila. You could probably catch the professor in his office."

Turning to face her, he said, "I know."

Sophia stroked her hand down his arm, worried. "Why do you sound the way you do?" As if he was holding something tightly in check.

He shuddered, bending his head so his forehead touched hers. "I'm afraid." A stark admission. "What if it isn't River? Or what if it is . . . and he doesn't want to see me?"

"Why would he reject you?" Max had fought for his brother, tried to save him.

"I've always thought that he went down the wrong path partly because of the guilt he felt at the way our mother always treated us so differently." River had been her golden child, Max the whipping boy. "I tried to shield him from it, but I couldn't, not in the end."

Sophia's fingers twined with his on the sheets between them. "If this is your brother, if he's the boy I saw in that flash of backsight, he cares for you to the depths of his soul."

"Sometimes, that isn't enough." Max knew he sounded harsh, but it was the only way he could handle this. If he allowed it to matter, it would hurt too fucking much. "I wouldn't blame him if he doesn't want to be reminded of the past."

Sophia squeezed his hand, leaving the decision up to him, those violet eyes warm with an intense, unbreakable loyalty.

In the end, there was only one thing he could do, his love for his tormented, damaged younger brother stronger and far more tenacious than the fear that sought to hold him back. Picking up his cell, he made the call—the conversation with the professor took less than a minute, with the elderly man promising to pass on Max's details to this River who might be his brother. Hanging up, Max released a long breath and drew the scent of Sophia into his lungs.

The temptation to curl up around her and just forget the world was almost overwhelming, but the cop in him wouldn't settle. He'd taken an oath, made a promise. "I should let you rest," he said to the woman who was trying so hard to make sure he had a family, "but . . . want to come on a stakeout?" His anger at being helpless in the face of her failing shields threatened to make him bitter, but he fought the ugliness, refusing to taint the beauty of this strange, beautiful joy between a cop and his J.

Sophia's face lit up with an almost childish pleasure. "Really? Yes!"

And he knew he'd do anything in his power to keep that light in her eyes.

"Okay," he said once he'd checked in with the manhunt team—no sightings, no information to help him narrow the search grid, his frustration as acute as theirs—and they were on their way through the darkening city, "word is, some Psy are having secretive meetings around town. No one knows why."

"We're going to observe one of these covert meetings?"

"Yes. Clay's informants say it's pretty certain the place we're heading to will be the gathering point tonight." The leopard changeling had sent through the message earlier. "For now—we're just going to watch, see if we can get an idea of what's going on, gauge if it might be connected to the Nikita situation."

Not that long afterward, Max brought the car to a stop in the exclusive Pacific Heights neighborhood, parking between two other similar black sedans. This particular street was a historical landmark, maintained much as it had been in the early twentieth century, the trims on the graceful Queen Anne–style homes decorative, the colors distinctive even in the muted light.

"This is exciting," Sophia said, wide-eyed, just as the streetlights sensed the approaching night and switched themselves on.

Max bit the inside of his cheek. "Yeah, and don't think I take all my dates on stakeouts. You're special." Such an impossibly simple statement to describe the depth of what he felt for her.

"I'm flattered." A husky chuckle. "Oh—I may have discovered what was bothering you about Quentin Gareth's file—I meant to tell you after you got off the comm, but we got . . . distracted."

Max's body purred at the thought of that distraction. "Still feeling tender?"

"Max."

Reaching out, he closed his hand over her thigh, gave a little squeeze. "So?"

"Yes." He could hear the blush. Then she said, "Are you erect?"

Hell. "I should know better than to tease you." Grinning, even as he shifted to ease the pounding erection she'd brought to life, he said, "So, Quentin Gareth?"

"Has a well-hidden discrepancy in his early records. It says he went to an Ivy League college from age eighteen to twenty-three, and he did. However, he wasn't actually at college for six months of his final year—he enrolled in no classes, took no exams.

"When I dug deeper, I discovered he'd won a place in some kind of work experience program." She touched her fingers to the hand he had on her thigh, rubbing her thumb over his knuckles. "There's nothing inherently suspicious in that, but the fact that he hid it instead of putting it on his CV tells me he either did so badly during the program that he wants it gone from his work history—"

"—or," Max completed, "he's got a secret he doesn't want us to uncover. Where was he posted?"

"That's the thing. There's no record whatsoever of where he spent those six months."

Max caught something with his peripheral vision. "Stay relaxed," he said to Sophia. "It's dark enough that they won't be able to see us." Though the streetlight in front of the target home made their quarry very visible.

Two men and one woman walked up from the other side of the street, entering the house after a quick knock. Two more women, middle-aged this time, followed. The sixth attendee was a much older man, his hair in tight gray curls.

Sophia jerked forward without warning. "Is that who I think it is?"

The individual who'd caught her attention paused on the steps of the house, glancing around as if conscious of being watched.

"Son of a bitch," Max murmured as Ryan Asquith shifted on his heel and walked inside.

CHAPTER 39

Councilor Kaleb Krychek was just getting into his car for the drive to his office in Moscow when he felt it. A telepathic ricochet. Catching the returning tracker with a psychic hand, he leaned against the vehicle. He had thousands of these invisible psychic constructs scattered throughout the Net, all of them primed to scan through billions upon billions of bytes for data for one name.

This was the first one that had returned since he began his search six years, five months, and three weeks ago.

He was careful with the old and fragile construct, not wanting to lose what it had brought back to him. It took him almost ten minutes to penetrate the layers of his own security—and then, there it was. *That* name, linked to information that had passed through a distant part of the Net two weeks ago. The information was fragmented, the trail would be difficult if not impossible to pick up, but that mattered little at this point.

Because at last, he had confirmation that his quarry was alive.

CHAPTER 40

I'm writing this as you sleep beside me, your breathing easy,
the lines of stress smoothed away—and I don't know how to
describe what I feel for you. I don't have those words. It hurts,
this emotion in my heart, this inexorable ache.

—*Sophia Russo in an encrypted and time-coded letter to*
be sent to Max Shannon after her death

Sophia lay in bed the next morning, her limbs loose and
her body utterly sated. So, this was what pleasure felt like,
she thought in wonder. This was what poets wrote about
and artists painted. This was why humans gave each other
secret smiles and changelings murmured in their mates'
ears.

The bathroom door opened to reveal a tiled enclosure
full of steam just as Morpheus jumped onto the bed and
padded around to sit right up against her abdomen. She
took the hint, stroking his solid form. "You shower in water
far too hot for you," she said to the beautifully muscled
male who walked out from the heat and headed to where
he'd thrown a change of clothes last night.

After they'd seen Ryan enter that stately Queen Anne,
she and Max had decided she should return home, tear
apart Ryan's file. Her cop had called up a white-blond
changeling male named Dorian to drop her home, while
he'd stayed on Ryan until close to three a.m., leaving only

when his friend Clay had arrived to take the watch for a few hours. She'd heard him return home, heard him confer with the manhunt team for over half an hour.

"Looks like Bonner's parents provided him with access to a private jet," he'd said to her when he stumbled into bed. "Bastard could be anywhere. I've alerted the local airports, let the cats know." He'd gone straight to sleep after that . . . but woken an hour ago with more than enough energy to make her gasp.

"You'll boil," she said, as another wave of steam escaped the bathroom.

An unrepentant wink. "Heat is good for you." Towel hitched around his lean waist and hair damp, he looked young, incredibly approachable.

A rumble against her palm as Morpheus began to purr. "I was thinking about calling Quentin Gareth's college." Having discovered nothing incriminating in Asquith's files, she was staying behind today to sort through the PsyNet data she'd cached—in the hopes of unearthing something that might tie Pure Psy directly to the attacks on Nikita's people. "But if he has alerts set in place, it could tip him off."

"Hold off on that," Max said, throwing the towel on the bed. "I might be able to get the information another way."

The intimacy of watching him dress was a tightness in her chest. "Come back to me, Max," she said quietly.

"How could I resist?" A solemn look, a kiss that held emotion that made her soul ache. "You're holding my heart hostage."

Ten minutes later and far too soon, Max walked to the door, with her behind him. "I'll be on the phone to the manhunt team throughout the day, too, so leave a message if you can't get through and I'll call back." Reaching out, he tucked a strand of her hair behind her ear. "Building security has Bonner's image—they know not to let him up to you under any circumstances.

"Enforcement's on alert, and Clay's also put the word out among DarkRiver's network of informants." A squeeze of her hip. "If you go out—and I'd rather you didn't—don't forget to take one of the security guys with you. Or better yet, call me, and if I can't get away, I'll call DarkRiver, organize a leopard escort for you."

Remembering the warped arousal she'd read in Bonner during the Gwyn Hayley scan, Sophia hugged her arms around herself, the tiny hairs on her body rising in primitive warning. "I plan to stay in." Being outside in the general population was becoming more and more unbearable. "And I won't be entering the PsyNet, so don't worry about that either."

He touched his lips to her temple. "How are you?" A rough question that held a thousand unsaid things.

She placed her hand over his heart, soaked in the incredible gift of his presence. "Still here." But her telepathic shields were so thin that *any* touch by an unstable personality could perforate them.

A hard kiss. "I'll check up on you every hour. Don't even try to stop me."

He was gone an instant later.

Knowing she should have protested, but reassured by his protectiveness, she fed Morpheus—who graciously permitted her to stroke him once—then took a quick shower. Afterward, refreshed, she changed into a pair of soft velour pants—they were like nothing she'd ever before worn. She'd bought them on impulse several months ago, in a decision so non-Psy she hadn't required a medic to tell her she needed to go in for reconditioning. But she hadn't worn them until now.

The dark blue material was velvety soft, delicate, and beautiful against her skin. Enjoying the tactile pleasure, she put on a stretchy T-shirt, zipping herself into a hooded gray sweatshirt several sizes too large for her to complete the outfit. It wasn't cold in her apartment, but the sweatshirt was Max's, carried his scent.

Her cop, she thought, would never understand the depth of what he meant to her, what he'd given her. It was at once a wild, earthy thing and an incandescent joy. The only shadow came from the knowledge that their time had almost run out, that one day soon, her mind would fill with noise and she'd lose Max, lose the tearing power of the emotion that had made her whole, every broken part of her accepted and cherished.

Her fingers clenched.

She forced them to open. It was no use being angry, no use railing at fate. Fact was fact—she'd gone through every manual, spoken to every one of her colleagues, all to no avail. Telepathic shields *could not* be rebuilt once they began to degrade from the core out.

"They use then discard us like garbage," a fellow J had said to her.

"Why did you accept the position?" As an eight-year-old girl strapped to a hospital bed, Sophia had had no choice, but other Js did.

"It was the only available job."

Sophia had understood. "Is it always the only available job when a J attempts to find work?"

"Yes."

Fury had made her gut twist. "In the past, before Silence," she'd dared ask, knowing the J opposite her would've been a historian if given the choice, "was it like this?"

"No. Js were only ever used in capital cases. Or if there was a hung jury where the crime fit certain parameters."

The load, Sophia had realized, would've been spread, placing far less pressure on each individual.

"Js still went mad, still broke," her colleague had continued, "but no more than the rest of our race."

But now the Council used them up in order to consolidate its power. In light of that brutal truth, Sophia wasn't sure she wanted to save Nikita, but Max was a good cop. He believed in justice, made her want to believe in it, too.

Her mind took that thought, connected it to a rumor tangled up in the information cache she'd begun to process while she got out the ingredients to prepare a breakfast drink of the hot chocolate Max had bought for her.

Interesting. Leaving the milk unopened on the counter, she found a piece of paper and, taking a seat on the sofa, began to note down the relevant facts as she smoothed out the "lumps" of raw data.

The click of her door being opened was quiet, but it shattered her concentration. "Ma—" But it wasn't her cop.

Her eyes took in the security override key in the woman's hand, the Center badge on her lapel. *No.* She went to lower her PsyNet shields, send out a psychic mayday, but the woman's male companion was already gripping her arm, slapping a pressure injector against the vulnerable skin of her neck, his naked hand mere centimeters away. Her concentration fractured—and they shot something into her bloodstream that turned her mind dull, sluggish.

"Useful that Js have such solid PsyNet shields," the woman said, supporting Sophia under one arm while her partner took the other.

"Why is she on the rehabilitation watchlist then?"

"Her telepathic shields are all but gone. If she isn't rehabilitated now, there's a chance she'll break on her own." They began to head down the corridor. "And the death throes of the fractured are always so disruptive to Silence."

Sophia tried to resist their hands, the way they directed her like a rag doll, but her mind was mired in thick fog, her body refusing to follow her commands. They "walked" her down to the garage level, each holding up half her weight. And the only thing she could think was that Max would never know how much she loved the scent of him.

Max jogged through the doors of DarkRiver's Chinatown HQ just as the skies opened up. "That's some storm," he said, shaking off the droplets that had managed to hit him.

"Forecast to clear sometime tonight," Dorian said. "So, what's up? Clay still shadowing that intern for you?"

"No, he had to switch with a guy named Emmett." Who

had texted Max a few minutes ago to say that Asquith had arrived at work.

"That's right." Dorian clicked his fingers. "Clay's holding a training session for some of the soldiers today."

Max nodded. "I hear you're good with computers." What he'd heard was that the blond sentinel was an expert hacker.

Bright blue eyes blazed with an intelligence many people missed, being taken in by looks reminiscent of some teenage surfer. "Yeah? Where did you hear that?"

Max tapped the side of his nose. "You have your sources. I have mine."

"I don't work for free." Dorian folded his arms and stared meaningfully at the box Max had carried inside. There was a very feline look of anticipation on his face.

"Thanks for driving Sophie home last night." Max handed over the doughnuts.

"I was working late anyway." He opened the box, drew in a long breath. "What do you need on the computer front?"

"Anything you can dig up about a Psy named Quentin Gareth during a particular period almost twenty years ago." Taking out a notepad, he jotted down the details of the six month gap.

Dorian took a bite out of a jelly doughnut. "Good call, coming to me," he said after swallowing. "Psy often forget about the Internet. Lots of stuff cached all over the place." Taking the torn off piece of notepaper, he slid it into a pocket. "I'll do the search now—have a few minutes free before a meeting."

"Call me on my cell if you have anything. I'm heading to Nikita's." But he'd only gotten to the door when he got a call from the head of the manhunt team. "Doctor's been found." Fury and pity intertwined. "We were right about the time and method of death. At least he didn't torture her."

It was, Max knew, a small mercy. "Was she found near the private airport where you think he boarded a jet?"

"Yeah. Parents are refusing to tell us where the jet might've gone. The filed flight plan says it's heading to Greece, but that's a load of bullshit. Air Control hasn't got it on its systems, which means the Bonners were fucking *ready* with a plane designed to evade radar."

Anger burned through Max's veins. "I've put a watch on some offshore accounts I know are his." Without a warrant and with the help of friends in the computronic crimes branch of Enforcement, but if it would help catch the Butcher before he killed again, Max wasn't going to sweat the ethics much. "He hasn't accessed them yet—his mother's probably supplying him."

"Bart's working on a warrant for her financials."

"Sightings?"

"Through the roof." A harsh sound. "People jumping at shadows—you know how it is."

"We'll get him," Max said, able to hear the other cop's frustration. "We did it once; we'll do it again." Hanging up after a few more words, he ran out to the car, the rain pelting against his body. Shrugging off his wet suit jacket, he was driving through Chinatown when he realized he'd forgotten his security keycard—which allowed him full access to the Duncan building—at Sophia's apartment. Figuring it'd be quicker to pick it up than have it reissued, he thrust a hand through rain-damp hair and turned homeward.

"Sophia?" he called out as he wandered into her bedroom. The keycard was on the dresser where he'd put his wallet the night before, but the bedroom proved otherwise empty. "Sophie? You in the shower?" However, when he knocked, the door swung inward.

Worried she'd decided to head out in spite of Bonner's possible presence, he pulled out his cell phone and placed a call to hers. It rang in the living area.

Ice crystals formed in his blood.

Closing his cell, he began to scan the apartment with the eyes of a cop. The food preparation area was clean except for the unopened container of milk on the counter. He stilled. Sophie was hopelessly neat, but it *was* possible she'd forgotten to tidy it away while distracted by something.

Living area undisturbed. Organizer on the coffee table.

And the bedroom, when he returned to it—

His head snapped back to the organizer. Sophia might forget her cell phone, but she was *never* without that computronic device. Gut clenching with a fear so visceral he couldn't afford to feel it if he was going to function, he ran out of the apartment and straight to the security hub at the heart of the building.

Entering using the override Nikita had programmed into his key, he had the Psy guard rewind the corridor feed. "Stop! Who are those two?"

The guard enlarged the view. "The facial recognition software places the female as an M-Psy attached to a local branch of the Center, while the male appears to be a security expert."

Max shoved down his raging worry, focusing only on the lethal clarity of his anger. "Why were they allowed up?" he asked, his tone a whip. "I fucking warned you all that she could be a target!"

The guard was already accessing the security log. "According to this, they had an authorization which overrode our—"

"Bring it up," he interrupted. "The authorization!" It was a snapped command when the man didn't immediately understand.

The screen filled with a crisp document mandating the removal of Sophia Russo, Designation J, to the Berkeley branch of the Center for Comprehensive Rehabilitation.

Rage burned an inferno across Max's skin, but his mind remained mired in ice. "What does that mean?" He pointed to what appeared to be a coat of arms or an emblem of some kind on the bottom of the page—a small square of black overlaid with a web.

The security guard went unnaturally still. "That's Councilor Henry Scott's new emblem."

Max was already coding in a call to Nikita as he ordered

the guard to send the location of the Center to his phone. "Nikita, Henry Scott is having Sophia rehabilitated," he said the instant Nikita answered, knowing Henry's interference would ensure Nikita's cooperation. Councilors, he'd learned, were as territorial as changelings. "She was taken an hour ago."

Nikita didn't ask useless questions. "Which branch?"

"Berkeley."

"Wait."

He was in the car and screaming out into the rain-dark city by the time her voice came back on the line. "They haven't yet reached the Center." A pause. "They should have according to the time frame you've given me."

He forced himself to think, to focus. The rain hadn't turned torrential until about twenty minutes ago—Nikita was right, they should've reached the Center by now. And then, suddenly, he realized that Nikita should've been able to contact Sophie on the Net. Everything stopped as he forced himself to ask, "Is she still alive?"

CHAPTER 41

"Her mind is present in the PsyNet," Nikita said, "but she's not responding to telepathic hails."

Relief mixed with a cold, cold anger. If the bastards had hurt her—"I need you to find out the make and model of the car the Center people were driving so I can ask Enforcement to put out an alert."

"You'll have the information in minutes. I've already notified the Center not to proceed with the rehabilitation order."

Thanking her, he hung up. But he knew Nikita's intervention wouldn't help, not if Sophia had been taken somewhere else. They could've already— *No.* "Hold on, Sophie. You just hold on." Opening his cell phone, he made another call. "Clay, I need your help."

The changeling male turned out to be at an indoor training facility at least twenty minutes closer to the Center than Max. "I've got several soldiers with me," Clay said, able to hear the incredible strain in Max's voice. But he knew from experience that the other man wouldn't appreciate sympathy, only practical assistance. "We'll head out now." Hanging up, he pulled a team together, and they drove out into the pounding rain.

"Pretty isolated," Kit said when they reached the road that led to the Center, his auburn hair appearing deep brown in the stormy light. "Visibility's low."

And getting lower as thunderclouds continued to roll in, their heavy weight making it seem as if it was late afternoon when it wasn't yet midmorning. "This is the only way to the place." The Psy had located their new lobotomy facility in an innocuous building set on a patch of fenced land that DarkRiver had kept an eye on, but hadn't considered a threat because it had no obvious military or tactical function. "If they're not on this route . . ."

"Stop!" Kit's cry came at almost the same instant that Clay pulled the car to a halt, reacting even before the proximity sensors detected the overturned vehicle on the road.

Getting out, Clay held up a hand to the packmates following in the vehicle behind them and ran to the wreck. "I have a male on this side, injured—fuck, it looks like his throat's been slashed."

"Same here, except it's a female." Wiping the rain from his face, Kit looked at him over the top of the car as Clay rose. "She had an ID around her neck, with an *M* in the corner."

Rain pelted Clay's back in hard little bullets. "I'll call Max, get him to send us the images—"

Max's car screeched to a halt behind the second Dark-River vehicle at that instant.

"Man." Kit whistled, his lashes dripping rain. "The cop must've driven at three times the speed limit. I didn't even know cars would let you do that."

"She's not in here," Clay called out as soon as Max exited his vehicle, knowing from the white look on the cop's face that that was what he feared.

Max peered into the overturned car as if to confirm Clay's words. A second later, he bent, bracing his hands on his knees, his white shirt so wet as to be almost transparent. "Thank God." Shoving a hand through rain-slick hair, he rose to his full height. "Sophie looked like she'd been drugged. If she got out, wandered off . . ."

"Jamie, Nico, Dezi," Clay said, pointing to the packmates who'd exited the second vehicle when Max came running over. "Do a sweep, see if you can find any trace of Max's J." The heavy canopy of trees around them could have protected the scent trail from the rain. "Kit, you, too."

"Max," Desiree said, her tone gentle. "Do you have anything of Sophia's?"

Max blinked rain from his eyes. "I had a shower before I left home," he said, obviously aware that intimate contact could leave a detectable scent, "just kissed her good-bye. The fucking rain's probably washed away anything that was left."

Frowning, Desiree stepped closer, her long, thin braids sleek ebony in the wet. "Do you mind?" At Max's distracted nod, she unbuttoned the top three buttons of his sodden shirt and pressed her nose to his skin, taking a deep breath. To his credit, Max didn't move. "Got it." A fierce grin. "She's in your skin, Cop."

Jamie, Nico, and Kit repeated the process—the men choosing to take the scent off Max's arm now that Desiree had confirmed it was in his skin—before they scattered. Max glanced at Clay, his gaze piercing even through the rain-lashed darkness. "Throats cut, what looks like oil across the surface of the road, this wasn't a simple crash." His words were practical, outwardly calm.

Clay understood—first the cop would find his mate. Only then would he give in to the demons tearing him apart. With that in mind, he followed Max's line of thought, his eyes on the oil. "You know anyone else who might want your J?"

Rage turned Max's blood to fire. "Bonner—the Butcher of Park Avenue." Forcefully wiping away the red haze that would just get in his way, Max moved around the car, checking for anything that might give him a clue as to where Bonner may have taken her. "The only good thing is—if the bastard does have her, he won't kill her." No, unlike with the doctor, Bonner would play with Sophia in the cruelest of ways.

His hand fisted.

"The car crash," Clay pointed out, raising his voice to be heard above the rain pounding on the wreck, "could've gone very wrong."

"No." Max shook his head. "It was planned very well. Look at where we are—right after a curve, so their speed would've been low."

"The car had to be on wheels for this to work," Clay said. "And they were—doesn't make sense with the rain."

Realizing the sentinel was right, Max examined the side of the vehicle, focusing on the section that he knew controlled the hover system. "Does that look like a bullet hole to you?" He pointed to a distinctive hole in the plasmetal.

"Here's another one," Clay said from the other side.

"He must've tailed them from the apartment, overtaken them at some stage to set up the oil slick," Max said, well aware of the Butcher's intelligence. He would've checked his vehicle's nav system, discovered this road had no turnoffs, no side streets. "All he had to do then was lie in wait and shoot." Squatting, he stared through the broken wreckage of the car. "The straps in the back have been cut through—but it's obvious Sophia was strapped in far more securely than either of these two."

"And if he was stalking her, Bonner would've seen them strap her in." Clay's eyes were leopard-bright in the rain dark. "Acceptable fucking risk."

"For him, yes." Rising, Max began to consider and discard options, refusing to let Clay's anger feed his own. Not yet. He had to think, had to find Sophie. "Bastard's got money. His family's helping him stay on the run. He won't be out in the open or even in a cheap motel, but he'll be close."

Clay walked around to stand beside Max. "It would

make more sense to take her as far as possible, give himself room to breathe."

"He's . . . impatient." Max swallowed his fury for the thousandth time, told himself he could scream at the heavens later. "He'll want to have her to himself as soon as possible." And if the Butcher touched her, the viciousness of him might just shatter her mind.

Forever.

No. Teeth gritted, Max hunkered down, blocking the rain with his body as he examined the vehicle again. Bonner had apparently had no problem with the front seat passengers. Either one or both had been unconscious at the time. There were absolutely no signs of a struggle.

He moved to crouch beside the window that Sophie had been dragged through. That was when he saw something glint in the headlights of Clay's car, right below the window itself . . . where Bonner might've braced his foot to gain leverage. He bent down, until his nose almost touched the earth, using the built-in light of his cell phone to illuminate the area.

Tiny particles that glittered and glimmered, having been hidden from the rain by the angle of the wreck.

Sand.

But there was something strange about it. Picking it up in between his fingertips, he brought it even closer to the light. Sparkles of yellow and crystalline red, along with the odd flicker of what looked almost like blue. "Clay!"

Max's eyes fell on a tiny white shell just as the leopard ran over. "What've you got?" the sentinel asked.

Max showed him what he'd found. "The sand's not natural. I don't think we're talking a beach house."

"Wait." Clay took the tiny shell, brought it up to keen changeling eyes. "I think this is coated with something. Protective plas would be my guess."

"You know of any place nearby that might use this stuff? It'll offer enough isolation that Bonner will feel comfortable—but won't be too rugged." That wasn't the Butcher's style.

Clay's eyes narrowed. "Kit and the boys were laughing about some kind of a fake 'beach resort' about an hour from here." He pulled out his cell. "I've still got the web address saved. There—says it has bungalows set 'discreetly apart,' laundry and room service."

All the comforts of home for a killer who liked to work without lowering his personal standards. It *fit*. Max rose to his feet, trying not to think about what Bonner might be doing to Sophia—if he did, he'd shatter, and Sophia needed him to hold it together. "Send the location to my phone"—he was already running to his car—"I'll hook it into the nav system."

"Done!" the cat called out after him. "We'll continue the search here, just in case!"

He was five minutes into the drive—too fucking slow—when his phone beeped. It was Nikita, wanting an update. "Councilor," Max said, telling her where he was heading, "how many teleporters do you know?"

He didn't expect help, not now that it was a human sociopath who'd taken Sophia, rather than another Councilor's interference. But she said, "I'll see what I can arrange."

Sweat trickled down Max's spine. *I'm coming, baby. Just hold on.*

Sophia's stomach roiled, nausea filling her mouth. Drugged, she thought. She'd been drugged. The Psy brain didn't react well to narcotics. A moan whispered out of her as she was jostled about, her already battered body unable to stop its jerky movements.

"Sorry." A smooth, charming voice with . . . excitement, yes, it was excitement that bubbled beneath the surface. "We're almost there. This road's the private one to my bungalow. Made to look like a natural pebbled road. They should've sealed it. At least the rain's stopped."

Sophia only understood about half of what he'd said. But she knew he'd taken her, and that he wasn't a man she wanted to be alone with. He smelled wrong.

A laugh, almost amused. "I'll shower when we get to the bungalow. Got a little sweaty and bloody saving your life."

A snapshot of memory, her legs kicking out in futile panic, her limbs too heavy to do much damage as he cut away the straps that held her in the car, as he pulled her out. Rain on her face. Glass on her legs.

Reaching down, she touched her thighs, touched the damp material that covered it.

"You're not injured," the man with the wrongness in him said as he brought the vehicle to a stop. "A few cuts and bruises from the crash, but otherwise fine. Not even that wet. My arms got nicely sliced up coming to your rescue—I'm sure you're dying to thank me."

A buzzing in her head, a dizzying splash of words and images, her mind twisting out of control for a frightening instant as the drugs punched at her again. But she came to enough to flinch when the man exited his side of the car and came around to hers.

"I'm not going to hurt you."

Lying, she thought, he was lying. "Don't touch me," she forced out through lips that didn't work right.

His expression changed, becoming mean in a way she couldn't describe. "I'm in charge now." His hand clamped over her upper arm, and he lowered his head, as if he would kiss her.

Even in the depths of her narcotic induced state, she knew that if she told him the truth, it'd give him another weapon with which to torture her. But if she didn't, he might inadvertently break her mind, kill her by making her relive the horrifying ugliness of his blood-drenched memories. And she had to survive. *Because Max didn't know.* "No," she whispered, swallowing the nausea inspired by his mere presence. "J. Can't . . . contact."

He stilled, his hand tightening on her arm. "You telling me direct physical contact can hurt you? Is that why you were always wearing those gloves?"

She tried to nod, but her head fell forward, and she had so much trouble bringing it back up. "Yes."

"Then I guess I'll just have to be careful." Unsnapping her safety belt, he lifted her out of the car and into his arms.

Her clothing protected her, but this close, her remaining telepathic shields shredded by the drugs, she couldn't help but drown in the fetid evil of him. He appeared normal, human. But he wasn't. He was so twisted up inside, so viciously mutated that he wasn't even close to human.

A slam, her body being laid down on some sort of a soft surface, that handsome blue-eyed face going in and out of focus. Her stomach revolted at the same moment, and she pitched over the side of what turned out to be a sofa, her stomach twisting in agony.

"There, there . . ." He was wiping her face with a wet cloth, his voice solicitous. "I'll clean that up. Let me take you into the bedroom." A smile that made her blood chill. "That's where we'll be playing our games anyway."

CHAPTER 42

Take care of my heart won't you, Sophie? It's a little odd having it outside my body—but I'm planning to steal yours to make up for it.

—Handwritten note from Max to Sophia

Max overrode his car's safety instructions for the fifteenth time but knew he was going to be far too late. By his calculations, Bonner was almost fifty minutes ahead of him. Even if he made the journey to the resort in half the time, that still gave the Butcher an eternity too long to torment a confused and drugged Sophia.

She'd survive, he told himself. J-Psy were tough in every way. And his Sophie had proven her strength over and over. He'd find her. There was no other option.

He'd just overtaken a sedan going at exactly the speed limit when there was a slight *shift* in the world to the right of him. He had his stunner out and pointed to the head of the Psy who'd teleported into the passenger seat before the thought cleared his mind.

"That won't be necessary, Detective." A voice so cold, it was beyond ice, beyond emotionless. "Nikita asked for a favor. Where do you need to go?"

Making a split-second decision, Max lowered the

stunner and crossed lanes to the blaring of warning signals, coming to a full stop on the verge. "To Sophia Russo," he said to the man in the passenger seat.

Councilor Kaleb Krychek wore a razor-perfect charcoal gray suit and had eyes of pure black filled with white stars. But unlike Faith's or Sascha's, his eyes were remote in a way Max simply couldn't explain. It was as if Kaleb had never felt, as if not even an echo of the boy he must've once been lived in his eyes.

"I need a lock," the Councilor said, and they could've been discussing the weather, not the life of a woman who had fought for her right to live every second of every day. "I can only teleport to locations I've either seen or have a recent visual of."

"Can you go to people?"

"Yes, with certain qualifications."

Max held out his hand. "Take her image from my head."

Kaleb didn't touch him. "You have a natural shield." His tone said that that made taking anything impossible.

Not giving in to frustration, Max quickly routed to the Internet using his phone. "There," he said, bringing up an image of the beach resort. "Can you get me there?"

Kaleb brought out a slim device that appeared to be a high-end organizer and pulled up several more detailed pictures of the place. "Yes."

There was no touch, no warning.

Max only just kept his balance as they appeared in front of the massive glass lobby that fronted the resort, the air heavy but clear of rain. The gaping doorman snapped his mouth shut. "Councilor Krychek," he managed to croak out. "I wasn't aware you had a reservation, sir." Max went through the door before Kaleb, heading to the desk.

Slamming down his ID in front of the receptionist, he brought up Bonner's photo—from a newspaper story—on his cell phone and showed it to the blond male on duty. "Which room?"

"Ah . . ." The man looked left, then right. "I have to ask my manag—"

"If she dies," Max said with absolute intent, "you die next."

Going sheet white, the receptionist shook his head. "I haven't seen—"

"Single male, probably checked in within the past twelve hours, isolated bungalow."

The blond began working his computer. "We've only had one arrival in the past twenty-four hours. But Mr. White's—"

The ice in Max's bloodstream turned to liquid fire at the sound of that name, a name the Butcher had no right to use. "Where!"

"Bungalow Ten, right at the end of the Eastern Route." The receptionist brought up a holographic image of the resort without prompting. "We're here. Bungalow Ten is here." He pointed out the locations. "About a twenty minute walk."

Max saw Kaleb walk in, turned to him. "Can you teleport there?"

"This image is representational—a 3D map," the other man said at once. "I need a shot of the actual building."

"I'm sorry." The receptionist spread his hands. "I don't have anything like that on hand. I could try our PR depart—"

But Max was already running through the doors.

Sophia rolled off the bed and began to stagger to the door. He hadn't tied her up when he went to have his shower, and that was his mistake.

Her leg went out from under her after three halting steps, her knee hitting the floor hard enough to send pain shooting up her leg. Biting off her cry, she gripped the edge of the bed and pulled herself up again. It took too long. She could hear him whistling in the smoked-glass enclosure a bare few feet away, obscenely cheerful, a man without a care in the world.

The bedroom door swayed then stretched sideways, making her grip the end of the bed for balance. Forcing herself to let go of the anchor, she lurched forward, desperate to get through that twisting, stretched door. She could almost hear it laughing at her. "Stop. Stop."

The laughter turned into chuckles. "And where do you think you're going?" Damp around her waist, skin so close to her cheek. She flinched, trying to hide her bare hands under her armpits.

"Now walk back . . . there you go."

She knew she had to do what he said, because his semi-nakedness was on purpose, a threat. "Why?" It came out raw, but it was also from the center of her brain, the part that hadn't been compromised.

He didn't answer until she was sitting with her back braced against the headboard, her legs stretched out in front of her. "You fascinate me," he said, stroking his hand down her thigh.

Nauseated, she tried to pull away, but he pinned her in place.

"When we talked before," he continued in a calm, clear voice, as if they were close acquaintances having an everyday conversation, "I used to wonder what you were like beneath that Psy surface. I wondered if you were like other women or if you were more."

"Drugged," she said, her mouth full of cotton wool. "Not myself."

Anger rippled across his features. "No. That's rather disappointing. I want to play with *you*. It doesn't matter—we have time." He leaned in. "Your skin is so clear, so lovely." His hand moved a bare centimeter away from the vulnerable flesh of her face. "I don't want to lose my playmate too quickly, but after so long, I just . . . can't resist." His fingertip brushed her flesh.

Gaping, screaming mouths.
Pleas. Whispers. Cries.

Earth, dark and dirty.
Blood spraying a wall. A thousand droplets of horror.

Sophia fought the spiraling whirlpool, knowing that this time someone *would* come for her, her cop would come for her. All she had to do was survive.

Max made himself come to a full stop a few feet from Bungalow Ten, his lungs burning after the sprint that had brought him here.

Instinct urged him to slam the door open and blast in, guns blazing, but he took two deep gulps of air, settled his breathing. "We have to be careful," he said to the cold-eyed Psy who'd run beside him with a lethal grace that made it inhumanly clear he was a telekinetic. "If he's near her with a weapon, he could decide to kill her if we startle him."

Krychek looked at the building, no change in his expression. "The windows are curtained. How will you know what's happening within?"

"Bonner's ego was always his undoing," Max said, walking silently to the door and twisting the old-fashioned door handle with care. As he'd hoped, the monster hadn't locked it—the possibility of escape a taunt to his victim. Pushing it back a fraction, he chanced a look. Seeing nothing and no one in the living area, he opened it enough that he could slide in.

Not sure what Krychek's interest was in this beyond a cool intellectual curiosity, he left the Councilor to make his own choices as he toed off his shoes and sodden socks and crossed the living area on quiet feet, heading toward the semi-open doorway he could see on the other end. Pressing himself to the wall, he glanced in through the crack on the hinged side of the door.

Sophie.

She sat propped up against the headboard, her hair tangled, her face grazed and bruised. But it was the way she sat that worried him. Her head kept flopping to the side, and she seemed to have to force it back up. Her hands lay by her thighs, bare and unprotected from the monster who sat in front of her, his own hand stroking the air bare inches from her face. Torturing her.

Shoulders rigid with the need to put the stunner in his hand to Bonner's skull, Max was about to chance a shot when Krychek appeared beside him. The Councilor gave him a single nod, and this time, Max was ready for the teleport. He found himself standing in front of Bonner, his stunner pressed to the Butcher of Park Avenue's temple.

Bonner froze. "Detective."

"Drop that hand," Max said in a flat tone that left no room for doubt, "or I'll press the trigger."

Bonner's blue eyes went wide. "You sound as if you mean that." He jerked his arm.

Twisting, Max shot him through the palm of his fucking hand before he could touch Sophia again, exposing the whiteness of bone. Sophia wrenched herself sideways on the bed at the same instant. The situation under control, Max was about to shove the Butcher to the floor and cuff him when a screaming Bonner was slammed across the room to come to a crumpled standstill in one corner.

Max, having thrown his body in a protective curve over Sophia's, raised his head. "He was no longer a threat." He got on the bed, cradling Sophia to his side.

"He'll be a threat as long as he lives," Kaleb said, turning to watch Max and Sophia with a detached kind of focus that made Max wonder if he'd exchanged one killer for another. "It makes logical sense to get rid of him."

"He's not dead?"

"Close enough as makes no difference."

Max made a ruthless decision. "Strip his mind. We need to know where he buried his victims so their parents can take them home, so they can grieve." He wondered if a Psy would understand.

But Kaleb Krychek asked no questions. "It's done. I'll note down the locations for you." A pause. "He's dead. Are you sorry?"

Max looked at Bonner's crumpled body and felt nothing

but a savage kind of satisfaction. "No." Maybe a better man would've answered differently, but Max had never claimed to be a better man. Holding Sophia tight, he looked down, "Sophie?"

She didn't answer, her eyes closed, her lashes dark-moon crescents against her cheeks. "I need to get her to a hospital."

Krychek didn't move a muscle but an instant later, Max found himself standing in the middle of what appeared to be a Psy medical facility, Krychek beside him. The medics went motionless for a second before moving into gear. Answering their snapped questions as to what had happened, Max gave over his custody of Sophia—but refused to move from her side.

He had no awareness of when Krychek disappeared.

Kaleb looked at the body of the human he'd just killed, his fingers playing with the small platinum charm—a single perfect star—that was always with him, no matter where he went. Glancing down at the star, he said, "For you." For the one person who he knew better than anyone else on this earth, and yet could not teleport to, no matter how many times he tried.

And he'd tried every single day for over six years.

If others had been present in the room at that moment, they might've wondered at the sweep of black that eclipsed the stars in his eyes, a black so absolute, it was beyond ordinary, beyond acceptable. But there was only a dead man in the room, so there were no questions.

Placing the star in his pocket, Kaleb contacted the authorities and made sure this incident wouldn't cause any problems. Given Gerard Bonner's predilections, he didn't have to push at all.

Then, when he was alone, he teleported to every location he'd ripped from Bonner's mind to ensure he had the correct coordinates. Cold and desolate, each unmarked grave reminded him of the lightless rooms used by another killer, a sociopath who'd groomed Kaleb to be his audience . . . and his protégé.

Kaleb. Nikita's voice came into his mind as he teleported away from the final grave and to the deck of his Moscow home.

It's done. Sophia Russo and Max Shannon are both safe. The gorge that fell away with jagged promise beneath the barrierless end of the deck called to him with the same whispered promise as the dark twin of the NetMind, the neo-sentience that was both the librarian and guardian of the Net. But Kaleb wasn't going anywhere yet. Not until he'd tracked his elusive quarry, discovered what awaited.

Nikita's telepathic voice fluctuated in strength for a second. *I apologize. I was speaking with the medical staff.*

The J?

She's in a coma—the drugs they used appear to have had a serious side effect. A pause. *Thank you.*

Kaleb could have reminded her it hadn't been a true favor, that he'd get his payment, but he didn't. Not today. *Are you certain, Nikita?*

She didn't ask him how he knew what she was going to do. *There's no use fighting the wave. Those who do will drown.*

Some will say that you're the one who'll drown, smashed against a wall of Silence.

And you?

Kaleb looked down into the blackness of the gorge, but it was another darkness that he saw, the light blinking out in a woman's eyes as she begged for mercy. *I think it's time.*

CHAPTER 43

Now that it's come down to it, I find I can't say good-bye after all, can't bear the thought of letting you go. It's a selfish, stubborn need, but it holds me hostage.

—Sophia Russo in an encrypted and time-coded letter to
be sent to Max Shannon after her death

Sophia felt painfully exposed, as if her skin had been rubbed off to bare her insides. Whimpering low in her throat, she opened her eyes. The lights stabbed and the voices, they were too sharp, too piercing.

"Sophie."

She turned her unseeing, dazzled eyes toward that voice. And when he wrapped his hand around hers, she held on. Because he was *quiet*. He made everything else quiet, too. Gulping in a breath, she tried to think, tried to focus. "What . . . happened?"

"They're using other drugs to counteract the narcotics," he said, and she knew then that his name was Max. "Medics say you're beginning to respond well."

Images, broken, disjointed, fell into her head. "How long?"

"Twenty hours," he told her, deep grooves in his face that she knew hadn't been there earlier. "I was starting to worry you'd never wake up."

Her brain fought to slough off the lingering effects of the drugs, driven by what she felt for this man with his dark male beauty and his tenderness. "My body shut down to deal with the drugs."

"That's what the M-Psy said." He glanced to his right.

Following his gaze, she saw the M-Psy beyond the glass, standing at a monitoring station. "I'm in a Psy hospital."

"It's a private one," Max told her. "Nikita's certain of the loyalty of the staff."

But no matter their loyalty, Sophia thought, they had to know she'd broken Silence. By the sheer fact that she was gripping Max's hand, they had to know. "They'll—"

"Shh." Leaning in, he lowered his voice. "I told them my natural shield seems to help anchor you."

She thought of that, pulling aside the cobwebs that threatened to suffocate her. "It's true." He was acting as a psychic wall, keeping everything at bay.

"Good."

But along with that understanding came another. "I can't spend my life holding your hand." Her fingers clenched around his strong, capable grip. "My telepathic shields . . . I can't quite focus enough to test them. There's no way they could've survived Bonner and the drugs."

His expression was grim. "You're not giving in on me, are you?"

"No," she said, and meant it. He was *hers*, the only person who'd ever been hers. And he needed her, this cop who held his pain so close, his scars hidden deep. "I'm not giving you up."

His eyes blazed. "Good girl."

She knew from the way he looked at her that he wanted to press his mouth over hers, meld them so closely that nothing would ever again tear them apart. It took everything she had not to beg him to act on the desire. Because when Max touched her, she became alive, became human. "I need you to know something," she whispered.

He shook his head. "No. Tell me on our wedding day."

Her mind swirled again, but this time, it was a different

kind of a dance, inciting an odd breathlessness. "I once tes-
tified in a case where the prosecutor showed a video taken
at a Greek wedding"—because the accused had been seen
there in the company of the woman he'd eviscerated an
hour later, but she didn't want to focus on the darkness
then—"and there was a part where they all threw plates
on the floor."

Max laughed, the lean dimple she so loved coming out
of hiding. "You want to throw plates on the floor at our
wedding, baby, I'll buy you a damn crate of them."

"No." She wanted to echo his laugh, trace her finger
over his lips. "I think I'd like to get married within the
walls of the place we decide to call home."

Max's expression changed, becoming savagely masculine. "Then that's what we'll do."

With the counteragents acting with remarkable speed,
Max intended to take Sophia home later that day so she
could heal in privacy, but the M-Psy refused to release
her. "Look," Max finally snapped, his temper hanging on
by a thread so thin, it was close to invisible, "she's got no
physical injuries aside from a few cuts and bruises, and the
side effects from the drugs are all but gone." In spite of
his wrenching need to hold her, he'd never have suggested
taking her home otherwise. "Why does she need to remain
here?"

The M-Psy looked at Sophia. "I need to discuss that pri-
vately with Ms. Russo."

"She's my partner." Max was going to have trouble
leaving Sophie alone for a long time coming. "And she's
already been subject to attack while in a supposedly secure
location."

"Let go of her hand," the medic said.

Max squeezed Sophia's fingers. "Are you insane?"

"No."

Sophia looked at the M-Psy, then back at Max. "Do it
slowly," she said. "I'll be able to tell if there's a problem."

Protective instincts rebelled. "Sophie."

"I must know." Her eyes said far more than her words.

Sweat broke out along his spine as he released his grip until only their fingertips touched—then Sophia broke even that contact. He was ready to clasp her wrist at the first sign of trouble but she stared at him before turning her attention to the M-Psy. "I should be dead. The voices should have crashed into my mind—but I can't hear even a whisper." The jagged, splintered thoughts that had stabbed into her mind when she first woke were held far at bay, her mind a clear, pristine pond.

"Exactly." The M-Psy put down the electronic file in his hand. "According to the records I've accessed, your shields were a cause for grave concern—to the point where you were on a rehabilitation watchlist. Yet according to my scans, those shields are now airtight."

Max sucked in a breath beside her, his tall frame held taut. "Is he right?"

"Take me outside, Max," she said, curling her fingers into the bed beneath the sheets when they would've reached for her cop. "I need to be certain."

A cool breeze stroked its way across Sophia's face as Max wheeled her onto the roof of the private hospital. It was tinged with the salt of the sea and the living beat that was the population of this vibrant city. A thousand smells lingered in the air, from the sweetness of cotton candy to the briny tang of fish, to the wild spice of some exotic restaurant. Noises, too, rose up from the ground. The smooth *shush* of vehicles, the heavy pulse of conversation flowing between thousands of people, the odd siren as emergency vehicles went about their tasks.

"It's all outside," she whispered, unable to believe it. Nothing crashed against her skull, or if it did, her shields were so incredibly strong that she didn't feel even an echo. "Take me farther, Max."

As he pushed the chair forward, she dared try and

manipulate whatever it was that was protecting her, opening the steel walls a mere fraction. Fragments of noise, slivers of thought. She snapped the walls shut. "There's no question—I have functional shields." Gripping the chair arms, she rose out of the chair. "*Highly* functional shields." Better than she'd ever had, even as a child.

Max had his hand out to catch her even as the M-Psy remonstrated with her. She didn't care. Standing shakily on her feet, she took a deep, deep breath . . . and let the beat of the city flow around her. "I'm free," she said, though she knew it wasn't as simple as that. The J Corps wouldn't release her, not now that she was useful again. But—"And I'll fight to keep my freedom." No more acid on her soul. *No more.*

Max's expression held mingled joy and determination, and she heard the words he didn't say, even as the M-Psy spoke. "You should sit back down, Ms. Russo."

Since her legs felt a little unsteady, she didn't argue. "Do you have any idea why my shields have regenerated?"

The M-Psy shook his head. "That's why I want to keep you here longer—shields as badly damaged as yours *shouldn't* regenerate. I've looked through all our archives without finding another case. I'm concerned the shield will fail again as quickly—"

"In that case," Sophia said, looking back out over the city, "I'd rather use this time as wisely as I can. Not many Js get a second chance."

The M-Psy glanced at his chart. "I can only release you if you'll have someone with you at all times over the next twenty-four hours. The drugs could rebound, trigger a blackout."

"I'll make sure she's never alone," Max said, his tone implacable. "Sign her out."

Ten minutes later, Sophia found herself in the passenger seat of Max's car, being driven back to the apartment. "I've lit a fire under security," he said, his jaw set in a grim line. "Nobody reaches you without having being cleared by me."

"Max, I know you said to wait for our wedding day, but I really want to tell you something."

Max's hands tightened on the wheel. "You're always in a rush, aren't you, sweetheart?"

With Max, yes, she thought, she was both impatient and greedy. "I love the way you smell."

A startled look. "That's what you wanted to tell me?"

"Yes." Smiling, content, she closed her eyes and gave in to the slumber that had been pushing at her ever since they entered the vehicle.

She had no awareness of reaching the apartment building, no awareness of being carried up to her bedroom and laid down in bed. Nor did she feel the kiss pressed to her forehead or hear the low, shaken whispers of a man who told her she was his everything.

Max sat on Sophia's sofa, able to think about Nikita's case for the first time since the nightmare of the abduction. After what Nikita had done to save Sophia, he owed the Councilor far more than what was obligated by his position as an Enforcement detective.

However, though Nikita had been in touch with him on and off over the past day, he'd withheld the information about Ryan Asquith's attendance at a Pure Psy meeting—gut instinct said the boy was no killer and he'd probably splinter under Nikita's version of a "chat." At most, the intern was a mole, one who might lead them to the kingpin.

But Max *had* told Nikita about Quentin Gareth, warned her to watch her back until they could determine where the prematurely silver-haired man had been for those unaccounted-for months in his past.

"Quentin's in Jordan for business," Nikita had told him. "He won't be back for three more days, so we have time to unearth the truth—I've already begun deep-level PsyNet scans in relation to this issue."

Wondering if she'd had any luck, he picked up his cell

phone and put through a call. However, the office comm line, her private line, the cell, they all went to voicemail. He was about to try her assistant when his phone rang in his hand. Glancing at it, he raised an eyebrow. "Ryan."

"Detective Shannon, as you kept our previous discussion confidential," the intern said without any lead in, "I feel I can trust you with this."

Max waited.

"I was approached by an individual associated with Pure Psy after my reconditioning last year—they believed I would be open to their message."

"Good way to pick up recruits." Ryan had killed when his powers went out of control, would've been—on some level—searching for something to make the world seem right again.

"Yes." Ryan paused. "At first, I went along, but I soon realized my goals didn't match theirs. However, just as I was about to resign my membership, I got the internship with Councilor Duncan."

"You're spying for her?"

"Not officially. She doesn't know." A long breath. "I wanted to bring her something that would make her more inclined to keep me on after this internship ends."

Either the boy was honestly pinning his hopes of survival on Nikita, or he was a very good liar. "What did you find out?"

"Nothing concrete . . . but there was an 'atmosphere' at the last meeting I attended, a sense of anticipation. I believe that while the members aren't aware of the details of what's about to take place, something is."

Hanging up after it became clear the intern could tell him nothing more, Max began to check the myriad of messages that had come in during the time he'd been in the hospital with Sophia, his hand locked tight around hers.

There was an e-mail from Dorian.

Found a cached note on an old server saying that Gareth won a 6 month internship at KTech Inc.

(London). Matches with the time period you're looking at. All legit. But someone went to a hell of a lot of trouble to hide it.

A second message showed up as coming in only ten minutes ago.

Cop, I hope your girl is okay. Call me.

Max input the code. Dorian picked up on the first ring. "How's Sophia?"

"Good, really good." His heart twisted, part of him still unable to believe his Sophie was safe. "So, what've you got?"

"I'm sorry this is coming in late," Dorian said. "A motorcycle slid in the rain, broadsided a couple of our soldiers a few minutes after I sent the first e-mail."

"They okay?"

"Broken arm, broken leg, but they'll be fine. I've been covering their shifts." A pause, the rustle of paper. "Anyway, I just did some more digging on this KTech Inc. It's owned by a shell company, which is owned by a shell company ad nauseum. But behind it all, KTech is part of Scott Inc."

"As in Henry and Shoshanna," Max completed, all the pieces clicking into place. According to the confidential file Nikita had given Sophia, Henry was the Councilor most involved with Pure Psy. It wasn't quite a smoking gun when it came to the murders, but it was close enough to put Gareth squarely in the crosshairs. "Thanks, Dorian." Hanging up, he was about to try Nikita again when he noticed a piece of paper by his foot, as if it had fallen off the coffee table.

Picking it up, he saw Sophia's handwriting.

Gareth. Rumor. Pr

There was nothing else. She'd clearly been interrupted before she could finish the thought. Fighting a rush of

possessive protectiveness when he realized it had to have
happened the morning of her abduction, he glanced into
the bedroom, saw that she was sleeping peacefully. There
was, he thought with a wrench deep in his heart, no need
to disturb her. Except . . . it had to be important if she'd
left the milk unopened on the counter to write it—and
his Sophie, the gutsy woman who'd refused to give in to a
sociopath, was strong enough to handle this.

Going to kneel beside the bed, he cupped her cheek,
the thin lines of her scars a familiar pattern. "Sophie?"
He couldn't help tracing the lines with a string of tender
kisses.

She stirred, her eyes obviously heavy as she opened
them. "Mmm?" Beside her, Morpheus—who hadn't left her
side since she came home—shot him a jaundiced look.

"You heard a rumor about Quentin Gareth." He dropped
little kisses on the corners of her mouth. "What was it?"

Another small sound, and she snuggled closer.

"Report from Prague," she muttered, as if in her sleep.
"Vague rumor." She turned toward his mouth, a kitten
seeking more affection.

"What about the rumor, sweetheart?" He brushed her
hair off her face, petting her with more kisses. "Sophie?"

"Gareth might've killed a student four months ago." It
was a crystal-clear statement. "Student was on a Center
short list."

"He was considered flawed," Max murmured out loud.
"Hmm."

If the rumor was true, Max realized, Quentin wasn't
simply a calculating, high-level mole for Henry Scott, he
was a fanatic who believed absolutely in Pure Psy. And
that kind of an individual could snap if he sensed any type
of a—

The doorbell chimed.

CHAPTER 44

The first thing Max realized was that Security hadn't
called up—every instinct he had went on high alert.
"Sophie, sweetheart, wake up." Shoving off the blankets,
he picked her up and carried her into the bathroom, sitting
her down with her back against the wall beside the sink.
Morpheus followed on silent feet.

Flicking a few drops of water onto Sophia's face, he
roused her. "Lock the door behind me, and stay here until
I come for you."

"Max? What's wrong?" Her gaze was still a little
dazed.

"Maybe I'm being a paranoid fool, but maybe we have
some bad company." Taking his spare stunner from his
boot, he put it in her hand. "Just press this if someone
comes for you. And take my cell phone—call Enforcement
if things turn to shit." The doorbell chimed again as he put
the cell phone in her lap. "Understand?"

At her nod, he pulled the door closed and waited until

he heard the lock snick into place before he walked out to the front. He wasn't surprised to check the surveillance and find Nikita on the other side, with Quentin Gareth beside her. "Nikita," he said, opening the door, his stunner hidden by his side. "What is it?"

"Quentin has a stunner held flush to the back of my skull," Nikita said, frigidly unruffled.

Max took a step back as Gareth urged Nikita into the apartment. Max saw Nikita's eyes sweep the room, wondered what she was searching for. "Sophia's not here," he said, testing Gareth's reaction. "The medics wouldn't release her."

"Her brain's likely mush by now in any case," the other male said, his eyes glittering in a way that spoke of a disordered mind that had lost any sense of reality. "Detective, if you don't want the Councilor's brains to leak out her ears, too, please place your own weapon on the coffee table."

Max did as asked, having caught Nikita's eye. For some reason, she was cooperating with Gareth. What, he thought, would make a woman of Nikita's power hold her fire?

"Good," Gareth said as Max drew away from the coffee table. "Stand against the counter."

Max did so, facing Gareth. "What're you planning to do now?" He heard something from the bedroom, felt his spine lock as he realized Sophia had exited the bathroom.

But Gareth didn't seem aware of anything but his mission. "Now we wait."

"For Henry, I assume," Nikita said. "Does he really think you have the ability to dispose of me?"

"I press this trigger, and your brain is so much liquid three seconds later."

"I've infected you," Nikita said quietly while Max, for the first time in his life, wished that he'd been born a telepath. What the fuck was Sophia thinking? "Your mind," Nikita added, "is already being consumed by a mental virus."

Gareth's hand didn't tremble, though the odd shine in his eyes seemed to flare even brighter. "I expected as much. It will be a small price to pay to save the Net."

Martyrs, Max knew, were even more dangerous than fanatics.

"Is Sascha dead?" Nikita asked, giving Max the information he needed.

"No. But she's in our control. She won't be harmed if you do exactly as ordered."

"If she's alive," Nikita continued, "I should be able to reach her telepathically, and I can't."

"You're a creature of habit, Nikita—I spiked the water jug in your office with a drug that's temporarily dampened your range." A pause. "It's a variant of Jax, still experimental, so I hope you didn't drink more than your usual single glass."

"How could you have possibly reached Sascha?" Max asked, hoping like hell that Sophia would keep herself hidden. Quentin Gareth was insane, but he was still in full control of that weapon. "She's surrounded by DarkRiver cats."

"We shot the DarkRiver alpha as he drove her home. It was easy to take her."

And Max knew without a doubt that Gareth was lying. Because if Lucas was dead and Sascha missing, Dorian would've been hunting Gareth down with the lethal rage of a leopard in stalking mode, not running a search for Max. "He's lying."

Nikita met his gaze. "I need to be certain, Detective. Quentin informs me that if he tells his superiors he's been taken, or if his star disappears from the Net, Sascha will be put to death."

Max saw the bedroom door begin to open. Shifting to the left in a sudden move, he made Gareth swivel toward him—though the man continued to use Nikita as a shield. "I wouldn't go for your stunner, Detective," he said. "We need to question you in order to ensure you didn't share classified information about our cause, but you're not indispensible."

A tiny squeak as the bedroom door opened farther, but Max was already talking. "What's your master promised you?" The choice of words was deliberate. "A position of power? Money?"

"That question shows you know nothing about me. I'm doing this for the good of the Psy race." And then at last, he confirmed his allegiance to Pure Psy. "Purity will save us."

"I called Faith." It was a husky statement from the bedroom doorway. "Sascha's fine."

What happened next was so fast, so deadly, Max was never quite able to put the sequence of events in order. A stunner blast hit Gareth from the bedroom, the pulse glancing off him as Sophia's arm trembled. At the same time, or an instant later, Nikita went to her knees, even as Max's hand closed around the stunner on the coffee table. He turned, his shot, set to stun, hitting Gareth square in the chest . . . but the male was already falling, blood pouring out of his ears, his eyes, his nose.

Rising to her feet as Gareth crashed onto the floor, his body twitching in the throes of death, Nikita coded in a call on her cell phone. "Sascha," she said as Max ran to Sophia, "I wanted to ask if you received the contracts I sent last night." A pause. "Excellent." Hanging up, Nikita looked down at Gareth's corpse with an utterly dispassionate gaze. "Henry is very good at telepathic wipes. He made sure Quentin carried no memories I could use to pin this on him, but I know he was behind it."

Max placed Sophia gently against the wall and looked up at the woman who'd just destroyed a man's brain in a splintered second. "I guess the drugs didn't dampen your range enough."

"A miscalculation on their part. It only affected my long-range sending abilities."

And Gareth had been standing right next to her. "He was the only one. Marsha's blood loyal and Tulane's clean—I'd keep an eye on the intern, but my gut says he's more apt to give you his devotion than anything else."

"I don't have time to keep an eye on everyone," Nikita said, redoing the single button on her jacket with an efficiency that told Max the dead man on the floor had already been dismissed from her thoughts. "However, you would be very good at it."

Max blinked. "Are you offering me a job?"

"I need a security chief. Think about it."

He didn't have to. "I'm a cop."

"You can remain one—Enforcement people have been known to be seconded onto a Councilor's private team. I'm willing to be flexible if you wish to continue to keep track of your old cases." Her gaze switched to Sophia. "Ms. Russo—the Corps has requested I release you as soon as possible so that you can be returned to the active roster."

With that detached reminder that Sophia was once again a functioning J, expected to walk into the abyss again and again and again, Nikita headed to the door. "A cleanup crew will arrive shortly. You may want to move into your apartment for the time being. And ensure that large black feline doesn't taste Quentin's blood—my viruses have never transmitted through organic matter, but I can't guarantee that."

With those chill words, she was gone. Helping Sophia to her feet, Max walked them out of the apartment and into his own. Morpheus had too much class to lick at Gareth's blood. Turning up his nose at the lifeless Psy, he padded into the neighboring apartment behind Max and Sophia.

Max was just taking a sip of his coffee the next morning before attempting to get in touch with Kaleb Krychek when security dropped off his mail. Checking it, he saw that his super in Manhattan had forwarded what felt like a couple of letters in a bigger envelope.

"What's that?" Sophia asked as he took a seat beside her on the sofa. She'd had a good night's sleep, shaken off the final side effects of the drugs.

Max reached out to run his hand through her hair, unable to stop touching her. "Probably bills," he said with a shrug that tried to be careless.

He knew he'd failed when Sophia touched his shoulder. "Max?"

"I've been trying to track down my father," he told her, admitting his final secret. "I don't know why. Maybe I'll know when I find him."

"Do you think the information is in that envelope?"

"No way to know—but each time I open a 'mystery' envelope," he said, looking down at the plain brown paper, "I hope."

Sophia shifted to snuggle by his side. It was automatic to put his arm around her, pull her tight against him. She fit perfectly. "There's something else." A soft statement from the Psy who owned his heart. "Your expression . . ."

He stole a kiss, needing her. "You're starting to read me like a book. By the time we're sitting in rockers watching our grandchildren play, you'll know my secrets before I do."

She smiled, and it hit him right in the heart, how fucking much she meant to him. He wasn't letting her go, wasn't letting the Corps drag her back down into the nightmare world of an active J—even if he had to fight Silence itself. "I know your secrets, too, Sophie," he said. "Who were you telepathing earlier?"

"Another J." A pause. "My shields, Max, I need to explain them, to assess if there's a chance they'll fail again."

His soul repudiated the idea, but he knew she was right. "What did your friend say?"

"That Sascha Duncan is supposed to be an excellent shield technician—he recommended I talk to her, see if she can figure out what's behind the regeneration of my shields." Lifting herself up a little, she pressed her lips to the tiny scar on his cheek, the one she seemed to love.

It made his heart smile each time she did that. Even today, now, he felt loved, adored.

"But we can discuss all that later," Sophia murmured. "Open the envelope."

Removing his arm from around her, he drew in the vanilla and lavender scent of her and slit open the paper.

He'd opened so many envelopes since he began this search, become so used to disappointment that it took him almost a minute to realize what he held in his hand. Letting the other pieces of mail fall to the carpet, he ran his hand over the crisp white paper of the single piece he still held. "See that?" he said, rubbing his thumb over the emblem on the top left-hand corner.

Sophia bent her head. "It's from the Department of Justice."

"Bart," he clarified. "I asked him for a favor." It could've gotten the other man fired, but the prosecutor had asked only the questions he needed to get the answer.

Sophia took a long breath, let it out. "You asked him to run your DNA against the central Justice criminal database."

He wasn't the least surprised that she'd guessed. "It was a logical step, given our socioeconomic circumstances, the history of the other men in the area at the time." He took a deep breath. "And it's a step I avoided for a hell of a long time."

"That's understandable," Sophia said, shifting to a kneeling position beside him on the sofa, her fingers stroking through his hair. "You're a cop. You've dedicated your life to upholding the law—discovering that your father was a criminal who broke those same laws will be a blow." Her words were calm, practical. "But Max"—her tone changed, gentled, her eyes shining—"it will alter *nothing* about the man you are, the man you've made yourself."

He slid one arm around her waist, his throat thick. "Yeah?"

"Yeah." Her forehead touching his in tender affection, her hands cupping his face. "You're the one who taught me that life isn't predestined. We are who we make ourselves."

Her faith in him tore him wide open, reformed him a better man. "Open it for me."

Sophia took the envelope, able to be strong for her cop, to give him what he needed. Sliding her finger under the flap, she slit it open to remove two pieces of paper. The first was closed around the second—which proved to be an automatically sealed printout with serrated edges which could be pulled apart to reveal what lay within. The first was a handwritten note.

"Max," she read out, "as far as the computers are concerned, this scan was never done. I don't know the results. Neither does the computer tech. We requested that the results be printed automatically sealed. I hope you find what you're looking for." It was signed with Reuben's name. But below that was another line—"P.S. A man's father doesn't make the man. If it did, I'd be a self-serving SOB with three wives and an inability to be faithful to any of them." Sophia put down the letter, her curiosity a wild thing. "I assume he means three consecutive wives?"

"Nope." At her gasp, his lips curved. "Bart's father founded his own religion."

"And how many wives does Bart have?"

"He's been married to Tasma since they were in law school. Got four brats they love like crazy."

Sophia smiled. "So."

"So."

"Ready?"

"Yes."

She broke the serrated edges but held the letter closed. "You should see it first." Passing it over, she waited as he read it, then put it on the coffee table. Nothing happened for the next few seconds . . . until Max gave a shuddering sigh and dropped his head, thrusting his hands through his hair.

Worry tore through her . . . until he lifted his eyes. Relief shone a beacon of sunlight through his irises. "Max?"

"I always thought," he said, his voice rough with emotion, "that there was something wrong with me that my mother couldn't love me. She could love River, and I think she even loved some of the men she brought home. But not me, never me."

Sophia's eyes went to the envelope, her brain making

connections out of the experiences of a lifetime spent in Justice. "Who was your father, Max?"

"His name isn't important," Max said, and she saw that to him, it truly wasn't. "But what he did to her . . . He raped her, was convicted of it, died in a prison fight." A short, brutal summary. Max shook his head. "The only thing I don't understand is why she kept me."

Sophia's hand clenched on his thigh. Looking up, he saw eyes huge with concern, with empathy. "Ah, Sophie." Pulling her into his lap, he nuzzled his face into the sweet curve of her neck as she wrapped her arms around him. "I'm not in shock." Part of him, somewhere deep inside, had guessed the truth a long time ago. "Now that I know why she couldn't love me, I can forgive her for it."

"You're a better person than I am," Sophia said, her anger a steel flame. "You were a *child*."

Max smiled, holding her tight, this woman who would fight for him. "But I've become a man." Looking back, he could feel only pity and sorrow for the tormented, haunted woman who'd been his mother. "And I'm a man who is loved. Who loves to the depths of his soul."

There was no way in hell he was ever letting anyone take Sophie away from him. She was his. The Justice Corps would have to just fucking get used to that. "Baby," he said, turning his relentless will to how to ensure no one would ever dare come between him and his J, "we need a plan."

Sophia's eyes gleamed. "I have an idea."

CHAPTER 45

Nikita entered the mental vault of the Council chambers knowing that what she was about to do would change the course of Psy history. Whether she'd come out of the change alive, time alone would tell.

Kaleb entered with her, Ming LeBon coming in just after.

"You're well?" she asked.

The militarily inclined Councilor didn't give much away. "Yes."

They stopped speaking as Henry and Shoshanna Scott entered, followed by Tatiana Rika-Smythe and Anthony Kyriakus in short order.

"Nikita," Shoshanna Scott said as soon as the psychic doors closed, "is this about the problems you've been having?"

"Yes," Nikita said. "The specialists I hired were able to track the assassinations to a Pure Psy zealot."

"I wouldn't term the members of Pure Psy zealots." Henry, joining in the conversation.

"Oh?" Nikita had played enough games. "The dictionary definition of zealotry is 'fanatical partisanship.' I'd say Pure Psy fits the definition."

Ming LeBon was the one who spoke next, and his words were nothing Nikita had expected. "I, too, have become concerned about the direction of Pure Psy."

"They seek only to protect our Silence," Henry said. "There is nothing of concern in that . . . not unless you wish to protect those who are flawed."

Nikita ignored the pointed reference to her daughter, focusing on Ming instead.

"However," Ming continued, "that goal is now being interlocked with a noticeably racial agenda. Pure Psy has begun to see the other races as 'unclean' for want of a better word. It's indisputable that Nikita was targeted because she has strong business ties with the changelings."

Well, Kaleb's voice whispered in Nikita's mind, *it seems this will make strange bedfellows out of us all.*

He may have an ulterior motive, Nikita replied. *Let us wait and see.*

"Keeping our people apart from the other races," Henry said, "is not the worst of choices. If we could achieve isolation, our Silence would soon be pristine."

"If you believe that"—Anthony Kyriakus's cool, considered voice—"then you're a fool."

Shoshanna's riposte was quick. "It's only the weaker members of our populace who are prone to breaks from conditioning—"

"So now you'll add two cardinals and a gifted scientist to that list?" Anthony's question was measured, no less lethal for its absolute calm. "It's time we faced up to the facts. Silence is beginning to crumble at far more than just the edges, and if we don't make a choice on how to handle it, we risk an uncontrollable breakdown."

"Surely," Tatiana Rika-Smythe said, entering the conversation for the first time, "it's not that urgent. Yes, there have been incidents, but nothing to suggest a Net-wide emergency."

Ming's mind swirled an icy razor. "I made note of an incident at the Sunshine mining station several months ago."

"The mass psychotic outbreak?" Nikita clarified, not having been immediately involved with the situation. According to the data she quickly accessed, the episode had resulted in over a hundred fatalities.

"Yes. It seemed an aberration at the time, but in the past three days, we've had another mass incident at a remote science station on the Russian steppes."

"How many dead?" Kaleb, speaking aloud for the first time.

"Three hundred," was the response. "And of the fifty survivors, at least thirty are candidates for total rehabilitation. Their minds are broken."

There was a moment's silence as they digested that. Nikita decided to speak first, draw a line in the sand. "We can't just keep rehabilitating people. It's akin to putting your finger in a dyke when the dam has burst."

"Rehabilitation is key," Henry argued. "It will remove the unstable part of the populace—"

"How many?" Nikita asked, holding her own Silence, holding the cold that had been conditioned into her as a child—a cold so deep and true that nothing would ever thaw it. "Stopping when all our people are dead seems rather pointless."

"A melodramatic statement," Tatiana responded. "It's still a minority who are experiencing problems, and you said yourself that more and more people are getting themselves voluntarily reconditioned, so the situation will correct itself."

"As to that," Anthony said, "it seems you haven't been reading your reports, Councilor."

Shoshanna spoke into the silence. "Anthony?"

"There's been a marked decline in the number of individuals choosing to have their conditioning checked over the past two months."

"How is that possible?" Henry asked. "I've been kept updated on all the numbers."

"Either someone is lying to you," Nikita said, "or you misinterpreted the data. The fact is, the Net is buzzing with new whispers of dissent—"

"The Ghost," Shoshanna interrupted, referring to the most infamous insurgent in the PsyNet. "He's been spreading his brand of rebellion."

"No," Nikita said, "he simply pointed out the truth—that the violence that began the reconditionings was planned, that the populace was being shepherded toward the Center. Even Psy, it seems, do not like being so openly manipulated." In truth, that had come as an unexpected realization. Nikita had begun to see their people as the herd of sheep they'd been for so long. But the tides were shifting. And Nikita did not intend to drown.

There was a moment of silence, and she knew telepathic messages were being exchanged, data scanned as her claims were verified.

"Silence," Henry finally said, "cannot fall."

"It is," Tatiana added, "the bedrock of our stability."

"Agreed." Shoshanna's voice.

"That stability is failing," Ming said. "There is no way to halt the momentum now."

"Then it may be time," Anthony murmured, "for Silence to fall."

"No." Three voices.

Ming said nothing.

"This isn't a decision we can make in a single day," Kaleb said, "wherever we stand. But Pure Psy is a problem that needs to be eliminated. Their actions are only muddying the issue."

"Pure Psy is composed of those who support Silence," Henry said. "If you're suggesting taking them out of the equation, that's unacceptable."

"Are you saying they're under your protection?" Nikita asked.

"Yes."

"And acting under your orders?"

There was a heavy pause, as Henry realized what his answer would reveal. They all knew, of course, that he'd been the one pulling Quentin Gareth's strings—at least for the past half year—but for him to admit it was a different matter.

Shoshanna "saved" her husband. "Pure Psy has its own set of principles. That Henry happens to agree with them is no cause to label him a conspirator in their attacks against you, Nikita."

So wifely. The low murmur of Kaleb's telepathic tone was filled with nothing, so empty that Nikita wondered what she was doing allying herself with him. But in a pit full of vipers, he was at least one she partially understood.

She's tied her sail to his, Nikita responded. *If he falls, so does she.*

Tatiana is with them.

Nikita agreed. *Ming is ambivalent.*

Anthony will stand with us—he has too many business interests tied up with the other races.

Nikita didn't mention the conversations she'd had with Anthony.

And you, she asked the most dangerous Tk in the Net. *What is your true allegiance?*

That, you will have to wait and see.

"It seems we are at an impasse." Anthony's intelligent voice. "It would be best," he said to Henry, "if you made it clear to Pure Psy that their ambitions of a coup d'etat would be better to be swiftly surrendered."

"And inform any members in my city," Nikita said, "that they have until the end of this meeting to leave. Or I'll eliminate them myself." She'd killed. Many times. And she'd do so again. Self-interest, she told herself. It had nothing to do with the fact that Pure Psy had tried to target her daughter, her unborn grandchild.

"One more thing—Henry?" she said, focusing on the other Councilor. She had a thousand strains of viruses in her head. One of them, she thought, would penetrate his shields. And she'd find it, no matter how long it took. "The next time you decide one of my people is flawed and order a rehabilitation without my consent, I might not act in so civilized a fashion. In fact, it might be better for your . . . health if you didn't set foot in my territory again."

"What of your pet J?" Tatiana asked, her tone silky smooth. "There is something severely wrong with her. Her shield is nothing ordinary."

"Is being extraordinary now a crime?" Nikita had survived in the Council far longer than Tatiana. If the younger woman had forgotten that, she'd get a lethal surprise one quiet day, when she thought herself safe. "She is one of my people—just like every other Psy within my territorial borders." The implication was clear.

"So." Shoshanna. "You're protecting the broken ones now. I suppose blood will tell."

Nikita didn't engage with the Councilor who'd made the fatal decision to stand by Henry. "I've said what I have to say."

The meeting ended less than a minute later. Nothing seemed to have been resolved, but Nikita knew that was a thinly veiled fantasy.

The Council had split in two.

Kaleb had attended the meeting standing on the deck of his Moscow home. Now, he turned to go back inside, to consider his next move—and to return Max Shannon's call, the message having come in just as the meeting began.

That was before he saw the package sitting in the center of his desk.

It hadn't been there when he'd walked out onto the deck.

Only one group of people had the skill to have breached his internal security without setting off the alarms.

Picking up a silver letter opener he'd been given by a human business associate, he slit it open. It held a wooden box. That box contained a pristine patch, such as might go on a uniform. The patch bore the image of two snakes in combat—Councilor Ming LeBon's personal emblem. But piercing the fabric was a small, perfectly formed black arrow.

The Arrow Squad, it seemed, had decided to terminate their allegiance to Ming.

Kaleb didn't make the mistake of thinking that allegiance had now shifted to him. No, this was a warning and an invitation in one. Removing the Arrow, he placed it on his desk. Then he put the patch back in the box, and teleported with it to an extremely secure location, 'porting out almost as soon as he arrived.

Two Arrows glanced up at once at the slight sound of something settling on the table to their right, a table that existed deep within the Arrow Squad's Central Command, and was known *only* to other Arrows. Neither man said a word, but they began working as one to dismantle the box and destroy the patch.

There would be no evidence for Ming to find, not until it was too late.

CHAPTER 46

Dream of me.

—*Handwritten note from Max to Sophia*

Sophia sat across from Nikita, conscious of Max's restless presence on the other side of the door. Three days had passed since he'd found out about his father, since they'd made their plan, and Max had spent most of those seventy-two hours in different parts of the country, talking face-to-face with parents whose lost daughters were now being found, thanks to the coordinates Kaleb Krychek had ripped from Gerard Bonner's dying mind.

"I'm not leaving you alone," he'd said after the information came through.

Sophia had shaken her head. "Your friends in DarkRiver will watch over me. Go Max, they hold a piece of your heart, each and every one." And that was okay with her, more than okay. Max remembered those lost girls, would always remember. "Go and tell their families they're coming home. It's *important*."

His eyes had filled with an angry protectiveness even as he nodded, and she'd known he'd heard the echo of the eight-year-old girl she'd once been. As a result, she'd spent the past seventy-two hours with a changeling in her living space—Desiree was smart and funny, Clay quiet, and Vaughn still made every hair on her body rise. It was as well that Faith had come with her mate.

Sophia's own mate, her Max, had returned exhausted an hour ago, with the news that while he'd been getting in often painful personal touch with the parents and relatives of the victims, the forensic teams had located each and every girl. "It'll take weeks to fully process the scenes, but the remains are in the morgue," he'd told her. "I'll go back when the parents have to come in to pick up their girls, but everyone's holding on to family right now. They don't need me—you do."

So now, dog-tired but determined, he stood outside the door while she sat a dangerously short distance away from a woman who had the ability to kill without remorse, without pity. But Nikita Duncan was also a woman who understood business, understood how to weigh costs against benefits. Sophia met her gaze. "I need a job."

"You're a J."

"Js have very short life spans."

Almond-shaped eyes filled with speculation. "I am missing several advisors as you're aware, but unlike Detective Shannon, you have no skills I can utilize."

"I have contacts across the Net." Js saw everything. And they talked to each other, because only another J understood the broken pieces within them. "As the situation with Quentin Gareth proved, you have a critical gap in your organization. I can fill a large part of it, organize a team that will round out the other aspects."

Nikita leaned back in her chair. "Is Detective Shannon part of the deal?"

"No." Sophia held the Councilor's gaze. "To be quite blunt, you don't want him working for you if he doesn't want to be here."

"No." Nikita was silent for several minutes. "Can you be discreet about your unorthodox relationship with him?"

Shock held Sophia silent for several seconds. Scrambling to make sense of the question, she decided to alter the plan and take the biggest gamble of her life, one that could put her back on the rehabilitation watchlist. "Yes, in public. However, I plan to marry him."

Again, Nikita didn't react as predicted. "Do it in private, file the legal paperwork through the slowest court system you can find—as a J, you should know precisely which one will fit the definition. Under no circumstance can anything you experience leak out into the Net. If it does, the Arrows will strike."

"My shields are impregnable." Sophia looked at the Councilor, suddenly aware that she had more of a capacity to understand this powerful woman than most. The darkness in her recognized the same in Nikita. "What's happening?"

"Change." Nikita rose to her feet, walked to the plate-glass wall that looked out over the city. "But change takes time, and always claims victims."

Sophia wouldn't ever again be a victim. "I will never like you," she said to the Councilor's back. "But I will never lie to you either. I think you could do with an advisor who's not afraid of you."

"Normal Psy do not feel."

Sophia said nothing. Not on that. "I've thought and thought about why you might've asked for me on this assignment, and I can only come up with one answer." And it was an answer beyond Silence, an answer to do with mothers and daughters, redemption and forgiveness. "But I can't make myself believe it. Not of you."

Nikita took five long minutes to respond. "Pick up the standard employment contract on your way out. And Ms. Russo?"

"Yes?"

"You should be scared of me."

"Perhaps." Sophia rose. "But once you've seen what I have, once you've lived in the abyss for that long, fear becomes nothing but another cage." Then she walked out and into the arms of a cop who waited only until they'd closed the door to his apartment behind them before crushing her into his arms and taking her mouth in a kiss that *demanded*.

She felt the lingering pain in him, the heavy sorrow of all those families, and gave him what he needed. Everything.

He ripped open her jacket, shoved up her skirt with rough, hungry hands that licked fire across her skin. "Stop me, Sophie." A harsh whisper. "I don't want to hurt you."

"It's okay." She pushed off his own shirt, baring the sleekly muscular beauty of his chest. "I missed you until I couldn't breathe. Come inside me."

Her panties were torn off her, his fingers urgent as he tested her slickness. Lifting a leg, she wrapped it around his hip. He swore, lowered the zipper on his pants, and then the hot, hard heat of him was thrusting into her, pinning her against the wall. She cried out, holding on, holding him tight.

The pleasure was a firestorm that erased the pain, wiped away the sorrow, left her limp, his face buried in her neck as that muscular back gleamed with perspiration. "Hello, my Max," she whispered.

"Hello, my sweet, sexy Sophie."

Later that day, after they'd spent most of it tangled up skin to skin, sleeping and loving and holding each other, Sophia took a deep breath. "I did some in-depth investigation of my new shields while you were away—I think I know their origin."

Her cop stroked her hair off her face, his expression intent. "Tell me."

"Part of this is because I'm an anchor, but part of it is because my mind is . . . unique." It had survived by doing the extraordinary. "You know about the NetMind?"

"I've heard rumors it's some kind of psychic entity that organizes the Net."

"Yes. The thing is, there's a DarkMind, too." She'd

searched, dug deep to find confirmation of her suspicions. "It's made up of all the emotions my race has rejected, and it's so angry, so scared, and so very, very lonely. I think . . . it's also a little insane."

Max didn't ask what others might have. He asked only the critical question. "This DarkMind is protecting you?"

"They both are in a sense." She took a shaky breath, swallowed. "At first I thought my shields were a psychic extension of the Net, that for some reason, the Twin-Minds had decided to look after me, but while that made sense with my Net shields, it didn't explain my telepathic protections—those *have* to come from within. Then I realized it's me." She hesitated.

"It's okay, sweetheart." A kiss on her forehead, arms that held her close. "No matter what, you're still my Sophie, still my J."

Her heart settled, quiet, content. "*I* am a living, breathing extension of the Net, Max." The tendrils snaked through her mind, fine threads, and not the dark alone. The light was there, too, simply less obvious to the casual eye. "I'm not just an anchor any longer—I've become some kind of a focus."

Two hours later, she shared the truth about her shields with Sascha Duncan over a secure comm link. The empath's face held no rejection, only concern. "But Sophie, the Net is going mad. If it's inside you on that level . . ."

"There's hope, Sascha." A blinding, beautiful hope. "As the Net passes through my anchor point, the light and the dark come together if only for a fraction of a second."

Comprehension dawned in a fracture of color in Sascha's cardinal eyes. "And for that instant, they're sane?"

"Yes." Her throat locked. "I may be the sole anchor who can give them that peace. And that's not right." Because outside of the tiny oasis of her mind, the Net *was* going inexorably mad, a dark rot seeping through its very fabric—parts of the PsyNet were already dead, places where neither the DarkMind nor the NetMind could go.

Sascha's own eyes shone wet. "No, they should've never

been split in two, but their sentience is formed and shaped by the Net. They can't, won't merge until Silence falls."

And that, they both knew, might take an eternity . . . and a war that could devastate their world. "Things are changing," Sophia whispered, holding the empath's gaze. The NetMind loved Sascha. The DarkMind knew the empath could give them something, but it didn't know how to shape its request, how to even convey its painful need. "You've felt it."

"Yes." A solemn gaze, but it held hope, the determination of a Psy willing to fight for her people. "Are you sure you're safe, Sophia?" So much care, the empath's huge heart there in the timbre of her voice, in every part of her.

At that moment, Sophia understood some of what the crippled, voiceless DarkMind was trying to tell her, understood that the Es *had* to be reawakened if the Net was to survive.

"I understand why it does what it does," Sascha continued, sorrow erasing the stars in her eyes, "but the Dark-Mind's need for vengeance has pushed it to spawn terrible crimes."

Sophia wrapped her arms around Max's waist, laying her ear against the solid pulse of his heartbeat, the warmth of him her own personal anchor. "In my mind, they're one." They were whole. As she was finally whole.

"They balance each other." Sascha's voice turned soft, thoughtful. "Yes, of course."

"And . . . I accept the DarkMind," Sophia said, hiding nothing of who she was, the darkness that had shaped her. "It has no need to scream, no need to fight to be known, to be remembered." She would never shut it away, never force it to be Silent.

Just like her cop had never asked her to be anything but what she was—a flawed, scarred J. Lifting her head, she reached up and pressed a kiss over that scar on his cheek, uncaring of their audience. Thanking him. Adoring him.

"I know," he whispered, his arms holding her tight. "I know, baby."

It was all she needed to hear.

EPILOGUE

I'm sorry, Max. Please don't be mad. I just can't be here anymore.

> —*Handwritten note from River Shannon to Max Shannon*

Sophia had never felt more content than she did at that moment, lying in the loose circle of Max's arms as they sat in bed watching the entertainment screen. The show wasn't important—it was background. But the warmth of Max, the scent of him, the knowledge that no one could ever steal this from her now . . . it was an almost vicious happiness.

Max rubbed his chin on her hair. "I can tell when you're thinking."

"Are you sure you're not Psy?" A kiss pressed to the golden-brown skin under her cheek. He was only wearing a pair of boxers, while she'd pulled on a tank top and a pair of pajama bottoms with dancing penguins on them.

Max's fingers massaged the back of her neck in an absent caress. "One hundred percent primitive human."

Tapping her fist against the hardness of his bare abdomen, she reached up to press a kiss against his jaw. "I like you primitive."

He took her mouth, stole her breath. And when he released her, he said, "I knew you wanted me for my body."

"That and your salary." Smiling, she tumbled him onto the sheets until she straddled him, her elbows braced on either side of his head. "Are you going to take the job Nikita offered?"

"It gives me hives to think about working for a Councilor." He scowled, his hands shaping over her hips. Lower. "But then I think about all the secrets I could learn, all the other cops I could help with the contacts I'd make, the access I'd have."

Sophia shivered at the way he stroked her, decided she'd have to get him in front of a mirror today. The fantasy was driving her to delirium. "I've already sold my soul"—that got her a grin, and she had to kiss his dimple then—"so I have little credibility, but Nikita seems to be better than some."

"Not saying much."

"No." She ran one hand down over his chest, loving the fact that she could adore him at her leisure, without worry, without fear. As long as nothing leaked out into the Net, no one would come hunting—not in Nikita's territory. "Max, do you mind that we have to continue to be careful?" Whatever change was happening, it was a slow, secret thing.

"I almost lost you to total rehabilitation," he said, his tone somber. "Compared to that, a little discretion is nothing. And"—a *Max* smile—"you know it turns me on when you're all prim and proper in public. I just want to take you home and strip you naked, teach you wicked, wicked things." Possessive hands shaping her flesh with sensual intent.

"Oh yeah?" She began to slide her hand south. "Maybe—"

The doorbell chimed, interrupting Max's groan of anticipation.

He scowled when she looked up. "Ignore it. It's probably Nikita's henchmen come to make sure I'm giving 'due consideration' to her offer."

"As if you'll make any decision but the one you want." She pushed him. "Go answer the door. They won't go away until you do."

A black look on his face, Max got up and pulled on his jeans, the tattoo on his back stunning. And, Sophia thought, it wasn't only because he'd had her name written on the blade. "I love you, Cop."

He turned to nip at her lower lip. "Good 'cause you've got life with no possibility whatsoever of parole." Then, barefoot and with sleep-tumbled hair, he walked out. She knew he'd done it on purpose—to irritate any assistants Nikita had sent.

Getting out herself, she pulled on a thick terrycloth robe and began to brush her hair. "Shall we go see who it is?" she asked Morpheus, who was snaking around her ankles.

As if he understood, he padded over, with her following.

Her hand stopped in midstroke when she saw the man in the doorway.

Max gripped the doorjamb, his knuckles going white. "How did you get past security?" It was the first question that came out, the last thing he cared about.

The blond man in the corridor clasped the wrist of one hand with the other. "I told them who I was at the desk, and they said I was on the list. So . . . I . . ." He swallowed. "Did you know? I mean, should I go? I thought—"

Reaching out, Max grabbed his younger brother in a bone-crushing embrace. "You fucking idiot. If you try to run off this time, I'm dumping your ass in jail."

River's arms locked around him. Max felt dampness against his skin, had to blink his own eyes, swallow the knot in his throat. Raising a hand after a long, long time, he messed up the hair on the back of River's head. "Where have you been, kid?"

River gave a sheepish grin as they drew apart. "Getting my shit together."

"You couldn't do that without disappearing?"

River dropped his head, shoving his hands into the back pockets of his jeans. It made Max grin, his heart full to overflowing. He knew this man, grown though he might be.

"Max?" Sophia's gentle voice. "Are you going to invite him in or interrogate him on the doorstep?"

River's eyes widened as he laid them on Sophia. "Wow, Max, what did you tell her to get her to let you in the door?"

Max cuffed his brother good-naturedly on the ear as River slid in past him and bent to kiss Sophia on the cheek. "Hello, are you sure you're with the right brother?"

Sophia had never had a younger sibling. But this man with his laughing eyes and bright smile . . . "Are you making me an offer?"

"I would"—a whisper—"but Max always was a little possessive."

Max's arm came around her waist, heavy, warm, real. "Don't you forget it."

River looked up at Max as her cop turned to press his lips to Sophia's temple, and for an instant, Sophia saw the truth of River's emotions laid bare. So much love, so much need, so much pain. Max's brother, she thought, *needed* them. "Welcome home, River."

His expression shifted into a wary kind of hope. "Yeah?" But he was looking at Max.

Max reached out to thump a fist on River's shoulder. "You're staying if I have to tie you to the furniture."

"No need," River said, dipping his head but not before Sophia saw the sheen in his eyes, "just tie me to your Sophia."

"I think," Sophia said as Max mock-scowled, "I'm going to like having a younger brother." Reaching out, she slipped her arm into the crook of River's elbow. "So, tell me all of Max's secrets."

Max curled his hand around her nape. "Hey now, no ganging up on me."

River laughed, said something. So did Max, the heat of his hold burning through to warm every part of her as she listened to the joy beneath their words.

Home.

Finally, they were all home.

Five things happened later that month. All of them momentous in very different ways.

One: Max decided there were medicines he could take for hives.

Two: Councilor Nikita Duncan met Councilor Anthony Kyriakus to draw up a plan to protect their territory against incursions by others on the Council.

Three: Sascha Duncan managed to stop a fight between ten six-year-old changeling leopards using her ability—though she couldn't figure out how she'd done it.

Four: Councilor Kaleb Krychek found the beginnings of a trail that could one day lead him to his quarry.

And five . . . Max bought Sophia some *very* naughty lingerie for their honeymoon.

Turn the page for a sneak peek at the next novel in the Psy-Changeling series, *Play of Passion*

Indigo wiped the rain off her face, clearing it for a split second, if that. The torrential downpour continued with relentless fury, slamming ice-cold bullets against her skin and turning the night dark of the forest impenetrable. Ducking her head, she spoke into the waterproof microphone attached to the sodden collar of her black T-shirt. "Do you have him in your sights?"

The voice that came back was deep, familiar, and at that instant, lethally focused. "Northwest, half a mile. I'm coming your way."

"Northwest, half a mile," she repeated to ensure they were both on the same page. Changeling hearing was incredibly acute, but the rain was savage, drumming against her skull until even the high-tech receiver she'd tucked into her ear buzzed with noise.

"Indy, be careful. He's functioning on the level of a feral wolf."

Under normal circumstances, she'd have snarled at him

for using that ridiculous nickname. Tonight, she was too worried. "That goes double for you. He hurt you in that first tangle."

"It's only a flesh wound. I'm going quiet now."

Slicking back her hair, she took a deep breath of the watery air and began to stalk toward their prey. Her fellow hunter was right—a pincer maneuver was their best bet for taking Joshua down without damage. Indigo's gut clenched, pain blooming in her heart. She didn't want to have to hurt him. Neither did the tracker on the boy's trail—the reason why the bigger, stronger wolf had been injured in the earlier clash.

But he'd have to if they couldn't bring Joshua back from the edge; the boy was so lost in anguish and torment that he'd given in to his wolf. And the wolf, young and out of control, had taken those emotions, turned them into rage. Joshua was now a threat to the pack. But he was also their own. They'd bleed, they'd drown in this endless rain, but they would not execute him until they'd exhausted every other option.

A branch raked across her cheek when she didn't move fast enough in the stormy weather.

Sharp. Iron. Blood.

Indigo swore low under her breath. Joshua would catch her scent if she wasn't careful. Turning her face up to the rain, she let it wash away the blood from the cut. But it was still too bright, too unmistakable a scent. Wincing—their healer would strip her hide for this—she went to the earth and slathered mud over the superficial injury. The scent dulled, became sodden with earth.

It would do. Joshua was so far gone that he wouldn't detect the subtle scent.

"Where are you?" It was a soundless whisper as she stalked through the rain-lashed night. Joshua hadn't taken a life yet, hadn't killed or maimed. He could be brought back—if his pain, the vivid, overwhelming pain of a young male on the cusp of adulthood, allowed him to return.

A slashing wind . . . bringing with it the scent of her

prey. Indigo stepped up her pace, trusting the eyes of the wolf who was her other half, its vision stronger in the dark. She was gaining on the scent when a wolf's enraged howl split the air.

Growls, the sickening clash of teeth, more iron in the air.

"No!" Pushing her speed to dangerous levels, she jumped over fallen logs and newly made streams of mud and water without really seeing them, heading toward the scene of the fight. It took her maybe twenty seconds and a lifetime.

Lightning flashed the instant she reached the small clearing where they fought, and she saw them framed against the electric-dark sky, two changelings in full wolf form, locked in combat. They fell to the earth as the lightning died, but she could still see them, her eyes tracking with lethal purpose.

The tracker—the hunter—was bigger, his normally stunning silver-colored fur sodden almost black, but it was the smaller wolf, his pelt a reddish hue, who was winning—because the hunter was holding back, trying not to kill. Aware that her drenched clothing would make stripping difficult, Indigo shifted as she was. It was a searing pain and an agonizing joy, her clothes disintegrating off her, her body turning into a shower of light before forming into a sleek wolf with a body built for running.

She jumped into the fight just as the red wolf—Joshua—slashed a line into his opponent's side. The bigger wolf gripped the teenager's neck. He could've killed then, as he could have earlier, but he was attempting only to subdue. Joshua was too far gone to listen; he reached out, trying to go for the hunter's belly. Teeth bared, Indigo leapt. Her paws came down on the smaller wolf, holding his struggling, snarling body to the earth.

She didn't know how long they stood there, holding the violent wolf down, refusing to let him go over that final destructive edge. The hunter's eyes met hers. A brilliant copper in his wolf form, they were so unusual, she'd never seen the like in any other wolf, changeling or feral. She glimpsed a piercing intelligence in that gaze, one that many people missed because he laughed so easily, charmed with such open wickedness.

Most didn't even realize he was SnowDancer's tracker, able to trace rogue wolves through snow, wind, and, tonight, endless rain. And though it was not their practice to call him hunter, he was that, too, charged with executing those they could not save. But Joshua understood who it was he faced. Because he went silent at long last, his body limp beneath theirs.

Indigo released her grip with care, but he didn't spring up, even when the larger wolf let go. Worried, she shifted back into human form between one instant and the next, her hair plastered to her naked back. The tracker stood guard next to her, his fur rubbing wet against her skin.

"Joshua," she said, leaning down to speak to the boy, determined to bring him back from his wolf. "Your sister is alive. We got her to the infirmary in time."

No recognition in those dark yellow eyes, but Indigo wasn't a SnowDancer lieutenant because she gave up easily. "She's asking for you, so you better snap out of it and get up." She put every ounce of her dominance in her next command. *"Right now."*

A blink from the wolf, a cocked head. As Indigo watched, he rose shakily to his feet. When she reached for him, he lowered his head, whimpering. "Shh," she said, gripping his muzzle and staring straight into those wolf-bright eyes. His gaze slid away. Joshua was too young, too submissive in comparison to her strength, to challenge her in that way.

"I'm not angry," Indigo said, ensuring he heard the truth in her words, in the way she held him—firm, but not in a grip that would cause pain. "But I need you to become human."

Still no eye-contact. But he heard her. Because the next instant, the air filled with sparks of light and a split second after that, a young male barely past his fourteenth birthday was kneeling naked on the earth, his face drawn. "Is she really okay?" It was a rasp, the wolf in his voice.

"Have I ever lied to you?"

"I was meant to be watching her, except I—"

"You weren't at fault." She put her fingers on his jaw, anchoring him with touch, with Pack. "It was a rockfall—*nothing* you could've done. She's got a broken arm, two broken ribs, and a pretty cool scar on her eyebrow that she's already showing off like a peacock."

The recital of injuries seemed to stabilize Joshua. "That sounds like her." A wavering smile, a quick, wary glimpse up at her before he dropped his gaze.

Smiling—because if he was scared about the consequences of his actions, he was back—Indigo gave in to her relief and nipped the pup sharply on the ear. He cried out. Then buried his face in her neck. "I'm sorry."

She ran her hand down his back. "It's okay. But if you ever do this again, I'll strip your hide and use it to make new sofa cushions. Got it?"

Another shaky smile, a quick nod. "I want to go home." He swallowed, turned to look at the tracker. "Thanks for not killing me. I'm sorry I made you come out in the rain."

The huge wolf beside Indigo, its tail raised in a gesture of dominance, closed its very dangerous teeth around the boy's throat. The boy stayed immobile, quiescent, until the tracker let go. Apology accepted.

Making a futile effort to shake the rain from her hair, Indigo looked at the boy. "I don't want you turning wolf for one week." When he looked shattered, she touched his shoulder. "It's not punishment. You went too close to the edge tonight. No use taking chances."

"Okay, yeah." A pause, a whisper of shame in his eyes. "The wolf's getting hard to control. Like I'm a kid again."

That, Indigo thought, explained his irrational response to his sister's accident. She made a mental note to kick some ass on the heels of that thought. Adolescents and young teens did occasionally have control issues—Joshua's teachers should've picked up the signs. "It happens sometimes," she said to the boy, keeping her tone calm and matter-of-fact. "Did to me when I was around your age, so it's nothing to be ashamed of. You come directly to me if you feel the wolf taking over again." She shifted into her other form as he nodded, his relief obvious.

The journey home to the den—a huge network of tunnels hidden deep underground in the Sierra Nevada mountains of California, out of sight of enemy eyes—was quiet, the rain letting up about ten minutes after they began. A human might've slipped and fallen a hundred times in the slippery terrain, but the wolf was sure-footed, its paws designed for increased stability, and it found the easiest route for Joshua.

Indigo, with the tracker taking position behind the boy, herded Joshua all the way to the wide-open door in the side of what would otherwise appear to be a sheer rock face—where his shaken mother was waiting with another wolf, a silver-gold one with eyes of such pale, pale blue, they were almost ice.

The boy fell to his knees in front of the SnowDancer alpha.

Indigo and the tracker backed away, their tasks complete. The pup was safe—and would be taken care of. Now, they needed to run off some of the strain of tonight. She'd really thought they'd have to kill Joshua. The boy had been all but insane when they'd managed to corner him earlier. Glancing over toward her companion at the memory—the larger wolf having kept pace with ease—she realized he was bleeding.

She came to a halt with a snarl. He stopped only a step later, circling back to nudge her nose with his. Shifting into human form, she bent over him, pushing back her rain-wet hair. "You need to see Lara." Their healer would be better able to check his wounds, ensure they weren't serious.

The wolf nipped at her jaw, growling low in his throat. She pushed him away. "Don't make me pull rank on you." Though to be honest, she wasn't sure she could—and that disturbed both woman and wolf. He occupied an odd space in their hierarchy. Younger than her, he wasn't a lieutenant, but he reported directly and only to their alpha. And as their tracker, his skills were critical to the safety and well-being of the pack.

Another growl, another nip—this one on her shoulder.

She narrowed her eyes. "Watch it or I'll nip that nose right off."

He made a growling sound of disagreement, his canines flashing.

Reaching out, she tapped him sharply on the muzzle. "We're heading back right now."

Color under her hands, the wolf with fur the distinctive color of silver-birch bark shifting into a human with lake-blue eyes and rain-slick hair. "I don't think so." He was on her before she knew it, cupping her face in his hands, his mouth on hers.

The caress was hot, hard, a slamming fist that held her motionless. And then . . . an inferno punching through her body, making her tangle her hand in that thick brown hair, tug back his head. "What," she said on a gasping breath, "are you doing?"

"I thought it'd be obvious." Laughter in his eyes, the lake seared by sunshine as his thumbs stroked over her cheekbones. "I want to lick you up right now."

She didn't take it personally. "You're high on adrenaline from the hunt." Pushing off his hands, she angled her head. "And loss of blood." It ran a clean, water-diluted line down his side. "You definitely need stitches."

"No, I don't." He kissed her again, pushing her down to the earth.

This time, she didn't back away at once. And got the full impact of the kiss . . . and of the rigid arousal nudging at the sensitive dip of her abdomen. Her heartbeat accelerated, startling her enough that she bit hard at his lip. "It's cold down here." Though the snow had melted away in this part of the range, the Sierra Nevada retained the chill kiss of winter even in the blush of spring.

A repentant look. She found herself on top an instant later. Still being kissed. Groaning at the stubborn wolf—who could kiss so insanely well that she was tempted to let him have at it—she pushed at his shoulders. "Get up before you die of blood loss, you lunatic."

A scowl. And then Drew kissed her *again*.

Love 👄 Sexy and ❤ Romantic novels?

Get caught up in an Angel's Kiss . . .

Vampire hunter Elena Deveraux knows she's the best – but she doesn't know if she's good enough for this job. Hired by the dangerously beautiful Archangel Raphael, a being so lethal that no mortal wants his attention, only one thing is clear – failure is not an option . . . even if the task she's been set is impossible. Because this time, it's not a wayward vamp she has to track. It's an archangel gone bad.

Enthralled by Angel's Blood?
Then get caught up in the rest of the series: Archangel's Kiss

For more Urban Fantasy visit www.orionbooks.co.uk/urbanfantasy
for the latest news, updates and giveaways!

Love 😊 Funny and 💗 Romantic novels?

Be bitten by a vampire

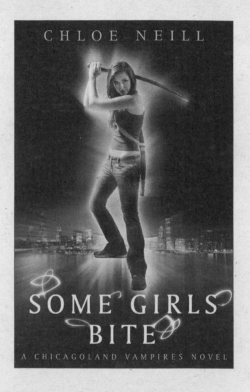

CHLOE NEILL

SOME GIRLS BITE

A CHICAGOLAND VAMPIRES NOVEL

Merit thought graduate school sucked – that is, until she met some real bloodsuckers. After being attacked by a rogue vampire Merit is rescued by Ethan 'Lord o' the Manor' Sullivan who decides the best way to save her life was to take it. Now she's traded her thesis for surviving the Chicago nightlife as she navigates feuding vampire houses and the impossibly charming Ethan.

Enjoyed Some Girls Bite?
Then sink your teeth into Merit`s next adventure: Friday Night Bites

Nalini Singh was born in Fiji and raised in New Zealand. She spent three years living and working in Japan, and travelling around Asia before returning to New Zealand.

She has worked as a lawyer, a librarian, a candy factory general hand, a bank temp and an English teacher, not necessarily in that order.

Learn more about her and her novels at:
www.nalinisingh.com